MASTER OF DESIRE

"This is Al. He didn't have a good night."

Jenna widened her eyes. She hoped she looked suitably naïve and stupid. "You didn't find any lost souls to save? How sad."

For a moment a predatory gleam lit his eyes, and then he smiled.

Jenna forgot to think, she forgot to blink, she forgot to *breathe*. She knew smiles, all the things they said and didn't say, all the ways they could manipulate. In the hands of a master, a smile could be the ultimate weapon. It could persuade, compel, destroy.

And Jenna was looking at a master. A woman could crawl on her hands and knees to a man with that smile. It was a soul-searching, sensual lifting of his lips, all savage beauty and frightening secrets.

"We found everything we were looking for tonight." On that cryptic note, he turned and walked from the room.

PRAISE FOR PARANORMAL QUEEN NINA BANGS!

ETERNAL PLEASURE

"It takes awhile to get used to placing this sort of character in the same sexy arena as wolves and vampires, but Bangs pulls it off with a deft hand and the right balance of menace and humor, weaving in Mayan prophecy for an unusual theme."

—*Booklist*

"This is the beginning of an exciting new series. It has it all... action, steamy sex and even some humor...This is a great book!" —*Affaire de Coeur*

ONE BITE STAND

"Bangs delivers another outrageously fun and scorchingly sensual paranormal romance." —*Booklist*

"Bangs's wacky tales never disappoint and her offbeat characters face danger with flair." —*Romantic Times BOOKreviews*

A TASTE OF DARKNESS

"The creativity and humor of Bangs's outrageously sexy paranormal tale is topnotch and consistently excellent. Her over-the-top scenarios are rich with adventure, fun and laughter. A guaranteed mood lifter!" —*Romantic Times BOOKreviews*

"Bangs continues her wildly imaginative Mackenzie vampire series with another deliciously dark tale that is...sizzling, sexy, and wickedly funny." —*Booklist*

NIGHT BITES

"Cosmic chaos and laughs abound in this latest romp from the always wonderful Bangs. Sexy and sizzling, this is paranormal fun with lots of spice."

—*Romantic Times BOOKreviews*

"Nina Bangs has written a truly fascinating romantic tale with *Night Bites*...everything from trickery, sorcery, sizzling sex, intrigue, and danger all rolled into one explosive package." —*Romance Reviews Today*

NINA BANGS

Eternal Craving

LEISURE BOOKS NEW YORK CITY

A LEISURE BOOK®

May 2009

Published by

Dorchester Publishing Co., Inc.
200 Madison Avenue
New York, NY 10016

ISBN 10: 0-8439-5793-X
ISBN 13: 978-0-8439-5793-8
E-ISBN: 978-1-4285-0665-7

Visit us on the web at www.dorchesterpub.com.

Eternal Craving

Chapter One

Kill. It was a primal scream filling his mind, blocking out things he should understand, remember. *Kill.* It was heat and rage and a pounding in his head demanding more, more, and still more death. It blazed hot and hungry, devouring him from the inside out. But nothing could burn away what lived in his soul.

His beast was free. No way was he forcing it back into its cave when there was still a demon left to tear apart. Shedding all human thoughts, he mounted his primitive soul for a last wild ride.

The demon was in its true form as it flapped leathery wings and rose above him. All its supernatural powers were useless against his beast, so now the demon was playing its last card. A straight-up physical attack. Dumbass

The demon plunged toward him, and he roared as he rose to meet it. It screamed, a long cry of shock and pain as he ripped one of those wings away. Its dark, thick blood flowed sluggishly across the churned-up grass and dirt.

The smell of demon blood drove him wild. Before the creature could scuttle away from him, he ripped off the other wing. Now all it could do was flop around helplessly.

It had all been too easy. In a killing frenzy, he ripped the creature to shreds, refusing to quit even after the demon's dying screams had ended.

"It's over, Al. Control your soul. Come back to us."

The voice in his head should make sense to him. He

knew that. But he resisted. Come back? What if he didn't want to?

Breathing hard, he looked around for more living bodies to tear, rend, *destroy*. Only a river of blood could drown the pain, the confusion, the need for never-ending violence.

"The killing is done. Obey me."

No. The killing would never be done. He looked down on the human standing by the tree, the one talking in his head. He didn't want anyone telling him to stop. He'd kill this one next. Then the voice would stop. The one that made him *think*, the one responsible for all those hated new *human* emotions.

He took a step toward the man. With no warning, an invisible force slammed into him. The earth shook as he crashed to the ground. Panicked, he fought to rise. Primitive instincts screamed at him to get up before something bigger and badder killed him. But the force held him down. The voice spoke again.

"Calm down."

He remembered. The voice had a name. Fin.

"Everything will be okay, Al."

He had a name. Al.

"I wouldn't lie to you."

Sure he would. It seemed like the murmur of Fin's voice had always been in his mind, even across the endless ocean of time. Fin had promised that together they could defeat the destroyers, that all would be as it was before. He'd make it happen.

See, now Al had a basic problem with that promise, because his world hadn't *had* any destroyers. Other than Al, that is. And Al's efforts had been strictly local, driven purely by the need to feed.

Then Fin had ripped Al's essence from his body and buried it deep in the earth. Al should've known better than to trust a voice in his head.

"You're human now, so it's time to return to human form. You'll get a chance to hunt again."

Right. Fin had promised that Al would again walk the Earth as the hunter he once was. He'd laid that lie on him just after he'd roused Al's soul from its long sleep far beneath Machu Picchu and given it a new body. Not the body Al wanted.

Afterward, Fin had stuffed Al's brain with every bit of knowledge he'd need to function in this new time. Fin had promised that Al was human now.

But he'd lied. Again. Al didn't feel human. He felt trapped.

And Fin's lies kept on coming. He'd promised that Al and the rest of the Eleven would be happy here once they defeated the immortals who wanted to destroy the human race. Evidently, these were the same immortals who had destroyed Al's world. Even though Al couldn't remember the event in question, Fin expected him to believe it had gone down just like he'd described. Fat chance of that. Besides, Al didn't give a flip about the freaking human race. And he'd *never* be happy here.

Up until now, Al had held it all together, fooled everyone into thinking he was okay with chasing the immortals from city to city with only brief fights to break the monotony. He'd stayed in control. But not tonight. Demons had been the fuse, and the battle his flame. He was ready to blow.

"Put your soul away before I have to hurt you."

Al tried to hold onto his soul, his *true* identity. He twisted and fought Fin's compulsion, but suddenly he was back in his human form. Filled with bone-deep disappointment, he climbed slowly to his feet and took a deep breath, reaching for the brittle shell of calm he pulled around him when others were near. Not that it would do any good. Everyone had just seen how close to the edge he was. Meltdowns weren't pretty.

Al wasn't ready to meet anyone's gaze. He stared at the ground.

Blood always looked black at night. Even demon blood. *Especially* demon blood. Too bad that's all that was left of the fight, just a few patches of black soaking into the earth. Not very satisfying. Al wanted bodies. Lots and lots of beautiful dead bodies.

Fin moved up beside him. "A good night's work." He must've decided to ignore Al's loss of control, at least for the moment.

Al accepted the change of subject. "Why did you come with us on this job? You could've stayed in your fancy new condo and just channeled your power through one of us." He gazed out over the dark waters of the Schuylkill River, away from his leader and those weird eyes that saw way too much.

"This was our first battle in Philadelphia. I felt the need to celebrate the moment with a hands-on experience."

Al could hear the amusement in Fin's voice. "Is that all?"

"No." Amusement gone. "Boathouse Row is just down the road from here. All those boathouses lit up like Christmas trees would be a magnet to you. The humans might be gone, but that wouldn't stop you. Property damage triggers investigations. We don't need that."

Al almost opened his mouth to throw a look-who's-talking at his leader. Fin had wiped a Houston landmark from the face of the Earth in a matter of seconds. But then he thought better of it. Another human characteristic: thinking about consequences. He liked his old life, a time of unrestrained savagery when the consequences never touched him, only his prey.

He'd been watching Lio emerge from the river, but now he turned his complete attention back to Fin. "You don't think we could control our beasts? You think we'd go on a killing spree?"

Al thought he knew what Fin would say, but he still needed to ask. The same way he'd poke at a sore tooth with his tongue. The pain felt so good. It let him know he was still alive.

Fin's long silver hair and matching eyes gleamed in the pale light of the full moon. The hair and eyes wouldn't help him keep a low profile.

Fin shrugged. "Not Ty. Now that he's mated to Kelly, he's mellowed a little. She's calmed him down. And Lio gets a rush from the whole thing, but underneath he's cold and contained."

"So it's me you don't trust?" He tried to work up some outrage, but it wouldn't come. Fin was right.

Fin met his gaze. "What would've happened if I wasn't here to call you back tonight?"

Al didn't answer. And yeah, he knew he had a sullen expression pasted on his face. He hated when Fin was right.

Fin's smile held a bitter twist. "Besides, you have lots of rage to work through."

Al didn't bother to deny it. Fin knew every corner of his soul. "So?" A lame answer, but it was the only one that came to mind.

"Don't work through your issues by running away from them, Al. That's what you're doing each time you block out your humanity. You don't want to become a liability to the Eleven." The warning was clear.

Ty joined them. "Hey, we kicked demon butt tonight. I haven't had this much fun since we left Houston." He thought about what he'd said. "Don't tell Kelly. She's never gotten the violence-is-fun thing."

Lio had pulled on his clothes and joined them. Tearing apart a bunch of demons hadn't put a wrinkle in his fashion-mag image. Al wondered how he did it. And why it even mattered.

"You are so whipped." Lio raked his fingers through hair that even damp looked perfect.

Ty turned on him with a growl.

Lio ignored Ty's reaction. "I froze my ass off in that water."

Fin held up his hand to stop whatever Ty intended to say. "Okay, it's over. We did the job. You guys ripped them up, and I tossed what was left back into hell. I'll get rid of this last one now. Once they pick up the pieces,"—Fin meant that literally—"they won't stick their noses or any other body parts through the portal again." He sounded sure of that.

"Why not? What's to stop them from getting their act together and making another run at it?" Al wanted that in a big way. He wanted a second chance to vent his frustration, his *aloneness* in mindless, savage fury.

"Because I told them not to come back."

Fin's voice was soft, reasonable, and the scariest thing he'd heard that night. Al just nodded.

"They belonged to Eight. He's the only one with enough power to make a bunch of demon dirtbags work together." Fin glanced at his men. "We needed information, but by the time you got through with them, they weren't in any condition to answer questions. Curb your enthusiasm next time."

Lio and Ty grunted their grudging agreement.

Al wasn't in the mood to agree with anything Fin said, so he opted for a question instead. "I don't get it. Back in Houston, you brought the Astrodome down without breaking a sweat. So why'd you settle for just sending the demons back into hell? Why not kill their asses?"

Fin turned his silver gaze on him. "I can't." His expression said the subject was closed.

"Glad you cleared that up. Thanks for the detailed explanation." Al's muttered sarcasm was meant to be heard.

Fin didn't get mad. He never lost his temper. And that's exactly what shoved *Al's* temper into the head-exploding range. What would it take to make the almighty Fin lose it? Something half remembered suggested Al wouldn't live through the experience.

In calmer moments, Al recognized that some of his anger probably came from being so close to Fin. None of them could be around the guy long without feeling their primitive emotions ratchet up. Fin had never explained why that happened. There were lots of things Fin didn't explain.

For just a moment, Al felt other thoughts intrude. Memories of times and places Fin never talked about. But then the pain in his head started, and the fog rolled in. His memories faded away as they always seemed to do.

Fin threw him a sharp look. "Demons are true immortals. Just like Zero and the rest of his crew. I don't have the power to destroy them. I can only change their home address."

Al pulled his calm a little more tightly around him. "Got it." He wished they knew the names of the damn immortals they were hunting, because he could never get used to calling them numbers. Of course, Fin got off on numbers, so he was probably in his happy place.

"Time to go." Fin stared at a spot in the center of the clearing and a portal opened. He sent the pieces of the last demon through, closed the portal, and then turned toward the SUV. "Get it together, Al. We'll wait." He didn't look back as he spoke.

For the first time tonight, Al was grateful to Fin. He knew Al needed a little breathing room and was giving it to him. Okay, grateful moment over.

Ty and Lio spared Al a curious glance, but they didn't ask any questions. He appreciated that too. He watched them until they'd climbed into the SUV before turning his gaze back to the river. A strong breeze was blowing off the water. It whipped his waist-length hair around him in a wild tangle, but that didn't bother him.

He always kept his hair braided, except when he hunted. It was a stupid symbolic gesture that didn't mean anything to anyone but him. Wearing his hair unbraided was a reminder—of what he'd been, of what he'd never fully be again. It meant freedom, an emotional cutting loose. He smiled. Well, not exactly smiled. More a baring of teeth. If Eight, the immortal they were hunting in Philly, had gathered enough of an army around him, maybe Al would get to cut loose a lot.

It would take too long to braid his hair now. Reaching into the pocket of his jeans, he pulled out a leather strip and tied it back.

Then he closed his eyes and just stood there for a minute while his soul slowly backed into its cave until it was swallowed up by the darkness. But his mind could still see its eyes staring out at him. Watching, waiting for the next chance to claw its way to the surface.

"Come on! Hurry it up! I'm starving!" Ty's shout echoed in the darkness.

"Yeah, yeah, I'm coming." Just to annoy Ty, Al took slow steps all the way to the SUV. In another time, Ty could've torn him apart. But now things were a little more equal. That was the only upside to *now*.

Once inside, he settled into the seat next to Lio. Al let the other men talk as Luke, Fin's human driver, headed away from Fairmount Park. They were damn lucky that both Houston and Philly had parks that covered lots of land. Plenty of private areas where no humans would be at night.

He glanced at the houses that made up Boathouse Row when Luke drove past them. Every house was outlined with strings of white lights. Pretty in the dark. Fin was wrong. He wouldn't have come down here and done a demolition act. He would've searched for something that could fight back.

Once away from the houses, Al sank into himself, his favorite place nowadays. But Lio ruined his attempt at some healthy brooding by punching his shoulder.

"Bet I could run up those steps faster than you could." Lio pointed.

The steps—lots of them—led up to the Philadelphia Museum of Art. Al recognized the building because Fin had made all of the Eleven study maps and guidebooks of Philly until their eyes crossed. His excuse was that if they ever had to drive themselves in an emergency, they'd damn well better know where they were going.

"Hey, knock yourself out. But you'll be puffing up them alone." The only thing that could motivate Al to exert himself that much would be if Eight was giving him the finger from the top step.

Lio shrugged. "What can I say, I love a challenge. Rocky ran up those steps."

"Who?"

"The movie?" He looked disgusted by Al's ignorance. "We all watched it in Houston. I thought you saw it with us."

"I don't watch many movies." Come to think of it, Al didn't do much of anything when he wasn't hunting or sleeping. Not great for his mental health, but he couldn't get into the rhythm of life in the here and now. His own fault. But what was the point? They were here to kill. He didn't think beyond that.

Fin turned to stare at him.

"What?" He didn't like the calculating look in Fin's eyes.

"When was the last time you had sex?"

Al didn't have to think long. "Sixty-five million years ago."

"Don't you think it's about time you had it again?" Fin wasn't smiling. "It might take the edge off you."

Lio stifled his laugh. Ty didn't stifle anything. He snorted his opinion of Al. "Jeez, no wonder you're such a hardass."

Al's soul thought that was a pretty good excuse to crawl out of its cave.

"Control it."

Fin's voice was a sharp blade across the heart of his rage. Al fought for calm.

"You know, sometimes you really *can't* go home," Fin said. "Sometimes you have to make the most of where you are."

Fin had returned to staring out at the darkened streets, but Al knew the comment was aimed at him. Because he was the only one of the Eleven who wasn't settling into 2012, who wanted to go back to where he'd been before, to *when* he'd been before. And he hated Fin for refusing to make it happen.

"You can't just show up here in Philly and expect me to welcome you with open arms. Why didn't you tell me you were coming?" Kelly paced—ten steps forward, swivel, then ten steps back—to emphasize how really ticked she was at her sister. "Where's the consideration?"

Jenna widened her eyes in her best fake innocent expression. "Ty's boss invited me."

"Fin?" Outrage gave way to confusion.

"The same." Jenna figured Kelly didn't need to know that she'd called Fin first or that the boss man hadn't specified when she should visit.

"Oh."

Kelly bit her lip, a signal that she was trying to think of a reason why Jenna shouldn't stay. Jenna was good at reading body language. She was also good at getting her way.

"You should've at least given me some warning."

"I decided on the spur of the moment. And I tried to call you from the airport, but your cell was turned off." Jenna took a chance on that, but she was betting on Kelly's habit of forgetting to turn on her phone. "Sorry to show up so late, but I couldn't get an earlier flight."

Kelly looked suspicious, but she didn't comment. She glanced around the condo's huge living room. "We don't have our own apartment yet. Fin is letting us bunk down here for a few days."

The insinuation was that Jenna wouldn't have anyplace to stay. Jenna didn't intend to let a weak excuse like that get in the way of her finding out what was going on in her sister's life. "Give me a break, sis. Hello, this is a penthouse suite. I bet Fin could fit an army of missionaries in here." Not that Jenna believed for a minute that Kelly's yummy husband was a missionary. "But if he doesn't want me to stay here, I'll just get a hotel room." There, let Kelly wiggle out of that.

Kelly glanced at Jenna's bags piled by the door and sighed. "Sit down."

Jenna recognized the expression in her sister's eyes. She wasn't buying into Jenna's spur-of-the-moment story. Instead of sitting, Jenna wandered over to the large window. The city lights glittered bright and cold. She shivered. Someone walking on her grave? She hoped not.

Turning to face her sister, Jenna smiled. "I'll stand. I sat too long on the plane." Besides, she thought better on her feet.

Kelly nodded and collapsed onto the couch. She curled her bare feet up under her and tied her robe shut. "So why are you really here?"

Jenna thought about lying. She was good at it. She'd had lots of practice on herself. But in the end, she decided to tell the truth. Lying took energy, and she'd had a long day. "I wanted to make sure you were okay."

Kelly frowned. "I'm fine. Why wouldn't I be?"

Jenna rolled her eyes up to the ceiling. "Gee, let's see. Uh, you met a guy, married him a month later, and then raced out of town so fast you left skid marks in front of the church. Oh, and did I mention that none of his family or friends came to the wedding? Add to that your pitiful attempts to avoid my perfectly reasonable questions about your new husband and, oh, I don't know, I sort of felt the need to get to know Ty a little better."

"Cut the sarcasm, Jenna."

Jenna turned to stare out the window again. "Right. No more sarcasm. You brought Ty to meet us three days before your wedding. I'd like to visit for a week so that I can go back to Houston and report to Mom and Dad how deliriously happy you are. I think they deserve at least that much."

"I'd call that meddling."

"I'd call it caring."

"I'd call it understandable worry." The deep male voice spun Jenna away from the city's lights.

The man standing in the doorway took her breath away. Literally. Big, about six eight, with a powerful body to go with the height. But that's where his comparison to other men ended. Long silver hair fell past his shoulders. Not gray. *Silver.* The strands gleamed in the light. Where could you get that kind of color job? She wanted one.

His eyes were silver too. They had their own kind of glow going on. The silver color should've made him look as though he didn't have irises at all, but she could see them clearly. As he drew closer, she realized his irises were outlined in black and there was a touch of purple deep in the silver. Cool contacts.

But it was his face that backed her up until she was pressed against the window. How could someone so beautiful be so terrifying? The journalist in her wanted to memorize details so she could get them right in her story—because anyone who looked like he did definitely had a hell of a story to tell—but the woman in her looked away. Jenna believed in woman's intuition, and that intuition was yelling at her to run and not stop until she got to the airport.

His soft chuckle raised goose bumps along her arms and down her back. "And I try so hard to be nonthreatening."

Taking a deep breath, Jenna glanced at him. "Yeah, well, you have to try harder." She glanced at her sister. "Introductions?"

Kelly was looking beyond the silver-haired man. "Jenna, Fin. Fin, my sister Jenna."

Jenna forced a smile. "The boss man. Glad to meet you." Glad to meet anyone, since Kelly had made a bunch of lame excuses to keep from introducing her family to the men who worked with Ty.

"You have no idea how happy I am to meet you." Fin managed to make the polite comment sound sinister. He reached for her hand.

Jenna fought the urge to bolt from the condo as his hand engulfed hers. She'd never thought you could physically *feel* a person's power, but power was the only word that came to mind as pressure built up around her, squeezing and squeezing and squeezing until she was gasping for breath. Just when she was certain her chest was about to cozy up to her backbone, he released her hand and stepped back.

Thank God. She had no idea what had just happened, but she couldn't get away from Fin fast enough. She sidestepped past him only to realize that three other men had entered the room with him.

She recognized Ty. He broke from the group to join Kelly. So she was left staring at the remaining two men. They both looked big and dangerous like Ty, but that's where the similarity ended.

One of them came forward to offer his hand. "I'm Lio. This visit is a surprise." His cold, dark eyes said it wasn't a good surprise.

She almost went limp with relief when his handshake didn't set off any seismic tremors.

Lio's hard face and unfriendly expression canceled out any points Jenna gave him for really knowing how to dress. From shoes to jacket, Lio was designer labeled all the way. And his brown hair showed what a great stylist could do.

If he expected her to feel guilty, he was doomed to disappointment. "Yes, well, Kelly will tell you I'm the queen of impulse." She offered him a friendly grin just to annoy him before turning to the last man.

The last man did *not* offer his hand. He wore a black duster that hung open. Worn jeans, a black T-shirt, and scuffed boots put him at the other end of the clothes spectrum from Lio.

But clothes would never define this man. He'd moved to the dimmest area of the room, where shadows cast the planes of his face into mysterious layers of light and dark. And his eyes were . . . terrifying came to mind. They blazed with so many emotions that Jenna wanted to hold her hands in front of her to block the force of his stare. No, glare was a better description.

Fin stepped into the uncomfortable silence. "This is Al. He didn't have a good night."

Jenna widened her eyes. She hoped she looked suitably naïve and stupid. "You didn't find any lost souls to save? How sad."

For a moment a predatory gleam lit his eyes, and then he smiled.

Jenna forgot to think, she forgot to blink, she forgot to *breathe*. She knew smiles, all the things they said and didn't say, all the ways they could manipulate. In the hands of a master, a smile could be the ultimate weapon. It could persuade, compel, destroy.

And Jenna was looking at a master. A woman would crawl on her hands and knees to a man with that smile. It was a soul-stealing, sensual lifting of his lips, all savage beauty and frightening secrets.

"We found everything we were looking for tonight." On that cryptic note, he turned and walked from the room.

"Gee, it was great meeting you too," she muttered to his retreating back. Final thoughts: his tied-back hair fell a lot lower on his back than she'd expected, and she'd been so mesmerized by the emotion in his eyes that she hadn't noticed their color.

The silence dragged on for a few beats too long. Then Fin walked over to lay his hand on her shoulder. She controlled her instinctive flinch.

"The room next to your sister's is empty. I'll have someone take care of your bags."

Jenna nodded. "I appreciate it." She glanced to where Ty had joined Kelly on the couch.

He grinned at her. "We're glad you could visit. Kelly needs someone to go out and do stuff with."

Jenna raised an eyebrow. Interesting. Why didn't *Ty* do "stuff" with his new bride? She wondered if Kelly still drove the mean streets with him while he looked for souls to save. If so, she'd evidently taken tonight off.

"What Ty's trying to say in his own male way is that I need someone to go clothes shopping with." For the first time since Jenna walked into the condo, Kelly sounded amused.

"Yes, well, I can do that." Jenna ignored Lio, who'd flung himself onto a chair, instead aiming a comment at Fin. "This is an incredible condo."

He strode over to the window and gazed out at the city.

"I chose it because it overlooks Rittenhouse Square. Not much of a park, but I like to be near trees."

Jenna could see him watching her in the window's reflection. "This must cost a fortune." Left unasked was, "Where the hell would a missionary get that kind of money?"

A rude comment. Too bad. She'd learned one important thing during the three years she'd spent writing for *The Scene*. You only got good answers when you asked questions that made people squirm. Besides, she'd ask this guy what color shorts he wore if that's what she needed to know to keep Kelly safe.

"I have a trust fund." There was laughter in his voice. "And they're white." She could see his smile reflected in the glass.

White? No, he couldn't have . . . Her knees felt a little rubbery. She resisted the need to sit down. "If you don't mind, I think I'll head for my room. It's been a long night." Turning away from Fin, she aimed what was probably a sickly grin at her sister. And she was definitely *not* running away.

Kelly looked troubled. "Sure. Maybe we'll go shopping in the afternoon."

Ty smiled. "I'll grab your bags." He leaned over to kiss Kelly before rising from the couch.

Jenna chalked one up for his side. He wasn't afraid to show affection toward Kelly in front of everyone. She could see why her sister had fallen for Ty Endeka. With that dark hair and those gray eyes, he was a great-looking guy. She chanced a quick glance at Fin. Even if he did have a strange boss.

Kelly wasn't smiling. She was worried. It was there in the crease between her eyes, the way she'd pressed her lips into a thin line, and how she avoided looking directly at her sister. Jenna tucked that fact away for further investigation.

Fin finally turned from the window. "I hear you thought

Ty was a vampire when Kelly first met him." He was still smiling.

Well, that was embarrassing. She glanced away from those silver eyes. "Umm, sometimes I let my imagination get away from me. I guess it was the whole mysterious, work-at-night thing." Along with some unexplained emotional hits her sister had taken when Ty was near.

Jenna didn't believe in vampires, werewolves, or alien abductions, but she never stopped hoping one would prove her wrong. In her line of work, fame and fortune were only one ET sighting away.

Suddenly, Fin was beside her. She hadn't seen or heard him move. She controlled a startled squeak.

"Your imagination needs an upgrade, Jenna. You have to think outside the box."

His murmur made her want to shrink away from him. And because there was no reason for her reaction, she forced herself to meet his gaze. "Sorry, I'm not too creative. Vampires are at the top of my woo-woo list."

"Hmm. Maybe we'll have to widen your horizons, then." He sounded thoughtful. And completely serious.

"Sure. We'll do that." As she followed Ty from the room, Jenna knew she was in full retreat. Fin was too beautiful, too strange, too . . . Too unearthly? Okay, so he scared her.

A short time later, as she lay in bed staring at the ceiling, Jenna was still thinking about the men she'd met. Once Kelly and she were away from this condo, she'd wring the truth from her sister, because there was nothing missionary-like about these guys. Any lost souls with a lick of sense would run and hide if they saw Fin and his crew coming. That's what she'd do.

She finally fell asleep on the promise that tomorrow she'd check out Al's eye color.

Chapter Two

Al's hair was braided today, as tightly controlled as his anger. That didn't mean the anger wasn't still simmering below the surface, though.

He paced the private elevator taking him up to the penthouse condo. Fin probably had security cameras watching his every move. Controlling bastard.

Lio and Ty might not have paid much attention to Al's brief defiance last night, but Fin had. The only question was how Fin would deal with him. And deal he would. Al never doubted that.

He stepped from the elevator and strode to the hand-carved door. Pretentious bastard. The thought almost made him smile. Almost. Guess he couldn't blame Fin for the door.

Then he stood waiting. Fin knew he was here. No need to knock. He probably also knew Al had called him a bastard twice. Fin wouldn't care. Mad, sad, glad—emotions didn't touch Fin.

While he waited, Al thought about what Fin might have lined up for him. Whatever it was, Al wouldn't like it.

Ty interrupted Al's thoughts by yanking open the door. He didn't look happy. But then Ty had spent the night here, so he'd been exposed for hours to whatever it was that caused the Eleven's aggression levels to skyrocket when Fin was near. Scowling, Ty gave him only a few seconds to step inside before he slammed the door shut.

Ty turned and headed for the dining room, complaining all the way. "He got me out of bed at ten. Said to meet him and the rest of you guys here in fifteen minutes. No explanation. My head didn't hit the pillow until five. Waking up before noon puts me in a crappy mood."

No shit. "Yeah. Hope this is important." Al was tired too. On a whole bunch of levels.

Ty paused in the doorway to the dining room. "It's bad when we're all together." He raked his fingers through his hair. "I want to kill something."

Al felt the wave of aggression from the nine men roll over him as he sat down at Fin's fancy antique table. Ten now that he was here. Ten plus Fin made up the Eleven, men with the souls of ultimate predators. The world didn't know it yet, but they were here to save humanity's butt. He nodded at his partner.

Car stared at him from bright green eyes that always seemed out of place in that savage face. He rubbed his hand over his shaved head.

"Where's the damn coffee?" Car's usual bad attitude was set on hyperdrive today. "Whatever the big man wants, it could've waited a few more hours." He swung his head to stare at the kitchen door.

Al figured Greer had better come through that door with a pot in his hand soon if he didn't want to be Car's main meal.

As if conjured from the lightning strikes of bad temper snapping and crackling around the seated men, Fin's cook pushed open the door and rolled his cart up to the table. Two big pots of coffee had a place of honor on it, along with a bunch of covered plates.

Greer wasn't a big guy, but his soul was tiger. A predator. That commanded respect from Al and the others. Too bad he was otherkin instead of a shifter. Otherkin had souls trapped in the wrong bodies, but they didn't have the power to change. Greer would never walk the Earth in the skin of his tiger. Al felt sorry for him.

While the others were busy shoveling food onto their plates and gulping their first shot of caffeine for the day, Al glanced around the table. Fin hadn't shown up yet. When Al realized what he was really searching for, he immediately stopped looking.

The woman wasn't there. He refused to recognize any disappointment in that thought. Jenna Maloy didn't belong in Philly with them. She had no place in what they were doing. Kelly's sister was nothing more than an annoying footnote to the battle the Eleven were fighting. Still, he kind of wished the annoying footnote was here so he could watch her try to play Fin. No way would Fin believe she'd come here for a friendly visit with her sister.

Al glanced across the table at Ty. "I thought you said Kelly planned to tell her family everything. Maybe it's just me, but I got the feeling her sister didn't have a clue about us."

Ty looked uncomfortable. "Yeah, well, she's waiting for the right moment."

"When's it going to happen? Some night when the sister sees what she shouldn't see? It'll be tough then to—"

"Shut up. It's none of your business." Ty's voice was a low growl. He half rose.

The men around the table grew still. Anticipation fed the silence.

Al started to rise too. "The sister is a danger to all of us."

"Sit the hell down. Both of you." Fin's voice sounded weary.

The pure novelty of that swung Al's attention from Ty. Fin took the seat at the head of the table. He exhaled deeply as he sat. For Fin that was tantamount to someone else collapsing from exhaustion.

Fin didn't waste time. "Finish your meal while I fill you in."

Everyone began eating again, but no one talked.

"Zero's looking for us."

Everyone stopped eating.

"When we showed up in Houston, Zero didn't think we were much of a threat. He took care of us sixty-five million years ago, so doing it one more time was no big deal."

Fin's silver eyes were flat, but Al knew that death lived behind them.

"Then we messed up his recruitment program and kicked Nine back out into the cosmos. One less immortal worker bee for him. That's a problem. The only way he wipes the human race off the face of the Earth on December twenty-first is if he has armies of nonhumans ready to rise up and destroy everyone. His guys already have thousands of shiny new recruits spreading the word across the rest of the world. But he needs more true believers. He can't afford to lose another one of his immortal flunkeys. Who'll do his recruiting then?"

"Does he know we're in Philly?" Utah glanced at his brothers. They all wore the same eager look.

Al figured the three brothers were the deadliest of them all except for Fin. He never let their spiky blond hair, bright blue eyes, and body piercings fool him into thinking they were less than they were. They were pack, and they thought and fought as one.

Fin closed his eyes as he took a gulp of his coffee. When he opened them, he looked a little less grim. "No. But he knows we'll be tracking down his guys. So he'll hit each of the cities where they're recruiting. I kept his mind off what we were doing in Houston with a bunch of psychic attacks. That won't work this time. He's motivated to wipe us out."

"Why don't we stop all the freaking games and make our stand here?" Gig's pale eyes gleamed with the same need that drove all of them.

Fin's gaze swept the table—cold, assessing, and always with that deadly calm. "We've gone down this road before. Get this straight. We can't kill them. We can only give them a one-way ticket home. And each of them has one and *only* one key to his house."

Gig made a rude noise.

Fin skewered him with a stare that pushed everyone back against his chair. Gig paled.

"I'm the one with the visions. I know which key will get rid of each of these guys. And you're not it. We track them down, kill their recruits, and get the key to *where* it needs to be *when* it needs to be. Any more questions?" His stare said more questions wouldn't be a smart idea.

I'm the one with the visions. For just a moment, a starburst of memory exploded in front of Al's eyes. *Fin, but not Fin. Speaking the same words. Not in the same language, but the same words. A feeling of hopelessness so terrible it brought Al to his knees.* And then it was gone, fading into the fog that always rolled in whenever he tried to remember. But there was something there, something just out of reach. And Al was convinced that Fin was at its center.

He glanced up to find Fin staring at him. No emotion showed in those silver eyes, but Al got the feeling Fin knew exactly what he'd just seen.

"The numbers aren't random, are they?" Lio evidently thought his revelation was worth the danger of asking a question. "I've been thinking. We don't know the names of these immortals, so you call them by numbers. I get that. But you're a number guy. I bet each of those numbers has a meaning to you."

For the first time since he'd sat down at the table, Fin really smiled. And even Al was swept away by the power of that smile. It made all kinds of promises that Al didn't believe anymore.

"You're right." Fin nodded at Lio.

Fin approved of Lio in a way he'd never approve of Al. Lio was cold and logical like Fin. But he was passionate enough about his fighting to fit in with the rest of the Eleven. He had the best of both worlds. Lucky Lio.

Fin leaned back in his chair, his expression thoughtful. "When the visions first hit me, they didn't make a lot of sense. They were like dreams where things were all mixed up. I saw each key and a hint of what it would do. I saw individual numbers and understood which city went with the numbers, even though the names of the cities meant nothing." He frowned. "The one thing I didn't see was the final outcome."

"Kelly was your key in Houston." Ty sounded accusing.

Al took orders from Fin, but sometimes the head guy's coldness made his veins ice up. The keys weren't people to Fin. They were tools. Al wondered what he and the others were. Just weapons?

Fin nodded. "And she did what she needed to do. Kelly took down Nine in the Astrodome, but not exactly in the way I envisioned." He shook his head. "That bothers me."

Of course it bothered him. Fin wanted a sure thing. Something they all wanted. Al spoke up. "So what did the number nine have to do with anything?"

Fin stared out the window. "Did you know that the first exhibition game played in the Astrodome was on April ninth 1965? Or that the last game the Astros played in that stadium was on October ninth, 1999? The Oilers played their last game there on December twenty-first, 1996. Nine, nine, twenty-one. Significant numbers. And I missed them."

Al laughed. "Oh, come on. You can find the numbers you're looking for anywhere. It's not your fault you didn't realize the Astrodome was the place where the big event would go down." He couldn't believe he was giving Fin an out.

"I should've known." Fin sounded like he meant it.

Al added god complex to Fin's sins.

"This time will be different. Eight is the number." His voice was packed tight with all kinds of intensity. "And we're looking for a bell."

"The Liberty Bell?" Lio had taken his guidebooks seriously.

"I don't know. Could be. But that might be too public."

Al pointed out the obvious. "And the Astrodome wasn't?"

Fin nodded. "Point taken. In my vision, I saw a woman reaching out to ring a bell. I couldn't see or hear it, but the *knowing* was in my head." He leaned forward. "I saw the number eight, and I knew it was in Philadelphia." He relaxed back into his chair again. "But I don't have a clue what kind of bell or where it is. It could be a damn doorbell for all I know."

Spin's bark of laughter sounded loud in the sudden silence. "Whoever gave you these crazy visions had a sense of humor."

"Yeah. Ha, ha." Gig would never be accused of having a sense of humor.

"Is that all?" Q glanced at his watch. "I have stuff to do before we hunt."

Fin took another swig of coffee. "Oh, there's one more thing. Car, you're switching partners."

Al felt like Fin had yanked the chair out from under him. "Hell, no. Car's *my* partner. I don't want anyone else." Not too friendly, but Car was his pack now. Not much of a substitute for the real thing, but Car was all he had.

Car frowned. "I didn't ask for a new partner."

"You two weren't together last night. Don't think you had any problems, Car."

Al noticed Fin didn't include him in the no-problems group. "I don't want another partner." He winced. Sulky wasn't a good sound on him.

Fin raised one brow. "Did I mention another partner for you?"

Uh-oh.

"I do what I think is best for the Eleven. Gig didn't have a partner in Houston. He deserves one this time around."

Al had opened his mouth to speak, but Fin held up a hand to stop him.

"Here's the deal. I want to keep Utah and his brothers together. Can't beat them as a team. So that means someone won't have a partner."

"Doesn't seem fair to me. Letting three guys stay together and then splitting others up whether they want it or not." Car tugged at one of the diamond studs in his ear, a sure sign he was pissed.

"Life isn't about fair." Fin's power swirled around him, pushing outward, pressing against them until breathing got tough and they had to lean away from him. He might not do a lot of shouting and stomping, but Fin had no problem reminding everyone that he was the big boss. "If life was fair, we wouldn't be here chasing nonhumans down every damn alley trying to find Eight."

Fin's expression never showed anything but calm. Only his display of power hinted that he might be a little ticked. "Don't worry about Al, Car. He won't be alone. I'm putting him in charge of keeping Jenna safe and ignorant while she's here." He looked at Al and smiled.

Gotcha. That smile said it all. Fin was taking him away from the fight until he got his act together. He knew Al would hate playing babysitter; he *wanted* Al to hate it.

"Follow her whenever she leaves the condo during the day and take her with you at night."

"Where the hell will I go at night if I can't fight? May as well sit on the couch, get fat on chips and dip, and watch the

Seventy-Sixers. I don't get it." Al didn't get anything because the angry roar in his head was drowning out reason.

Fin's smile faded. "This isn't about you. Get over yourself."

Al forced himself into tight-lipped silence. He gripped his coffee mug to have something to do with his hands.

"She thinks we're missionaries. Or maybe not. But whatever she thinks, you're going to prove that we really are trying to pull people out of the gutter and make productive citizens of them. You'll take her with you every night, you'll find humans passed out in dark alleys, and, by God, you'll save them. Whether they want it or not. By the time she leaves here, she'll think we're freaking saints. And you're the man who'll make it happen."

His soul crept closer to the mouth of its cave, but Al wouldn't allow a repeat of last night. He tightened his grip on his control. Squeezing, squeezing, squeezing . . .

Hot liquid spilled over his fingers. Shocked, he glanced down. His mug lay in pieces as coffee soaked into the tablecloth.

"Very good." Fin sounded surprised but pleased that Al hadn't gone primitive on him.

Al could only nod as Greer rushed to mop up his precious table.

How could you hate a guy while at the same time knowing he was right? Al understood that Fin had to shut him down. One loose cannon could out them and throw every human in the city into a panic. Fin couldn't take a chance on that.

With the violence option off the table, Al satisfied himself with silently cursing Fin. He used every word Fin had poured into his head and some that he hadn't.

"Inventive. I'm impressed. Just make sure when you're with Jenna you keep your emotions under control. Don't broadcast,

and for God's sake don't turn your soul loose. Ty made a mistake with Kelly because he let her feel his rage and lust, and then he let his soul escape. She didn't have to do a damn thing. He connected all the dots for her."

The voice in his head didn't surprise Al. He welcomed it. After all, what fun would mental curses be if Fin wasn't listening?

Then Fin turned his attention back to the others. "I know being around me and close to each other is working on your tempers, but keep it cool. I want Jenna to see a bunch of really kind and gentle guys." He seemed to think about that for a moment. "Okay, that might be tough. But at least talk a good game. Make her think you'd throw yourself in front of a bus for your fellow man."

There was a collective groan that was cut off suddenly as Jenna entered the room.

Coffee. Jenna needed a shot of caffeine before she could think about last night. Following her nose, she paused in the doorway to the dining room.

Kelly hadn't told Jenna she would have to eat breakfast with the savage hordes. Missionaries, ha. Jenna took a deep breath and scanned the men sitting around the long table. Eleven pairs of eyes stared back at her. None of them looked friendly except for Ty's and Fin's. And Fin's friend-liness was dipped in sinister.

Jenna propped up the walls of her determination with some false bravado and tried to decide where to sit. There were two empty seats next to Ty. Probably for Kelly and her.

Ty was still smiling, but his eyes looked worried. Why? Interesting. He pointed to the seat beside him. Jenna shook her head.

She'd never find out the truth of what was going on here if she attached herself to Ty. She had to set up shop in the belly of the beast. So taking a last survey of the empty chairs, she walked around the table and settled herself next to the guy Fin had called Al.

Jenna didn't look at him, but she could feel the virtual darts of dislike he was sending her way. And beneath that, she sensed something stronger, emotion that raged and roared, fought to escape. She did some mental eye-rolling. Talk about an overactive imagination.

But she hadn't imagined his dislike. Too bad Al hadn't talked to Kelly about her. Kelly could've told him that Jenna only had one reaction to anything negative flung her way. She caught it and heaved it back.

Jenna poured herself a cup of coffee, added sugar and cream, stirred it, and then took a gulp. A sip wasn't big enough to get her through the next few minutes. Turning her head, she smiled at him, showing lots of teeth. "So how long have you been a missionary?"

She had to keep her smile from wobbling because . . . Wow, just wow. Last night she'd been dead on her feet, and he'd been standing in shadows. In the bright light of mid-morning, he was a sight to behold.

Jenna had already done her body inventory of him last night—almost as tall as Ty, muscular, über alpha-type, but she'd missed his more subtle points . . . "What's your last name?"

"Endeka."

The ghost of a smile touched lips so sensual she wanted to reach up to skim her fingers across them.

"We're all Endekas. Ty's my cousin." The smile disappeared completely. "I'm into the missionary life. It's been such a blast that it seems like only minutes ago I first took my vow to help others."

Yeah, right. Jenna's bullshit hat was planted firmly on her head. She spent lots of working hours squeezing stories out of people who were professional liars. No matter what Al's luscious lips were saying, he wasn't one of life's nice guys.

She knew that because? His eyes. He had eyes that could lure a woman into all kinds of sexy or possibly even illegal situations. Maybe both at once. They were hazel. She'd wondered about that. A lot. It was a little unsettling to realize how much she wondered. And if eyes truly were the windows to the soul, Al's soul was a scary place. So many emotions, all of them dark.

Jenna blinked and broke eye contact. "I admire someone with your kind of calling." She didn't even try to sound sincere.

His soft laughter walked up her spine on silent predator's paws. "You'd be surprised at what I do for my 'calling.'"

No, I wouldn't. And I'll find out soon enough. She shifted her gaze to his hair. Dark brown. He'd braided it, and the braid fell almost to the base of his spine.

She wondered on a purely impersonal level what that hair would look like freed and falling around his shoulders. Things got a little less impersonal as she wondered what those silky strands—they'd have to be silky because he was that kind of a guy—would feel like skimming across her bared body. Drawing in a deep breath, she banished that thought to the trash bin where it belonged.

"Kelly told us you were a journalist. What kinds of stories do you write?" His expression said, "Making meaningless conversation here."

Jenna smiled. She always loved this part. "I write about vampire attacks, werewolf maulings, ghost infestations, and alien abductions." Her theory was never act defensive about what you do. Always attack first.

Instead of the expected snort of derision, he simply nodded and continued eating. How . . . disappointing.

It didn't look like he intended to hold up his end of the

conversation, so she shifted her attention to the man on the other side of her. He had the requisite great body and face that was evidently required to join this missionary society, but there his similarity to Al ended.

He had short spiked blond hair, brilliant blue eyes, and a gorgeous smile. But she wasn't sure she believed that smile. She glanced past him and realized the two men who sat next to him were carbon copies.

She grinned. "Triplets?"

"Yeah." His smile widened. "We do everything together."

Jenna didn't find that particularly comforting.

He nodded at the two other men. "These two are Tor and Rap. I'm Utah."

She didn't ask him to explain who was who because she'd never be able to tell them apart anyway. Jenna leaned forward and smiled at the other men.

Tor, or maybe it was Rap, spoke up. "How long do you think you'll be here?" The unspoken addendum was, "I hope it won't be long."

She was sure of that. He was still smiling, but his eyes had a "get lost" gleam to them. Ah, it was great to be wanted. "A week or two. I don't have to worry about my job. My laptop's in my room, and I bet Philly has as many weird stories as Houston."

Jenna could've sworn they all looked a little wary, but maybe she was imagining it. Could be she was seeing deceit everywhere she looked because she was worried about Kelly. Maybe she should back off and give these guys the benefit of the doubt until they proved they didn't deserve it.

She considered that for a nanosecond.

Nope, couldn't do it.

Her intuition was scarily accurate, and her intuition was pointing fingers and taking names. And so far it had the names of everyone she'd talked to since she'd arrived last night, including her loving but lying sister.

Utah's smile faded, revealing a face that could only be described as predatory. "Some stories shouldn't be told."

A warning? It sure sounded like it. Jenna had never considered herself a coward, but she quickly shifted her gaze to the man across the table from her.

Jenna recognized Lio from last night. There was something really sexy about his square-neck chunky sweater. It wasn't the color. Dark gray wasn't a huge turn-on. It was the way he wore it, as though he could stride down any street in the country and women's heads would turn. His hair, his clothes, his attitude said, "I'm too rich for any woman's blood, but for the woman who dares . . ." Jenna couldn't finish that line, because she didn't know what would happen to a woman who dared.

Lio's smile was cool, his gaze assessing. "What do you want to do while you're here in Philly?"

She tried to look casual as she took a sip of coffee before answering. "Visit with Jenna, see Independence Hall, maybe take a look at your soul-saving techniques." Jenna deliberately met his gaze. "Just in case I ever have the urge." Okay, that sounded ridiculous.

Lio dismissed her comment with a contemptuous twist of his lips. "We don't save *souls*, Ms. Maloy."

She opened her mouth to blow his sarcastic butt off the chair when Fin saved him.

"We're not missionaries in any religious sense, Jenna. I'm sorry if you got that impression. We search the night for people who've been cast aside by society, who need a second chance at life, and we give them that chance. We're sort of hands-on philanthropists."

Jenna nodded. "That makes more sense. You guys don't fit the missionary mold."

"And what's the missionary *mold*?" Al sounded as though he was holding back laughter.

She hated anyone laughing at her. Always had. Jenna turned on him. "Gentle, kind, caring, and good." And yes, she'd just insulted all of them, but maybe they needed to know from the beginning that she wasn't a naïve ninny.

He watched her from eyes backlit by something savage and hungry. "What *are* we then?"

Jenna wasn't sure who was more surprised when the truth popped out. "Hard, predatory, and . . ." She shrugged. "Only as good as you need to be." Fine. So she wasn't sure about the last.

"An interesting judgment." Fin's voice was the purr before the pounce.

Suddenly, Jenna knew she had to get out of there. Panic was an invisible hand clapped over her mouth, her nose, smothering her until she didn't think she could take another breath. Where, how . . . She never panicked. "I think I'll pass on breakfast."

With no other explanation, she pushed her chair away from the table. Fin watched her from those strange eyes, and for a moment she thought she saw satisfaction there. "I want to save my appetite for a Philly cheesesteak." She kept her walk to a slow stroll even as her breaths came in short gasps. These guys wouldn't see her run.

Jenna was leaning against the wall outside the dining room trying to catch her breath when Kelly showed up. Her sister looked a bit wild-eyed.

"Where were you? I knocked on your door, but you'd left." Kelly must've realized she sounded a little strident, because she smiled. "I thought we could have breakfast together, just us."

"That's okay, I grabbed something. Ty's waiting for you in there." Jenna wanted to talk to Kelly alone but not right now. She needed time to recover from whatever had just happened. "I have a couple of things to do in my room. Knock when you're ready to go shopping."

Once back in her room, she avoided all thoughts of breakfast as she turned on her laptop and pulled up her file on the Endekas. She'd put it together back in Houston, but no matter how hard she had dug, she'd found zip. Fin and the others seemed to have sprung up fully grown from, well, nothing. No record of parents, past jobs, or just plain living.

For a short while, she immersed herself in adding the details of who had said what at breakfast and a description of each man.

Finally she shut down the computer, leaned her head back against the couch, and allowed herself to think about the panic. It hadn't come from inside her. No amount of psychobabble would convince her it had. Then where the hell did it come from?

Jenna had no answer to that. Yet.

Chapter Three

Hell was shopping with her sister at the same time she tried to wring information from her. Jenna knew this for a fact. She'd been working at it all afternoon. But Walnut Street had too many damn stores. Every time Jenna brought up Fin or his men, Kelly ducked into another shop and bought something expensive.

So now it was almost dark, Jenna's feet hurt, and she hadn't squeezed even a squeak out of her sister. The thought of walking back to Fin's condo carrying a mountain of bags made her want to groan.

She played with the idea of letting Kelly win this round, but too much was at stake. Sure, Jenna had avoided things in her life when it suited her, but this wasn't one of those times. This time the safety of her sister was involved.

Without giving her sister a chance to fight her, she steered Kelly into a small restaurant. "Look, you've dragged me to every store on this street, and now I want my reward." Once they went back to the condo, Jenna would have Ty's presence to contend with. This might be the last time today to get her sister alone.

Looking weary for the first time, Kelly allowed herself to be led to a dimly lit corner of the restaurant. With a huge sigh, she piled her bags beside her.

Jenna waited until the waiter had taken their order before easing into what she wanted to say. "Jeez, sis, I can't believe you bought all this stuff. Why didn't you go shopping with Ty sooner if you needed clothes and shoes and purses and everything else under God's blue sky?"

Kelly cast a disgusted glance her way. "Oh, come on, you're smart. How long do you think Ty would've lasted after I hit the first shoe store? Only a woman can shop with a woman."

Some women weren't born to buy, and right now Jenna hated Ty for sacrificing her to the gods of obsessive shoppers. He'd given Kelly this idea. Only her need to ferret out the truth about Fin and his tribe of really weird but beautiful men had kept her trudging from store to store. "Yeah, well, I think the shop owners of Walnut Street are going to erect a statue to you and your credit card." She took a deep breath. "Okay, sis, you know what I'm going to ask. What the hell is going on with Ty and his relatives? Oh, and by the way, I don't believe that relative crap either."

The expected denials didn't come this time. A promising sign. Kelly seemed to wilt in her seat.

"This isn't the place, sis. I've got a lot of things to explain, and I don't want you going ballistic in a public place."

Whoa, that didn't sound good. "Have you read the kind of stuff I write? There isn't much that can shake me." Jenna hoped.

Silence stretched between them as their waiter brought the food. Afterward, Jenna poked at her salad, waiting for Kelly to begin. When she didn't, Jenna gave her a gentle sisterly nudge. "For God's sake, stop with the mysterious silence. Just spit it out."

Kelly abandoned what she was trying to eat and leaned back in her chair. "Fine. Don't say I didn't warn you."

"Hey, mind if I join you?" The voice was deep, male, and had "in bed" tacked onto the end of that sentence.

No, no, no! Jenna turned with a snarl on her lips to the

man who'd interrupted them. And then she blinked. Somehow she'd thought he'd be one of Ty's "cousins." She was wrong.

What was it with Philly? There must be some kind of magnetic field around the city, because Jenna had never seen so many extraordinary men gathered in one place before. He towered over them, at least as tall as Ty. Hair that blended shades from intense to pale blond fell in a tangled glory around a face that at first she didn't think could possibly exist outside the imagination of an artist. Al and the others were great looking, but in an earthy, savage, *human* way. Except for Fin. He was different. Like this man was different. Both of them had a kind of unearthly—had she really said that?—beauty that made them hard to describe. It was in this guy's icy blue eyes. Stare into them long enough and you'd freeze solid.

Exhaling deeply, Jenna let the bullshit go. She wasn't writing one of her tabloid pieces. This was just a stranger who'd interrupted her very important talk with Kelly. "Do we know you?" She tried to send a "get lost" message his way, but it was hard to sound imperious while she was sitting down and he was looming.

Not waiting for an invite, he slipped into one of the two remaining seats. "No, but I think you'll want to, Jenna."

She stiffened. How did he know her name? Not only had she never seen him before—and she certainly would have remembered that face and body—but this was her first visit to Philly.

Jenna got her second shock when she looked at her sister. Kelly had turned white as she stared up at the man.

He smiled at Kelly, and the temperature in the whole place seemed to rise a few degrees. No matter how cold his eyes might be, that smile was pure sizzle.

"Kelly knows me." His attention returned to Jenna. "We met back in Houston."

"Kelly?" Jenna looked to her sister for an explanation.

"Jenna, this is Seir." There was something in Kelly's voice. Not exactly fear, but a deep wariness.

Which immediately raised all of Jenna's be-careful antennae. "Since I *didn't* meet you in Houston . . ." She wasn't going to give her sister a chance to explain this man away as no one important. Every journalistic cell in her body was screaming in caps that he was very IMPORTANT. "Why don't you tell me a little about yourself so we can be on the same page?"

Amusement gleamed in his eyes as he glanced at Kelly. "Why don't you explain who I am? Ty must've told you."

Jenna didn't like this guy. She didn't like the way he'd managed to upset Kelly, and she sure didn't like the way he'd taken a seat with them and made himself comfortable. On the other hand, he might open a crack in Kelly's information box that so far had remained locked down tight.

Kelly refused to meet Seir's gaze. She stared fixedly in Jenna's general direction. "Seir knows Fin. I guess they're not on speaking terms. The last time Ty met up with him, Seir had Ty pass a message to Fin."

"Coward." On Seir's lips, the word wasn't an insult. It was a warm caress and irresistible temptation. "You know more than that."

Jenna agreed. Kelly was talking in half-truths. She saw it in the way her sister's eyes darted from side to side, never quite looking directly at her.

When Kelly didn't open her mouth to defend herself, Jenna spoke up. "Uh-huh. And who are you when you're not busy passing messages to Fin? And by the way, since no one will tell me anything, who the hell is Fin? I know who he says he is, but who is he *really*?"

Seir laughed. It was a good laugh, low and sexy enough to make all the women in the restaurant shed a layer of clothing. "I'm the man who's watching out for you. For example, I can tell you that someone's been tailing you all day. Thought you might want to know."

Even surrounded by people, Jenna felt a chill. "To know that, you had to be tailing us too." What was going on here? It was her job to follow people, not the other way around. The cloud of doubt and suspicion that had been building ever since Kelly first told her about Ty might just be ready to rain on her. She chanced another glance at Seir's eyes. Change that prediction to snow. One thing for sure, they weren't walking the rest of the way to Rittenhouse Square. She'd call a taxi before they left here.

Kelly reached over and touched Jenna's hand. Jenna shivered. Her sister's fingers were ice cold.

"Don't talk to him, Jenna. You don't know what he is."

"*What* he is?" Jenna thought this whole conversation was getting weird.

Seir didn't look upset by her sister's hints of something dark in his background. He stared at Kelly. "You couldn't even begin to guess what I really am, sweetheart." That sounded almost like a threat.

Jenna pushed her plate away and tried to catch the waiter's eye. "I think it's time for us to head home, sis." If she'd been alone, Jenna would've made a scene and had his ass thrown out of the restaurant, but Kelly really looked upset. And her sister didn't let too much bother her, so this guy must be serious bad news.

"Eating and running? Now you've hurt my feelings."

From the expression in his cold, hard eyes, Jenna figured it would take a lot to put a dent in Seir's feelings.

"Then I guess I'd better give you my message," he added.

Ah, the important stuff. In Jenna's mind, her tabloid self's fingers were poised over the keyboard, ready to pound out a headline.

"Tell Fin he has a mole in his organization, and Zero is trying to eliminate one of the Eleven in retaliation for

Fin's getting rid of Nine." He shrugged. "I don't have the mole's name, but I guess you'll know soon enough if Fin doesn't find him."

Nine? The Eleven? What was that about? Code names. Ah, she got it. Organized crime. It couldn't be anything else.

Suddenly, another man slid into the remaining seat. "I don't know who you are, but I think you need to leave." Al's voice was a threatening growl.

"Hey, Al. Taking a chance coming in here, aren't you?" Seir glanced toward the ceiling. "Not much expansion room."

Al's eyes flared with shock. Then they narrowed. Fury sharpened the lines in his face. He was death in high definition.

Seir didn't look scared. Jenna sure was. But her curiosity, which didn't respond to piddling emotions like fear, waited breathlessly for more info. She'd opened her mouth to ask a question, but Seir spoke first.

"Handling all that inner rage okay?" His smile lifted his lips, but his eyes remained frozen and flat.

Al looked like he'd taken a blow. But where Jenna would've moved away from Seir, Al reacted by leaning across the table and locking eyes with him. "Who. Are. You?"

Seir's expression turned thoughtful. "Looks like Fin made Ty keep his mouth shut." His gaze shifted briefly to Kelly. "But Ty wouldn't keep secrets from his loving wife."

His attention moved back to Al. "I'm Fin's brother. I'm deeply hurt that he never mentioned me."

Al couldn't hide his surprise. "Why didn't Fin tell us about you?"

Seir shrugged. "Black sheep of the family?" He waved that explanation away. "No, that's not right. I'm definitely not the blackest sheep in our family." He smiled. Evidently that thought amused him.

"How do you know me?"

Al seemed awfully intense about the whole thing. But then, she supposed everything in organized crime was about life or death. Not too many shades of gray. Jenna didn't want any part of it, and she sure didn't want Kelly mixed up in it any more than she already was.

"I met you a long, long time ago, Al." Seir's gaze captured Al's. "You don't remember, but then you don't remember a lot of things." After watching that last missile explode in Al's face, he stood. "I've done my good deed for the day, so I'll be on my way."

"So you're on our side?" Al's voice suggested that being on anyone else's side would not be a good thing.

Seir looked surprised. "No. I'm on my own side." His expression darkened. "Never forget that. I only do what will make my life better. Maybe you should hope we have a lot of common goals." And he simply walked away.

Jenna could track his path by the women's heads turning to stare at him. There was a lot to stare at. Even though he was just wearing jeans, a T-shirt, and a leather jacket, no man could even begin to compete with his wow factor.

Except for . . . Jenna looked back at Al. Sure, she was furious at him for following them and wary because of his possible criminal ties, but she hoped she could still be objective about some things. Al didn't have Seir's unearthly beauty going on, but he definitely called up a woman's primitive memories. His face had a primal savagery that would send most women searching for a cozy cave. This was a man who could make a woman drown in everything female about herself. He was a hormone enhancer.

Al was still staring at the door where Seir had disappeared. Finally he looked back at Kelly. Jenna might've been invisible for all he seemed to notice her. And that bothered her on some level.

"Why didn't Ty or you tell the rest of us?" His voice was hard, suppressed rage behind it.

Now that Seir had left, Kelly's courage seemed to have returned. "It wasn't my call. Fin didn't want anyone else to know."

"So? Last time I checked we still had free will."

Kelly glanced away. "Look, you're going to have to talk to Ty or Fin. This is about the Eleven, not me."

Jenna frowned. The Eleven again? She mentally added that to the list of all the things she wanted to ask Kelly next time she got her alone.

Then Jenna forgot about her list as she remembered she was really ticked at Al. "If what Seir said is true, you've been tailing us all day. Who gave you the right?"

Fin did. But Al couldn't tell her that. Damn Fin to hell. He glanced at Kelly, but she only looked away. She'd understand why Fin had put a tail on them, but she wasn't about to keep his ass above water. So he was on his own.

"I don't need anyone's permission to go wherever I want." Attack first had always been his motto. But that was in another time. It might not work so well now.

Jenna seemed puzzled by his reply. She looked as if she was waiting for him to tack an excuse on to his statement. Well, she could wait until her pretty behind took root on that chair.

Pretty behind. Not a safe thought. But once locked onto the mental image, his mind went crazy with it. He remembered the torture of watching the swing and sway of that behind as he followed her all day. Small, round, and compact, each cheek would fit his hands perfectly. And from there he could . . .

Both Kelly and Jenna's eyes widened and focused on him. Crap. He was broadcasting. Thank God they could only lock on to his emotions, not his thoughts.

Kelly's eyes narrowed as she glared at him. "Stop it. Stop it now."

Jenna was on that so fast her mental processes must've been just a blur. "Stop what?"

"Nothing." He and Kelly answered at the same time.

Al expected Jenna to demand an explanation, but she only nodded. Probably figured she'd corner her sister at home and get lots of answers to her questions. He didn't envy Kelly that interrogation.

"I called for one of our drivers right before I came in here. He's probably parked close by waiting for us to come out. Want to ride home with me? Save taxi fare, and I get to lug all those bags to the car."

"I guess so."

Kelly didn't sound enthusiastic, but she must have figured that Jenna wouldn't ask any questions while they were in a car with the driver. He wouldn't bet on it.

Al waited for Jenna to reject the idea, but instead she nodded. Unexpected, but he wasn't going to question his good luck. He waited impatiently as both women finished their meals. Kelly's appetite seemed to suffer in his presence. Not so Jenna's. She ate almost defiantly, as though by stuffing herself she could reject any idea that he made her feel uncomfortable. He admired her defiance.

The transfer of all those bags to the car and the short drive back to the condo were completed in silence. Kelly looked worried, and Jenna swung between puzzled and angry.

Him? He just felt pissed at Fin for forcing him to do this. And if Fin had kept his brother's existence a secret, what else hadn't he told them?

Yeah, yeah, that's not all he felt. Sexual attraction was alive and well in his world. Desperately he tried to think of other things—Fin lying bloody and defeated at his feet,

Fin waving his hand and returning Al to what he once was—but his thoughts always came back to Jenna.

He might not like her, but he definitely wanted to have sex with her. He could almost feel her long legs wrapped around him as he plunged into her, deep and hard, burying himself in her heat and passion.

Jenna made a small sound, and he looked in his mirror to find her eyes, wide and startled, staring back at him. Instantly he switched his thoughts to carrots. Hard, tasteless carrots that Greer insisted on putting in the salads. Al hated salads. Anything without meat wasn't worth eating.

Fin was waiting for them when they reached the condo. Al made sure his mind was open so Fin could root through his memories of the day. He didn't try to hide his thoughts about Jenna. Fin would expect sexual fantasies.

Al knew from his expression exactly when Fin found Seir in Al's mind. Fin's gaze sharpened, but nothing of what he was feeling reached his eyes. Without comment, he turned to Jenna. Kelly had already made her escape to find Ty.

"Let's get comfortable. I want to talk to you." He shot a glance at Al. "You too."

Leading them into the living room, Fin relaxed into his favorite chair and waited for them to find seats. Predictably, Jenna chose another chair. Al pointedly dropped onto the couch. He knew his expression said that eventually she'd have to get close to him.

Once seated, Jenna went on the attack. "Why did you tell Al to follow us around all day?"

Fin cast Al a sharp glance.

"Don't blame Al. He didn't tell me. But it didn't take much to figure out that you're the boss. You had to give the order. And what's with this Seir? Is he your brother? And why doesn't he deliver his messages in person? Or at least pick up a phone, send a text message. Why so cryptic?"

"Messages?"

For one of the few times since Al had known Fin—

Suddenly, one of Al's elusive memories tried to surface. How long *had* he known Fin? He'd never seen Fin before rising to this time. Fin had only been a voice in his head before that. Then why did he feel he'd known Fin's face in another time?

The question was followed immediately by a quick stab of pain. He rubbed his forehead as the thought faded into the gray mist rolling through his mind.

Al shook his head to clear it. What had he been thinking? Oh, yeah. For the first time since he'd known Fin, those silver eyes lost their calm expression. Emotion flared in them—shock, fury, *love*.

Love? Not Fin. Al must've gotten that one wrong. Looking at Fin again, Al only saw what he always saw. Nothing.

"Message. Singular." Jenna's sharp gaze said she was storing away every careless comment or unusual reaction so she could take it out later and examine it. "Seir said you have a mole in your organization. Someone called Zero wants to eliminate one of your guys to get even for Nine."

Fin didn't comment. He stared into space while he tapped out a rhythm on the arm of his chair. Al would've loved to get a look at his thoughts, but the mind stuff was all one way. Fin could, they couldn't.

Jenna didn't give Fin much thinking time before she started with the questions. "Zero? Nine? You've got to be kidding. And the whole mole and eliminate thing sounds suspicious. Are we talking organized crime here?" She took a deep breath. "Stupid question. If you tell me, you'll have to ruin Ty's marriage by chopping his sister-in-law into tiny, easily disposed-of pieces."

Fin waved her suspicions away. "We're not organized crime. But we do have enemies. And no, I don't want to elaborate. Since we don't know the names of these guys, I've tagged them with numbers. Makes sense to me."

It must've made sense to Jenna too in a twisted kind of way, because she nodded.

Fin got down to business. "You wanted to see what we do, so I'm sending you out with Al tonight."

She cast Fin a startled glance. "Can't I go with Kelly and Ty?"

"No." Fin's no always had an unspoken "and that's final" attached to it. "Al's the only one going out tonight, and he's going out because you won't leave this alone until you see exactly how we operate. The rest of us will be in a meeting."

Al pressed his lips into a thin line. Damn him. Fin was making it plain how little he was needed. The meeting would be about rooting out the mole. Fin didn't feel the need for Al to contribute anything. In Fin's mind, Al was simply a problem with a soul he couldn't control.

"If you're ready, we can get started now." Al threw the comment at her. What did he care about being gracious? She didn't want to be with him any more than he wanted to drag her around Philly looking for lost freaking souls.

She seemed a little uncertain. "Maybe I should tell Kelly."

Fin stopped tapping his fingers. "She'll try to talk you out of going. Do you want to be talked out of it? It's your only chance to see us in action."

"Us? You mean the Eleven? Why'd you give yourselves that name? You sound like you have a number fetish."

"You ask a lot of questions. Just like Kelly. It must be an inherited weakness. She could tell you I don't answer many of them." Fin glanced at his watch. "Sorry, I'd love to stay and be grilled by you, but I have a meeting to attend." He rose and started toward the door.

Jenna looked ticked. "Did anyone ever tell you you're a

secretive jerk? Okay, I'll go." Her body language promised that she might go with Al, but she'd make everyone pay for Fin's high-handedness.

And a fun time would be had by all. Al stood.

"Wait." Fin paused and walked back to them. Something in his expression said the other shoe was about to fall. "I'm sending someone else with you guys. He's visiting from Houston, but he knows his way around Philadelphia. He'll do the driving."

"I can drive." Al was dying to get behind the wheel. Any wheel. He hated having a human driver even though he accepted the need for one.

Eight and the rest of his immortal friends could sense the Eleven, but not when they were close to humans. Only humans could keep the immortals off their backs, so Fin had ordered that they stay near one whenever possible. The Eleven couldn't guarantee humans would be around when they hunted the dark Philly streets, but they could be damn sure a human was in the car with them. So Fin hired human drivers and told them that the Eleven were new to the country and didn't know the city. That excuse wasn't needed tonight.

Fin shot Al a pointed stare. "I want you to take care of Jenna and look for people to save. You can't concentrate on all that if you're driving."

Right, and Al believed that. Fin probably wanted someone along to make sure Al didn't go all prehistoric on Jenna. "Yeah. Fine. So who's the friend?"

"I am." Jude's voice swung Al around.

Great. Just what his little soul-hunting party needed, a vampire. "What brings you to Philly?"

Jude's gaze slid past Al to rest on Jenna, who still sat in her chair. Her eyes were riveted on Jude. No surprise there. Even Al recognized that Jude was spectacular in a way that impressed females. All that long black hair and the way he looked at women. Al wondered how impressed they were when he broke out the fangs.

Jude abandoned his study of Jenna for a moment to focus on Al. "I have business in town."

Probably a lie. Al didn't believe in coincidences. Jude was here because of the Eleven.

"I thought I'd stop by while I was here to find out how everyone's doing. Fin asked if I'd do him a favor and drive you guys around tonight." His attention returned to Jenna. "And this is?" He turned that smile on. The one that invited a woman into his bed and promised she'd never want to leave it.

Al didn't give anyone else a chance to answer. "Jenna Maloy. Kelly's sister. You remember Kelly." There was no reason for the anger bubbling inside him. None at all. And yet there it was. He focused on inner calm, trying to convince his soul that there was nothing for it to attack here. He was lying, and his soul knew it. Gleaming eyes watched from that cave in his mind.

Jude stepped past Al and moved over to Jenna. "Hi, Jenna. I'm Jude. I'm going to enjoy tonight." The vampire oozed sensuality from every undead pore.

Al's soul inched closer to the mouth of the cave. It sensed real possibilities in the situation. Al forced his feet to stay in one spot when all he wanted to do was stride over to the vampire, pick him up, and heave him through Fin's expensive condo window.

"Al." Fin's sharp warning came at the same moment Jude and Jenna turned their gazes on him. Jenna looked scared. Not surprising, since she'd picked up on his emotions when he was careless before. Jude just looked amused.

"I have a question." She smoothed her fingers over her jeans with fingers that shook slightly. Her voice *didn't* shake. "Why am I feeling the same emotions Kelly told me she felt when she first met Ty?"

Al looked at Fin. No way was he touching that question even if he was the cause of it. He might not agree with Fin on a lot of things, but he trusted Fin to be able to talk himself out of anything.

"Emotions?" Fin shrugged. "You've been under a lot of stress since you got here. Maybe it's made you more sensitive to what others are feeling. Or maybe it's your imagination."

Jenna narrowed her eyes to insulted slits. "I don't imagine things."

Well, Fin had certainly handled that with style and tact.

Fin looked at his watch again. "Time to get moving. There're people on the streets who need you." His glance at Al clearly said, "Get her the hell out of here."

Al thought that was a good idea. Any minute Kelly might come searching for her sister. He didn't think Kelly would let Jenna go off with Jude and him without a battle. Reluctantly, he tossed Jude the car keys he always carried with him just in case he ever got a chance to drive.

The silence in the elevator as it took them down to the ground floor was about as uncomfortable as it got. Jude looked lost in his own thoughts, Jenna looked suspicious as she darted glances at Jude and him, and Al knew that he just looked grumpy. The scary part was that he was beginning to realize what would put a smile on his face. But he didn't think Jenna would ever be ready for that.

Once in the parking garage, Jude slid behind the wheel while Jenna climbed into the backseat. Al left her there alone because he'd be tempting more than fate by getting in beside her. He grabbed the passenger seat.

And as they drove into the night, Al wrestled with a whole bunch of conflicting emotions. He didn't like her, but he admired her courage. He didn't like her, but he longed to be on more than speaking terms with her luscious body. He wanted her to go home. He wanted her to stay.

Yeah, and he wanted to put his fist through the car window too.

Jude glanced over, laughter gleaming in his eyes. "Fin would take the cost out of your ass."

Al agreed. Maybe he'd get more satisfaction from punching his mind-reading driver in his big mouth.

Chapter Four

"Have everything you need, boss?" The worker peered at him from the darkness. Stake should probably remember the man's name, but then names weren't important to him. Only recruitments mattered. Fine, so he was lying. Only *death* mattered.

"Of course. Sketch pad, pencil, iPod. What else would I take to a slaughter?" Stake laughed at his own joke. He didn't expect the worker to understand.

Tonight he was hoping for lots of beautiful blood spatters cast in complex patterns over every solid surface. His artistic soul cried out for fulfillment.

"iPod? What do you listen to?"

Stake smiled at him, and if his smile looked a little predatory, well, all the better. "I listen to the music of death—the sounds of suffering in a symphony of screams." A lie. But his answer went with his image. Perception was all-important when dealing with underlings.

Actually, he listened to sounds of the sea. He'd always felt the pull of the ocean—the ebb and flow of its tides, the crash of waves beating against the shore. It was a coming-home sound. If he didn't know better, he could almost believe he was birthed from the sea.

The worker frowned. "I like Maroon 5 myself. But that's just me."

Another worker appeared out of the darkness. "Everything's set up. Dave has everyone quiet and ready to listen.

The fools think they're getting paid a few bucks to listen to a motivational speaker." His chuckle held all the maniacal glee that Stake demanded in his people.

"Excellent. You've done well, worker." Already his blood sang with the promise of death.

His setup was simple but brilliant. Bring in a few human sheep. Add in some possible nonhuman recruits to his cause. Mix well. Allow workers to kill humans in front of possible recruits. Give recruitment speech. Sign up nonhumans who thought killing humans was tons of fun. Personally kill nonhumans who refused to sign up—the best part for him. He'd do it slowly and with great creativity.

First, though, he'd watch his workers tear the humans apart. While he sketched the carnage, he'd look for true artists among his workers, the ones who didn't just dispatch the humans but made the whole process into an artistic triumph.

The first worker frowned. "My name's Carl. Why do you call everyone worker?"

Because your name isn't important enough to remember. You're *not important enough to remember.* "I've had a problem with my memory since I was young. I can't remember names." He shrugged. "Don't take it personally."

The worker Carl looked at him as though he wanted to make more of his stupid name, but he must have seen something in Stake's eyes that changed his mind.

"Why don't you ever help with the killing? It's a helluva high." The second worker's eyes glowed red in the night.

Ah, a vampire after his own heart. Maybe he'd promote him. Maybe he'd even remember his name. "What's your name again?"

"Keith—" The guy looked surprised. "I've been your assistant for a couple of weeks now."

"Keith. Yes." Stake would watch how well Keith killed tonight.

Stake turned to the shadowy figures behind him. They were a collection of the dregs of Philadelphia's paranormal society. Homicidal vampires, bloodthirsty shifters, and a few Fae and demons who were in it for the thrill. His kind of men—beings. Couldn't be a sexist. There were a few females mixed in with them. Yes, fifteen motivated killers were more than enough to create wonderfully bloody mayhem in a small enclosed space filled with clueless humans.

"Yeah, why don't you ever join in the fun, Stake?"

His first in command, old what's-his-name.

"I'm an artist. I choose to hold myself above the fray. I prefer to observe and record." He freaking *couldn't* kill humans. Some stupid rule made up by the idiots, er, powers who ruled them all. Stake could only orchestrate their deaths, something he did very well.

He'd have to limit his own pleasure tonight and make sure he only destroyed the nonhumans who refused to join his cause. Anything more would lower the morale of his merry band of killers.

A whispered signal came from the worker planted by the entrance. Yes. It was time to begin the dance of death. A sashay he never tired of.

His workers all crowded around the door. Stake held up his hand. Everyone paused as he carefully spun a magical suggestion that no one should even think about entering this place. That should take care of any latecomers.

Then he slipped inside. He'd dressed for the occasion. Gray pants, an expensive sweater, and a long leather coat. He enjoyed the texture of clothes. The sweater was soft, the coat cool and smooth. He sighed his regret. Too bad it would all be over in twelve months. Not even that, because they were already into January, and December 21 would come much too soon. Through the millennia, he always looked forward to his short times on Earth.

He motioned his workers into the room. "Try to look nonthreatening. Keep them calm as long as possible."

They trailed inside, pretending to be just more of the audience. But a few of the victims must've sensed something, because Stake felt the first tendrils of fear. The fear energized him, as it always did.

He took his time climbing onto the stage. He had such a short while on this planet that he savored every moment. Being an immortal had its downside. Sure, you had the perks of being indestructible, but the whole endless cycle of years could be a monumental bore. Only in death did he feel alive.

He held his arms up to still the babble. Stupid, stupid animals. Stake respected no one but himself and his leader. He secretly suspected that his fellow immortals were less than he was. They didn't deserve his respect either. Look how easily Fin and his minions had taken out one of them in Houston. That would never happen to him.

Everyone had quieted except for a woman whimpering softly in the crowd. Good grief, they hadn't even gotten to the scary part yet. He hoped his workers took care of her first.

Stake cleared his throat and began to speak. "The humans here need not listen. This offer doesn't apply to you."

"Humans? Offer? What the hell are you talking about? You trying to sell us something?" a big guy in the back shouted. "I'm outta here." He turned to push his way past the workers.

Stake smiled. He hadn't thought the fun would begin so soon. "Leaving isn't an option." He nodded at the worker closest to the man.

The vampire reared back, eyes blazing red, fangs bared, and grabbed the guy. The human only had time for a high-pitched scream of terror before the worker tore his throat out. Ignoring the blood spatter and gore, the vampire drank.

The crowd reacted as crowds always reacted, with blind panic. You had to love it.

Time for some crowd control. Stake thought the thought and it became real. The crowd froze in place, humans and nonhumans alike. He smiled at them. "See, now isn't that better? All that wild-eyed shrieking and running is so unnecessary. Everyone will now calmly and quietly listen to what I have to say. When I'm finished, I'll release you."

Behind the crowd, his workers covered all exits and formed a circle around his captive audience. Nodding, he spoke.

"I hate to bore everyone, but it's really necessary for you to understand why I'm here." He smiled benignly at them. A really stupid woman in the front row looked relieved, mistaking his smile for a sign that she was safe.

"You're truly fortunate, or unfortunate as the case may be, to be living in 2012. The ancient Maya created a calendar that ends on December twenty-first of this year. They understood it would be a time of challenge for humanity, but even they didn't know the full significance of this day. On December twenty-first, all humans will be wiped from the face of the Earth." Stake picked up a glass of wine from the table behind him and lifted it high. "I celebrate the brilliance of the Maya. I toast their ability to foresee what was to come." He drained the glass in one gulp. "I bemoan their inability to stop it." Did his sad face look authentic?

Along with his wine, Stake drank in the horror on every human face in the crowd. *That's right, now you understand. You're going to die, and you can't do a thing about it.* He continued with his speech. "I and eight of my immortal compatriots are here to make this a memorable time for everyone on Earth.

"I'm afraid the nonhuman members of the audience

will have to stay frozen until I get some old business out of the way." He nodded to his workers at the same moment he freed all the humans. Then he put in his earplugs and sought inspiration from his iPod and the horror unfolding before him. Stake picked up his sketch pad.

The humans were like ants, scattering in every direction, but his workers were faster. He ignored vampires ripping out throats. Clichéd. His werewolves tore chunks of human flesh from still-screaming bodies. He yawned. The demons were a little more creative, tearing heads off and propping them on tables like place keepers in some ghoulish game. But he'd seen heads torn off before. Could he help it if he felt a little peevish?

Then he saw something new. With a grunt of satisfaction, he began to sketch. He should've known the male Fae would be the fun one. They seemed to have a higher intelligence than the other races.

Stake's pencil flew. What emerged was the angelically radiant face of the Fae, its golden hair sticky with human blood. Ah, it would take all of Stake's talent to show the texture of that hair with only a few strokes of his pencil. The intensity of the Fae's expression amazed him. Could he capture the wondrous evil that shone from those eyes? What an incredible challenge.

The Fae was slowly taking the human male apart one piece at a time and then laying out the pieces to form an immensely creative new form. Unfortunately, the human had lost consciousness the moment the Fae tore off his arm.

Stake's pencil flew over his sketch pad. He cursed his frustration in not being able to fully illustrate the gushing blood that settled into thick puddles all around the Fae.

Finally, there was nothing left but a bloody torso. Stake threw back his head and roared with laughter as the Fae placed the last part of the dismembered body in place on the floor.

The human's head now wore a set of antlers made from his forearm, hand, and spread fingers. His entrails had become a long flowing tail. Note to Fae: deer didn't have long, flowing tails. But Stake would forgive him the mistake because of the total entertainment value.

He labored over his sketch, ignoring the rising gore around him. Stake had amazing concentration when necessary.

With a flourish, Stake added the four legs of the new animal the Fae had fashioned out of the two lower legs and the two thighs. He'd formed an utterly unique creature, a man-deer.

Stake dropped his pad and pencil onto the table and then pointed at the Fae. "Bravo, bravo!" He'd fuck this superb creature later. Male or female had no meaning for him. It was only the sexual experience that mattered.

The Fae saluted him with a bloody hand.

Stake finally took stock of the slaughter. Finished. The humans were nothing more than anonymous bits of flesh. His possible recruits still stood frozen, but their eyes screamed their own terror.

He chuckled. *Not to worry, my new little workers. You're safe. For the moment.* Stepping to the edge of the stage, he addressed his future employees.

"Forgive me for holding you hostage. What you just saw was a demonstration of the kind of entertainment you can expect in your very near future. If you haven't guessed, this is a recruitment meeting. We need more true believers to fan across the city, and then the whole Earth, carrying our message of a shift in world power." He smiled what he hoped was a benevolent smile at the faces staring up at him. "And *you* will be in the vanguard of the shift."

Excitement over the coming apocalypse made him unable to stand still, so he slowly paced back and forth across the stage. "I'm part of a group of immortals who've returned to Earth after a long absence." He mourned the fact that they'd ever had to leave at all. "We've successfully engineered other great overthrows of dominant species. Now we're about to do the same for you. Humans will disappear from Earth forever on December twenty-first. On that day, the massive armies we'll have created will rise up and wipe them out." Just saying the words felt almost orgasmic.

He wagged a playful finger at them. "I bet I know exactly what you're thinking. 'If this guy and his friends are so damn powerful, why don't they kill everyone themselves?' " Stake shook his head sadly. "Oh, that we could. See, we have a slight problem. The powers that be forbid us to destroy humans directly." Stake wanted a minute, just one freaking minute alone with the anonymous powers that be. That's all the time it would take for him to scoop their stupid brains from their heads and put in the brains of something smarter.

Stake blinked and forced himself to concentrate on the job at hand. "That's where you come in." He reached out with his mind to everyone beneath him, smoothing over panic and fear with feel-good emotions that would give all of them a false sense of safety.

He smiled. *Stupid nothings.* They thought because they were nonhuman that they were superior to the ones who'd died. They were only a blink of the eye to Stake's leader. For a nanosecond Stake allowed himself to wish the leader had shared his name with him. Then he forgot about it. The leader could do anything he damn pleased. After all, names were power. Stake never for a moment considered giving his real name to any of his workers.

"You will be our army. When the hour comes, we will lead you in an uprising that will rid the Earth of all humans and put you in their place." He watched their eyes carefully. Their eyes would tell him who would join and who would not. The nots would die, of course.

Good, most of their eyes held expressions of excitement

and anticipation. The few that didn't? They'd serve as a lesson to the others.

"For any who don't see the value in what I'm proposing, think of the possibilities. No more hunting the night for prey while trying to hide your existence from the dominant species. They may be less than you, but there are a lot more of them. Think peasants with pitchforks. And then think of a world where *you* are the powerful ones, the ones who make the rules." *The ones who, after the humans are gone, will happily turn on each other while the world descends into chaos.* The very thought put Stake in his happy place.

"Now I'm going to release you so you can voice your support or rejection." He lifted his arms to signal that they could once again move. The arm-lifting was simply showboating, but it gave his workers a visual of his power. Lower beings needed such demonstrations.

A babble of voices all trying to be heard at the same time hurt his ears. He raised a hand to still them and everyone instantly shut up. Good. They could take direction.

"Any questions?"

The expected hand went up. "I don't wanna be part of any damn army. I get everything I need without your help." The demon had "dumbass" printed in bright neon letters across his tiny brain. "So whatcha gonna do about that?"

Stake smiled gently. "I'm going to send your stupid ass back to hell."

The sudden flash made everyone gasp. Then they took a few seconds to look around the room. When they realized the demon was truly gone, their gaze returned to him. He didn't miss the new respect in their eyes.

"Let me clarify things. I can't kill humans directly, but I can dispose of nonhumans quite easily." His smile never wavered.

Another hand went up. A tentative hand. "Umm, what should we call you?"

Supreme leader? God? Stake resisted the temptation. "Just call me Stake. Not my real name. Only a fool hands out his real name. I like Stake because it reminds me that I have a huge stake in your success." Always make the workers think you're doing it all for them.

"Anyone else want to walk away from my offer?" No one raised a hand. The example of one dumb demon had done the trick. Too bad. The demon hadn't been any fun. Anything that didn't involve blood couldn't be classified as entertainment.

"Good, good. My people will pass out forms to everyone. Name, address, phone number, that kind of stuff. Fill out the forms and leave them on the small table by the door as you leave. Someone will contact you in a few days. And I'm going to stand by the door to shake every one of your hands."

The forms meant nothing. The handshake was everything. As he touched each hand, he'd slip into the worker's mind and know immediately if he or she was truly committed. Any who were lying or planning to betray the movement would be dealt with.

He'd let them think they'd fooled him. But once he'd touched them, they were his. They couldn't run far enough to escape him. He could call them to him, or if he didn't feel like taking the time to destroy their betraying butts, he could send other workers out to do the job for him.

And when he'd completed his recruitment duties in Philadelphia and was ready to move on to the next city, he'd use the memory of that touch to gather them together one last time. By then he'd have a well-oiled organization in place to carry on in place of him.

Once finished with the handshaking, he allowed his

thoughts to wander. Fin and the other Gods of the Night had to be dealt with. Gods of the Night? His leader had chosen that name, but Stake thought it gave them a lot more importance than they deserved.

"What do you want done with the body parts, boss?"

Stake abandoned his thoughts to deal with the worker's question. "Move them, then come back and clean up this place. Find a public building and dump them there to be found in the morning. Make sure you smear lots of blood on the walls and floors. It's time for the real fear to start. Wars are won on many levels. A terrified enemy is an easier enemy to defeat. Philadelphia is about to get its first taste of battle waged on a level it can't begin to understand. Or stop."

Seir stood in the shadows and watched. Perhaps he'd show up at Stake's next party. Maybe he'd even offer his help. After all, he'd been a big help to Nine. In a twisted sort of way.

Of course, he was playing both ends against the middle. He'd played the game so long, he'd almost forgotten which side he was really on. Loyalties were a bitch. Oh, wait. He didn't have any loyalties. That made things a lot easier.

He watched as they all came out, the ones who had survived that is. Finally, Stake, aka Eight, emerged. Self-satisfied bastard. All eight of them were. Zero was the exception. Zero had his head screwed on right. Could he help it if the hired help was less than he was? Jeez, it was hard to find good immortal flunkeys nowadays.

The thought dragged a grin from him. His grin died, though, when he realized Stake's followers were carrying body parts out in big plastic bags. Seir could smell the coppery scent of blood. He scanned their thoughts. Looked like Stake was firing the first major shot in his war against Philly's human population. The terror was beginning.

"As you knew it would."

The voice in his head startled him. Balan. Seir slid his gaze to the many shadowed places not lit by the lone security light. There. Amber eyes glowed intense and intelligent as the blacker shape of the jaguar almost, but not quite, blended into the shadows.

Why was Balan here? Seir knew he was the immortals' messenger, but he owed his allegiance to the head guy. Allegiances could be fluid, though. He should know.

Balan had hung around the edges of the action in Houston. What did he know? Had he been in the Astrodome on that final night when Fin wiped out Nine's recruits? Seir didn't think so. He would've sensed the big cat.

The important question was how much did Balan know about *him*? Nothing, he hoped, other than that he wasn't human. Balan could sense that much. After all, Seir had changed everything about himself. He wasn't what he once was. If Seir's luck held out, Balan would never know who he was or what part he'd played in Nine's exit from Earth.

He reached out to the cat with his mind. *"Who are you and why are you here?"*

"I'm Balan. I'm here to observe and report. Nothing more at the moment."

"At the moment" was the operative phrase. Seir knew what Balan was capable of. Now for a little probing. *"Why did you speak to me? Have we met before?"*

Balan's soft chuckle made Seir uneasy.

"I know you for a demon. I know you worked for the one the Gods of the Night called Nine. That is all I know."

Seir felt some of his tension drain from him. But Balan's next question ramped up the tension again.

"Why did you leave Houston?"

"Yeah, I worked for Mr. Wyatt." Think. *"Too bad he failed in Houston. I don't like failure. So I watched the news until I found a*

*city where the murder rate had skyrocketed. Figured that was a good
clue that another one of the immortals had set up shop. I'm here to
help finish what Nine started."*

Balan was silent for a moment. *"Then good luck . . . with
whatever you plan."*

What the hell did he mean by that? Seir sensed rather than
saw Balan leave. One minute the jaguar was there and then
he wasn't. Now that Seir knew Balan was in Philly, he'd
move more carefully. It wasn't just coincidence, though, that
Balan had been in Houston when Fin was there and now
once again he'd shown up in the same place as the Gods of
the Night.

But wondering about Balan was pointless. Seir walked to
his car, his footsteps echoing along the dark, empty street.
Somewhere in Philly, the dead were being left to be discovered by the living.

Once in the car, he drove toward home. He didn't need a
vehicle, but it was a prop like everything else in his life,
something that made him look normal if humans saw him.

Seir had the ritual down pat. He parked his car as close as
he could to his small apartment—unlike Fin, he was into
keeping a low profile—and then dematerialized only to
reappear in the park at Rittenhouse Square. With no humans around at this hour of the morning, he didn't need to
play the "normal" game. Then he sat in the shadow of a
large tree and stared at the windows of his brother's condo.

Chapter Five

Jenna stared at the back of the men's heads and wondered what she'd gotten herself into. Maybe she should've insisted on telling her sister where she was going. But Fin was right. Kelly would have tried to stop her. And even though her sister had promised to tell all, Jenna got the feeling she'd avoid it as long as possible. This would have been a wasted night waiting around for Fin's meeting to be over.

She compromised by pulling out her cell phone and trying to call Kelly. No luck. Phone turned off. She and Jude and Al had been driving around for hours now, but better to let her sister know late than never. Jenna sent a text message. There. Duty done. Not that she didn't trust Fin. Okay, so she *didn't* trust him. But thinking that he'd knock her off and dump her lifeless body in the Delaware River was a bit of a stretch.

She wasn't totally unprepared for trouble. All the women in the Maloy family carried pepper spray in their purses. And of course, she always had her cell with her.

She glanced out the window. Jude was driving slowly down a dark street with far too few streetlights. Or maybe it was just that half of them looked like they'd been shot out.

"So what're you looking for?" She aimed the question at anyone who'd answer.

"Someone who's lying around on the sidewalk or staggering down an alley." Al didn't sound enthusiastic. So far, they'd found no one in need of saving.

Jude stayed silent.

Jenna returned to staring out the window. Well, that had been informative. She hugged herself. Even with her heavy coat, she was cold. Maybe if Al would shut the damn window, she'd warm up a little.

"Why do you have the window open? It's freezing in here." She'd promised herself she wouldn't complain about the open window. No way would she give either of them an excuse to go back to Fin with tales about Kelly's whiny sister. But enough was enough.

Jude answered. "He has preternatural senses. So he's trying to catch a scent or hear something."

Al swung his head around to stare at Jude. Jenna didn't have to use her intuition to know that Al was ticked at what Jude had revealed.

Jude shrugged. "Sorry. I forgot."

Forgot what? "Preternatural senses? Want to explain?"

"No." Al sounded definite about that.

"Why not?" She prided herself on being persistent. It was part of who she was. No one got a dynamite story without being a pain in the ass at least part of the time.

He didn't answer. Instead, he said, "Stop."

Jude obeyed, stomping on the brake.

Jenna braced her hand against the back of Al's seat. "Jeez, thanks for the warning."

With no explanation, Al shoved his door open and got out. Then he leaned into the open window. "Stay here. Both of you. Do not even *think* about getting out of the car." He speared Jude with a hard stare. "Don't let her do anything stupid."

"Jerk." Unfortunately, he'd disappeared into a small park they'd been passing and hadn't heard her opinion of him.

Jude pulled to the curb, put the car in park, and closed the window. Then he cranked up the heat.

"You're my hero." Jenna meant it.

He turned and flashed her a grin. Being amazed at every great-looking guy she met in Philly was starting to get old. But she couldn't deny the facts. If she used her fave dessert, ice cream, to compare the men she'd met, Jude would be smooth dark chocolate. Long dark hair that flowed over broad shoulders, eyes so dark they seemed black, and a face that had all the necessary angles to capture shadows and women's imaginations. And Al? Al was Rocky Road. Delicious but never predictable.

She was busy trying to decide what flavor Fin was when the shouts and screams began.

Her first thought was that saving souls sounded like a violent business. Her second thought was that maybe Al might need their help.

"Believe me, he doesn't need our help."

Startled, she met Jude's gaze and quickly looked away. Something in his eyes seemed to have changed. They were still dark, but a hungry gleam had crept into them. And wait, how had he known what she was thinking?

He laughed softly. "Don't worry, I wasn't reading your mind. Your expression said it all."

"I thought helping the downtrodden was a more peaceful business. Either one of the down-and-outters is beating our guy to a pulp"—not very likely—"or else Al is making a little too compelling an argument for change. Either way, I think we should take a look."

"No."

Okay, now she was ticked. Her business was gathering info and crafting it into an interesting story. Well, a story was happening out in the darkness, and she wasn't there. But she would be. "Come on, Jude. I want to find out what's happening. If you won't come with me, I'll go alone."

The click of the remote locks was her only answer.

"I don't believe you!" But she didn't get a chance to give him a piece of her mind, because suddenly a shadow emerged from the stand of trees.

Distracted from her mad, she glanced out her window. And froze.

Oh. My. God! Whatever was coming out of that park was so huge she had to look up to get the full effect. It wasn't close enough yet to see details, but she recognized the shape. Every person who ever saw *Jurassic Park* recognized that shape. As she stared in unblinking horror, she could *feel the vibration* as massive feet brought it closer and closer and closer . . .

Jenna screamed. Not a polite ladylike squeak, but a full-throated bellow.

"Son-of-a-bitch. What the hell does he think he's doing?"

Jude's response made no sense at all, but neither did the monstrous thing bearing down on them out of the darkness.

"Drive! Get us the hell out of here."

Instead of obeying her, Jude did the unthinkable. He shut down the engine, pocketed the keys, unlocked the doors, and got out of the car.

"Are you crazy?" Her shriek was drowned out by an animal roar like nothing she'd ever heard before or wanted to hear again.

In response, he leaned back into the car. But he was a different Jude. And this one scared the crap out of her. The eyes that a few minutes ago had promised sensual nirvana now glowed red. Then he opened his mouth and hissed at her. He sure didn't have those sharp fangs the last time he opened his mouth.

"Stay here," he ordered, and ran around the front of the car to confront the thing that now towered over them.

"Get your fucking head screwed back on! Stop right

there!" Whatever Jude was, smart wasn't part of it. He was about to get either torn apart or stomped on.

She was in a waking nightmare. Jenna had always wondered what she'd do in a crisis situation. Would she calm everyone around her while she called the bomb squad, talked the jumper off the ledge, or saved the woman who'd fallen onto the tracks? She'd always liked to think she'd keep her cool and do the right thing.

Jenna panicked. Pure and simply freaking panicked. Her breaths came in great wheezing gasps as she flung open the car door and ran. Wildly and without any thought about where she was going. Her pounding heart was so loud she was sure the creature would be able to track her by that alone. She imagined the thud, thud of its massive feet gaining on her.

She didn't think. Thoughts were beyond her. *Run, run, run.* The words took on a rhythm in her mind as she matched her pumping legs to the cadence. If she could just run fast enough, far enough, the nightmare would go away.

And then, unexpectedly, there was light. One of those all-night convenience stores, a beacon in a lost world. Finally, the first thoughts trickled into her mind.

There was only one person she trusted in this strange city. She had to call Kelly. Oh, God, she'd left her purse in the car. Frantically, she tried to think of a lie to tell the clerk. She glanced behind her. Would the monster follow her here? Would it hurt anyone in the store?

Jenna forced herself to breathe more slowly, channeled inner quiet to her completely berserk mind, and tried to think calm thoughts as she pushed open the store's door.

She didn't have to try hard to look traumatized as she walked to the checkout counter. "Please, you've got to help me." *A monster is chasing me.* "Someone just mugged me. Took my purse. Can I use your phone to call my sister?" Did she sound pitiful enough?

"Not going to call the cops?"

She shook her head. What would it accomplish? If what she'd seen was real, lots of people would have called the police by now. They'd be too late to save Al and Jude anyway. *Al*. Her heart gave a primal scream of despair. What had happened to him, and why did she care so much?

It was a testament to the neighborhood that the clerk didn't look shocked. "Shouldn't be on the street this time of night, lady." His expression said she was too stupid to live. But at least he let her use the store phone. "Make it short."

She offered him a watery smile—when had the tears started?—and quickly punched in Kelly's number. *Please, please have your phone turned on.*

"Hello?"

The familiar sound of her sister's voice almost made Jenna's knees buckle.

"Kelly, you have to come get me." She couldn't keep the panic from sliding into her voice.

"Where are you, sis? I got your text message. I had my phone turned off during the meeting."

Good old Kelly. She didn't waste precious time asking what happened. "I don't know. I heard Jude say we were in North Philly." Jenna glanced at the clerk. "Address?"

He gave it to her, and she passed it on to Kelly.

"Ty and I are on our way. Stay where you are. Will you be okay until we get there?"

"Sure. But hurry. I'll explain when I see you." Now that she'd calmed down a little, reason told her that neither Jude nor Al—if he was still alive—knew where she'd gone. And since the monster hadn't shown up yet, she felt a little safer.

Jenna ended the call and handed the phone back to the clerk.

He propped his elbows on the counter and studied her. "Been lots of homicides around here lately. Weird stuff. You're lucky he just took your purse." Unspoken was the belief that someone stupid enough to be on the streets alone after dark didn't deserve much luck.

Jenna just nodded and wandered over to the window to watch for Kelly or anything else that might come out of the darkness.

Her brain had finally returned to a functioning organ, and she allowed herself to think about what had happened. *What had happened* was impossible. Had she just gone through a mental breakdown? Was everything some demented brain burp? No, she felt normal. *You'll never feel normal again.*

Every story has a past. And the past often explained the present. Jenna focused on everything that had happened since Kelly first met Ty. All the unexplained little things that had made Jenna suspicious from the beginning. Up until to-night, she'd been leaning toward Fin and the others being part of organized crime. She should be so lucky.

She shook her head to clear away the stuff that didn't make sense. Couldn't do it. Because tonight *nothing* made sense.

Were Jude and Al still alive? Just thinking about Al being dead made her stomach flip and then drop. Nausea rose on a wave of dread. What had happened to him? And why had she panicked and left him behind? She'd failed him.

And what about Jude? Had she really seen what she thought she'd seen, or were the glowing eyes and fangs all a result of an imagination gone wild? She shuddered.

The story she might have was only an afterthought right now. *If* she was ready to accept what she'd seen as real. She didn't know. God, she just didn't know.

It felt as though she'd been looking out at the parking lot for hours, trying to make sense of the madness, when Ty finally pulled up to the store.

Jenna's relief left her weak and shaky. She wanted to fling herself into her sister's arms and bawl like the baby she felt she was. In all her imaginings, she'd never believed that in a time of crisis she'd run away, abandoning another human to God knew what. She'd have to come to terms with her new diminished self-image. But not now.

Not wanting the clerk to hear any part of the coming conversation, Jenna ran from the store to meet her sister. Kelly flung her arms around Jenna and hugged her tight.

"What happened?"

Jenna stepped away from Kelly and waved Ty back into the car. She climbed into the back while her sister returned to the passenger seat.

Then both Ty and Kelly turned to stare at her.

"Let's hear it." Ty looked grim.

How could she tell them what she'd seen without both of them looking at her like she was crazy, without her *feeling* like she was crazy? But if Jenna trusted anything, she trusted Kelly's belief in her. *This time you have a whopper to believe.*

As calmly as she could, Jenna told her story. When she finished, there was a charged moment of silence.

Then Ty exploded. "Damn them to hell! The dumb shits. What the fuck were they thinking?"

Jenna cringed. She never cringed. Not even when the main crazy in one of her stories had told her that giant bugs the size of rats were crawling through the sewer lines and would soon pop up in her toilet.

Kelly's reaction was more subdued. "Oh, no. They didn't."

This wasn't the reaction Jenna had expected. For once in her life, she had nothing to say. She fell back against the seat with a startled *oomph* as Ty peeled out of the parking lot.

"Get Al on his cell," Ty threw at Kelly as he drove way too fast in the general direction Jenna had indicated she'd run from.

Other than a terse, "Where are you?" from Kelly, Jenna didn't get any other information, but at least it seemed as though Al was alive. *Thank you, God.*

A few minutes later, Ty pulled up to the curb at the park where Jude and Al waited. Panic shadowed Jenna, a sense that something horrific still lurked in the darkness, ready to pounce.

"What about Jude? Don't let him into the car." What if Ty and Kelly *didn't* believe her story? Panic slithered closer. Her gaze darted from tree to tree, searching for the menacing shadow and finding none. Self-doubt crept in. Had there ever been a shadow? Had Jude ever had glowing red eyes and fangs? Was she the victim of a psychotic event?

"They're both getting in." Ty seemed definite about that.

"They have their own car." Jenna hoped she sounded calm, rational.

"Not anymore." Ty sounded a lot less calm and rational than Jenna did.

"What?" For the first time, Jenna glanced at the car Jude had been driving. The front end was crushed. Flat. She swallowed hard. Ty didn't give her a chance to ask any questions.

"We'll discuss it back at the condo." His voice was clipped, angry.

Kelly shifted in her seat so she could look back at Jenna. Worry shadowed her sister's eyes. "I should've talked to you sooner. But I didn't know you were going out with Jude and Al tonight. You should've told me." She quickly waved away Jenna's response. "No, it's not your fault. It's mine. I should've told the family when I was still back in Houston. But I thought I'd have lots of time to work it out."

Told her what? For the love of God, told her *what*? Jenna was too confused, too upset at everyone, to make any reply. She just nodded.

But when Al pulled open the door and slid in beside her and Jude went around the car and got in on the other side, panic shook her. She clasped her hands over her stomach to hold everything in.

"Did anyone see you?" Ty scanned the darkness.

"Don't think so. At least no one came out or called the cops. Not surprising in this neighborhood." Jude sounded matter-of-fact about the whole thing.

Al watched her from eyes filled with emotions that tore at her—rage, regret, sadness. None of them made sense.

She didn't think she could even look at Jude. She would've sat in Al's lap to avoid touching Jude if she wasn't almost as afraid of Al. Because whatever had happened in that park had involved him as well. And where had the monster gone?

"Do you need a cleanup?" Ty sounded like he was suppressing a lot of anger.

"Yes." Al didn't elaborate.

Kelly punched in another number on her cell. No greetings. She just said, "Cleanup," and then gave the address.

No one talked for the rest of the way back. Jenna wasn't going to be the one to speak first. Besides, she had too many thoughts racing around in her head to concentrate on a conversation.

"Look at me, Jenna." Jude's voice was low, compelling, and she found herself turning to stare at him even as her brain screamed at her not to look.

"Leave her alone." Al's voice was a rumble of savage threat.

Jude shrugged. "I was just trying to help."

"You can help by shutting up until we get to the condo." This came from Ty.

"Watch it, human." Jude was all smooth menace. "Respect who I am."

Human? Jenna couldn't even begin to process the meaning of that one word. Her memory laughed hysterically and whispered, "Yes, you can."

Now that Jenna was actually facing Jude, she forced herself to study him. He looked like the same gorgeous man

she'd met a few hours ago. He smiled. No fangs. She relaxed just a little. But she knew in her heart of hearts that
only the calm presence of her sister kept her from screaming like a banshee. And that's about all she'd be able to do
hemmed in by both men.

Jenna should've felt relieved when they reached the
condo, but she could only think that inside were more men
like Al and Jude. She forced herself to climb from the car
and not run away from all of them. When Al offered his
hand to help her out, she pointedly ignored it. No touching.
She didn't know why that was important. He wasn't going
to infect her with whatever he had.

The uncomfortable silence lasted all the way up in the elevator. The mirrored walls reflected everyone's tense faces
back at her. Thank heaven Kelly stood beside her. Kelly
wouldn't be so calm if there was danger anywhere near.
Jenna had to believe that.

Fin met them at the door. And if Jenna thought she'd felt
fear earlier, it was nothing compared to the mindless terror
she felt looking into those silver eyes. Something cold and
merciless moved in them. She shivered.

He swept his gaze over them. "All of you. In the media
room." As Jenna started to follow Kelly, Fin put a hand on
her arm. "You, come with me."

Kelly swung to face Fin. "I should be the one to tell her."

"You gave up that right when you put it off so long that
this happened."

Fin's voice dripped with cold fury. Even Kelly seemed
to wilt beneath it.

Ty joined his wife, pulling her to his side in a protective
gesture. "Don't blame Kelly. This isn't something that's easy
to explain. Besides, you're the one who invited Jenna here."

Jenna felt like a volleyball being lobbed from one side to
the other. "Hey, guys, I'm right here." She looked at her
sister. "It's okay. Fin can do the telling. He's such a cold

bastard that he'll keep me from going all emotional."
There, problem solved, with the added bonus of letting
Fin know what she thought of him.

There was a long silence, and Jenna got the weird feeling
that some kind of conversation was going on without her.

Finally, Ty turned toward the media room again. Kelly
stepped up to Jenna and hugged her. "Everything will be
fine. Listen to Fin and what he says. He's telling the truth.
And I'm sorry."

Sorry for what? She asked herself that question all the way
to Fin's office. And what an office it was. Huge with soaring
ceilings and a bank of windows that looked out over Philly.
The lights of the city looked bright and magical. She glanced
at Fin as he took his seat behind his massive oak desk. If the
lights were bright and magical, then Fin was dark and demonic, even with his silver persona. She sighed. Okay, time
to shut down her imagination. She sat stiffly in a chair facing
him across the endless expanse of his desk.

Instead of facing her, he swiveled his chair so he was
looking out the windows at the night. "I had a better condo
in Houston. Higher. It felt like I was in the stars."

What a whimsical thing for him to say. Didn't fit his image.

"And what *is* my image, Jenna?" He didn't turn to face
her but continued to stare out the windows.

Shock clogged her throat, taking away her breath and
her voice.

Fin waited patiently for her to answer.

She was finally able to croak, "You read my mind."

"Yes. But I asked you a question."

Slowly, her heart calmed. After what had happened at the
park tonight, this didn't seem worthy of total collapse. Besides, she'd had a demonstration of his mind-reading ability
last night. She'd just chosen to forget it. "I think you're

cold, calculating, and hiding emotions that would probably scare the crap out of me. I also think you must be incredibly powerful to lead the kind of men I saw today. Now will you tell me the truth about all this?" Good, anger pushed some of the fear aside.

He finally swung his chair around to face her. "I'll tell you, but I have to make one thing clear. Only my respect for Kelly kept me from wiping your mind clean of what happened tonight."

"You can't do that." Her response was more instinctual than reasoned. No one could take another person's memories away.

Fin smiled. It was slow and so glorious it made her want to cry. Did that make any sense? No. But after the park, she had every right to get emotional over whatever she wanted.

"Tell me about tonight, Jenna." His gaze speared her, reached inside her, and did weird things to her thoughts.

Okay, now that impression was definitely the product of a deranged imagination. She'd just opened her mouth to answer when a stabbing headache caught her by surprise. Where the hell had that come from? It was like an ice pick to her brain. But she tried to fight past it. "Kelly and I came home from shopping and you said I should go with Al and Jude to see . . ." See what? She frowned, straining to remember. There was an important reason why she was supposed to go with them tonight. Where had they gone? What had they done? Jenna closed her eyes, tried to picture the night, tried to reclaim her memory of what had happened. Because every instinct screamed that something important *had* happened.

Fin nodded. "Now I'll return your memory. Then we can get down to business."

Suddenly, it all came flooding back, and the headache disappeared. The park, the monster, Jude. She breathed out a horrified breath. Fin had done what he'd promised. How? "Who are you?" It sounded like a cheesy line from some grade-B movie, but it fit the moment.

He shrugged. "Who, what, it doesn't matter. Let's not waste time. I'll tell the story, and you'll keep quiet until I'm finished. Then you can ask questions." Fin looked as if it pained him to grant her any questions at all.

"Go ahead." Jenna forced herself to relax as she slid a little farther down in her chair.

"The Maya Long Count calendar ends on December twenty-first of this year at exactly 11:11. The Maya believed that time is cyclical. The present time period ends at that moment. Time then resets to zero and begins again."

She nodded. Lots of apocalyptic myths were attached to the 2012 date. But some people saw the final days in everything. Jenna didn't.

"The Maya understood the importance of numbers." He paused. "So do I. I have an affinity for them. They guide my existence."

Jenna thought that was a bit extreme, but then everything about this group of men seemed extreme.

"We're the Eleven, and our destiny balances on that number. At 11:11 on December twenty-first, we'll be at our most powerful. And that's good for humanity. Because if we're not successful in what we're doing now, mankind will cease to exist at that moment." He spread his hands in a symbol of inevitability. "Time will go on without you, your family, or any other family on Earth. And a new dominant species will arise. One that will bring chaos and destruction to this world."

Wow, he did bombshells well. Jenna knew her mouth was hanging open, and she felt like she'd never blink again. He had to be crazy. Then she thought about his mind-reading and memory erasing. Maybe not.

Jenna automatically started to ask a question, but he put

his finger over his lips, and she shelved the question for the moment.

"Who are the enemy?" He steepled his fingers and stared at the opposite wall.

Memories? Her intuition said yes. From his expression, they weren't good ones. For no logical reason, her thoughts slid briefly to Al. Did he share those memories? Was that why she sensed all those emotions hiding behind the angry stare he showed the world? And why did she even care?

"They're a group of ten immortals. At the end of each time period, they appear to do what they do best—destroy. Not directly. They can't personally lay hands on the dominant race. The last time this happened, they used an asteroid strike along with volcanic eruptions to get the job done. Now they're getting nonhumans to do their work for them. The minute the new time period begins, they're banished from Earth. But they always come back."

"Nonhumans?" Okay, mental overload alarm ping, pinging away in her brain. She thought about Jude. "Vampires?"

Even saying the word out loud sounded stupid. When she'd told Kelly she thought Ty was a vampire, she hadn't really believed it. She'd just *wanted* to believe, so she could get an awesome story. But she'd never thought—

"Yes."

She took the concept a step further. "And others?"

"Yes."

With that one word he shattered the shell of what she'd believed was her world. But what she'd believed in had only been a pretty veneer. The cracks revealed something dark, frightening, and totally impossible to accept in a few minutes. She'd need lots of time to think through this new vision of the universe.

"Since I have no names for them, I call the immortals by numbers. They were granted access to Earth about six months ago. They've spent their time here traveling to major cities where they're recruiting an army of nonhumans who'll be ready to rise and destroy all humans on December twenty-first. They have no problem with their recruits starting to kill now. It helps to spread terror, and terror is their friend. We came to Philadelphia because I knew Eight was here."

"Eight?" His explanation was making her head ache again. The fingers she pressed to her forehead shook.

"We banished Nine from Earth back in Houston."

"Banished? Not killed?"

"They're immortals. We don't have the power to destroy them."

"You've left a bunch of holes in this plot. Why can't—?"

Fin exhaled wearily and leaned back in his leather chair. "Did I not explain the silence and question rules thoroughly enough?"

"Right. Silence." But questions about Al, about all of them, tripped over each other in her mind.

"We existed sixty-five million years ago when the immortals last visited Earth. They met no resistance that time. We had no weapons that could defeat them."

A slow smile tipped up the corners of those marvelous lips, and for just a moment, Jenna saw another man inside Fin.

"This time we can fight. And fight we will. This time we have—"

Whatever he would have said was cut off when someone knocked on his door.

"Just a minute, Shen." Fin didn't sound any happier about the interruption than she was.

It said a lot about her acceptance of his power that she didn't wonder how he knew who was on the other side of the door.

"Find Al. He'll tell you the rest of what you want to know."

"I can ask Kelly."

"No, you can't. Kelly and the rest of the Eleven were called out for something important." A shadow dimmed those silver eyes for a moment.

"Something important? Kelly didn't say anything about going back out when I just saw her. How do you know she was called out?"

"I always take a look into the mind of anyone standing on the other side of my door. Safety issues. Shen is about to give me the details."

That scared Jenna. "Kelly isn't in danger, is she? Why does she have to go with Ty anyway?"

"Your sister isn't in danger. But she's Ty's driver. She has to be with him." He held up his hand. "Let me reword that. She wants to be with him."

"Why does he need a driver? I—"

"Enough." It was an order. "You're like your sister, an endless stream of questions. Al can answer all of them."

Endless stream of questions, hah. If she weren't so traumatized by everything tonight, she'd give him questions until they squirted out his ears.

She rose and headed for the door, determined to track down Al and wring every last bit of information from him.

"Jenna."

She looked back at Fin.

"I hope you decide to stay."

"Maybe." Definitely. Unless she could find a way to drag her sister back to Houston without Ty. Fat chance of that happening, though. So she'd be staying here as long as Kelly might be in danger. And from what Fin had told her and what she'd seen, there was a whole lot of danger going around.

"I don't invite many people to my condo. I invited you."

"Thanks?" What was he getting at?

"Sixty-five million years ago, I had a series of visions.

You were in one of them. You're very important to the Eleven, Jenna." With that parting shot, he twirled his chair around to stare out at the city again.

She knew a dismissal when she heard it. That was fine, though, because she couldn't have gotten a word past the shock clogging her throat. Numbly, she opened the door and almost knocked down the man on the other side.

He was about six feet tall and lean, with dark hair, dark eyes, and a big smile. "Hi, I'm Shen, Fin's assistant. And you're Jenna. If you need anything while you're here, let me know."

All she could do was nod dumbly and slip past him. Then she went in search of Al.

Chapter Six

Al didn't even pretend to be amusing himself. Things were happening, and he was sitting in front of a freaking TV.

Someone had slaughtered—and slaughtered was the only word for it—a bunch of humans and left the body parts in a used furniture store.

A member of the local werewolf pack had caught the scent of death as he walked past and investigated. Almost buried under the stench of blood and body fluids, he'd caught a fading whiff of nonhumans. He'd reported to his pack leader.

Luckily, Fin's relationship with the Houston pack leader had paid off in timely info from the Philly pack leader.

Fin had ordered all of the Eleven except for Al onto the streets to see if they could track down any of the killers. When a mass murder happened in a city where the immortals were at work, it probably could be traced back to them. Eight must've had a busy night.

Shen had taken care of mobilizing a cleanup. If the ones who did the slaughtering were hoping to make a splash on the news with this, they were in for a disappointment. Yes, there would be missing-person reports, but the bodies would never be found, and no sign of the murder would remain at the store.

And what was *he* doing while everyone else was out

being useful? He was sitting on a couch staring at a blank screen. He wasn't even motivated to turn the damn TV on.

Grounded like some kid. He tried to work up a healthy rage, but for once he had other things on his mind beside his soul.

What was Fin telling Jenna, the truth or an elaborate lie? She'd seen too much tonight, so he must be laying out the truth. Would she pack her bags and take the first flight out of town? She'd panicked tonight, but who wouldn't? She might stick around for her sister. *But she sure enough won't ever relax around you again.*

Footsteps coming toward the media room warned him that he was about to lose his precious solitude. Good or bad? He wasn't sure, because before she even entered the room he knew it was Jenna. Her distinctive scent of cool mint and hot temptation went before her. She wouldn't be happy to know how easy she was to identify.

She walked into the room, glanced around, and then hesitated when she realized he was the only one there. A ripple of bitterness touched him. Yeah, Fin had told her the truth. She was afraid to be alone with him now.

But he was in a defiant mood, so he patted the spot beside him on the couch. "Have a seat. What do you want to watch?"

Jenna hesitated for just a few beats too long before walking to a nearby chair and sitting. She didn't look like she was here to watch TV. Her expression said she was a woman with a mission. Crap.

Smoothing her fingers over the arm of her chair, she leaned back and crossed her legs. Must be trying to look relaxed. It wasn't working. He could smell her fear. It was a scent he'd always gloried in, as long as it wasn't his. It had always meant he was close to a kill, and the kill was what his life had been all about in that other time.

Her scent made him feel defensive—not a familiar emotion—and that made him mad. He shouldn't care what she felt about him. "Okay, I get that you're not here to watch TV or because you want to be with me."

Jenna narrowed her gaze on him. She had to recognize the aggression pushing at him, and she didn't like it. Too damn bad.

"I just got through talking with Fin. He explained the basics of what's going on with you guys, but he left a lot of blank spots."

Al empathized. "Fin is all about blank spots." How many times had Al felt that Fin lived in his own hidden world? Their beloved leader was a font of nonanswers. Al hated being manipulated, and deep in what passed for his heart, he believed Fin was using all of them.

"Fin didn't get to answer all my questions because someone named Shen interrupted. Fin said you'd fill me in on the rest."

Al wanted to be anywhere but here. Exactly how much had Fin told her? Did she know what he was? She might have a clue, but she probably wasn't certain, because if she was certain she wouldn't be here at all. *Thanks, Fin, for laying this load on me.*

Somewhere in his mind, he heard Fin's laughter.

"Sure, what do you want to know?" *Do you want to know how much I need your long bare legs wrapped around me? How about if I tell you how much I want to bury myself in your heat and feel your soul-deep shudder as I drive deeper and deeper? Sure, ask me anything.*

She nodded but didn't quite meet his gaze. "What are you?"

Ah, she was starting with the money ball. "What do you think I am?" Coward. He wanted her to say it first. He didn't want to be the one to put the word out there and watch it scare the shit out of her.

"I hate game playing." Jenna finally met his gaze. Her eyes were cool and controlled.

Brave lady. He shrugged. "Otherkin have nonhuman souls trapped in human bodies. Our cook, Greer, is otherkin. He has the soul of a tiger."

Al studied her expression. So far no panic, just intent interest. She nodded for him to go on.

"Greer has all the instincts of the tiger, but he'll never walk the Earth in the form of his beast. His soul is trapped. The Eleven are a kind of otherkin, but we have the power to release our souls." And sometimes their souls escaped and ran wild.

Some emotion flooded her eyes and then was gone. "The shadow I saw tonight."

"Yeah."

"What happens when you release your soul? Do you shift?" She edged forward in her seat. She'd stopped stroking the arm of the chair. Her gaze was intent.

"My soul manifests its physical form with every scary detail in working order. It's a flesh-and-blood ancient predator stalking the city streets looking for prey. But it's not powerful enough to completely overwhelm the human part of me. If you look closely, you can still see the shadow of my human form within the . . . beast." That hurt. Not because he was ashamed of what he was, but because of how she'd react to that word.

"Fin talked about sixty-five million years ago. That's when the dinosaurs went extinct." She swallowed hard, a brief sign of what she must be feeling if he could only get past the calm exterior. "So your soul is a T. rex?" She blurted it out as though the word burned her tongue.

"Allosaurus." He waited a beat. "Ty's the T. rex." Then he held his breath and watched her.

Hours and years passed before she slowly nodded. "I see." Did she? He didn't think so. She didn't see his agony at being an abomination in a time he despised. She didn't see his aloneness without his pack, his failed attempts to fit in with this new pack. She didn't see his disgust at his rage and inability to control it. "Anything else you want to know?"

Then the most surprising thing of all happened. Jenna laughed. Sure, it was a shaky laugh, but a laugh all the same. And as far as he could tell, it didn't sound hysterical.

"Yes, I have lots of questions. But first let me savor probably the biggest story of my life." She dug her nails into the arm of her chair.

Okay, maybe she did have a little hysteria going on.

"The biggest story of my life and absolutely no one would believe it." She looked thoughtful. "Of course, no one believed my alien abduction stories either. But in this case, I probably wouldn't even get the story written."

"Why not?" He watched her wiggle her beautiful little behind into a more comfortable position on the cushion. Without warning, desire exploded, and his soul awoke.

Oh, hell. Al forced his gaze away from her. He stared out the window, tried to concentrate on the city lights. *Count them. One, two, three—*

A small gasp brought his attention back to her. She stared at him from wide, startled eyes. But he didn't have any trouble reading the emotion churning behind those eyes. Lust. So strong that it practically oozed from her pores.

While he stared at her, she wrapped her arms around her stomach and rocked forward. "Stop it. Just freaking stop it."

It took him a second to realize she was talking to him. Taking a deep breath, he imagined stepping into a giant bucket of ice. At the same time, he forced his soul deeper into its cave. When he felt nothing more than a normal sexual attraction, he looked at her again.

Jenna had straightened and was staring at him with a mixture of fear and outrage. "What the hell was that? It was coming from you. I know it was, because I've never felt that kind of arousal before, didn't think it was possible to feel it. It . . . it *hurt*." She looked amazed by the revelation.

It was time to ramp down the intensity. "Hey, sixty-five million years is a long time to go without sex. Besides, I have a big soul with the big emotions to go with it. Promise, I won't broadcast around you again."

"Broadcast?"

"Let my emotions get away from me. They're strong enough for someone else to feel. Sorry that happened." Not sorry. He wanted to share more than just some sexual emotions with her.

Her gaze skittered around the room, never resting on him once. Not surprising. Fin and he had turned her world upside down tonight. She was handling it a lot better than he'd expected. He hadn't had much experience with putting people at ease, but that's what he wanted to do now. He didn't want her to jump up from that chair and run from the room. He wanted her to keep talking to him.

"You never finished telling me why you can't write your story." Fin had probably threatened her. But it wouldn't be with violence. Fin was more subtle than that. And he wasn't stupid. Kelly was married to Ty. A threat to Kelly's sister would impact Ty and through him the rest of the Eleven.

"He'd probably take away my memory of what happened. Can't write about what you don't remember."

Al stilled, every instinct telling him something important was about to happen. "What makes you think he can do that?"

She looked surprised he'd have to ask. "He gave me a demo. Very impressive. One minute I remembered what happened tonight, and then I didn't. And since he can jump into my mind and root around, he'd know if I was thinking about putting out a story. I'll keep my memories, thank you very much." She sounded like she was taking Fin's demonstration lightly, but her eyes said something else.

He couldn't imagine what *his* eyes were saying. Rubbing his hand across his forehead, he tried to think. All those times when bits and pieces of memories started to surface and then wham, the headache struck and the fog rolled in. Everything gone. Had that been Fin? Could the bastard have done something like that to his own men? If so, why?

"I still have some questions."

You're not the only one. Al pulled himself from the brink. Racing off to confront Fin wouldn't achieve anything. He had to think things through. Uncontrolled rage had already gotten him into trouble. "Ask away."

"Why does Kelly have to be with Ty? He doesn't need her. I saw that tonight. He can drive himself."

Al forced himself to concentrate on the answer. "Eight can sense us when we're alone, but his signals don't work when we're close to a human. Solution: keep a human near in the form of a driver."

Jenna nodded as though she'd added his answer to some inner notebook. "One last thing. Fin said you guys got rid of Nine back in Houston. He's immortal, so you just tossed him out into the cosmos. Why doesn't he come back?"

Al didn't want to talk about Nine. The only way he could push the bone he had to pick with Fin under the rug for the moment was to concentrate on something just as powerful. And that meant Jenna. He wanted to know more about her. Wanted to get closer to her. Who was he kidding? He wasn't good at getting close to anyone. Not since Fin had taken him from his pack.

He shrugged. "I don't have a clue. Guess they have a boss somewhere pulling their strings, because these guys only seem to get one shot at the end of each time period to mess with Earth. Once they're here, they stay until the start of the new period and then they have to leave. If they leave before that, it must count as an official visit. They won't be back until the end of the next period."

"Nine must've been totally ticked."

"Yeah." He couldn't help it; he smiled. He'd never thought of it from the immortal's viewpoint. "I didn't see the actual event, but Ty said Kelly kicked butt that night."

"Kelly?" Horror filled her eyes. "She was there? She was in danger?"

Uh-oh. "She was the key."

"The key?" Jenna didn't like the sound of that. Up till now, she'd been running on adrenaline and emotion. Most of the emotion since she'd entered this room had centered on the man sitting across from her. With that intriguing braid she itched to undo so she could slide her fingers through all that hair, the strong hard face with those hazel eyes that bled sadness when he wasn't guarding his expression, and the muscular body exposed by the clingy sweater he wore, he was a major distraction.

The things Fin had told her, along with the holes Al had filled, gave her a picture of life that could only exist in some alternate universe. She was in shock. That's the only reason she was still here.

No, you're here for Kelly. And what Al had just said about her sister needed expanding. But she wouldn't ask him; she'd ask her sister. "Well, thanks for answering my questions. Guess I'll head to my room." She stood, swaying a little from exhaustion.

"It isn't real to you yet, is it?"

His voice was warm and husky, with a sensual pull that softened her insides like bread dough ready for baking. But there'd be no baking going on in her life as long as she was here in Philly. Because everything still had a crazy feel to it, and she didn't intend to cozy up to her insanity.

"No, it doesn't." She met his gaze directly. "Will you make it real for me?"

Wariness crept into his eyes. "How?"

"You know how. I only saw a shadow tonight. I can't believe in shadows."

He stared at her for a long time and then nodded. "Come with me."

Be careful what you wish for. Dread stalked Jenna as she climbed the ornate staircase with him. She hadn't been up here before. "How much condo does Fin have?"

"As much as he needs. I don't know where he gets his money, and I don't ask." He turned to smile at her. "The guy's saving humanity, he deserves his perks."

There was only one door at the top of the stairs. Al pulled it open. He motioned her into the room. Inside, all she saw was one towering space—several stories high and spacious enough for a marching band to practice in. No windows.

Al led her back outside. "Fin makes sure every condo he buys has one floor he can remodel. We use it as a cooling-down area. Anyone whose soul gets out of hand is kept in here until things return to normal."

The rest was obvious to Jenna. No dinosaur—it was hard to even say the word—would be able to escape from this room to tear up Tokyo. She'd watched all those corny monster movies; she'd just never thought she'd be playing a part in one.

Monster. She slid a glance at Al. Big, hard, and so sensual he made her teeth hurt. Did she think of him as a monster? Jenna hoped she was more rational than that. But her job had taught her that sometimes seemingly rational people could act in weird ways.

"Okay, I'm going into the room. Close the door behind me and keep it closed. No need to lock it. I can't get through it when my soul's running the ship."

She could only nod. What was she doing? What in the name of God was she doing?

For the first time, Al reached out to her. He rested his hand on top of hers. She closed off all thoughts, only allowing herself to absorb the heat and texture of his skin.

"Everything will be cool." Turning, he strode into the room and didn't stop until he reached the middle. Then he turned to face her.

Drawing in a deep breath for courage, she shoved the door shut. Then she stared through the small window at the man still standing in the middle of the huge room.

Deep inside where small hopes still lived, she prayed it wouldn't happen, that this whole thing had been one gigantic hoax. A stupid hope for someone who chased the impossible on a daily basis, who made her living by giving people something wild and weird to read with their morning coffee.

When the change happened, it was so fast she would have missed it if she'd blinked. One minute Al was standing there and the next an Allosaurus filled the room.

For a few too many heartbeats, Jenna didn't breathe at all. And when she finally did resume breathing, it was with hard gasps of panic she tried to hold down and control.

Big. He was so damn big. From head to tail he had to be almost forty feet long. With a massive head, S-shaped neck, and short arms that ended in long claws, he was a primitive killing machine. Then he opened his mouth and roared. She stared in unblinking terror at his lethal serrated teeth. Every primal instinct in her body screamed, "Run, run, run!"

She fought down the need to flee and looked, really looked, at him. There was something strange, something not quite right. Then she spotted it. Within the body of the animal was a faint human form. She couldn't make out features, but she knew it must be Al.

"Do you believe now, Jenna?"

Fin's voice behind her drew a startled squeak. She didn't take her gaze from Al though. "Don't ever creep up behind me like that again."

"I don't creep."

It wasn't worth arguing the point with him. "Yes, I believe. That's Al inside the dinosaur, isn't it?"

She sensed rather than saw his nod. "His soul isn't strong enough to completely overwhelm his human form."

"He has to have a human essence. A dinosaur couldn't act human, even with a human body." Jenna turned over all the impossibilities of Al's existence.

"When Zero and his immortals returned to Earth sixty-five million years ago, I took the souls of the Eleven from their bodies and placed them in safe places, places of great power. Al was beneath Machu Picchu in Peru. They remained there until a few months ago when I called them forth again. I gave them all the knowledge they'd need to function in this time."

"That doesn't really answer my question. No matter how much knowledge you gave them, it wouldn't do a bit of good if they had the brain of a dinosaur."

"Maybe I gave them a new brain too." His words were a soft murmur, and she didn't imagine the humor in them.

She didn't believe the brain claim. It was just too great a leap of belief for her human mind to grasp. "You know, you sort of give me the creeps." Okay, so he was her host. "In a good way, of course."

His quiet laughter was really scary. "Your intuition serves you well, Jenna Maloy." Something about the cadence of his speech seemed wrong, not the same as his usual way of talking.

Now she did turn to look at him. Chills danced along her nerve endings. "What are you, a god? Or maybe you're not one of the good guys at all. Do they think you're one of them?"

His expression never changed, but Jenna got the feeling that danger stood only inches away.

"Not a god. If I were, I'd get rid of the immortals and be done with them. Good? Bad? Who knows? It's all in your perspective." Fin shook his head and walked away.

Bemused, Jenna turned back to the window in time to see the Allosaurus body literally dissolve in a cloud, and then Al was standing there. He started walking toward the door.

At that moment, Jenna snapped. Al was literally the last straw, or in this case, the last dinosaur. Events and voices from the past two nights were a kaleidoscope of mind-blowing, panic-inducing sights and sounds in her head. She pressed her palms against her temples to keep her brain from exploding.

He was coming. She stared as the door opened, saw him standing there, watching her, waiting for her response. Then he reached for her hand.

No, she wouldn't let him touch her. To let him touch her was to admit that everything was true, that he harbored the soul of a millions-years-old predator, that immortals were planning to destroy mankind as a preholiday treat, that vampires and other assorted things that went chomp in the night really existed.

Jenna backed away from him, shoving her hands out in front of her to stop him from touching her. Shaking her head, she wordlessly turned and hurried away from him. This was the second time tonight she'd fled. It was becoming a habit. Instinctively, she took refuge in her room. She locked the door. Not that it would stop anyone in this condo from getting in.

Time crawled. Kelly called Jenna from her cell phone,

and Jenna calmly lied and said she was fine. She spent some time Googling all she could find about the Allosaurus. Her journalistic mind turned up one discrepancy in Fin's story. He said he'd taken the souls from his dinosaurs 65 million years ago. Sure, that was the right time for the extinction event, but the Allosaurus had disappeared from Earth 145 million years ago. There was a bit of a time lapse between those two dates. Out of habit, she wrote it down in her notebook for future investigation.

She spent some more time trying to match up the names of the Eleven with their dinosaur counterparts. After all, time used on research was time *not* used thinking about the unthinkable.

Then she sat by her window gazing out at the real world until Kelly rapped on her door. She'd barely gotten the door open before Kelly rushed in and yanked her into a bone-crushing hug.

"I'm so sorry this all happened to you at once, sis. I should've stayed here, but I had to go out tonight with Ty." Something in her sister's eyes said whatever had happened tonight had been bad.

When Jenna was able to disentangle herself from Kelly, she wandered over to plunk herself on the sitting area couch. Someone had started the fire in the fireplace before she got to the room. It should've made her feel all cozy, but she couldn't look into the flames without seeing the Allosaurus staring out at her, its eyes dark and predatory. She tried to see Al in those eyes, but he wasn't there.

Kelly sat beside her but wisely remained quiet.

"Why didn't you tell me sooner?" Sighing, Jenna finally looked at her sister.

"How, sis? How could I say that I'd fallen in love with a guy who had the soul of a T. rex? And that he'd risen from some sort of stasis so he could save mankind from a group of murderous immortals who intended to kill all humans on December twenty-first of 2012?"

Jenna nodded. Kelly was right. She wouldn't have believed her.

"I wanted to tell you and the rest of the family, but I didn't know how." She looked away, her trembling hands the only clue to her emotional state.

"Al said you were the key in Houston. What did he mean?" Jenna had an idea what it meant, but she wanted to hear the full explanation from her sister's lips.

Kelly looked at Jenna. "I don't know how much Fin told you, but I assume it was enough for you to get the general idea of what's at stake."

"Yeah, between Fin and Al I know pretty much everything." Jenna wasn't sure she believed her own statement. Even though she worked for a tabloid, she was a good journalist, and her intuition was telling her there were still secrets to be uncovered. For example, she could've sworn that Al didn't know anything about Fin's power to wipe her memory before she'd told him. Why would Fin not tell his men *that* little fact?

"Back when the men were dinosaurs, Fin had these visions."

Jenna nodded. "He told me."

Kelly looked surprised, but then she went on. "In each vision, he saw a possible way to defeat the immortals."

"Where did the visions come from?"

"I don't know." Kelly looked impatient. "Now let me finish."

Jenna subsided.

"One of his visions showed me playing my flute, and he knew that was the way Nine could be defeated. He wasn't sure what tune I was playing, but he knew it was music from inside me, not an ordinary tune. He finally realized it was my brain music."

"Brain music?" Okay, this was officially at the upper end of weird.

"I had a scan made of my brain waves, and Fin had someone make it into music. Only that music would send Nine back into the cosmos." She smiled. "In the end, it didn't play out exactly the way Fin saw in his vision. Anyway, I was the key to Nine's defeat. I guess there's a different key for each of the immortals. Fin's heavy into the power and symbolism of numbers, so each key's success is bound up with a certain number pattern."

In a night filled with breathtaking events, this newest revelation left Jenna speechless.

Kelly filled the silence. "The only thing that worries Fin is that his visions didn't show the outcomes. Plus things didn't work out with my flute exactly like his vision predicted. Fin's a control freak—he doesn't like the unpredictable."

"I feel for him." When in doubt, resort to sarcasm.

Her sister sighed. "What're you going to do?"

Jenna countered with a suggestion. "Come back to Houston with me, Kelly. Stay with me until Ty gets this immortal problem straightened out." Her plea would probably fall on deaf ears, but she had to ask anyway.

"I love him, sis. No way would I run and hide when I might be able to help him." She bit her lip in concentration. "But I think you should go home. There's nothing you can do here. And I'd feel guilty knowing you were in danger." She offered Jenna a shaky smile. "I have Ty to protect me. It doesn't get safer than that."

Jenna nodded. "I'll think about it."

Kelly rose, gave her another hug, and walked to the door. She turned. "Tell Mom and Dad I'm happy, because strange as it may seem, I am." Then she left, closing the door quietly behind her.

Jenna turned off the lights, got undressed, and climbed into bed. *"Sixty-five million years ago, I had a series of visions.*

You were in one of them. You're very important to the Eleven, Jenna." She spent the few hours left of the night staring into the darkness and thinking about Fin's words.

Just before dawn broke, someone banged on her door. She crawled out of bed to answer it. When she opened the door, Al stood glaring at her. He'd pulled on a T-shirt, and his jeans rode low on his hips. She sighed. This wouldn't be a happy visit.

His hair was a tangled glory falling over his shoulders, and those hazel eyes had a wild look to them. "I've done some heavy thinking, and I've come to a conclusion."

"I'm sure you're going to tell me what it is." No, she wouldn't invite him in.

He leaned against the doorjamb and crossed his arms over his spectacular chest. "You need to go home."

"No."

"You won't be safe here."

"No."

"We can take care of your sister."

"I'm sure you can. But the answer is still no."

He was all frustrated male. "Why the hell would you want to stay?"

She rolled her eyes to the ceiling. "Let me count the reasons. First, my sister. Second, my sister. And last, umm, my sister." *And maybe you.*

Now where had that come from? He was a great-looking guy with a predator's soul. Incredible in an alpha kind of way, but not the man she was looking for. There wouldn't be any steady job or home back in Texas for him. Life with Al would be unpredictable, dangerous, and . . . exhilarating. No, scratch the last. She didn't want that kind of excitement.

"There's nothing I can say to change your mind?"

"Nope."

With a muttered curse, he pushed himself away from the doorjamb and walked off.

She smiled as she crawled back into bed. A magnificent ass. But he wasn't much of a persuader. He could be, though. Once he learned how to use all his assets.

Chapter Seven

Well, that had been a half-assed job of persuasion. He should've tried harder. He had a tough job concentrating, though, when he was so hot for her that he probably melted Fin's damn security cameras at the end of the hall with the heat generated by 65 million years of sexual abstinence.

Al needed to cool down. Climbing the stairs to the roof, he stared out over the sleeping city. Fin had raised all of the Eleven back on November eleventh of 2011. Eleven, eleven, eleven. Their leader's obsession with the number eleven never ended. He'd brought them straight to Houston where they'd gotten rid of Nine. They'd spent December cleaning up the mess that Nine had left behind him before moving on to Philly.

He shivered in the January dawn. Not the temperature he was used to. Houston had been a lot warmer. But the cold sure cleared his mind.

Al's thoughts returned to Jenna. Okay, cooling-down period was over. Houston might have had warmer weather, but it didn't have Jenna. And she heated things up just fine.

Leave it to him to decide he wanted sex with a female who not only feared him but also didn't like him much. Now he'd be babysitting her until she *did* decide to leave. Then he brightened. His first night on the babysitting brigade had sort of sucked. Maybe Fin would stick someone else with the job.

Fin. Thinking about Jenna had taken his mind off the

bone he had to pick with their freaking fearless leader. Now was as good a time as any to confront Fin with what Jenna had let slip. As he headed for the stairs, he reviewed the implications of Fin's power.

All the way to Fin's office he reminded himself to control his temper. Fin wouldn't let him hunt again until he showed he could hold it together.

But as he stood outside the door, his rage was close to liftoff. He raised his fist to knock, not for a minute doubting Fin would be there. Al didn't think the guy ever slept. He knocked. Not a pounding, just a plain knock. Al was proud of that.

"It's open."

Al didn't need more of an invite. He turned the knob and stepped into Fin's office. Fin was seated behind his big-ass desk, but he'd swung his chair to face the windows. He didn't invite Al to sit down.

"Every time I see you, you're staring out those windows." Not what Al had thought he'd say first.

Fin didn't turn to look at him. "The sky never changes. Yes, I guess stars come and go over millions of years, but who'd notice? When I look up there, I can pretend everything's the same as it once was."

That observation silenced Al for a moment. It had never entered his mind that Fin might have feelings about his past. Fin wasn't a nostalgic kind of guy. Come to think of it, he didn't have a clue what Fin's past was. Al had been an Allosaurus with a dinosaur's needs, and he hadn't wondered about much of anything beyond his next meal, his next mating, and his pack. Fin had been nothing more than a voice in his head that he'd obeyed.

"What were you back then?" Why hadn't Al ever asked that question before? Probably because he'd assumed Fin was a dinosaur like the rest of them.

Fin finally swung to face him. "I was a voice."

Al grunted his disgust. A typical Fin answer. But he wouldn't let Fin get away with it this time. "What was your physical form?"

"My form doesn't have a name in this time because my fossilized remains were never found. There were only a few of us, so chances are they'll never be found. But I was big, bad, and liked to kill." He shrugged. "Not much different from you."

Hah. Al would bet that whatever Fin was, he wasn't like anyone else. But enough small talk. Time to get down to business. "Jenna said you could wipe her memory. You never told us you had that power."

"She didn't waste any time telling you that." Fin sounded mildly surprised.

"Stuff the surprise. You can jump into any of our minds. Are you telling me you didn't know she'd told me?"

Fin pinched the bridge of his nose between two fingers. That very normal sign of weariness shocked Al. Twice now in the last two days Fin had looked tired. If Fin felt normal emotions like everyone else, he'd never before shown them to his men.

"Here's the deal, Al. Zero is headed for Philadelphia. I can't stop him from coming. The best I can do is annoy him with a few psychic jabs to the brain. That takes more energy than you can imagine. Then I have to keep track of everything that's happening out on the streets, especially when some of you get too enthusiastic about your job."

Al glanced away. Fin would never forget the demon thing.

"So I don't use my spare minute or two checking into everyone's thoughts." His smile was no smile at all. "I even sleep once in a while."

Al refused to admit he'd thought of Fin as this all-seeing omnipotent godlike figure. No, he'd always believed their leader was just like the rest of them only . . . more so. He scowled. Lying to himself left a bad taste in his mouth.

Al got himself back on track. "If you can wipe minds, why didn't you wipe Jenna's? That way you wouldn't have to worry about her writing about us for her tabloid or telling me things you don't want me to know."

"First, I don't think she'll write her story. Yes, the temptation will be there, but it would put her sister in even more danger than she's in now. Jenna's a smart lady. She'll figure out that her sister and the future of mankind are a little more important than a byline. Once we take care of all the immortals, I don't care what she writes." He shrugged. "And maybe I don't care if you know."

That all sounded great. Too bad Al didn't believe it. Fin always had layers and layers of motivations. He'd just given Al a peek at the top layer. Not good enough.

"Now what's your real reason?"

Fin actually laughed. It sounded pretty normal to Al. But he'd never make the mistake of believing that laugh.

"You're a suspicious son of a bitch. That's a mixed bag. You're always looking for a reason to nail me. So that makes you a pain in the ass. On the other hand, suspicion is one of the most important survival skills. You'll live when others around you die because you don't believe anyone."

Al frowned. It sounded like Fin had just complimented him. A moment to be savored. Okay, moment over. "I'm waiting." He did some virtual finger crossing. Fin didn't have to tell him anything, and they both knew it.

Fin shuffled a few papers around on his desk. Al decided Fin was trying to decide what lie to use.

"I didn't wipe her memory because she's the key to Eight's trip home."

Fin's admission was a fist to Al's jaw that rocked him back onto his heels. He didn't ask if Fin was kidding because Fin never joked about the immortals. Al's instant reaction was disbelief followed closely by fear and then anger. And wasn't that a freaking shock. All those emotions centered on a woman he hardly knew. Warning bells almost deafened him.

"Getting rid of Nine came close to killing Kelly." Al clenched his fists at his sides, digging his nails into his palms to keep from lashing out at Fin.

Fin's expression was calm, detached. "We all do what we have to."

"Kelly won't let her sister walk into danger." *Neither will I.*

"What's meant to happen will happen. Kelly can't stop it." His gaze clawed a ragged hole in Al's gut. "You can't, either."

Cold bastard.

Only a brief twist of Fin's lips acknowledged that he'd heard Al's thought. "I know you tried to get her to go home. If you'd succeeded, I just would've had to go after her myself. She can't leave until we take care of Eight." Fin abandoned his papers to stare at Al. "You have no other job from now until Eight is gone except to keep Jenna safe. When she's not in this condo, you'll be with her."

"What about Kelly and Ty? Kelly will tear your head off if you try to keep her away from her sister,"—Al paused to enjoy the mental picture—"and Ty can take care of them both." Jenna wouldn't need him. Why did that scenario bother him? And why did he hope Fin rejected it?

"I've found an apartment for Ty and Kelly in the same building with Q. Partners need to stay together for mutual protection. Besides, North Philly will keep both of them busy."

Way to go, O Great Dispenser of Bullshit. Remind me that I don't have a partner.

Fin's stare was one part amusement and two parts frustration. Good, he was still tuned into Al's thoughts.

"Kelly will want Jenna to stay with her, but I'm giving that a thumbs-down. She'll be pissed, but it can't be helped. This condo is a lot safer than any apartment. And by the way, why don't you stop blaming me for everything you think has gone wrong with your life? If you weren't here with us, you'd be dead."

Al's impulsive side wanted to throw the I'd-rather-be-dead line at Fin, but the honest side of him admitted he *didn't* want to be dead at all. In fact, since Jenna had arrived, his interest in living had improved a whole lot. He wasn't sure if that was because she drove him crazy in a good way or because he wanted her body. Maybe both. So Al decided to ignore Fin's challenge.

"What if Kelly refuses to accept your order?" Ty's wife was a force to be reckoned with.

Fin's gaze grew intent, the silver going molten and the hint of purple darkening. Without moving a muscle in his face, Fin suddenly became frightening enough to give even Al pause.

"I lead the Eleven. I protect the Eleven. And I make the final decisions."

Al nodded. Okay, he had two more questions and then he was outta here. "You can erase memories. Why didn't you ever tell us?" How many times had Al seen bits and pieces of things half remembered only to have them fade away? He asked the second question before he could lose his nerve. "Did you ever take away any of *our* memories?"

And in the silence stretching between them was the understanding that Fin could take away Al's memory of even asking the question. Al waited to see what Fin would decide.

Finally, Fin answered. "Yes."

Yes? Just *yes*? "What memories?"

"Ones that are better left forgotten. Right now we have one goal—to save humanity's butt."

Al was too mad to stop his question from popping out. "Why? I don't think you give a crap about saving humanity. I think all you care about is bringing down the immortals. You're all about revenge." He waited for the fist of Fin's anger to drive his ass into the floor. Nothing happened. Figured. Fin didn't react to insults.

"Wrong. I care a lot about humanity's butt, because no matter what our *souls* are, everything else about us is human. From here on, it'll always be human." He held up his hand to stop Al's denial. "And here's a secret. In the end, your soul is what you want it to be."

That didn't make a hell of a lot of sense. He'd always want his soul to be Allosaurus. He couldn't imagine anything else. "Forget the humans. Who gave you the right to take my memories?"

"I don't need permission from anyone to do what I think is right. The memories I hold might well tear us apart. I won't sacrifice that for you or anyone." There was no give in Fin's gaze.

As much as Al might rage against Fin's arbitrary decision, he knew he couldn't force him to explain. "Will you ever let us remember?" Al felt like a guitar string being tightened and tightened and tightened. At any moment, he might snap and catch someone in his whiplash.

"After it's all over, if that's what you want."

Why the hell wouldn't he want his memories? Good or bad, they were his. "Does anyone else know this?"

"Ty and Kelly."

"And they never told anyone?" He worked to control his surge of anger. Ty was one of the Eleven. He should've shared what he knew.

"Ty didn't share because he knew how the rest of you

would react. We're not fighting an ordinary enemy. A moment's distraction could be your last. Sure, you won't be dying from natural causes anytime soon. And yes, you're pretty much invulnerable when your soul's in control. But if someone takes your head while you're in human form, you're dead. Or at least your body is."

Al noted the distinction Fin made, but he didn't bother commenting on it. Turning, he headed for the door. "I need some space." He didn't offer a good-bye as he left the office, but he didn't slam the door behind him either.

He made note of two things: Fin had let him keep the memory of their conversation, and he hadn't made Al promise not to tell the others what he'd learned. Right now, Al wasn't sure what he intended to do beyond falling into bed.

A short while later, as Al hovered between waking and sleeping, he thought about what it would take to keep Jenna safe from the immortals. He also wondered who would keep her safe from him.

His soul had never denied itself anything in his former life. It was into instant gratification. Sex had been a violent mating. Tenderness and caring were foreign concepts. How would he keep his soul from being the third party in any bed he and Jenna shared? He'd work on that problem. Sleep ended his planning session.

Jenna opened her eyes to late afternoon sun. A glance at her clock verified that fact. She never slept this late. But as the events of last night leaped gleefully into her memory, she decided she deserved that extra time.

Crawling out of bed, she staggered into the shower. A short time later, dressed and awake, she went in search of caffeine.

No one had told her when meals were served, so she figured she'd just slip into the kitchen and grab something from the fridge. Unfortunately, a tiger was guarding it. What Greer lacked in body size he made up for in ferociousness.

"Make some coffee? Fix a sandwich? *Yourself?*" Greer's glare said to get her hand off his fridge or lose it. "Go." He pointed in the direction of the dining room. "Sit."

Beg, roll over, jeez. Jenna huffed and puffed herself to the dining room table and sat down.

A short time later Greer emerged with a huge plate of sandwiches complete with pickle slices, chips, and potato salad. He held a pot of coffee in his other hand. "I'll be back." He disappeared again.

While she considered drinking the coffee directly from the pot, Al walked in.

Forget the coffee, she'd just gotten a sensual jolt of wake-me-up. With all the excitement of the past few nights, she hadn't had much time to sit quietly and study him. She did that now.

Worn jeans, a black T-shirt, and biker boots molded and accentuated the long muscular length of his body. Bottle whatever constituted "male" and it would have his picture on the label.

He was a sexual time bomb ticking down the final minutes till his personal detonation. She didn't know how she knew this, she just did. It was in the sharp stabs of tension she felt from him along with a sense of heat and male arousal she couldn't possibly be feeling. And overriding everything was her conflict—run from the impending explosion or fling herself onto the bomb.

His hair was still braided. "Do you ever wear your hair loose?"

He looked surprised at her question. "When I hunt."

"No hunting tonight?"

He moved with a litheness she didn't associate with his soul.

"I'll be with you tonight." That said it all.

This had to be Fin's doing. She couldn't picture this man choosing to be with her when he could be out chasing enemies. "What if I decide to sit and watch TV?"

"Then I'll watch TV with you." He sat across from her.

Not by even a tic of his eye did he betray how much he'd hate that, but she knew he would.

Neither of them spoke as Greer returned with more sandwiches, along with everything else they'd need. Jenna waited until Greer disappeared back into the kitchen before returning to the subject.

"Why you? Why not one of the other guys?"

He shrugged. "I'm out of the hunting business until Fin says otherwise."

"Why?" She watched as he reached for a sandwich.

He had strong hands with long fingers that could as easily strangle an enemy as paint a masterpiece. And that was a bunch of crap. He had hands, ordinary hands.

"I lost control of my soul. I didn't return to my human form after a kill. Fin had to force me. So I won't be hunting for a while until he's sure I understand what's at stake." He delivered his speech calmly, but there was a bitter undertone woven through what he'd said.

"You don't like Fin?"

"I don't know if I trust him. Oh, I trust him to lead us. I don't know of anyone who'd mess with him in a fight. But there's just something . . ." He shrugged. "This isn't a logical thing. It's just a gut feeling."

She nodded. "And what happened in the park last night?"

"Luck. I smelled blood, heard sounds of general merrymaking, so I took a look. Six ghouls were just finishing a late dinner."

Her stomach turned over. "Ghouls?" She didn't bother asking if they existed. Obviously they did.

"Eight must be encouraging his recruits to run wild. He wants to spread terror in the city. Terror leads to chaos. He's all about chaos."

"The slaughter last night?"

Al nodded. "I heard it was bad."

A night in front of the TV was looking pretty good. But something inside her insisted on whispering, "Coward." She'd tried to run twice now. Running could become a habit. It could also mean survival, and she was all for survival. Besides, there wasn't a thing she could do that a prehistoric predator couldn't do better.

"Are you still afraid of me?"

Was she? She looked at him, *really* looked. Hard face, cool hazel eyes, muscular but not bulky, and an overwhelming sensuality that made her want to nibble every inch of his bare body and then wrap herself in his freed hair. Afraid? Yes. On a whole bunch of levels.

He reached across the table for the salt, and she put her hand over his. He stilled.

"I'm not afraid of *you*, Al Endeka. But I'm not too sure about your soul. It doesn't know me, and its capacity for violence is pretty scary."

Al smiled as he withdrew his hand. "Al Endeka doesn't know you either, but he'd like to. So how'd you end up writing for a tabloid?" There was nothing but casual interest in his tone.

"I come from a family of exceptional people. Dad is the head honcho at the Houston Zoo, Mom is a vet there, and Kelly is brilliant in every way. Me? I'm just normal. Average grades. Not too motivated to excel at anything in particular. Went through college with a major in English Lit. Didn't really prepare me for anything. So when the tabloid offered me a job, I grabbed it." Did *she* sound casual enough?

He stared at her for so long, she wanted to squirm. She didn't, though. Maloys didn't squirm.

"Was it really lack of motivation?"

No. It was like if I said I didn't care often enough, Mom, Dad, and Kelly would lay off trying to push. She was ordinary in a family of overachievers. And if she couldn't be the best at something, then not caring worked for her. "Yeah, it was really lack of motivation."

Al didn't look as though he believed her, but what he believed didn't matter in the end. Her secret was tucked safely away where no one could find it.

Just as it seemed he was getting ready to dig deeper, the triplets burst into the room. From the neck up they looked exactly alike, but they had different tastes in clothes. Thank God.

They planted themselves at the table. One of them stole a sandwich from her plate.

"Utah," the thief identified himself. "Our car's down. We're stuck here until it's fixed. Hey, let's all go someplace interesting. We don't want to sit around until it's time to hunt." He grinned at Al. "We'll take your car."

His smile was beautiful and happy, but Jenna knew what savage soul hid under all that sunshine. "Fin explained about the Eleven. I know that Ty is a T. rex and Al is an Allosaurus. Who thought up your names?"

"Fin," they all said together.

She bit her bottom lip as she thought about their names. She stopped biting it when she noticed Al's gaze fixed on her lip. The hunger flooding his eyes shocked her, throwing her off stride.

Taking a deep breath and refusing to dwell on his look, she blundered on. "Okay, we have Utah, Rap, and Tor. So you're all Utah raptors?"

"Got it. And I'm Tor." He smiled at her. "I think I'll grow

my hair as long as Al's so no one will mix me up with these other two jerks."

Utah and Rap made threatening noises around the sandwiches they were devouring.

"So what does Fin stand for?"

Rap, who was wearing a heavy sweater, a scarf around his neck, and had a wool coat hanging over the back of his chair, answered. "Infinity."

"Strange. Why not a name like you guys have?"

Rap shrugged. "Never thought about it. Guess if you're all about numbers, Infinity's a great name." He looked at the others. "Let's go to a movie or do something inside. I hate the cold."

Greer had come out of the kitchen to listen. "If you have a few hours to blow, stop by the Academy of Natural Sciences. You can see stripped-down versions of yourselves."

Jenna thought that sounded kind of gruesome, but she was evidently the only one, because a short while later she was staring out the windshield in unblinking terror as Al and his GPS unit navigated the Philly streets. She'd offered to drive because she realized none of them had more than a month or so of experience. She should've known better, though. The four men had fought over who would own the wheel, so she'd let them go at it. Now if she could just survive the ride.

They made it in one piece. Barely. A few hours later they emerged from the Academy to a cold winter night. Jenna braced herself for another wild ride back to the condo. Tor was in full whine.

"Gig and Ty were in there. Why weren't we there? We weren't important enough?"

Gig. Okay, she could match that up with the Giganotosaurus they'd seen. No one had introduced her to Gig yet. But from what she'd seen today, Jenna hoped she never got an intro to his soul.

Rap leaned over the seat to hand Jenna a card. "Let's go to South Philly and get some cheesesteaks. Guy I was talking to back at the condo gave this to me. Says this place has the best food in Philly. They're running a special. Buy one get one free. It expires tomorrow. I say we hit it tonight."

Al pulled to the curb and took the card from Jenna. He put the address into the GPS before handing the card to her and then steering back into traffic.

Another death ride finally landed them at a place in what Jenna assumed was South Philly. They pulled into the small parking lot and got out.

God, it was cold. She'd never complain about Houston's heat again. She wrapped her coat more tightly around her. When Al put his arm across her shoulders and drew her close to his side, she didn't think of his soul once. She was just thankful for the extra warmth. Jamming her hands into her pockets, she imagined hot sandwiches and somewhere warm to eat them.

Once in front of the restaurant, the three brothers headed for the door.

Al stopped. "I can't go in there. If anything happened, I couldn't free my soul. The place is too small."

Utah made a rude noise. "Oh, give it up. We'll only be in there for a little while. Just long enough to eat. What could happen?"

Al backed up a few steps. "Something doesn't feel right here."

"It's a restaurant, see? A public place. Nothing dangerous. I'm starving, and I'm freezing my butt off. Let's go inside." Utah pulled open the door.

Al peered into the place. "No one's in there. Why?"

"It's too early for a crowd, and the waitress is probably in the kitchen." Utah's brothers stepped inside.

Al looked worried. "This place doesn't want us."

Jenna thought that was a weird thing to say. "Look, while

we're here arguing, I'm losing feeling in my fingers and toes."

Utah made one last attempt. "Turn off your inner beast. You don't have to be on guard every damn minute. Relax a little. I don't sense anything dangerous."

Al finally made his decision. "Jenna and I aren't going inside. If you still want to eat your sandwiches here, we'll go back to the car and wait. Just make sure you bring some back for us."

Jenna thought he was crazy, but she wasn't going inside without him. Sitting at a table surrounded by three strange predators could be an appetite suppressant.

After Al handed them money for takeout, he started to guide her away from the restaurant.

Jenna had opened her mouth to do some heavy-duty complaining about him and his weird "feelings," when she tripped and dropped her purse. It wasn't closed right and all the junk inside, including her pepper spray, scattered over the sidewalk.

With a muttered curse, she bent down to scoop everything up. Al started to help her. That's when they heard the shouts.

Shoving everything back into the purse, she rushed over to where Al was already yanking on the restaurant door. It stayed closed.

"What the fuck?" He flung himself at the door. It didn't budge.

The noise of battle rose, both human cries and the sounds of what Jenna assumed were the raptors. Horrified, she backed away from the door and looked around. The street was dark and empty. Why was it empty? It wasn't that late.

Al abandoned the door. "Get out of here, Jenna. Run!"

She didn't waste time telling him that she'd run away enough lately. She wasn't running again. Besides, where would she run to? She didn't have the car keys. But she did have her cell. She pulled it out.

"Don't bother. Fin knows." Even as he spoke the words, he freed his soul.

Jenna stood frozen. So close. All she'd have to do was stretch out her hand to touch his massive hind leg. She couldn't force her hand to move. Her heart didn't have that problem. It was galloping along at Kentucky Derby speed.

She looked up. Way up. Above her, the long-extinct predator roared its challenge. The sound echoed along the darkened street. Frantically, she strained to see Al's form within the beast, anything to assure her that humanity lived inside. It was too dark.

Then the dinosaur took one stride and crashed through the front of the restaurant. Glass and loose debris rained down around him. She could see the inside of the room now that the front was gone. Two of the raptors were leaping among a group of shadowy figures that moved way too fast to be human. Two? Where was the third? She didn't have a chance to finish her thought, because at that moment, the Allosaurus backed out, holding a human figure in his massive jaws.

Jenna didn't look away fast enough. The predator tore the body apart in front of her. The hot spray of blood was a shock against her ice-cold skin. She should've been strong. She wasn't. Turning away, she bent over and vomited.

When she was finally able to look again, everything was still, and Fin stood staring into the restaurant's ruin. She didn't question how he'd gotten there. He hadn't brought any of the others. Why not? He should have brought all of them.

There was something eerie about Fin's stillness. With his silver hair lifting in the slight breeze and those scary silver eyes, he could have been the frost king standing in the cold darkness.

Why hadn't the noise brought people into the street? Why hadn't any cars driven by? Jenna gave herself a mental shake. That wasn't important now.

Al. She shifted her gaze to the restaurant, afraid of what she'd see. Jenna was just in time to watch the cloud drift away in the frigid air, leaving Al standing there. She didn't question her surge of relief. He didn't waste any time rushing into what was left of the restaurant.

Jenna didn't want to go inside. Didn't want to see what had happened. But because she was terrified, she forced herself to go. She needed to be with Al. She'd run away enough.

She edged in behind Fin.

"Oh my God." She couldn't help it. There were bodies everywhere. No, not bodies. Body parts. Blood ran in crimson rivulets down the black-flocked wall. Blood lay in puddles on the floor among arms, legs, heads, and unidentifiable pieces of flesh.

Jenna recognized one of those heads. Utah? Rap? Tor? She didn't know. Oh, God. Oh, God. Tears ran down her face, but she didn't care. She had nothing left in her stomach to throw up, but that didn't stop her from bending over racked by dry heaves. *He was dead.* Which one?

At some point she knew Al was there, felt him put his arm across her shoulders and pull her close. And in the horrible, horrible silence, she looked up.

The two remaining raptors crowded against the back wall, dangerous, with wild eyes that looked about as far from human as she'd ever seen any eyes look.

Fin offered them only a glance; he seemed to be searching for something. The something was the third brother's headless torso. They'd caught him in human form, and he hadn't had a chance to free his soul. She'd seen how fast Al could change, and she couldn't imagine anything human moving fast enough to catch him by surprise. But then she remembered the speed of the shadows she'd seen.

Jenna looked away from Fin to watch Al. He'd left her to walk toward the two raptors, and something deep inside her bled fear for him.

Each of the raptors had to be close to twenty feet long, with bladelike claws and deadly teeth. The bodies scattered over the ruins of the restaurant attested to their power and fury.

"Utah, Tor, it's over." Al's voice was softer than she'd ever heard it. "You've avenged him. Now it's time to mourn. Control your souls."

Rap. It had been Rap. He'd hated the cold. Now he'd never be cold again. God, she was crying for a man she hardly knew, but it felt as if she'd known him forever.

Both animals raised their heads and screamed, and the scream was a tortured cry that transcended human or animal. All living things would recognize the agony of it.

And then their forms dissolved, leaving only the two men.

They stumbled past Al to get to Rap. Jenna turned to follow them, wanting to comfort them but not knowing how. And the tears still coursed down her face. Then she felt warm fingers lock with hers. She knew Al's touch as a coming home. It was comfort, safety, and the strangeness of that feeling shattered her control.

Jenna clamped her hand over her mouth to keep any sounds from emerging and lifted her gaze to Al's face. She saw him through a watery film. His face was all harsh lines and planes, his eyes filled with barely controlled rage, pain, *sorrow.*

But when he saw her looking at him, he seemed to make a conscious effort to soften his expression. It didn't work.

She reached up to slide her fingers over his clenched jaw.

Jenna wanted to say words of comfort, but none came to mind.

"Fin wants us." His words came out as a harsh rasp.

They took the few steps needed to reach Fin. Jenna forced herself to look. These men had come from a distant time to make sure humanity survived. Humanity owed them. And so now she'd witness for her whole race. She *would* watch.

While Al had been trying to talk the two remaining raptors back into human form, Fin had laid Rap's head and the rest of his body out in a macabre imitation of life.

Fin looked up at her from where he crouched over what remained of Rap. For the first time since she'd met him, emotion flowed in those eyes. They were no longer silver. Deep purple glowed with so much emotion that it backed her up a step. The universe moved in those eyes. Jenna thought she'd experienced sadness, anger, regret. But what she saw in Fin's eyes made her puny emotions seem worthless. She couldn't stand it; she looked away.

"I'm including you, Jenna Maloy, in our final good-bye to Rap's mortal form because you are the key to his revenge."

Jenna swung her gaze back to Fin's face. He simply nodded.

The key. She had a horrible feeling a date with Eight was in her near future.

Chapter Eight

Al watched Jenna try to push her panic away. How much violence, how much terror could she absorb before she broke? She was strong beyond anything he would have expected. That was surprise number one.

Surprise number two? He felt . . . sorrow. For someone who wasn't pack, who wasn't even a friend. After feeling only rage for so long, the sorrow seemed strange. Frightening. Was it a sign of weakness? Al hadn't decided. But now wasn't the time for decisions.

"You okay?" He wanted to touch her, stroke her shining hair, *comfort* her but feared her emotions were too fragile to withstand contact with him, with his soul.

Her hand shook as she pushed a strand of hair from her face. "No. *Not* okay. Hysteria is this far away." She put her thumb and index finger close together. Very close. "It's like a swarm of bees. Bat one away and five more take its place. I'm no Superwoman. I've never been great at anything. And putting my life on the line doesn't give me a rush."

Not great at anything? Al didn't believe that. But her fear gave him even more reason to be pissed at Fin.

Fin evidently took her key status as a done deal because he shifted his attention to his three followers. "I mourn with you."

Al blinked back what felt suspiciously like emotion leaking from his eyes. Even Al, who woke up each morning with the hope of finding some new sin to drop at Fin's feet, couldn't deny the reality of his leader's grief.

"I will now take Rap's soul from his human shell and return him to a place of safety." Fin's words sounded stilted, ritualistic, and totally removed from the emotion of the moment. But his eyes held all the emotion his words lacked.

Utah stepped forward, his fists clenched so tightly that Al saw blood dripping from where his nails dug into his flesh. "Give him a new body. Now."

"I cannot." Fin's denial was remote and strangely formal, as if he'd slipped into someone else's skin.

Al felt Jenna tense beside him. God, this must be a nightmare for her. He almost gave into his need to wrap her in his arms, protect her from what Fin had in store for her. No. He resisted the urge. This moment belonged to Rap.

"Sure you can. You're a fucking god." Tor's voice was thick with tears. "We're pack. We've been pack for millions of years."

"And you will be again. But not now. I don't have the power to keep Zero at bay and put Rap's soul into another body. Zero must be controlled, so Rap's soul will wait."

"How long?" Tor edged closer.

Fin just shook his head. "I must speak the words now or else his soul will escape to a place I cannot follow."

"He's our brother. We want to take part." Utah's eyes were great pools of pain.

"I will give all of you the words in your mind. Accept them without asking questions." Fin speared Jenna with his gaze. "Do you want to take part?"

Al felt her hesitation, and then she nodded.

Fin began. He rested one hand on Rap's bloody forehead and the other one over his heart. Suddenly, Al felt a door opening in his mind. He was in a place he recognized but couldn't see, spoke in a language he didn't know but understood. The words flowed into the place of death the restaurant had become, but they came from somewhere lost in time and memory. They spoke of love and friendship, sorrow and despair, hope and redemption. And then they were done. The door closed, and he was back.

Everyone's eyes looked glazed for a moment until Fin caught their attention. He held out his hand to them, and nestled in his palm was a small glowing ball of light.

"Touch your brother one last time before I send him on his journey."

First Utah and then Tor reached out and stroked a gentle finger over the light. It shimmered, growing brighter at their touch and then dimming.

Suddenly Al knew he had to say good-bye too. He'd thought he felt no kinship with any of the Eleven, but he was wrong. Friendship was a funny thing. He hadn't known it was there until it was gone.

He reached out and touched the light. All that Rap was flowed through Al—his laughter, his temper, his love of Philly cheesesteaks. And his tormented need to return to his brothers. Al made a promise that he'd see Rap's need fulfilled and let it flow back into the light.

Then a real shock. Her hand shaking, Jenna touched Rap's soul. Tears streamed down her face. She spoke her words aloud. "I'll buy earmuffs for you so you won't be cold when you get back." Her eyes widened. She slowly removed her finger and stared at Al. "He said he'd hold me to that."

A smile touched Fin's eyes, and the purple faded a little. Then his gaze grew distant, and Al knew Fin was somewhere else. "I send you to your place of safety, Rap Endeka. May time treat you gently, and may your sleep be peaceful." The light winked out.

Al frowned. Those words didn't sound like Rap would be rejoining them anytime soon.

Jenna broke the silence. "Why hasn't anyone called the police? People have to have heard or seen something."

"Whoever planned this wove a spell that repelled humans from wandering into the area. Didn't any of you feel it?" Fin's eyes had returned to their usual silver.

Utah and Tor seemed unable or unwilling to talk. Al didn't blame them. "I didn't like the feeling of the place, but I thought I was just being overly cautious." He frowned. "Jenna didn't feel anything." He glanced at her for confirmation.

Jenna shook her head. "I was so miserable from the cold, I would've chalked up any bad feelings to that." She glanced out at the dark street. "But I did notice there weren't any people or cars around."

"Where did you send him?" Utah's voice was hoarse; his breathing sounded loud in the stillness of the room.

"There's a place beneath Sedona in Arizona where he'll rest until I can call him forth again."

Al broached the unthinkable. "And if you don't survive Zero's attack?"

Fin didn't look upset by the question, but then Fin never looked upset. Except for a few minutes ago. Rap's death had gotten to him.

"If I don't survive, then Rap will sleep for eternity." Fin didn't give any of them a chance to think about the finality of that statement. "I've contacted Shen. We're lucky that everyone on his cleanup crew has magic skills. By morning when the spell fades, all that'll be left is a burned-out building. No bodies will be found. No one will remember seeing how the fire started."

"They were vampires."

Tor's voice was almost a whisper, but Al had never heard so much hate packed into such a quiet tone.

"They were fucking vampires, and I'm going to make sure all the bloodsuckers in Philly find their final deaths before I'm done." If Tor had his way, Philly would lose its title as the City of Brotherly Love.

Fin moved toward the rear of the restaurant. "Let's go out the back. I don't sense anything out front, but I don't know if Zero's in town yet. I'd have trouble picking him up if he wanted to hide his presence. And I don't want to face him until I'm ready." He didn't look at them as he stood in the shadowed alley behind the restaurant. "We'll meet back at my condo. I've called in all of the Eleven."

"We're not eleven anymore." Al didn't know why he had to voice the obvious, but it seemed important. Fin had always made a big deal about the number eleven. It was a master number. It was *their* number of power. He wondered what power the number ten had going for it?

Suddenly, Fin's expression looked unutterably sad, but Al thought that might just be a trick of the shadows slanting across his leader's face.

"Perhaps. Perhaps not." Fin stared into the darkness as though he saw something none of the others could see. "There's one who stays close, who might . . ." He shook his head. "But I don't know. Not yet."

What the hell was that about? As Al guided Jenna to their car, he thought about Fin's words. The Eleven didn't know anything about Fin or each other. Except for the raptors, none of them had physically met in that past life. Kind of weird.

He had lots of time to think on the way back to Rittenhouse Square because Utah and Tor sat in the backseat, frozen in their silent agony. Jenna remained quiet too. He wished she hadn't seen any of this. She should've stayed in Houston.

But then you never would've known her. A selfish part of him, the part that answered to his predatory soul, thought he was damn glad she was here and had every intention of sating his sexual hunger with her. His soul's savage need drowned out any softer thoughts.

That was good, because sex was all they could ever share.

What woman would ever accept what he'd been, what he was, what he would always be? *Kelly accepted Ty.* Al pushed that truth away. Ty was a nicer guy than he was.

Once back in the condo, Al, Jenna, and the two remaining triplets gathered around the dining room table in silence. Fin sat at its head. Shen solemnly placed eleven candles on the table, lit ten of them, and then turned off the lights.

The flickering flames cast shadows across their faces, changing them in subtle ways. As Al glanced around at those he thought he knew, he realized he didn't know them at all. Not really. Familiar and yet unfamiliar. An unsettling revelation.

Slowly, other members of the Eleven arrived to join them.

Al didn't question the fact that Jenna and Kelly were at the table with them. Surprisingly, Jenna didn't get up to sit with her sister when Ty and Kelly arrived. She remained beside him. And something that felt a lot like satisfaction touched him.

Shen offered to serve coffee, but no one took him up on it. Finally, everyone had arrived. Utah and Tor sat together as they always had, but they'd left an empty chair between them.

Fin stood. "We have lost one of us tonight. We will mourn him now."

The men rose as one. Then all except Fin opened their mouths and roared their pain, their sorrow, their anger. And it wasn't their human voices that emerged. It was the voices of their souls, sounds from a primal past they'd once ruled. The room shook with the sound and fury of that emotion.

Finally, Fin joined them. His voice rose above them all, and it was like nothing Earth had ever heard. It carried beyond that room, that building. A night that a few minutes before was cold and clear suddenly lit with zigzag flashes of lightning. The whole building shook with the booming cracks of thunder. It went on and on, and then it stopped.

Everyone sat except for Fin.

The silence was a deep well of despair, and Al knew they'd all have to make the climb out of it to continue their pursuit of Eight. To say they were motivated now was a gross understatement.

The despair was so human it scared him. And it had come from their *souls*, the ones that shouldn't feel this kind of emotion. Could souls change, become something else? He shook his head to clear away the question. He didn't know, didn't want to think about it now.

Al looked at Jenna. Her face was bleached white in the dim light, her eyes wide and staring. But it wasn't fear he saw in those eyes. It was the sorrow they all felt. And he wanted to enfold her in his arms and hold on.

He didn't. His soul wouldn't let him. Even as he mourned for Rap, his soul roared for blood, for death, for destruction. He beat it back into its cave, but Al knew it wouldn't stay there long.

Fin still stood at the head of the table, calm now. Nothing remained visible of the being that had cried out his grief for Rap. "I've asked Jude to come tonight."

"No." Utah half rose from his seat. "I don't want any fucking vampire here after what they did to Rap."

"This isn't your decision. We need to know what happened. Jude proved his loyalty in Houston. We need a friend in Philadelphia's vampire community." Fin was once more in his cold, calm, and commanding mode.

"Should I stay?" Jenna's voice was strung tight with tension.

"Do you want to stay?" Al tried not to let his expression influence her.

"Yes."

Al nodded. "Then stay." He marveled at the rush of pride

he felt in her. She wasn't his, so why all the emotion? Sex was one thing, other feelings weren't part of the deal. Besides, Jenna wouldn't want his touch after seeing what he was capable of. Tonight she'd let him close because she'd been terrified. Tomorrow everything would be back to normal.

Jenna watched Al watch her. She couldn't read anything in his expression. But he was there beside her, and for whatever it was worth, that's where she wanted him to be.

She glanced over at her sister. Kelly met her gaze and offered her sister a tremulous smile. This sudden death had to be a lot harder on Kelly. She'd known Rap longer than Jenna had. At least Kelly had Ty to share her sorrow with. Jenna was glad for that.

Shen came in and whispered to Fin. Fin nodded and then sat down. "Jude is on his way up. He's being careful tonight. He has bodyguards with him."

A low rumbling growl spread around the table.

Fin shook his head. "He's not stupid. What happened tonight has to have sent shock waves around the paranormal community. The humans may be blissfully ignorant, but our nonhuman friends aren't. And the outcome of our battle will affect all of them." He leaned back in his chair, looking relaxed and nonthreatening. "I don't want anyone causing trouble, no matter what your soul tells you." He cast Utah, Tor, and Al hard glances.

Jenna heard the door to the condo open. Evidently Shen was also playing doorman tonight. And then Jude and five other male vampires strode into the dining room.

Just as it had the first time, Jude's beauty took her breath away. He'd dressed for effect tonight. Leather pants, a black silk shirt open halfway down his chest, and knee-high boots. With his pale perfection, darkly wicked eyes, and flowing black hair, he would be every woman's evil pleasure.

Except for her. That surprised Jenna. She cast a quick glance at the man beside her. Where Jude's threat was hidden beneath smooth temptation, Al's was upfront and in your face.

His was a harsh and unforgiving face with eyes that said, "Danger, run like hell." Al's raw sensuality called to the primal need in every woman. The need that wanted a man to rip her clothes from her body and drive into her until she writhed, screamed, and tore bloody furrows in his sweat-sheened back with her nails.

Startled by her thoughts, Jenna quickly shifted her gaze away.

Fin didn't rise, but he did smile. Who knew what that smile meant? It could mean, "Welcome to my home, I'm really glad to see you," or it could mean, "I'm glad you could make it because I was getting tired of waiting to kill you."

Jude seemed to feel the same way, because he paused in the doorway. "You invited me here tonight. I assume I'm here as a trusted friend." His men crowded around him.

Fin's smile widened. "Friend, yes. Trusted? Not too sure of that." He motioned toward the empty chair to his right. "But I'm not harboring murderous intentions toward you." The word "yet" hung in the air.

The vampire nodded at his men. They fanned out around the room, ready to rush into action if anyone threatened their leader.

Then Jude approached the table. He eyed the seat Fin had offered him before dropping into the one at the far end of the table.

Fin shook his head. "I can reach you as easily there as here."

Jude shrugged, the motion accentuating his broad shoulders. "Indulge me. Distance gives the impression of safety."

Fin nodded. "Vampires killed one of the Eleven tonight."

Wow, Fin didn't beat around the bush. Jenna watched Jude's reaction. Which was none at all. He'd known about Rap before he came here.

"I'm sorry." Jude was lobbing the ball back into Fin's court.

"Remind me again why you're here in Philadelphia when Pennsylvania isn't one of the states you have authority over." Fin tapped his finger on the table in a slow, deliberate beat.

Jenna caught herself following the up-and-down motion of that finger, getting caught in its even pacing, wondering if Fin's thoughts were quite as calm and ordered.

"If anything happens, I'll get you out of here." Al's whisper fanned the sensitive skin behind her ear. Prickles of awareness spread from there. Or maybe the prickles were fear, because Jenna couldn't even begin to imagine what would happen if the polite conversation exploded into violence. She thought about the restaurant. Maybe she could.

"Perhaps I felt a need to offer my help to the vampire queen of Philadelphia. After all, I had an inside view of what happened in Houston." Jude never took his attention from Fin.

Smart vampire. Jenna probably would've held this conversation by phone.

Fin nodded. "I've got a short memory. How did you know we were in Philadelphia?"

This time Jude grinned. "I have people that work at the airports. You don't fly out of Houston without me finding out. I run a tight organization."

"Vampire queen of Philadelphia?" A smile touched Fin's cold eyes. "You're kidding, right?"

"Afraid not. She became vampire when the word royalty meant something. Katherine oversees a ten-state area just as I do, but she thinks of Philly as her royal seat."

Fin nodded. "How much do you know about what happened tonight?" His voice had lost its casualness. It cut the length of the table, slicing to the point of Jude's visit.

"I know a group of Katherine's vampires laid the trap. Evidently Eight paid them well. She wasn't part of the plot."

Utah growled low in his throat. Fin ignored the sound.

"How do you know she wasn't part of the plot?"

"Katherine is . . . Katherine. She says what she thinks, and she doesn't care who she insults. If she'd planned the ambush, she would've been damn proud of it."

"I need information from Katherine."

"And if she doesn't want to talk to you?"

Jude's temper was rising. Jenna couldn't miss the glowing eyes and the slight lift of his lip to expose fang.

"Then we start pulling in vampires and doing our own brand of investigating."

"You're a cold son of a bitch."

Fin actually smiled at that. "See, I knew if I waited long enough you'd say something nice about me."

"You'll have to go to her." Jude looked downright scary. Unlike Fin, he wasn't amused.

"Not really. I think I'll send my representative." Fin scanned the table. He stopped at Al. "Tell Her Majesty that Al Endeka, my personal rep, will meet with her."

Jude simply nodded. Then he rose from the table, waved his guards to him, and left the room.

"That went well, don't you think?" Fin didn't wait for anyone to voice an opinion. "No, neither of you can go. I couldn't trust you to control your beasts around the vampires." He aimed his comment at Utah and Tor.

"And you *can* trust me?" Al sounded incredulous.

"I'm trying, Al. I'm really trying. You listened to your gut tonight and didn't go into that restaurant. That's a point in your favor." Fin motioned to Greer, who'd been standing by the kitchen door. "I think I need some coffee now. How about the rest of you?"

A half hour later, Jenna was awash in caffeine and full from stuffing herself with the sandwiches Greer had made for all of them. The sandwiches made her think of the cheesesteak she hadn't gotten. And that of course reminded her of Rap. It was time for this day to be over.

Fin had spent the time going over ideas for finding Eight. So far they knew he was smarter than Nine had been. They also knew he went in for big splashy parties. Bloody ones. There was nothing subtle about Eight. What they didn't know was where to find him.

Jenna was just about to give up and excuse herself from the table—after all, she wasn't going to be the one to engage Eight in hand-to-hand combat—when Fin banished thoughts of sleep.

"Wherever you go from now on, make note of any unusual bells you see. The ringing of a bell will send Eight back home, but that doesn't help us if we can't figure out which bell."

Suddenly everything clicked into place. And she wished it hadn't. Fin saying he'd seen her in one of his visions. Fin appointing Al as her personal protector. And now the bells.

Her whole world cartwheeled, and when it finally came to rest, she wasn't a tabloid writer anymore. She slowly rose from her seat. Gripping the edge of the table to keep from swaying, she faced Fin.

"I'm your freaking bell-ringer, aren't I?"

Chapter Nine

Oh, shit. Jenna looked ready to self-combust. Al placed his hand over hers. But he didn't get a chance to say anything comforting—not that he had any practice at it anyway—because Kelly leaped to her feet.

"No, you're not putting my sister anywhere near that bastard Eight. She could've died tonight. Jenna's human. She can't pull out a prehistoric soul to protect herself." Kelly pointed a shaking finger at Fin. "If you need someone to ring a damn bell, then *you* ring it."

Ty reached up to calm his wife, but she slapped his hand away. "The Maloy family has already done its share to save humanity. Leave Jenna alone!" Then her eyes widened. "You had your visions millions of years ago, so you knew about Jenna back in Houston . . . You never said anything to me."

Jenna slowly sank back into her seat, her eyes fixed on her sister.

Kelly was just getting started. "You knew she'd show up here to check on me." She pushed away from the table so hard her chair toppled over with a clatter that sounded extra loud in the silent room. "You manipulative jerk! I don't care how powerful you are, you're worthless as a human being." Kelly ended on a watery gulp. Her last words before she stormed out were aimed at Jenna. "You get on the first plane out of here." And then she was gone. Ty rose and followed her. He didn't ask Fin for permission to leave.

Al watched them until they left the room and then he switched his gaze to Fin. If Kelly's tirade had touched him, no one would know. He studied Jenna and the rest of his men with a calmness that said being a human being wasn't at the top of his priority list.

"Anyone else have anything to say?"

"We want Al in our pack." Utah spoke into the silence.

Beside him, Jenna gasped. He couldn't tell whether from shock or horror.

"Al won't be hunting while he's with Jenna. So he can't be part of your pack." Fin's glance touched Jenna. "Unless she decides to go home. In which case we may as well move on to where Seven is, because Jenna is the key here."

"That's right, play the guilt card." Jenna's comment was an angry snarl.

Utah didn't give up without a fight. "We're pack. We've hunted with three from the beginning. Three's an important number—past, present, future. We need a future. You're the numbers guy. You should know. Al hunted with a pack before, so we want him."

"He's not the only one," Fin replied.

"But he's the one who misses his pack the most."

Al wondered how Utah knew that. He'd never talked about his old pack with the Eleven.

Fin held up his hands. "Okay, I'm finished for the night. Utah and Tor, talk to me tomorrow. Jenna, I'll see you at breakfast."

He delivered his message to Al mentally. *"Don't let her leave."*

Then he pushed his chair away from the table and left them sitting there.

Q said it for all of them. "Let's quit for the night. Being around Fin and you guys this long has revved up my aggression way past safe. We don't need a fight to top off everything."

"Good idea." Al wanted to get Jenna out of there. She'd experienced enough tonight to last ten human lifetimes. He also wanted time to think over his feelings about joining the raptors' pack.

Q stood and offered Jenna his hand. She accepted it, but she looked a little shaky.

"We've never officially met. I'm Q, Ty's partner. Don't let Fin bully you." His gaze shifted to Al as he said the last.

Jenna seemed to rouse herself as she worked up a smile for him. "Q? What's that stand for?"

Al wasn't sure he liked Q's smile. Was it a little more than friendly? And if it was, why should he care? Oh, right, he was a possessive prehistoric jerk who wanted to kill anyone who looked at his mate in the wrong way.

But wait, Fin had proclaimed them human, so he wasn't supposed to be having these feelings. Well, fuck Fin. Al sort of liked the sound of that.

Then he remembered. Jenna wasn't even close to being mate material. She was Fin's key, and all Al wanted to do was have sex with her. Somehow though, his last thought didn't have the ring of truth.

Q dropped Jenna's hand, just in time as far as Al was concerned. "I'm a Quetzalcoatlus. Fin wanted to call me Quetz, but I don't answer to anything that weird. So I call myself Q."

"A what?"

Q laid his smile on her, the one all women seemed to like. Al growled low in his throat. Q heard and sent him an anytime-anyplace look.

"My soul's a giant pterosaur. A flying reptile." Then the asshole had to brag. "The biggest flying animal that ever lived. Most of us had thirty-seven-foot wingspans. Mine was closer to forty-five."

"Wow, that's incredible."

Al hated the look of awe she sent Q's way. "Yeah, yeah,

we're all impressed. Except, last time I looked we didn't have tape measures way back when, so how do you know what size your freaking wingspan was?" He couldn't believe the words coming out of his mouth. Jealous words. He hoped to hell they were just a normal primitive reaction to another male trying to take away his personal dessert.

Q's expression turned dangerous. "At least I was the biggest of something. You were nothing beside Ty, Gig, and Car."

"Look, it's been a long night, guys. And if you're going to get into a pissing match over who's the biggest, then I'm out of here right now." Jenna sounded exhausted.

Al took a deep calming breath and tried to think nonviolent thoughts. "Guess you're right about one thing, Q. Being near Fin and the rest of you guys is working on me. Time for everyone to leave." Yeah, that was it. He wasn't really jealous. He was just reacting to being around the others.

Q nodded, and with one last smile for Jenna, walked away.

She looked at Al. "I have to talk with Kelly." Nothing in her expression gave a hint whether she intended to stay in Philly or flee back to Houston.

He'd be an optimist. "See you sometime this afternoon then." As she walked away, he thought about following her to her room, following her into her bed, and there in the darkness touching her in all the ways a man could touch a woman. His soul offered a few opinions on what *it* wanted to do.

Al decided maybe he needed to step outside before heading to his room. Glancing around, he realized everyone had left. Most of the other guys had their own apartments. Their drivers would've been waiting for them to leave the meeting.

He purposely didn't bring his duster with him. Al needed a blast of Arctic air to freeze the sensual images of

Jenna that bubbled and boiled in his mind. And in other places.

All the way down in the elevator, he thought about how he'd feel if she stayed—tempted, distracted, conflicted. *Happy.* Then he thought about his emotions if she left—bored, focused, still conflicted. *Not happy.* Well, that sort of summed it up.

In the lobby, the guy behind the desk was reading a book. He looked up long enough to nod and then went back to his book.

Al paused, "You new here?"

"Nah. I sub when anyone quits or goes on vacation."

Al left him to his book as he stepped outside. January in Philly was cold enough to freeze the devil's ass. Just what he needed. Crossing Nineteenth Street, he moved silently among the shadows of the small park. A tough thing to do since the park was pretty well lit up. He was just getting ready to turn around and go back to the condo when he saw Fin.

Obeying his instincts, he slipped farther into the shadows to watch. He'd probably never react like a human. His soul's habits were too ingrained.

What the hell was Fin doing? There was enough light in the park to cast a shine over all that silver hair. But Al stopped worrying about Fin's hair as something moved in the shadows near him.

Suddenly a big cat slid into view. Al instantly accessed all that info Fin had poured into this head when he first rose. Jaguar. Black. Carnivore. Dangerous. Fin didn't seem worried, though. Instead of keeping his attention on the jaguar, he looked toward where Al stood.

"Don't just stand there staring." Fin motioned to him. "Come meet Balan."

Al emerged from hiding and approached. He never took his attention from the big carnivore. "How did you know I was there? I thought I was quiet." Al knew he'd been quiet. He'd had a lifetime of moving a very big body silently so he wouldn't startle his prey. He and his pack had never been fast enough to run down smaller and lighter dinners.

"I always know where all of you are." Fin sounded amused. "Think about that when you walk past Jenna's room later on."

Al grunted. Talk about a buzz kill. "Who's Balan?" He remembered Ty talking about meeting the jaguar back in Houston, but he wanted the info directly from Fin.

The voice in his head wasn't Fin's, and it startled the hell out of him.

I am the messenger for the ones you call numbers. My masters are not pleased with how you've named them. Numbers show lack of respect. The jaguar watched Al from unblinking golden eyes. *They have shown their respect for you by naming you as Gods of the Night. My masters wish to be called Lords of Time.*

Al stared blankly at Balan and then shifted his stare to Fin. "He's kidding, right?"

Fin wasn't smiling. "No, he's very serious. Balan would have you think he's a glorified messenger boy for Zero and the rest of them." He paused for an aside to Balan. "If your masters would tell me their names, I wouldn't have to call them by numbers. They could even make up names. So what name is Eight going by while he's among the humans?"

Balan opened his mouth in a silent snarl, exposing big sharp teeth. *Do not mock my masters. Names have power. They will not give you that power.* Then some emotion that looked a lot like humor appeared in his eyes. *I cannot tell you the mortal name the one whom you call Eight is using because it would help you find him. Personally, I think his name lacks dignity.*

"Why are you here tonight, Balan?"

Good. It was about time Fin got down to business. As far as Al could see, Balan was working for the enemy. It never helped to get chummy with someone who wanted to kill you.

Balan swung his great head to study Al. *"I do not kill. I simply——"*

"Observe and report," Fin finished for him. "I don't know what part you're playing in this whole thing, cat, but it's not the part of a spy. Is Zero in Philadelphia?"

Balan made a coughing sound that might have been a laugh. *"Do you think I'd tell you if he were? But I will tell you this. The one who calls himself Seir watches your windows from this park each night."*

Al couldn't tell from Fin's expression whether this was a surprise or old news to him.

"How do you know this?"

"Because I also watch."

Fin laughed, a harsh bitter sound. "Just great. Pretty soon I'll have a freaking party outside my windows. Maybe I'll have to put on a show to make it all worthwhile. Let me know when you're freezing your butts off and I'll send down hot chocolate."

Balan blinked his gold eyes. *"Is that why you came here to-night? Did you hope to catch Seir here?"*

Fin glanced away from Balan to scan the surrounding trees. "I don't have to go searching for Seir. He knows where I'll be if he wants me."

Al couldn't figure out whether that was a threat aimed at Seir or not.

"So is there anything else you want to tell me?"

Balan remained silent for a little too long. Then he spoke. *"My master, the one you call Zero, wants you to know that things need not be like this between you. Now that the one named Rap has been eliminated, all is even between you. He was payment for Nine. Stop interfering in what will be, and you along with your men will reap the benefit when humans no longer walk the Earth."*

At the mention of Rap's name, Al's fury fought for expression. Fin threw him a sharp glance.

"Do you believe that, cat?" Fin seemed really interested in Balan's answer.

"I do not believe or disbelieve. I only report." The jaguar sniffed the night air. *"There will be snow."* Then without a backward glance he faded into the shadows.

"What was that about?" As hard as Al stared, he couldn't see where the cat had gone.

"I don't know." Fin looked thoughtful. "He guards his real thoughts."

"You seemed pretty cozy with a being that admits working for Zero and the rest of his trash."

"I've known about him for a long time. And he doesn't work for anyone. He chooses a side." Fin finally looked at him. "But he can be persuaded."

Al walked beside him as Fin headed back to the condo. "You said you've known about Balan for a long time. I don't remember him. Guess you and I didn't move in the same circles. Or maybe I just *forgot*."

As Fin turned his head toward him, Al caught a glimpse of something that looked like shock in his eyes. Now what had he said to cause that reaction?

"You never met him. There was nothing to forget."

Al nodded, not completely convinced. "Tell me about him."

"The Mayan civilization got some things right. They may not have understood the greater implications of some of their beliefs, but they had the basics. Balan means jaguar in the Mayan language. Some believed that Balan was a helper to Bolon Yokte, a Mayan creation lord."

"And this Bolon Yokte did what?"

Fin cast him a don't-be-stupid look. "He created."

Al thought about that. "Well, if I have a piece of land

with an old house on it, and I want a new house, I guess I'd have to knock down the old one to make room for the new one. I might even enjoy the knocking down as much as the putting up."

"That's the way it works." For just a moment, Fin looked at him as though he was seeing beyond the man and his soul to something more, something older.

"What about this Seir?"

Fin shrugged. "I'll deal with Seir when the time comes. And no, I'm not going to discuss him."

Before Al could work up another question, they entered the condo's lobby and Fin stopped to talk to the guy with the book. Al didn't wait around. He caught an elevator and headed up to his room.

Kelly answered her door on the first knock. "You took long enough getting here."

Jenna walked past her sister and into the sitting area. She glanced around. "Where's Ty?"

Her sister nodded toward French doors that led to the balcony. Drapes had been drawn across them. "Sometimes being closed in too much makes him feel claustrophobic. He threw on his heavy clothes and went out to sit on the balcony so he could 'breathe.' His word, not mine." She dropped onto the couch and waved for Jenna to join her. "He functions so well in this world that I often forget what he came from and how much of a culture shock this whole thing must be."

Jenna wasn't here to discuss the Eleven's assimilation issues with Kelly. "I thought about this all the way to your room. I'm not leaving."

Kelly leaned toward her sister. "You. Are. Crazy. After I found out what these guys were, I decided to stay too. Want to know what happens when you team up with them?"

"Why *did* you stay?"

"It's tough to walk away when you know you can help save humanity."

"And you were falling in love with Ty."

Kelly didn't deny it. "I ended up in the Astrodome, the unwilling guest of Nine. His entertainment for the night was a fight to the death between Ty and Gig. You haven't seen either of their souls. The fight wasn't a pretty sight. *I* was the key that night."

Jenna let anger roll over her. The fury felt surprisingly good. "And you never thought to share with your family that you were in mortal danger?"

Kelly looked away. "I couldn't. It wasn't safe for you to know too much. Besides, you would've tried to help."

"Did Ty talk you into it?"

"No. I had a heart-to-head talk with Fin. My heart, his head. Sometimes I think his heart takes extended vacations. Anyway, he promised to keep all of you safe if I helped to get rid of Nine. He pointed out that even if I quit, Nine would know I'd worked for the Eleven and target the whole family. Besides, if I didn't help, Nine's recruits would take over the city, Zero would win, and all of us would be dead anyway." Her laugh was a little unsteady. "No pressure there."

Jenna figured Zero and Fin were evenly matched. They were both bastards to the nth degree. "So now you want me to go home even though I'm the key to kicking Eight's butt. It won't matter if *I* fail humanity."

Kelly looked stricken, but she didn't back down. "I've done a lot of thinking, and I wonder if the people Fin saw in his visions really matter. Okay, for Nine it had to be me because only my particular brain waves could do the job. But this bell-ringing thing. Anyone could ring a damn bell. So Fin doesn't really need you." Desperation was starting to creep into Kelly's voice.

"Will you go back to Houston with me?"

Kelly looked at her sister from wide eyes glistening with unshed tears. "You play dirty, sis."

"Will you?"

"You're going to make me choose between my sister and my husband?"

Suddenly Jenna felt unutterably weary. She couldn't do it. She couldn't tear her sister from the man she loved, no matter how much she wanted to get Kelly away from the danger.

"No, you won't have to choose. I'm staying. I never thought of myself as a hero, but if Fin says I'm the only one who can ring that bell, hey, I'll go for it."

"I want you out of here." Kelly swiped at her eyes and then reached for a tissue.

"You know, the more I think about it, the more being a hero appeals." *God, please give me the right words.* "Do you have any idea what it was like for me growing up in our family?"

Kelly seemed puzzled. "We have a perfect family."

"See, that's the problem. I'm *not* perfect. Everyone else is. Dad's the zoo director, Mom's a vet, and you're a genius at everything you do."

"That's not true. We all love you, and everyone's life path is different. Different doesn't mean less important." Kelly looked horrified. "I never knew you had these thoughts."

I never wanted you to know. "I love all you guys, but I wanted to be great at something too. I wasn't. Average grades, no motivation to excel, no drive to get an awesome job after college. I majored in English Lit, so when I graduated I could tell you a lot about books, but that didn't prepare me for a spectacular career." She shrugged as if it didn't matter. It mattered a whole lot. "So I took the first job I was offered."

"But you always acted like you didn't care. You said

grades didn't matter. You said you liked your job at *The Scene*; you didn't want to try to move up to the *Chronicle*."

"I didn't. I don't." Lord, what had she gotten herself into?

Her sister was no fool, and Jenna saw the exact moment when she put everything together. Which proved how really smart Kelly was, because Jenna had only just put it together herself.

"You're afraid of failure."

Okay, Jenna was finished with listening to her sister's amateur analysis of her personality. "Look, this isn't getting us anywhere. I just wanted to let you know I'm staying. If you could do your part to make sure humanity gets to see December twenty-second, then I can too." *But what if I can't? What if no one finds the stupid bell? What if I trip and go splat right before I ring it? What if . . . ?*

Jenna shut down all negative thoughts. They just gave credence to Kelly's theory. She'd accepted a lot since she'd hit Philly, but she was done with all self-analysis for the night. She stood and started toward the door.

Kelly rose to follow her. "Shen told us he's gotten an apartment for Ty and me in the same building as Q. Fin likes partners to live close to each other so they can cover each other's butts. Move in with us, Jenna."

Jenna thought about it briefly. "It wouldn't work, sis. Fin probably has other plans for me, and even if he doesn't, I'd just get in the way. When Rap died, all I did was hang around and heave, not necessary talents for hunting vampires and immortals. I'll stick here with Al and hunt bells instead." She smiled weakly. "Be happy. Hunting for bells is a lot safer than what you're doing." *I hate what you're doing.*

Her sister finally nodded. "I guess this condo is safer than any apartment. Fin is here. Try to do your bell hunting during the day. Not all of the bad guys hunt at night, but some of the worst do." Kelly's expression said she wasn't happy about any of this. "And just so you're clear about my feelings, I hate that you're staying in Philly."

Finally. A meeting of minds on something. Jenna softened as she recognized the worry on her sister's face. "I'll be careful, sis. I need to survive so I can save humanity."

At least Kelly was smiling as she closed the door. Now her sister could collect her husband from the patio where he'd most likely frozen his ass off. That made Jenna smile, and she appreciated Ty giving Kelly and her some time alone.

She was still smiling as she neared her door. For whatever reason, she paused just as she reached for the knob. The hall was brightly lit, but some people carried shadows with them. Al was that kind of guy. He stepped forward from where he'd been waiting.

Jenna hoped she didn't show how startled she was. Funny, but startled was the right word, not scared. Al was a frightening man, but she wasn't afraid that he'd hurt her. *At least not physically.* Now where had that thought come from?

She smiled at him. "Waiting for me?" Duh?

He nodded as he moved into her personal space. Jenna was taller than her sister, but Al loomed over her, a muscular tower of testosterone. She'd have to remember that description for one of her articles.

"I had to make sure you were okay after everything that happened tonight."

Jenna stepped back until she was flattened against the wall. "I'm fine." Although "fine" was pretty fluid right now.

"I'm glad." His voice lowered to a husky murmur.

Unspeakable sexual hunger. The emotion hit with enough force to draw a gasp from her. She opened her mouth to try to say something, but Al took that option from her.

Flattening his palms against the wall on both sides of her, he trapped her in a vortex of spiraling heat and desire. "Yeah, that's me you feel. Right now my soul's crawling from its cave, searching for prey, sensing what it wants is near. I don't know if I can force it back into that cave, but I'll have to. Because what it wants is primitive, savage, and sexual in a way you couldn't possibly handle."

Jenna met his gaze. "You have no idea what I could *handle*."

His soul's need bled into his smile. "Okay, so maybe it can play for a few minutes before I put it away." Lowering his head, he covered her mouth with his.

Sex had never been much of a contact sport for Jenna. She dated, had a good time, and walked away with no emotional scars. Kelly would say she was looking for the perfect man. Not true. Jenna *wasn't* looking. At all. Period. She liked being with men, but a permanent arrangement didn't appeal.

This wasn't a game, though, contact or otherwise. This was a primal taking: of her mouth, her mind, her will. She couldn't think past the feel of his lips moving over hers—soft seduction, firm demand. Heat that spread, a slow slide of rising anticipation.

He didn't try coaxing her to open to him. No A, B, C, or none-of-the-above options for him. The pressure of his lips increased in direct proportion to her own response. He was sex and power, and her heart pounded out its recognition that she needed all the help she could get to survive this assault on her senses.

When she opened her mouth to gasp for breath, he took full advantage. His tongue explored and claimed everything it touched for its own.

Jenna had no idea at what point she mounted a counterattack. Reaching out, she gripped his shoulders and pulled him closer until her breasts pressed against the hard wall of his chest. Eyelids heavy with sudden arousal, she swayed back and forth, her nipples hard points of screaming sensitivity as they scraped against her shirt, his shirt, his *body*. Her senses exploded on contact. Oh my God, the two shirts had to go, because only skin against heated skin could ease the ache growing low in her stomach.

She immediately forgot about the shirts, though, as he leaned into her. She parted her legs to accommodate him. He had a lot for her to accommodate. Jenna clenched around the promise made by the size and strength of him. The spot where his cock pressed hard and demanding between her legs became a combustion point. At any moment the whole condo could burst into flame—he was just that hot.

And then, without warning, he ended it. He broke the kiss and pushed away from the wall with arms that seemed a little shaky. Jenna hoped so. She wouldn't want to think she was the only one held upright by just a thin thread of pride.

He might have controlled his body, but his eyes said his soul was fighting the good fight. Or bad fight depending on your point of view.

His soul stared out at her from eyes filled with carnal and predatory intent. Those eyes were like nothing she'd ever seen, a window to a time before history, when death walked the Earth in its most elemental form. It wanted what it wanted. And if his soul won, nothing would stand in its way.

Just when Jenna thought it was all over, a second emotion ripped through her. Fear. Irrational, primitive fear. She had one advantage, though. Kelly had described the same emotions when she was with Ty. Jenna wrapped her arms around her stomach and held on.

"Why are you doing this? *How* are you doing this?"

Al didn't answer immediately. He stood, breathing hard, until his eyes returned to the hazel Jenna was used to. Her fear faded. His soul had lost. This time.

"I'm still what I was back then. Inside." He laid his palm flat against his chest to demonstrate. "My soul was one of Earth's great predators. You don't banish it just because you change forms. When my emotions spike, the beast crawls out of its cave and tries to take over." He looked uneasy. "I have to fight it. It would make an uncomfortable threesome in bed."

Jenna knew whom he was including in that cozy threesome. Right now she was still thrumming with bottled-up sexual tension, so she wanted him with a part of her that didn't give a damn about his soul. But she had a feeling that once she was alone and had time to think things through, she'd change her mind. What she'd seen in his eyes was a scary proposition.

Since she couldn't think of anything meaningful to say, she turned toward the door. "I'm going to get some sleep. Good night."

She half expected him to argue with her. He didn't.

But as she closed the door behind her, she heard his quiet murmur.

"I'm not sorry, Jenna. I'm not sorry at all. And neither is my soul."

Chapter Ten

Today would be better for Jenna. Al would make it so. He'd eaten breakfast with her, and even if the memory of that kiss sat at the table with them, they'd managed to talk around it.

Unfortunately, he couldn't control his mind as easily as his mouth. His thoughts skulked around the image of her body, bared and open to his touch, with all the enthusiasm and focus of a starving wolf.

Only half listening to Fin, Al had escaped the table with no more than a reminder to check out places that might have bells.

Now they'd finished a late afternoon lunch and come out of the restaurant to snow flurries. The winter night was already falling, but the snow made the growing darkness seem almost festive.

Jenna spun in a circle. "This is so great. Houston isn't the snow capital of the world. Everything looks beautiful."

His soul said the snow was good for hunting. Falling snow would hide a predator's presence until it was too late for the prey. The human part of him was enjoying it because it made Jenna smile. How long was it since he'd cared whether anyone around him smiled? Try never.

"Do we have time to see the Liberty Bell?" Her eyes gleamed with the joy of the moment. "I mean, if Eight needs a bell, that would be the obvious one."

Al glanced at his watch. "It's getting late. I don't know. We can take a look."

At some point during their walk, the hunter became the hunted. It was an instinct honed in countless life-and-death situations. Al never ignored those feelings. "Keep walking, Jenna. We have visitors joining our group."

She gasped and started to turn around.

"Don't look. They aren't vampires, and there are plenty of people around."

He knew the exact moment when one of them drew up beside them.

"Katherine, queen of all vampires, wants to talk to you." The voice was tough, a voice attached to someone who wouldn't mind leaving a few bodies lying around on the sidewalk.

Only two of them. He relaxed a little. If he hadn't had Jenna with him, Al might've found this whole thing funny. Queen of all vampires? Talk about visions of grandeur. "Why us? Your queen should be talking to our leader. I'm nobody."

"Yeah, that's what I think too. But she just said to snatch any of you we could find. You're it, bud."

Al kept walking as he reached out with his mental link to Fin. *"We've received an invite to an audience with her majesty, Katherine, the queen of all vampires. The invite was delivered by humans. The thug kind. What do you want me to do?"* If Fin wanted him to talk to the vampire, he'd hail a taxi and send Jenna back to the condo.

"Queen of all vampires?" Fin sounded amused. *"Go with them. I want to know where her vampires stand. She obviously doesn't want to talk to me."*

"I'll send Jenna back to the condo in a taxi."

"Take her with you."

Al knew Fin was a cold bastard, but he didn't think he was stupid as well. *"Why?"*

"She might see a bell that needs ringing." The humor was still in Fin's voice.

Al ground his teeth in an attempt to quiet his soul, which thought that Fin needed eating. *"Even if you don't give a rat's ass about her safety, you're going to need her for your vision to happen."*

Fin was making a big deal about sounding patient. *"First, even if no one else survives this visit, she will. If she died saying hi to Katherine, I wouldn't have had a vision of her ringing the bell. Second, she'll be safer with you. Anyone who knows she's with us might be looking for a chance to catch her alone. A cab would be perfect."*

Yeah, that kind of made sense, but Al still didn't want to take Jenna with him. *"Send someone to pick her up."*

"She'll be safe. I'm sending Spin your way, but not to take Jenna. He should catch up with you in about two minutes. And Jude has risen. I've contacted him, and he'll be there with the queen when you arrive."

"And you trust Jude?"

"He helped us in Houston."

Al had run out of arguments. But God help any vampire that tried to touch Jenna. He met her wide eyes. "You stay with me."

She nodded, but he could sense her fear.

They were just approaching a Hummer parked in a side street when Spin came up behind him.

"Hey, Al. Think I'll tag along with you guys." Spin waved at Jenna. "Hi, Jenna. I'm Spin. We never met. Too bad. Al has all the luck."

Even with everything that was happening around him, Al experienced a stab of something that felt a lot like jealousy. Which made no sense at all. Sure Spin looked great. Women turned to look at that long blond hair. But Al didn't own Jenna.

The guy next to Jenna turned to glare at Spin. "We don't need anyone else along."

Spin laughed. "Sure you do. Besides, you can't stop me from going with you. Want to try?" That last held a dangerous edge no one could mistake.

With a few mumbled curses, the two men gave in. As Al held the door for Jenna, he wondered what these guys would think if they knew who shared the Hummer with them.

When they pulled out into traffic without anyone mentioning blindfolds, Al's suspicions revved up. "Don't you care if we see where you're going?"

The driver shrugged. "Doesn't matter. This is a one-time event. The queen won't be back here again."

Spin laughed. "Gee, and here I figured you planned to kill everyone when the meeting was over."

Both men grunted. Al figured they wished it would happen but weren't sure they could count on it.

Jenna didn't say anything.

When they finally reached their destination, an old abandoned church, it was completely dark. Al had no idea where they were in the city, just that they'd twisted and turned through a warren of streets. Probably meant to confuse them. It'd worked.

The driver stopped the Hummer behind the church and waited while Jenna, Spin, and Al climbed out. Then he drove away with his companion.

"Guess this is an all-vampire get-together." Spin didn't seem worried about being odd man out.

Jenna moved closer to Al. "When does Buffy show up?"

"Buffy?" He searched through his store of human pop culture. No Buffy. Fin had slipped up. It was little things like this that brought home exactly how *not* human he was. And the thought that he had no Buffy memories in common with Jenna made him surprisingly sad.

"Vampire slayer." She waved the comment away. "Never mind."

Al might have believed her cool, calm exterior if he couldn't hear her heart pounding away in triple time. He put his arm across her shoulders and pulled her tightly against him while he bent to her ear. "We *will* keep you safe. After all, you have a bell to ring. If we have to, Spin and I can pull this place down around their undead ears." Then he moved away from her. "Don't make yourself a target by getting too close to me, but don't get out of my sight."

She managed a smile. "Right. Close, but not too close."

Al exchanged a get-ready glance with Spin and then he knocked on the back door of the church.

It was opened almost immediately. If Al's senses hadn't told him the man standing there was a vampire, he never would've believed it. The vampire didn't have Jude's great looks or the big-muscled body of some of Jude's guards. This guy was short, round, and wearing a huge smile. He was the undead version of a fanged Santa Claus, and he had the jolly part down pat.

"Welcome, welcome." He motioned them into the church. "I'm Kenny. My wife is Queen Katherine."

"Wouldn't that make you Prince Kenneth?" Jenna's heartbeat had started to return to normal.

Al figured Kenny could be deadly in his own right, but right now he was showing them his "human" face.

"Nah. Come on, come on, everyone's excited to meet you." He led them down a long, dark corridor toward the front of the church. "I'm just plain old Kenny Colaccio. Always will be. Born, raised, and died in South Philly. Maybe if we get together again we can drink some wine, and I'll cook up some lasagna like you've never tasted before. *Magnifico.*" He kissed the tips of his fingers. "I was a cook before I became vampire. I might not be able to eat it, but I can still cook it." His chuckle sounded friendly and open.

But Al wasn't really paying too much attention to Kenny's rambling. Probably bullshit anyway. He kept his focus on everything around him. Doors to rooms long abandoned hung from one hinge or were gone completely. Trash littered the rooms, and a heavy layer of dust and grime covered everything. Al wasn't about to take a closer look at what was in that trash. Most of the windows Al could see were cracked or missing.

This would be a bad place for Spin and him to be if a fight broke out. Neither of their beasts would fit in the narrow corridor.

Jenna seemed to feel comfortable enough with Kenny to ask a question. "Uh, this is a church. I thought vampires couldn't go into a church."

Kenny chuckled. "Fiction. I've been going to mass at Old Saint Joseph's for over a hundred years. Never went to this church, though."

Al felt enormous relief when they suddenly entered the main part of the church. Thank God for big open spaces. The ceiling soared several stories high. At least fifty vampires sat in what remained of the pews. He glanced at the altar. The woman posed regally on a portable throne must be Katherine.

With a sense of relief he wasn't sure was warranted, Al spotted Jude seated in a front pew. He took a few seconds to scope out the doors. Nailed shut. Not that the doors were important when there were so many broken windows for fleeing vampires to jump through. The church was lit by only a few candles. Probably didn't want to advertise they were here. He started to swing his gaze back to Katherine when he caught the coppery scent of blood.

"Son of a bitch." Spin's exclamation warned Al of trouble to come.

Al felt Jenna stiffen beside him and then heard her heart speed up.

"What the . . ." Quickly he scanned the whole church.

That was when Al saw the naked vampire to the right of Katherine. His wrists had been bound, and the rope that was tied to an overhead beam held him suspended about a foot off the floor. There didn't seem to be a spot on his body that wasn't burned or cut. His cock was gone, and from the blood still streaming from the wound, Al figured he'd be dead from blood loss in a short time. No way would his body be able to heal before he bled out. The guy's head hung onto his chest. Didn't look like he was conscious.

Killing didn't bother Al. He'd spent his whole life hunting down prey and tearing it apart. But this kind of killing bothered him. He preferred a clean kill. Torture wasn't his thing.

Jenna. She'd seen Rap killed last night and now this. He wished he'd defied Fin and sent her back to the condo. Her body was pressed against his side, and he glanced down. Her face was so pale she would have fit right in with the vampires in the pews. But other than that, she looked calm. Unfortunately, he could hear her racing heartbeat and her quick shallow breaths as she tried to keep her nausea at bay. He could feel her body trembling with fear she had every right to feel.

He leaned down to her ear. "I'll *always* keep you safe. That's a promise."

Jenna raised her gaze to his. He could see the silent scream in her eyes. "Always is a long time. Be careful what you promise." She looked away, making sure her glance didn't stray back to the altar and its gruesome scene. "Let's get this over with fast before I throw up or pass out. And if Katherine is responsible for that unspeakable cruelty, then she needs killing." A new hardness had crept into Jenna's voice.

"Bring them to me, Kenny." The vampire queen's voice was as imperious as she looked.

Katherine was a big woman. Not heavy, just tall and

solid. She looked like she could take out her smaller husband with one punch and not even break a sweat. Did vampires sweat? Something for Al to check on later.

Kenny seemed nervous as he led them onto the altar and over to his wife. Al decided he didn't care what protocol demanded, he wasn't doing any bowing to this woman.

Katherine studied them from eyes so black that Al couldn't read any expression in them. He opened his link to Fin so his leader could see her. Fin would get past the surface stuff to what lived in her soul.

"Be careful. She's dangerous, and she doesn't have any allegiances. She'll go to the winning side. Oh, and she's thinking about asking for Jenna as a gift."

The rage that exploded in Al caught him by surprise. His beast was already half out of its cave by the time he got his emotions under control. Al didn't try to push his soul all the way back in; if he was honest with himself, he wanted this woman dead.

Katherine nodded at Al. "Introduce yourself and your friends." Her gaze lingered on Jenna for a few seconds too long. Al's beast growled.

He pointed at the others. "Spin and Jenna. I'm Al." He'd offer as little info as possible.

The vampire queen's thin-lipped smile didn't give off any warm and fuzzy vibes. "I understand you lost a friend last night."

Al tensed. He knew Spin would be doing the same, readying himself for his soul's release and that first leap. "What do you know about it?"

Katherine glanced toward the suspended vampire. "He's the only one of the ambushers who escaped. He was working for someone other than me. I demand loyalty from those who are mine."

Suddenly Al felt a lot less sympathy for the tortured vampire.

"After a little . . . encouragement, he told us how he and the others lured some of your men into the trap. Of course, he exaggerated your ferociousness. And I don't for a moment believe the dinosaur tales. Utter nonsense. I know all the shape-shifters in the area, and none of them can shift into anything bigger than a lion."

Jude had evidently kept his mouth shut about the Eleven. Good. "We're not shifters." *And we're a damn lot bigger than a lion.*

She shrugged. "Whatever. Now, let's get down to business. From what my reluctant informant told me, you're battling a group of immortals who intend to wipe humans from the face of the Earth on December twenty-first. And the immortal who's recruiting nonhumans in Philadelphia to help do the job is encouraging his followers to start indulging their murderous impulses against humanity now. Is that correct?"

Al nodded.

Katherine leaned back in her throne. "Then it looks like I have a choice to make. I can support you and your leader, who've offered me no incentive to join your cause, or I can throw my power—and I control most of the vampires in this country—toward these immortals."

She tried on a benevolent expression. It didn't work.

"Before I make my choice, I'll allow you to return to your leader so you can tell him that I would make a powerful ally or a deadly enemy. It's his decision. Kenny will contact you with the time and place to meet me again. I'll expect a generous offer."

Fin was still in Al's head, and he'd already decided. *"Your leader will offer her a kick in her self-important ass."*

Al risked a quick glance toward Jude. The vampire looked more than pissed at Katherine's claim to national dominance. Al wondered if Katherine was too puffed up with her own importance to realize how dangerous Jude really was.

She evidently decided to end her presentation by demonstrating her power. Turning her head toward the hapless vampire, she snapped her fingers. He immediately burst into flame. No screams, so he was dead or unconscious.

Then she returned her attention to Al and the others. Al didn't need to read the expression in her eyes. He could see the hunger and greed in the twist of her lips.

"And as proof of my good faith, I'll tell you that our dearly departed friend said the immortal operating in this city calls himself Stake." She scowled. "A rather insensitive name. I'll have to suggest he change it."

Spin spoke up for the first time. "What do *you* want?"

Katherine slid her gaze to Jenna, and Al knew what she'd say before she said it. He allowed his soul to crawl a little farther out of its cave.

"Leave the woman with me as a token of *your* good faith. I'll return her to you when you deliver the offer from your leader."

"Bitch." Jenna said it loud enough to carry to the queen.

Katherine smiled. "Spunky. I like that."

The vampire was a coward and a liar. Al knew Jenna would be dead or worse ten minutes after Spin and he left the church. And Katherine had made it clear she didn't want to meet Fin in person. She wasn't taking any risks with her royal person. Her mistake was in thinking that Spin and Al weren't powerful enough to threaten her.

"Sorry, Jenna stays with us." Al made sure Katherine saw that he wasn't sorry at all. "And you might not want to hold your breath waiting for our leader's offer. He doesn't hire mercenaries. They can't be trusted."

Katherine's face twisted into an ugly glare. As vampires went, she was an unattractive specimen. She stood, her gaze fixed on them.

Then she turned to her followers. "Kill them. Stake will

reward us when he finds that we eliminated two more of the Eleven. In a few minutes, they'll be the Eight."

She'd made a fatal mistake. She'd said too many words. She should have stopped after the first two. All the extra babbling gave Spin the time he needed to turn his soul loose.

Al grabbed Jenna and dived for the door.

"Aren't you going to help?" Jenna didn't take her gaze from Spin, who stood facing the queen. "God, he'd better change before she can snap her fingers."

The only thing I'm going to do is keep you safe. "Only one of our souls will fit in this room, and she won't snap her fingers. She wants her followers to rip us apart. I see someone with a camcorder back there filming this. A bunch of vampires ripping three people apart makes for great footage." Besides, Spin was fast. By the time she thought about snapping her fingers, it would be too late.

Al stopped talking as Spin's soul burst free. For just a moment, a random thought hit him. He didn't remember ever seeing a Spinosaurus when he'd last walked the Earth. And Spin was distinctive enough that Al wouldn't have mistaken him for anything other than what he was.

Spin was an impressive sight. Over fifty feet long, he had freaky skin-covered spines sticking up at least six feet from his backbone. And even though he had the same powerful hind legs and short forelegs as an Allosaurus, his head was something else. Spin had a long narrow snout with equally long sharp teeth.

And Spin put those teeth to good use. He was probably thinking about Katherine and her snapping fingers too, because before the screaming could even begin, he leaped on the vampire queen and tore her head from her body. Then he turned on her followers.

Except her followers were gone. Or at least in the act of

leaving. They'd evidently taken one look at the massive dinosaur filling up most of the church and decided not to stick around to see if they could take it down. And with their queen dead, they were left rudderless. In the ensuing confusion, Spin had no trouble picking off the stragglers.

Al fought his soul. The scent of blood, the battle, the dying tore at the thin tether connecting him to his human body. He wanted to roar his challenge and lose himself in the slaughter. Gritting his teeth, he held it together as his soul shredded his insides with its need to be free.

Then he glanced at Jenna. She stared at him, horror in her eyes. He knew exactly what she was seeing—all the bloodlust of an ancient predator trapped behind the eyes of a man. Not something she'd soon forget. He tried to convince himself that he didn't give a damn what she thought of him.

Within a few minutes Jude was the only living vampire inside the church. But the danger wasn't over. In their rush to escape, the vampires had knocked over the candles. A healthy fire was feeding on the old wood of the building.

"Let's get out of here." Al grabbed Jenna's hand as they fled back down the corridor, Jude and Spin—back in his human form—close behind.

"Use one of the windows," Al shouted over his shoulder. If any of the surviving vampires felt particularly brave, they could be waiting at the back door to try a surprise attack.

Al guided Jenna into the first empty room and then kicked out what remained of the window. Spin and Jude went out the windows of other rooms so they wouldn't be caught all together.

"Someone's probably called the fire department by now." Jenna didn't sound as though she was about to fall apart.

"Yeah. We need to be away from here when the trucks

arrive." He edged along the outside wall toward the back of the church.

By now most of the building was blazing, and the heat was growing unbearable. When he finally got close enough to see the parking lot in the back, the only ones there were Spin, Jude, and Kenny. But there was also a car. That was important.

Jenna said it for him. "Kenny?"

Al didn't have time to puzzle over the presence of the vampire queen's husband. He ran toward the group. "We need to get out of here right now."

Kenny nodded. "That's my car. Climb in."

"Why would you help us?" Jenna was learning fast.

Kenny wasn't smiling, but he didn't look devastated either. "Hey, I don't hold a grudge. Katherine liked to throw her power around." Something in his expression said he'd been the recipient of some of his wife's power blasts. "And after what I saw tonight, I'm throwing in with you guys." His gaze slid to Jude. "And whoever the new leader is."

Jude must've seen Al's hesitation. "From what I've heard, Katherine wasn't a beloved ruler. She wouldn't have allowed Kenny to walk away even if he wanted to." He glanced at Kenny. "And I'm guessing he wanted to."

Al didn't sense any danger from Kenny, so he got Jenna into the car and climbed in beside her. The others piled in, and Kenny didn't waste any time peeling out of the parking lot. They heard the sirens when they were a block away from the church.

"Where'd you leave your car?" Kenny aimed his question at Jude, who sat in the front passenger seat.

Jenna was squished between Al and Spin in the backseat, but Al was enjoying her closeness. The only bad part was that Spin was probably enjoying it too.

Within a few minutes, Kenny pulled up beside Jude's

white Lexus. "Umm, when you want to get everyone to-gether, call me." He pulled a smudged card from his pocket.

Jude smiled. "I'll remember your help, Kenny. Sorry about your wife."

Al didn't think anyone was sorry about Katherine, espe-cially her husband, who was looking pretty liberated at the moment.

Once Jude pulled out into traffic, Jenna spoke. "What was Katherine's official title?"

Jude glanced in the rearview mirror. "She was in charge of a ten-state area like I am. Only it seems she liked to think of herself as a lot more powerful than she was." He shook his head. "Not too smart. Only someone stupid would meet with strangers without a lot more protections in place. Only someone stupid would underestimate you guys. She didn't deserve those ten states."

"Who does deserve them?" Spin sounded like he knew the answer.

Jude's smile was wide and for once sincere. "I guess I do, for the time being. But as much as I like the power trip, I don't want the added responsibility. So I'll give it up as soon as someone can take it from me."

"Take it from you?" Jenna wiggled her behind as she worked herself into a more comfortable position.

Al's body reacted to the stimulus in a predictable way. He suspected, though, that Spin would have a similar reac-tion. Bastard.

"We earn leadership over an area by being stronger than everyone else." He shrugged. "So when someone stronger comes along, they can have Pennsylvania and the other states."

"How do you decide who's stronger?" Jenna wasn't go-ing to leave it alone.

"We fight."

That silenced Jenna. Her expression said the whole idea

was barbaric and she'd thought better of Jude. Personally, Al's opinion of Jude had just gone up. Call him primitive and savage, but Al respected a man who fought for his territory, or his mate. He sent a glare in Spin's direction. Mate? He'd better lose that thought fast.

When they finally got back to the condo, Fin was waiting for them in the media room. Jenna took the decision of who would sit next to her out of Al's and Fin's hands by dropping into a leather recliner. She sighed her relief.

Al masked his disappointment by taking a nearby chair. Then he waited for everyone else to be seated.

For once, Fin seemed satisfied. "Things worked out a lot better than I expected."

Jenna didn't agree. "A power-hungry vampire bitch set one of her own on fire just to prove she could. After that she threatened us with death and Spin had to kill half a church full of vampires to save our lives. I don't know about you, but I expected a better ending to my day."

Al wondered what held her together, and why she didn't run. Just a few days ago she was an ordinary woman living an ordinary life. Now she was witnessing death and horror everywhere she turned.

If she was staying just for her sister, then why did she agree to go anywhere with him? She could refuse. Fin wouldn't drag her kicking and screaming from the condo. Fin might be able to keep her from going along with Kelly and Ty on their nightly hunts, but he couldn't stop her from visiting her sister each day. And that was all she really needed to do to assure herself that Kelly was okay.

"We have to look at the big picture." One of Fin's favorite phrases. "We got rid of Katherine, who would've signed up with Eight, and replaced her with Jude, who'll fight on our side. This Kenny guy looks like someone we can use. And we even found out what name Eight is using." He shook his head. "Dumb name."

"Speaking of names, Infinity is an interesting choice." She looked as if she was trying to work through something. "Numbers are a big thing with you, so naturally you'd see yourself as a forever kind of guy." Her gaze sharpened. "Infinity also means something that's not subject to any limitations. Do you see yourself like that?" The questions kept on coming. "You call your enemies immortals. What about you guys? Are you immortal?"

Fin held up his hand to stop her. "No more. This whole question thing must be a genetic weakness in the Maloy family. You're even worse than your sister."

Al wondered how many of Jenna's questions Fin would answer. Fin only gave out information on a need-to-know basis. But he *was* loosening up a little. Al now knew that Fin had manipulated his memory and that Jenna was the ticket to Eight's trip home.

"Our enemies are true immortals because nothing can kill them. Our only hope is to ban them from Earth until the end of the next time period. In a few million more years we might have the power to keep them out permanently." His expression spoke of his frustration with the good guys' limitations. "The Eleven? They don't die natural deaths. Old age, disease, or even life-threatening injuries can't destroy them. But they *are* vulnerable." The silence was filled with the memory of Rap. "They can still lose their heads."

Jenna mentioned the obvious. "You said 'they' not 'we.' You didn't include yourself."

His smile was classic Fin—warm, open, and as fake as the rest of him. Al shook his head. He needed sleep. Fin might not be his favorite of the Eleven—okay, so his feelings came close to hate sometimes—and Fin might drive him crazy with the things he refused to tell them, but Al always held onto his core belief that Fin was on their side. Fin was the only reason they'd survived to fight in the year 2012.

"I *didn't* include myself, did I?" Fin yawned. "I'm tired. See you all in the afternoon." Then he simply rose and left them all sitting there.

Al glanced at Spin to see what he thought of Fin's side-stepping. Spin was fast asleep. He looked at Jenna.

Her eyes were alight with excitement. "I'm going to find out what Fin is."

Al closed his eyes. Oh, hell.

Chapter Eleven

Jenna was having a quiet crisis. She sat cross-legged on the couch in the sitting area of her room trying to figure out why the formula that had worked her entire life was no longer enough.

When she'd realized she couldn't be as perfect as Kelly in school, she'd stopped competing and proclaimed she didn't care. When she'd recognized that she'd never be as good with animals as her parents were, she'd given up on her plans to be a vet and switched to an English Lit major. It was for the best. She never could stand the sight of animals suffering.

The only thing that *had* been perfect for her was her tabloid job. What had started out being another I–don't–care moment had morphed into a damn–I'm–good–at–this job. Her perfectionism had translated into awesome articles. The best part? She wasn't competing with any of her family.

So what was she doing competing with Kelly again? Her sister had saved the day in Houston, and now Fin expected Jenna to do the same in Philly. If she didn't ring that damn bell, it was bye-bye humanity. And this time she couldn't walk away and pretend she didn't care.

The last two nights proved she wasn't ready for a prime-time performance. Last night she'd wasted her chance to shine by heaving up her stomach. Tonight she'd just stood frozen trying to breathe past the boulder in her throat.

Kelly probably would've picked up a candlestick and splattered some vampire brains over the floor.

Then there was Al. He terrified her on a level so primal, her modern mind couldn't wrap itself around the emotion. She'd looked into his eyes tonight and seen death. He'd wanted to join Spin in the killing, and he'd had a tough time resisting all that fun. His soul had recognized her tonight. And she had a gut feeling it was trying to decide where to file her. She hoped it wasn't under "prey."

So if she was that afraid, then why did she want to rip his clothes from his body and do things with him she'd never wanted to do with any other man? She didn't just want sex, she wanted SEX—rough, raw, and savage. No holds barred. Was there something in the carnal, elemental male of him that called to the primitive remnants of her essential female? She was a thinking person, and something that spoke to instinct and not reason made her nervous.

Even though she was physically exhausted, her mind was awake and trying to dissect everything Al had said and done today even as it analyzed how those things related to her.

And when her mind took a breather from thinking about Al, it brought up all the violent images from the church. In living, or more accurately undead, color. God, she didn't want to think about that.

So she did what she always did when she wanted a mental distraction: she turned to her laptop. First she checked her e-mail. Penis enlargement, hair replacement, sexy singles, and a message from her editor. She needed to up the level of her spam filter. Delete, delete, delete, and read.

Martha had succeeded as editor of *The Scene* by holding the strings to tipsters all over the world. When a tip came in, she found someone to check it out. This time she'd tapped Jenna.

Two tips had popped up from anonymous sources in

Philly. Luckily, she had Jenna right in the city. Martha wanted her to see if there was anything to them.

Jenna glanced at the tips before saving them to her work file. Aliens were planning to steal the Liberty Bell, and some restaurants in Philly were fronts for vampire activity.

She'd had personal experience with the vampire restaurants. But the Liberty Bell lead held special interest. And just for a moment, she enjoyed the irony of her treating the tips as real when a few days ago she would've done lots of eye rolling.

Next order of business, Fin. Jenna didn't know where to start learning about him, so she shut down her computer until her mind was clearer. Wait. There was something she'd meant to follow up on. Opening her notebook, she checked her facts. Yep, Al had been extinct by the time Ty rolled onto the scene.

She'd tell Kelly and Al about her finding first. Jenna didn't trust Fin. He had the power to make her forget all about her discovery. But this could wait until the afternoon.

After taking a shower and pulling on her nightgown, she turned off the light and climbed into bed. If she could turn off her brain too, maybe she could fall asleep.

She was just dozing off when someone knocked on her door. The temptation to ignore it lasted all of ten seconds. Kelly? Not bothering to even run her fingers through her hair, she pulled on her robe, stumbled to the door, and flung it open. "What?"

Then her brain caught up with her mouth and she just stared. Al stood in the darkened hallway. He wore jeans and . . . jeans. His chest was sculpted perfection, and she'd always craved perfection. His feet were bare, and his skin gleamed damply as though he'd just gotten out of the shower.

And his hair wasn't braided. It was a dark curtain that fell down his back and flowed across his shoulders. It looked clean, shiny, and just blow-dried.

He smiled at her, a sensual lifting of his lips that changed the hard lines of his face into something softer but just as dangerous. "I was heading straight to bed, but I started thinking about what happened tonight. I need to talk to you about it."

"It can't wait until this afternoon?" She wanted him to stay. She wanted him to leave. The message was different according to which part of her body she asked. Her brain thought the faster he left the better. Other body systems thought she should open her door wide and invite his gorgeous ass in.

"I think it needs to be now." His face might look softer, but he still had the eyes of a predator.

Now Jenna knew how Little Red Riding Hood's grandma felt, because she was tuning out her brain even as she held the door open for him.

He shook his head. "Not here. The walls are starting to close in. The roof is good. I can see the sky."

She glanced back at her nice warm room, her nice warm *bed*. "A little chilly up there."

Al laughed, and there were no undertones, no unspoken messages. "Come see." He held out his hand.

Jenna knew she looked doubtful. "Give me a minute to change and—"

"You don't need to change."

"I'm from Houston, the land of hot weather and thin blood." But she wanted to stay with him, so she let him pull her toward the stairs at the end of the hallway. When they reached the roof, she expected to be met by a blast of frigid air. Instead they stepped into a heated glass room—four glass walls and a glass ceiling. No lights.

"Wow." She spun in a circle, taking in the 360 degrees

of city lights and night sky. The snow flurries had stopped. Too bad. "Did Fin do this?"

"Yeah. He has an ongoing psychic battle with Zero, and lately he's had trouble unwinding enough to sleep. Being able to see the sky relaxes him."

"Okay, that explains the floor." The floor that was one big mattress. Great to sleep on, hard to walk on. Since there weren't any chairs, she dropped onto the mattress and leaned back against the glass. Jenna watched as Al stared out at the night before turning toward her.

"If I ever have a place of my own, I'd like a room like this." It was the first time he'd ever hinted there might be an "after" for him. "I don't like feeling trapped."

"You were an apex predator. I thought fear wasn't in your vocabulary."

"Maybe the human in me is bleeding through." His gaze settled on her, impersonal but with intimate waiting in the wings. "Anyway, being up here drives the shadows away."

You bring the shadows with you. "Well, it sure is spectacular." *Like you.*

He stared at her in silence for so long she had to resist the urge to squirm.

"I saw your expression when you looked at me tonight. Do I scare you, Jenna?"

"You scare the hell out of me. I looked into your eyes while Spin was tearing through the vampires, and I saw your soul. That would be scary for any human."

For a moment she thought she saw regret in his eyes.

"But that doesn't mean I don't trust you to keep me safe." *It doesn't mean that I don't want you deep inside me.*

Al nodded. "I guess that's better than nothing." He settled down next to her. "No matter how much knowledge Fin poured in here"—he tapped his forehead—"when I get emotional, my soul tries to take over." He shrugged. "I can fight it, but I don't always win. Fin says as we spend time in our new bodies, human nature will exert more power over us." His smile didn't look convinced. "The upside is that I can call my soul out at will. That's a good thing."

"Are you saying that *all* emotions trigger it?" What would it be like making love with this man? Would he bring his soul into the bed with them? Not a comfortable threesome. But even as she told herself she absolutely did *not* want to deal with the danger, a primitive part of her was anticipating the rush of so much primal energy focused on her.

He must have seen something in her expression, because his smile was all heated temptation. "Rage and sexual hunger. That doesn't mean a woman will wake up with a dinosaur beside her, but it does mean we bring the same intensity to mating as we did millions of years ago."

She took that to its obvious conclusion. "Not long on foreplay, huh?" Jenna smiled so he would know she was trying to lighten a conversation in danger of getting out of control.

His eyes darkened, "I wouldn't know."

Uh-oh. "How long have you had your human body?"

"I rose on November eleventh of last year and now it's January, so about two months."

She stopped herself before she asked the next question.

He answered it. "Sixty-five million years ago."

A random thought cut through sexual tension so thick Jenna couldn't have hacked a hole in it with a machete. According to her research, it had been more like 145 million years.

"Oh." But what were a few million years between lovers?

Suddenly, he turned his head to stare directly at her. Those predator eyes seemed to gleam in the darkness. She suppressed a nervous giggle. She *never* giggled. "When you look at me like that, my over-the-top imagination kicks in. Did you see *Jurassic Park*?"

"Yeah. We rented it." He smiled. "We cheered every time one of us ate one of you."

"Not funny." But she smiled back. "When I look into your eyes, I think of the scene where the power fails and everyone's stuck in the tour cars. It's dark and suddenly you feel the ground shaking as though something massive is moving through the trees. We all know the T. rex is coming. Nearer, and nearer, and nearer . . . We wait for it, wait for it . . ." Thud, thud, thud. She shook her head. Just the pounding of her heart. "And then all at once it's there. So big it takes your breath away. And those teeth." She remembered her terror when she'd first caught a glimpse of the Allosaurus's massive shadow looming over their car as Jude scrambled out to face it. She shuddered.

He must have sensed a little of what she was feeling because he slid down until his head was lower than hers.

Jenna choked back a laugh. "Making yourself look smaller doesn't help." She shook her head. "You're a dangerous man with or without a prehistoric soul. And I was damn glad of it in that church."

He nodded, but Jenna couldn't read the expression in his eyes.

"Take a chance and go out with me again. This time without Jude."

"I won't find any bells by hiding in the condo." She couldn't help it; she had to know. Reaching over, she slid her fingers through the long, glossy strands of his hair. It was as smooth and soft as she'd imagined. So *not* like the rest of the man. The way it framed his face, the clean smell of it, touched a primal part of her soul. "I thought you only left it free when you hunted."

Something hot and hungry moved in his gaze. "Who said I'm not hunting?"

She didn't know where to go with that line.

He glanced away from her, searching for something in the

night sky. His past? His future? "One of the guys in *Jurassic Park* said something that's true. He said the T. rex didn't want to be fed, it wanted to hunt. He nailed it. What makes us so dangerous is our need to attack, to kill. It's hardwired into our souls. The man in me loves to sit down to a rare prime rib with mashed potatoes and gravy. My soul would rather stalk a nice fat heifer as it grazes out on the range."

More info than she needed to know. Time for a change of subject. "It must've taken you a long time to grow your hair that long."

"I wouldn't know. The body wasn't mine when the hair started growing."

"I see." Jenna decided not to ask how Fin had acquired the bodies. She was trying to think of something to say to keep the conversation flowing when he put his hand on her thigh. But then, who needed conversation?

"I don't play games, Jenna. I want you. And if I broadcast my emotions, it's because they're that strong, so strong that I can't hold them down. And sometimes they get all mixed up. My soul strings emotions together. One leads to another. That's why you might get feelings coming from me that scare you on a whole bunch of levels. Sex, rage, hunger. All primitive emotions, and all churning in my head at the same time."

"So when you're lusting after a big juicy steak, you might hit me with one of your emotional punches without meaning to?"

He smiled. It was slow, and beautiful, and so sensual she had to remind herself to breathe. She'd met more gorgeous men since coming to Philly than she'd ever seen in her entire life, and they all had incredible smiles. But Al owned her with his. It was tuned into every erotic fantasy stashed away in that dark little corner of her mind with the sign reading: Never Gonna Happen. His smile made her think it just might.

"I'm not lusting after steaks."

She had a hard time concentrating on his words as he pushed her robe aside and slipped his hand beneath her gown to massage the flesh high on her inner thigh. Thinking was becoming hard work.

But the voice in her head that separated truth from fantasy was stubborn. In her line of work, she was always searching for the angle. Did he have one?

Shut up. But her mind wasn't that easy to silence. Even though mind and body had their own agendas, mind kept on blabbing in the background. A man got turned on at the drop of an innuendo. A man didn't need to even like a woman to get aroused. A man wouldn't hesitate to use sex to manipulate. And a man with the soul of a prehistoric predator would expect to always get what he wanted.

Enough. She didn't care.

Leaning over, she drew one finger down the side of his jaw and watched it clench. His eyes burned with need, and she felt the heat and heaviness building low in her stomach. Her mind might be ambivalent about him, but her body didn't have any doubts.

She waited for the blast of desire from him she'd experienced before. Nothing. So maybe this was an act. If Al was just shoring up his companion status with her because of Fin's order, then she didn't want any part of his seduction.

Her head was firmly back in control. They'd settle this some other time when she was more prepared. "Look, I think we're both tired. Let's call it a night."

He was still sitting, his back propped against the glass wall, when she started to stand.

"No." The one word was the angry growl of a predator not to be denied its prey.

She was the only prey in the room. "Yes." Well, this antelope had attitude.

Wrapping his arms around her hips, he pulled her back down to the thick mattress. Then he loomed over her. Hunger tightened the muscles in his face until every line stood out starkly. His eyes burned with what he held reined in for the moment. "You don't dismiss what I'm feeling, what *you're* feeling, with just a few words. I thought I could control it this time so I wouldn't scare you. Can't do. Too bad, sweetheart."

Okay, no words. Then what? She swallowed hard as he lowered his head. If she was lucky, she'd stirred up the perfect storm.

The moment his lips touched hers, every suppressed emotion she'd locked away since coming here exploded in one focused attack. She reached up, tangled her fingers in all that glorious hair, and pulled him closer.

Whatever his motive might be, his reaction matched her intensity. His lips moved hard over hers at the same time his tongue demanded unconditional surrender. He tasted of mint toothpaste and aroused male. Her favorites.

When he finally broke the kiss they were both breathing in short gasps. Gripping her robe, he peeled it off. Her gown followed close behind.

With her last bit of rational thought, she scanned the area to make sure no one could possibly see them. Safe.

Then she fumbled at his jeans. She wanted to see the powerful muscular whole of him exposed for her enjoyment. With an impatient sound, he stripped them off and flung them aside. No underwear. Good.

His soul finally made its appearance. And if she wasn't already flat on her back, his emotional punch of amped-up lust would've knocked her onto her deprived butt. The blast of desire wrung a cry from her. It left Jenna wet and clenching at the image of her legs wrapped around him while he plunged into her again and again and again.

He didn't speak. He didn't need to. She knew what

watched her from Al's human eyes. His beast wouldn't see any use for sensual words or sexy compliments. Ruled by its senses, all it wanted was to hear her panting and screaming as she climaxed.

Jenna welcomed him, no matter who was in the driver's seat.

He leaned over her, and all that shining mass of hair skimmed her bared body. Jenna shivered as she gathered it into her fists, rubbed it between her fingers, savored its silky texture and clean scent, then let it spill out of her hands again, a dark waterfall for her pleasure alone.

There was no playfulness, no teasing foreplay in his sexual dictionary. His mouth touched her everywhere—breasts, stomach, and a long sensual nibble from the back of her knee and along her inner thigh.

Her breathing came hard and fast as he gave her no chance to do anything except dig her nails into his broad shoulders and hang on.

He was a silent lover. No doubt his beast saw no reason to make useless noises. But it did crave as much contact as possible. Al straddled her and then lowered his body until it was barely touching hers. He supported his weight on his forearms as he lightly scraped his torso over her breasts and stomach. Back and forth, back and forth. The friction against her nipples and stomach drew a moan from her.

When he moved down between her legs, she opened to him. He knelt, slipped his hands beneath her buttocks, and lifted her to his mouth.

Even as she felt her orgasm gathering low in her belly while his talented tongue teased and tortured, she knew there needed to be more. Where was her part in all this? She wanted to touch him, talk to him, slow down the pleasure. This may have been how males did it millions of years ago, but he was about to get a sexual update.

"Stop." Her voice was breathy, and parts of her body wanted to know what the hell she was doing.

Within the blink of an eye, Al shut down everything. It was as though someone had turned off his motor. Except for one part. That part remained long, hard, and hopeful. "You've changed your mind." His voice was flat, expressionless.

But she knew how hard it must have been to obey her. "No, I *want* to make love to you. Now listen carefully. *I* want to make love to you. *I* want to touch you. *I* want to tell you what I'm feeling." She paused, trying to think of how to say this in a way he'd understand. "In this time, men and women give each other pleasure. It's not a one-way street. Let me touch your body the way you've touched mine."

In the silence that followed her announcement, she could almost hear his mind trying to make sense of what she'd said. Time for a demonstration.

"Lie on your back and spread your legs." She smiled as his eyes widened.

But he did what she asked. Omigod, she didn't know if she'd survive touching all that beautiful flesh. As he lay there in the darkness, hard muscle moving beneath smooth skin, she could truly believe he was a god of the night.

"I talk when I make love." Jenna knelt and then leaned over to kiss his neck. She felt him swallow hard beneath her lips. She smiled. "Feel free to talk back."

Remembering how sensual his hair felt, she purposely trailed her hair over his chest, his stomach, between his spread legs. He jerked as the strands slid across the head of his cock.

"It makes me hot watching you react to the things I do to your body." If her voice was a little hoarse, it could be blamed on all that want clogging her throat.

"How long do you expect me to last?" He sounded a little desperate.

"Oh, for a little while longer. I haven't even started yet."

Even his beast couldn't stop his groan. "You're killing me, woman."

"Really?" She swept her tongue over his collarbone and then flicked each of his flat male nipples with the tip. He flexed those perfect pecs in response. "See, now that makes it all worthwhile." She leaned down to whisper in his ear. "Want to know a secret? I don't think I can last much longer either." She tugged on his earlobe with her teeth.

Al's breaths came in harsh rasps as his chest rose and fell while a sheen of sweat made his naked body glisten in the darkness.

She skimmed the tips of her fingers over his ridged stomach and watched the muscles clench. "Touching you is magic."

He couldn't stay still any longer. Arching his hips, he dug his fingers into the mattress. That put his amazing male package on full display.

For a moment, the wonder of him overwhelmed her. She could barely see past her own need. Had she ever been this wet for a man, felt such powerful anticipatory spasms for one, knew that she'd go crazy if she didn't relieve that heavy desire low in her stomach?

But he was touching something else, something that yearned toward his sudden vulnerability. She'd bet he'd never laid himself open like this in his previous life. And his trust. No matter how quickly he could change, right now he was *not* thinking about home security. If she whipped out a knife, she could kill him before he knew what was happening to him.

He trusted her with his life. And she . . . She wanted to trust him with her heart. Jenna almost chuckled. And wasn't that the most ridiculous thing she'd ever thought? Sex did strange things to the human mind.

"Jenna." Her name on his lips was a tortured cry.

She abandoned wayward thoughts and turned the show over to her senses. Kneeling between his legs, she cupped his balls. He shivered, but didn't move. Leaning over, she slid her tongue slowly over each and felt them tighten in response.

Giving him pleasure upped her own excitement level a thousand times. That hadn't happened before. With the few other lovers she'd had, touching them had been pleasant but not like *this*. This was . . .

Oh, forget it. She was still thinking. Turning her attention to his cock, she grasped him and ran her tongue from base to head.

He bucked beneath her. "Damn it, keep doing that and I won't—"

She circled the head with her tongue and enjoyed the tactile sensations of velvety smooth skin and heat. So much heat. Then she planted a kiss right on the tip.

"I won't be responsible for what happens." He pushed each word out between clenched teeth.

She kneaded his inner thighs, and if she dug her nails in a little too hard, it was just a demonstration of her slipping control. Taking a firmer grip on his staff, she placed her lips over the head and slid lower and lower and lower. Then she tightened her lips and began the up-and-down motion she hoped would give him so much pleasure that he'd never again yearn for his past life. Faster and faster, swirling her tongue around him until . . .

With fingers she could feel shaking, he reached between her legs and touched her. She might as well have stuck her finger in a light socket, because her reaction was the same. The low moan of unbearable need couldn't have come from her mouth. She didn't make sounds like that.

And when he slid his finger back and forth over that sweet, sweet spot, she lost it.

"Now, now, now." Her strangled cry bore no relation to the Jenna Maloy she knew, but then maybe she hadn't known herself as well as she'd thought she did. This was someone driven by all that was savage and primordial. He didn't waste the opportunity. With enough strength for two men, he slipped his hands under her behind and lifted her into the air. Then he planted her firmly on his cock.

She would like to have said she wiggled and teased, eased herself down a little at a time to prolong the pleasure. But Jenna couldn't say any of those things. She was so wet and ready that she ground herself down on all that hot male flesh and howled her happiness.

The female-on-top position might not have been a natural one for Al, but he adapted quickly. He grunted with effort as he drove up into her at the same time she slammed down on him. The ancient rhythm of sex caught them in its claws and tore away the fabric of civilized behavior. Jenna and his beast were on equal footing right now.

Jenna didn't even have time to anticipate her orgasm before it was on her, a violent spasm that flung her high and tumbled her end over end. Why all the glass walls didn't shatter was a mystery to her.

She hung on to the moment, milked it of every drop, and then rolled into the slowly weakening aftershocks. Somewhere she remembered hearing Al's roar of release.

But as she came down after that ultimate second when she knew she was going to die, because anything that felt so incredible had to kill you, Jenna realized there should've been more.

As she breathed in hard gasps and listened to the heavy thud of her heart, she thought about it. Okay, total mystery. Nothing could've been more. More was impossible.

Why then did she feel like she should've *touched* something? Not physical. Sort of like if she'd stretched her emotions a little more, reached out as far as they'd go, she would've connected with . . . Connected with what? She didn't know, but it left her with a vague sense of incompletion.

"You are wondrous, woman."

Jenna had collapsed on top of him, and now she could feel his voice vibrating in that beautiful chest. She rolled off him to lie flat on her back staring up at the night sky.

Al's words seemed strangely formal, almost from another time, but they made her feel special in a way ordinary words wouldn't have.

"You were . . ." Rarely at a loss for words, she searched for the right ones now. "You were more. More than I've ever known, more than I could ever have imagined. Just *more*." She turned to look at him.

Whatever he would have said went unspoken, because suddenly his gaze grew distant. Then with a grunt of disgust, he pushed himself to his feet and reached down to help her up. "Fin wants us to come to his room. He needs to discuss something." His hands were clenched tightly at his sides.

"Now? Both of us?" She let him slip her gown over her head and wrap her robe around her.

She didn't question how Fin knew they were awake and together. The old Christmas song about Santa knowing when you've been good or bad came to mind. The thought almost made her smile. Fin would make a warped Santa.

Al nodded. "I'll wait while you get dressed." He pulled on his jeans and guided her down the stairs and back to her room.

"Doesn't anyone ever say no to Fin?"

He didn't reply; he just stared at her.

"Right. I'll throw something on." But she couldn't help wondering what happened to the ones who refused Fin. Well, she wouldn't be tempting fate tonight.

A few minutes later, they were at Fin's door. Al's body was still thrumming with its memory of Jenna. His hunger for her was a many-headed monster. Back when his soul had ruled him, all hungers were the same. He hunted, he killed, he ate, he fucked. No mixed emotions about any of his actions. There hadn't been a lot of thinking going on back then.

Now that seemed like all he did. He wanted her body, but he didn't want the emotions she made him feel. He wanted her body, but he didn't want the complications that went with caring about her. He wanted her body, but why would she ever want anything to do with his rage and his soul? Most important of all, something had almost happened up on that roof that must *never* happen. But how could he stop it when he was determined to have a next time? The conflicts went on and on.

Jenna might not realize it, but Al had no doubt the timing of Fin's call hadn't been an accident. Next time he was with her, he'd have to remember to lock Fin out of his thoughts for the duration no matter how pissed it made their fearless leader. In this life, Al was beginning to realize that Fin didn't need an all-access ticket to his mind.

And in the second before Fin threw open his door, Al dragged his thoughts from their lovemaking long enough to wonder why they were meeting in Fin's room instead of his office. No one got into Fin's room.

As Fin swung the door wide, Al's immediate impression was that for the first time in his memory, the godlike Fin looked almost human. His jeans hung low on his hips, and he wore a sleeveless T-shirt that had seen better days. And the cold calmness of his eyes didn't look so remote in the early hours of the morning.

Fin didn't say anything, just waved them in. If Al had been expecting lots of expensive things to go along with Fin's status as leader of the Eleven, he was in for a disappointment. The setup looked the same as Al's room, but there wasn't one thing there that spoke of Fin's personality. It was a blank slate. Somehow Al had thought that Fin would have tried to power the place up with a few pictures or something. Nothing.

"Have a seat." Fin had his fireplace lit, and he took a seat in the chair nearest the crackling flames.

If Al was the imaginative kind, he'd find something demonic in the way the shadows played across Fin's face with the fire in the background. But he had his feet firmly on the ground.

Jenna sat on the couch, and Al defiantly dropped down beside her. His possessiveness didn't seem to bother her.

"This is an odd time to call us in to see you." Jenna glanced around. "And why not your office?"

Al knew as soon as he saw the sly lift of Fin's lips that Jenna had asked the wrong question. But then, she wasn't used to Fin-the-control-freak.

"You were awake. I was awake. So why not meet? And one place is as good as another. Did I interrupt anything?"

The lift of Fin's brows was so patently fake that Al wanted to . . . Al frowned. Why hadn't he ever had thoughts of violence toward Fin before rising to this time? One of those unpredictable memories tried to surface, a memory of Fin's face and his own helplessness. He didn't even try to hold on to the memory, because he knew the pain and the fog were coming. Al wasn't disappointed. But one day he'd push back that fog and see things the way they'd really been.

What the hell was he thinking? It'd been a long day and his brain was way past due for some down time.

"Yes, you did interrupt *something*."

Jenna was matching Fin sarcastic comment for sarcastic

comment. Al felt pride in her, and that too was an unfamiliar emotion. Human feelings were dangerous. They distracted him from the important things, like survival.

"What's up?" He was too tired to play Fin's games.

"Jude called. He's received a challenge for his leadership of the states ruled by Katherine. He wants you there, Al."

Al nodded. He didn't know why the vampire needed him, but the Eleven owed Jude for favors rendered.

"He also wants Jenna to be there."

"No." The word was out of Al's mouth before Jenna could react.

"Why does he want me?" Jenna was a little less emotional in her reaction.

"It doesn't matter. You're not going with me." Al was certain of that. "For God's sake, haven't your recent vampire experiences been enough to convince you to stay home?"

She turned a cool gaze on him. "I don't like other people making my decisions for me."

Angry, he turned his frustration on Fin. "Why does she need to be there?"

Fin looked really interested in both their reactions. "I don't know. Jude said he didn't have time to explain." He shrugged. "Jenna will be safe. I think you and Jude can manage to protect her. Just to make sure, I'll have Utah and Tor wait outside in case you need backup."

"Are you crazy?" Okay, maybe he shouldn't have worded it quite like that. "Utah and Tor are torn up from losing Rap. They'll look for any excuse to wipe out every vampire they see. Who's going to control them?"

"I will. They'll only kill if I say so."

Fin's eyes didn't even flicker, but Al got the feeling he'd enjoy the killing. Al could never figure Fin out. The rest of the Eleven loved violence. It was as strong a drive as sex and hunger. They had to constantly keep their souls submerged to function as humans.

But Fin wasn't like the rest of them. He was cold, calculating, and used violence like an ice pick. If he needed it to get the job done, so be it. But if he could get the same result from just letting the ice melt, he'd choose the melting.

If Al wasn't so pissed, he'd be intrigued. Was the great Fin actually experiencing an emotion like the rest of them? "I still don't want her there."

"*Her* is sitting right here. And *she* chooses to go."

Al didn't know what was driving Jenna to do something she couldn't possibly be looking forward to, but someone had to save her from herself. "Give me one good reason why you need to be there."

"Because I don't *want* to be there." She raked her fingers through that beautiful dark hair that was all tousled and tempting.

Al quickly jerked his mind from that particular precipice. Sex wasn't on the agenda right now. His first instinct was to react sarcastically to her statement. But one look at her face stopped him. She was dead serious about this. "Explain."

Jenna sighed and seemed to sink farther into her chair. "I've tried a lot of things that I wasn't good at." She shrugged. "But that's okay, because they didn't matter."

Was Al imagining it, or did her they-didn't-matter comment ring false? He blinked. Was some of his humanity asserting itself? Because his soul would take her at face value and not care if she was lying.

"But I *am* good at writing articles about the weird and wacky. Not that I'm going back to my room to start writing about what I've seen and heard—although I'm keeping my options open for the future—but I take pride in going where the story is." She dropped her gaze from his.

Al saw where this was headed and tried to cut her off. "This is different. You can't expect to—"

"Yes, I can." She met his gaze directly. "I can expect to

face each story directly and not let my emotions get in the way. She swallowed hard, and Al felt her reluctance to reveal anything further.

"Every time I've faced the reality of the battle you guys are fighting, I've become a useless pile of frightened crap. I ran from Jude and you in the park, all I did was throw up while Rap was being killed, and I was so scared at the church that I just stood staring instead of helping." She was in full disclosure mode now. "I *hated* that you had to stand and watch with me because you knew I couldn't take care of myself." Her expression was filled with self-loathing. "But that ends as of now. I'm going tomorrow, and someday I'll write about it. And it won't be a secondhand report."

"We have something in common." Fin sounded as if his thoughts were elsewhere. "We both feel that if we can just be perfect enough, we can control everything around us." Humor crept into his voice. "That's not true, you know. And there are just so many times in life that we can walk away from a situation we can't control and convince ourselves we didn't care anyway." An underlying bitterness said Fin didn't think any of this was funny at all.

Al had never thought about what Fin felt. He'd never wondered what Fin had left behind in the place he'd come from. He'd never even thought about Fin coming from anywhere. Fin just . . . was. Al blamed the fog for his lack of curiosity about Fin. He turned his head to find Fin staring at him. Al turned his attention back to Jenna.

Jenna didn't even try to hide her discomfort with what Fin had said. She stood and was already headed toward the door as she spoke. "I'm tired. I'll see you guys in the afternoon." But she paused before leaving. "Oh, and I have a question for you, Fin. You're supposed to have saved everyone from extinction sixty-five million years ago. But the Allosaurus went extinct one hundred forty-five million years ago. It must've been tough saving a soul that was already gone." Then she left.

And left her bombshell sitting between them. Al didn't wait for the fog to envelop him. "What's that mean, Fin?"

Fin leaned his head back against the chair and closed his eyes. "It means that I manipulated the truth."

One thing Al had to hand to Fin was that he used the hard words. "Manipulate" was about as negative as you could get. He could've found a word that wouldn't sound so damning.

"No kidding." Al could feel the familiar fury churning in him. "Aren't you going to make me forget everything now? That's how things work, isn't it?"

"Maybe I'm tired of keeping up with all the questions. As Jenna said, maybe it doesn't matter. So what do you want to know?"

"Everything."

"Everything would take a long time to explain. Guess I'll just tell you about the time difference." Opening his eyes, Fin speared Al with a gaze that was more purple than silver right now.

Al remembered Fin's eyes had been the same color when Rap died.

"When your souls became beast, I had to spread you out over different time periods so you'd be harder to find."

"I guess it wouldn't do any good to ask why anyone would want to find us? I mean, we weren't a threat to these immortals." A thought hit him. "Or were we? None of us know what we were before the dinosaurs."

"Right. It wouldn't do any good to ask."

Al's rage was close to the surface now. "You never mentioned that you could move through time."

"It never came up." Fin sounded like his patience was wearing thin.

"That's why I could never remember seeing Spin or Ty.

They didn't exist in my time. So when you took me, you weren't saving me from extinction. You could've left me to live out my life."

Fin ignored his outburst. "All time exists at once. I took you when I needed to take you."

"Why put us in the ground for all those years when you could've just zapped us from our time to this time?"

Fin's laughter lacked a lot in the humor department. "You give me credit for a lot more power than I have. I was burned out. I couldn't zap you anywhere. I needed lots of downtime to power up my batteries again for this fight. Without the rest, I never would've been able to put your souls into new bodies."

Al could only focus on one thing. "Could you send me back to my time as I was then? Could you do that now?"

"Do you want it? Knowing what you know about the future here? Could you go back to being what you were?"

Al had already opened his mouth to say yes after Fin's first question when the second question struck him. Al closed his mouth. He'd never had one doubt about what he wanted. He didn't like the twenty-first century, didn't like having to ride herd over his soul, didn't like always feeling closed in. And *alone*. He missed his pack.

But going back meant never seeing Jenna again. It meant leaving humans to their fate when he had the power to do something about it. For the first time he considered the option of accepting the rest of the Eleven as his new pack. Why? Because he couldn't stand the thought of never seeing Jenna again. Stupid. He'd bet she'd be just fine with never seeing him again.

"Well? Do you want to go back?"

In that moment, Al had the feeling he'd reached a tipping point. It was the moment when he decided he wanted to stay. "I guess not."

Fin grinned. "Good, because I couldn't expend the energy to send you back."

Al rose to leave. He considered going back to Jenna's room but decided she needed some time away from him. He asked one more question before leaving. "What about this Seir that Balan said was watching you from the park?"

Fin's expression hardened, and his eyes turned glacial. "I don't talk about Seir. Ever."

Which meant that Al would find out everything he could about the guy. Anyone who could put that expression on Fin's face was worth investigating.

Chapter Twelve

"Where did Fin get the bodies for you guys?" Jenna knew everyone was fed up with her questions, but while she'd lain in bed last night trying to make sense of everything, she'd come to a conclusion.

She wasn't staying just to protect her sister. Lord knows she wasn't much protection for anyone. Kelly had made her choice to involve herself in this battle, and Jenna couldn't change that. Jenna was staying for herself. For the first time, she was accepting her lifetime of avoidance for what it was. She was admitting that perfectionism combined with competitiveness created a person who not only had to be better than everyone around her but also could never make mistakes. Well, her whole attitude sucked. So, she'd stay here and probably make all kinds of mistakes. But as of right now, she was going to start doing her job. And asking questions was part of her job.

"Fin says he searched for bodies that had just lost their souls, and he stuffed our souls into the empty shells. Then he tweaked our features. He says he did the tweaking to make us better, but I think it was so no grieving relatives would ever run across us on the street and think they were seeing ghosts."

"So he only took dead bodies?"

"That's what he said." Al never took his attention from the road. He drove with the same intensity he brought to his lovemaking.

"He didn't get impatient and kick out a few souls so he could claim the bodies?"

"He might've. Fin keeps his eye on the big picture. He doesn't sweat the small stuff."

"So you're saying he's ruthless enough to kill an innocent to achieve his goal?" Jenna was pushing it, but she wanted an honest opinion.

"Yeah, I think he would." But Al's expression said he was conflicted about that answer.

Jenna would have asked the silent Utah and Tor the same question, but she was too scared of them in their present mood. Neither had said a word since they'd climbed into the backseat of the car. Ravaged by grief, both their faces were carved with their determination to kill and kill some more. Maybe that was the only way their souls knew how to work through their loss.

So instead of trying to make more conversation, she forced herself to take out her final reason for staying and examine it from all angles. That wasn't too hard since the reason was sitting right next to her.

She was staying for Al. That wasn't as selfless as it sounded. Because Al was giving her something. And, no, it wasn't an orgasm that would kill her with its pure intensity of pleasure. Okay, so that was part of it. But there was something about the way he looked at her, spoke to her, made her feel, that hinted of things to come. Maybe bad, maybe good. But she wanted to stick around to find out.

When they pulled into the parking lot of a club that was tucked into a courtyard off the main street, Jenna glanced around. Dark, dark, and more dark. She could see a light on in the club, but the buildings surrounding it looked empty. "Sexy Bites? This is it?"

He shrugged. "This is where the GPS took us, so I guess this is it. Jude owns a vampire club in Houston, so maybe these kinds of places are everywhere."

Jenna had lots of questions to ask about that but decided to hold them for now.

Al twisted to look at Utah and Tor. "One of you watch the front, the other the back. Don't come in unless there's trouble."

Utah bared his teeth. "We should kill them all."

"Look, I know how you feel—"

Utah interrupted. "No, you don't have a clue how we feel."

Jenna felt Al's surge of anger as cold terror, her instinctive reaction to a threat from an ancient predator. Did other humans pick up the same emotion from him? And why did she feel it so intensely, *physically*?

"Don't give me that crap. When Fin took my soul he left my pack behind. At least he kept you with your brothers. So don't tell me I don't understand." Al pushed open the door and climbed out without giving Utah and Tor another glance.

Jenna got out before Al could charge off without her. Even so, she had to run to keep up. Damn Fin for insisting she dress up for this visit. Sure her heels and black dress looked sexy. But when she ran, the heels made her wobble and her oh-so-tight dress rode up her thighs. Sexy didn't help when you were fleeing a mob of enraged vampires.

Al stood at the entrance waiting for her. "Jude told Fin they were keeping the club closed tonight. I don't know anything else about what's going to happen here. Jude will fill us in. Spin put on an impressive show last night, so hopefully they'll treat us like honored guests."

She could've told him that *he* was the only thing that could make her feel safe in this place. But now wasn't the time. Jenna walked beside him into the club and tried to look coolly elegant.

Al didn't have to put any effort into how he looked. His black pullover sweater, jeans, and long leather coat would take him into the dark alleys of Philly as easily as a trendy club.

Of course, Jenna didn't know if this place was trendy or not. She didn't hit the clubs much in Houston. The décor seemed to be dark and intimate. Polished mahogany plus dim lighting gave the impression you could meet anyone here, and probably would.

The vampire at the door was huge, hulking, and looked like he chewed up steel girders to exercise his gums. But he must have expected them because he waved them through. And judging by the flaring of his eyes, he recognized Al from last night. That could be a good or a bad thing depending on how tonight turned out.

Jude waited for them just past Cerberus. Jenna tried to take a closer look at the inside of the club, but she still got the impression of dark and rich. No Goths welcome here. It was very big, and the ceiling in the center was very high. Jude would have demanded a spacious locale so that in a worst-case scenario Al's massive body would fit. Stairs led up to a balcony that circled the room where customers could sit quietly, drink, and watch what was happening below. What was happening now was a mob of vampires crowding the main floor and lining up along the balcony railing.

When Al and Jenna walked into the room to join Jude, every vampire eye turned their way. Jenna imagined hunger lighting those eyes. Jude motioned them into a small side room. He closed the door behind him.

The vampire dropped into a nearby chair. His smile was so seductive, so completely beautiful male, that if Jenna hadn't been currently into the primitive predator look, she might've tumbled. A dangerous thing to do around a vampire leader.

Jude wore his black tux and black silk shirt with the same ease that Al wore his clothes. Both men were comfortable in their skins.

Al remained standing. Jenna sat. She was storing up pain-free memories against the time when her feet would begin to complain about the heels.

"So what's happening?" Al leaned against the closed door. No one would be interrupting their talk.

"Tonight we do some acting." Jude looked completely relaxed. "Katherine and Kenny's daughter has challenged me for leadership. Lia wasn't close to her mom . . . Actually, she hated her. But Lia feels this obligation to the vampires her mother ruled." He shrugged broad shoulders that hinted at strength and muscle. "Go figure. They never did anything for her."

"Cold, Jude." Jenna thought that loving a man like this would take lots of courage, because she wasn't sure there was a softer side to him. And the hard side was terrifying.

"Hey, I do what I have to for me. And I've decided that I don't have the time to take care of my own ten states, let alone Katherine's ten. I want out."

"Then go out there and tell everyone you're resigning your post and Lia can have it." Jenna thought about that. "Wait. Would this Lia go over to Stake's side?"

"No. But she wouldn't help you either. She wants to take the vampires in a new and gentler direction." Jude snorted his contempt of Lia's new and gentler approach. "No more killing, no more feeding from humans, no more acting like, well, vampires."

"I don't see a problem."

"You wouldn't." Jude glanced at Al for support.

Al tried to explain. "She's asking her people to go against their instincts. Believe me, I know how it feels when someone asks you to suppress your nature.."

"Yeah, I guess you're right." Jenna looked back at Jude. "So what's going to happen when we leave this room? Can you just say 'I quit'?"

"It doesn't work that way. I'll have to battle her for the leadership."

"Why? Sounds like a stupid way to find a leader. The strongest isn't necessarily the smartest."

Jude exhaled deeply. "I know, but vampires live a long time. The oldest are the most powerful in our society. And they still cling to the old ways. Try to tell a Viking that fighting isn't the best way to settle things."

Jenna didn't like the way Al's expression brightened. "Guys, this is *not* a smart idea."

For a moment Jude looked regretful. Jenna suspected it wasn't because he'd have to fight Lia but because he'd be giving up power.

"The decision is made. There's no going back." Jude leaned forward in his seat. "We'll fight with swords. The loser is the one who dies first."

"Dies?" Jenna saw a flaw in his plan.

"This is where it gets dangerous."

"No kidding." She looked at Al. He only shrugged.

"Lia's insecure even though she'd never admit it. She has the brains to rule, but if she ascends, she'll have to show she also has at least a little of her mother's viciousness. It's sad but true that the old ones admire a certain savagery in their leaders."

Jenna didn't see where Jude was going.

Al evidently did, because he nodded. "That's where I come in."

"Got it. I have to lose this fight in order to win." He grimaced. "I hate losing. Anyway, when Lia finally stands over me with her sword at my throat, she has two options. She can stab me in the throat in a symbolic gesture or—"

"*Symbolic* gesture?" She was horrified. "What's symbolic about it?"

"It'll hurt like hell, but as long as she doesn't slice my

artery, I can heal myself before I lose too much blood. But there's a segment of her advisors encouraging her to take my head as a show of strength. That would be too permanent for my taste."

"She's a murdering little bitch." Jenna hadn't realized she felt so strongly about Jude.

Jude shrugged. "You have to be able to do the tough stuff to rule vampires. We like to brag that we're superior to humans, but we're way behind the curve when it comes to civilized behavior."

"So what do you want me to do?" Al probably didn't see anything wrong with the vampire way of doing business.

Remember this when you're having all those hot thoughts about him. Along with the sexual sizzle came his predatory soul.

"I'll have to put up a good fight so no one will suspect anything when she wins." His expression said he doubted anyone would believe he could lose.

Jenna wondered about that. Was Jude just that good, or was ego playing into his opinion?

"When I go down, you'll have to move fast." Jude speared Al with a hard gaze. "Watch her sword arm. If she intends to merely stab me, she won't raise her arm. But if you see her swing her sword arm back, you'll have to interfere."

Jenna had a good idea what form that interference would take. "Why Al? Couldn't one of your friends come forward?"

"These are all Katherine's people. None of my vampires were allowed in. I could invite only two people who'd represent my interests."

"I don't get it—" Jenna was cut off by someone knocking on the door.

"It's me, Kenny. Can I come in?"

Jenna recognized the excited voice of Katherine's husband. And Lia's father?

Jude nodded at Al, who moved away from the door and then unlocked it. Kenny burst into the room and shoved the door closed behind him.

"Everyone's getting restless." He cast an anxious glance Al's way. "You won't hurt her, will you?"

Evidently Kenny realized where the true danger would come from. Jenna had a question, though. "If Lia's your daughter, why didn't you talk to her about all this? I don't think Al's boss will be too happy if your daughter offs an ally." Jenna didn't want to call Jude a friend, because she didn't think Fin had any friends.

Kenny did everything but wring his hands. "She's all wrapped up in taking over her mother's place. Lia sees Jude as the enemy. She thinks he'll carry on the same way Katherine did. She loves me, but she thinks I'm too weak, unwilling to do what needs doing to take our people in a new direction. Besides, she's been listening to friends who think she can only win the respect of her people by showing no mercy to Jude."

Jenna huffed. "Let me get this straight. She wants her vampires to be kinder and gentler, and to demonstrate her own kindness and gentleness she's going to try to chop Jude into little pieces? Hey, works for me." And yes, the situation called for sarcasm. "Vampire logic is a thing of beauty."

Kenny's face fell. "Please, I don't want to lose her."

Okay, now Jenna felt officially small and mean. "She's a vampire, so I'm sure she's strong enough to come through this fine."

Kenny looked stricken. "But that's the problem."

Jenna stood; the others looked like they were ready to leave. "Problem?"

"Lia is human."

Jenna stopped dead to consider the impossibility of what Kenny had just said.

"I was still human when I hooked up with Katherine.

My swimmers must've been a lively bunch, because Katherine got pregnant and had Lia. Once we figured out that Lia didn't act like Katherine—thank God for small favors—we had all the tests done." His voice grew bitter. "Instead of treasuring her daughter for the miracle she was, Katherine rejected her. Said she was inferior. Do you know what the chances are of a vampire as old as Katherine getting pregnant?" He answered his own question. "Let's just say I wouldn't put any money on the odds."

Jenna had lots of questions bubbling up from her bottomless well of curiosity, but she figured now wasn't the time to ask them.

As they left the room for the dimly lit club, it was tough for Jenna to make out expressions, but both Jude and Al looked worried.

"I hope she's at least half decent with a sword. My reputation will take a major hit if it looks like I was so bad I lost to a human." If Jude wasn't a big bad vampire, Jenna would have said he was pouting. "Any perception of weakness on my part will bring challengers out of the woodwork when I get back to Houston. Not that any of them would have a chance, but I have better things to do than humiliate losers."

That's what Jenna liked about Jude, he was such a humble guy.

Al had other worries. "Once my soul takes over, I'm still in control, just . . ." He seemed to be searching for the right word. "less so. I don't think like a human. So any decisions I make might not be completely appropriate."

Jude smiled. "In other words you think like a prehistoric predator loose in a candy store. All that prey trapped in one spot. The temptation must be unbearable."

Al looked relieved that someone understood him. Jenna was feeling a little miffed. *She* understood. Then she took a good look at Al and Jude, thought about what they were, and realized she could never understand their urge to kill.

Did that make her totally incompatible with Al? Probably. Did it matter to her? No.

Kenny beckoned them from the center of the floor, where a floodlight formed a large circle. Vampire eyes bright with excitement shone from the darkness around the ring.

This was so far out of Jenna's experience, she couldn't wrap her mind around the reality of it. She turned to Jude. "Why am I here?"

"Lia is human. I thought she should have a human to cheer her on."

"And?"

He looked almost embarrassed. "She's grown up know-ing only vampires. I thought you might give her more of a . . . human perspective on things."

Jenna smiled. "Well, well. Is that a spot of kindness staining all that wicked vampire darkness?"

He looked insulted. "No. I don't do kindness."

"It's time to begin."

Kenny's announcement ended the discussion. They turned to watch as he stood in the pool of light.

"The challenge for leadership of the Northeastern Vam-pires is about to begin." Any fear Kenny was feeling for the safety of his daughter wasn't showing. "Lia Colaccio chal-lenges Jude."

"No last name?" Jenna scanned the darkness looking for Lia.

"Last names aren't important."

"Which means yours is very important." Al seemed to accept Jude's avoidance policy as no big deal.

Since all of the Eleven had the same last name, Endeka, she understood his thinking.

Kenny took a deep breath, which Jenna found strange for a vampire. Maybe it was just a remembered human reaction to stress. Even in this bizarre and frightening situation, she couldn't turn off her curiosity. She'd have to ask Kenny about what happened to human reflexes he no longer needed.

"When the challenge ends—"

Challenge? He made it sound so civilized. She wondered why he didn't call it exactly what it was, a barbaric fight to the death. Fine, so political correctness wasn't her strength.

"The winner may allow the defeated to live or may kill him or her without consequences."

Jude grunted. "Like hell, no consequences. If the little bitch managed to destroy me, my organization would have this whole city drowning in vampire blood within hours. Unlike Katherine, who never allowed anyone control but herself, I have a well-oiled machine in place to take over." With that threat hanging in the air, he strode toward the circle of light.

Al glanced around. "I have plenty of headroom as long as I'm close to the circle. The vampires will need every bit of their preternatural speed to get out of my way if I free my soul."

No one was paying any attention to them. Everyone was focused on the circle of light. "I wonder why no one seems to be afraid of you? Some of these vampires had to have been at the church when Katherine bought it."

He shrugged. "We're not the main attraction. And Spin was the one who did all the damage. They didn't see my soul." He made that sound like a threat.

Jude stepped into the light, all fluid grace and wicked beauty. He'd picked up his sword at some point, and light glinted off its sharp blade.

Lia finally made her appearance. She surprised Jenna. What was a daughter of Katherine supposed to look like? Jenna had pictured long, flowing black hair, long pointed bloodred fingernails, and a long slinky black gown. Okay, so she was picturing Morticia in her mind.

Lia was small, curvy, with short curly blonde hair. She had on jeans and a loose red T-shirt. She looked like a soccer mom in training.

Until you looked at her eyes. They were big and blue and filled with intense determination. Her full lips were drawn into a thin line of hate. And Jenna figured all that hate was aimed at Jude. Maybe some of it would have been spared for Spin if he were here, but he wasn't. Jenna would bet that Lia didn't know Al was here.

There was no splashy opening ceremony. Kenny just wished both of them good luck and backed out of the light. Jenna could hear the rustle of vampires moving to get the best view of the battle.

Lia moved first, stepping in and slashing with a sword that looked a lot lighter than Jude's. Jude parried her move, the clanging of the swords setting off an excited buzz among the watching vampires.

Fifteen minutes later, Al and Jenna had worked their way through the crowd until they were just behind those in the front row.

Jenna felt like she'd traveled back in time to some primitive point in history. Who fought with swords, anyway?

There was blood. From both Jude and Lia. But the cuts inflicted on each didn't seem to slow them down. The wounds were making Jenna a little queasy, though. Al, on the other hand, seemed excited by the battle. If opposites really did attract, then they were perfect for each other. If they had points of compatibility, Jenna hadn't found them. She thought about the glass room on the roof. Okay, so maybe one.

Lia was impressive. She moved fast for a human. And the emphasis was on the word "human." For a vampire? Not so fast. Jude was working hard to make Lia look good—slowing down just enough, missing his swing by just a little, and looking like he hated her guts every moment of the fight. Which he probably did. Jenna didn't think Jude liked to look weaker than anyone, even if it was his own decision.

"He'll give Lia her chance any moment now."

Al's whisper warmed the side of her neck and took her attention away from Jude and Lia. "How do you know?"

"Because that's what I'd do. He's kept the fight going long enough to make it look real, but if he drags it on too long, the human will tire."

Jenna tensed. *The human.* Once again a reminder that Al didn't count himself as part of the human race. He needed to take a good long look in the mirror. His soul was what he chose to make it, but he wouldn't want to hear that from her. She edged away from him and returned her attention to the battle.

Which ended suddenly. Jude took a step back and pretended to stumble. Jenna wondered if this was the first ungraceful step he'd ever taken. He went down with Lia's sword at his throat.

Lia smiled, flushed with victory, but Jenna saw what maybe the others didn't—uncertainty in her eyes. Did she suspect anything? Jenna would have. It had to occur to Lia that a human beating an ancient vampire wasn't the norm.

The crowd roared its approval, and Lia's uncertainty disappeared. Jenna held her breath. Would she let Jude live?

When she drew back her sword arm, Al reacted. Ohmigod, no. Al thought Lia was going to take Jude's head, but Jenna was still watching the other woman's eyes. Death wasn't in Lia's eyes, only joy. She was simply flinging her arms into the air. Jenna reached for Al.

Too late. Before she could even blink, Al freed his soul. Jenna was the only one who screamed as she scrambled away from the monster taking up the space where Al had stood. The vampires scrambled too, but they did it silently. Humans were much more vocal.

The Allosaurus roared, and Jenna's blood ran cold as she

looked way, way up at Al's soul. No matter how many times she'd seen dinosaurs in movies and on TV, nothing came close to seeing one live and in person. They'd never looked this big from the safety of her living room. And only the shadow of Al's human shape within the beast kept her from running panicked into the courtyard. Which was what most of the vampires were doing.

As Lia stood frozen in place with her sword still raised, Jude leaped to his feet and strode to Jenna's side.

"Someone needs to take this group of bloodsuckers in hand. Look at them all run. They look like someone stomped on their anthill. If my people were here, they'd be attacking Al with every power they had. And he wouldn't be just standing there looking bored." Jude shook his head in disgust.

"Uh-oh." Jenna realized before Jude did that there was one person who wasn't fleeing the scene. Lia took a deep breath and charged Al with nothing but her puny sword. That girl needed to get some common sense. Jenna watched horrified as the Allosaurus lowered his head and took a stride toward Lia. A very big stride. Who was in control inside that gigantic head with its supersized teeth?

"Stop!" She ran toward Lia, who'd at last had the sense to take refuge behind the bar. Fat lot of good that would do her. "He's upset because he thought you were going to take Jude's head."

Then Jenna turned back to where the allosaurus had just made fire kindling out of most of the tables on the ground floor. Now he was looking up at a few vampires who'd taken refuge on the balcony. But when Al rose up he was at eye level with them. Not a safe place.

While Al was eyeing the tasty treats on the balcony, Kenny had reached his daughter and was dragging her into a back room.

Jenna sighed her relief. Al must've seen Lia's escape too,

because suddenly his soul was gone and he was once again standing beside her.

He didn't look at her. "Scared?"

"No." Then she amended that. "Okay, at first. You trigger an instinctual fear, but I could see *you* inside, and I had faith that the human part of you was in control." She wouldn't add that her faith had been a little shaky. But at least this time she hadn't thrown up or run like crazy.

Al glanced at Jude. "You okay?"

The vampire nodded. "The little bitch was going to take my head after I handed her the crown. She'd better not show up in any of my states. Ever." He drew his lips back from those fangs and hissed his fury.

"She wasn't going to take your head. She'd just thrown her hands up in the air to show she'd won." Jenna didn't think Jude would believe her.

"You're human. You want to believe the best about everyone. But I know vampires. She wanted to kill me." With that, Jude turned and headed for the door.

"But Lia's not a vampire." Jenna's comment was lost in the crash of the door as Jude kicked it down on his way out.

She looked up at Al. "That went well, didn't it?"

Chapter Thirteen

Al led Jenna from the dimly lit club into the complete darkness of the courtyard, and it just felt natural for him to take her hand. Natural? For *humans*. There were no symbols of affection in the pack. Sex was an itch to be scratched and forgotten.

It was *human* to examine emotions and assign reasons for everything you felt. Pack life was simpler. Hungry, kill, eat, happy. Angry, fight, kill, happy. Aroused, choose, fuck, happy. Everything in his previous life had ended with happy, or what passed for that emotion. Thinking back, it was more satisfaction than happiness. Yeah, there had been times when pack members died, but he only recalled them as brief times of puzzlement and then acceptance before moving on. Not real grief. Not the way he'd felt when Rap's body died. *Not the way you'd feel if anything happened to Jenna.* Maybe he'd thought about emotions long enough.

Since Fin wanted him to act more human, he'd think about this holding-hands thing. He felt the protective instinct of the male for the female. Not a feeling he was used to. The females of his pack had been as ferocious as the males. They hardly needed protection.

Touch? Yes, he enjoyed the feel of her hand in his—the warm smoothness of her skin, the sense of intimacy and possession it brought. Intimacy, a human feeling. Possession, very much part of his soul's time.

Suddenly, he realized it was too quiet. Instinct formed in a world where even a moment's inattention meant death shouted that something was wrong. Without thinking, he pushed Jenna behind him so she was sandwiched between his body and the wall. Then he looked for the threat.

All the vampires who'd left the club, including Jude, had crowded together on one side of the courtyard. On the other side of the lot two really pissed raptors stood poised to attack. Utah and Tor had let their hate get the better of them and turned loose their souls. Crap. If they'd shut off their mental connection to Fin while he was busy playing head games with Zero, then their leader didn't have a clue that the two were about to start a freaking war.

"Tell your guys to back off before I hurt them." Jude spoke to Al without taking his gaze from the raptors. "Tonight hasn't been too great for me, and I'm in a lousy mood. Don't make me show them what I've learned in eight hundred years." He nodded at the other vampires. "These guys might not be the bravest bloodsuckers on the block, but trap them in a corner and they'll fight your raptors."

Al caught a glimpse of Kenny and Lia leaving the club. They froze. Hell. He'd have to do something before Lia decided it was her job as vampire leader to face off against Utah and Tor. "I'll have to become an allosaurus. They'll only understand physical force."

Jenna wiggled out from behind him. "Whoa, wait. You can't always use your soul as a universal problem solver." She looked up at him from wide, frightened eyes. "What would Fin do?"

Wrong thing to say. "Damn what Fin would do." Al wanted to free his soul. He wanted to attack all of them, the raptors and the vampires. He wanted to coat himself in blood and forgetfulness. For one more time, he wanted to know the excitement of a kill uncomplicated by emotions and consequences.

"Maybe you could try talking to them first." She didn't sound hopeful about his response.

"You want me to *talk* to them?" Yeah, that's what Fin would do. But then Fin could scare the crap out of anyone with just a stare.

"I don't know." She looked uncertain. "I think a few words could avert a bloodbath. I don't want to see another of the Eleven die. And I sort of like Jude."

Like Jude? A stab of jealousy startled him. He scowled.

"Forget it." She shrugged. "Do what you think is best."

Great, lay the responsibility on him. He'd had everything worked out. Free his soul, kick butt, pick up the pieces, and go home. Now Jenna had pointed out possible consequences. Now he had to *think*.

His first thought shocked him. He'd talk to them. Because *she'd* asked him to. That was setting a dangerous precedent. But he didn't have time to wonder when she'd gained so much power over him.

Whatever he was going to do, though, he'd better do it fast. Utah sprang off his powerful back legs, landing within easy striking distance of the closest group of vampires. All the vampires hissed in unison and crouched, ready to fight back. In one graceful leap, Jude landed atop the roof of an empty store. His eyes glowed as he curled his lip to expose impressive fangs.

Al took a deep breath and strode to a spot between the two groups. He focused on the human forms he could see within the raptors, not their outer souls. "Utah, Tor, don't make asses of yourselves." Okay, so maybe that wasn't the most diplomatic beginning. "If you think these vampires will go down easy, think again. Some of them will die, or one of you may. How's that going to help the cause? We end up with one less of us or a few less of them.

"We don't have a bunch of friends in the paranormal community. Do you want to make sure we add a big group of enemies? And how will one of you feel if the other one dies like Rap died?" Not that it was likely to happen while they were in raptor form. But once back in human form, a vengeful vampire could take them out with one good swipe of a sword. Sort of like the one Jude was carrying. Couldn't regenerate a head.

"Even if you both survive, you'll have to face Fin. He'll ground you just like he did me. He doesn't want any loose cannons out here making trouble for the Eleven."

That last argument must have hit home because Al saw the first uncertainty in their large raptor eyes. "Come back now before this goes too far." He controlled his need to add a more violent warning, one that included his Allosaurus kicking their butts all the way back to Rittenhouse Square.

While the moment of indecision seemed to stretch on forever, Al glanced over at Jenna.

She wasn't there.

Jenna had watched the unfolding drama almost paralyzed with terror. She didn't have preternatural speed and strength like the rest of this group, but she did have old-fashioned human common sense. The question was, did she have the guts to put it into action?

Glancing around the small courtyard, she'd made her decision. A guy she was beginning to care about was standing smack dab in the middle of two warring groups. Sure, he could free his soul in the blink of an eye, but Rap could too. It hadn't helped him.

Everyone was watching Al as she'd slipped away. She'd run to an old fire escape that zigzagged up the side of a dilapidated apartment building. She'd started climbing.

Now, as she struggled upward, her old insecurities trailed behind her. Was she doing the right thing? Was there a better solution? Would her plan backfire? Maybe she should let Al do it his way.

No. She fought back against the habit of a lifetime. Maybe what she was about to do wasn't the perfect or even the only way, but she wouldn't walk away from her decision. Not this time.

She found the spot she was looking for on the fire escape. The second landing. High enough that no one could get to her too fast. Low enough for everyone to hear her.

While she stood gathering her courage, she saw Al glance at where he expected her to be. When he didn't see her, he scanned the area. If she was reading his body language correctly, he was worried.

Whether he was worried or not, the thought gave her a warm feeling inside. She must be going crazy, because no way should an ancient predator make her feel anything except mindless terror.

He hadn't looked up yet.

Jenna put her fingers to her mouth and whistled. Everyone below her stared up. After the first shock passed, Al looked furious. Too bad.

She waved at them. "I don't like to interfere in your little war here. I mean, you all have your own way of settling things. But I really don't think killing each other's the answer. Sure, it'd be a lot of fun, but the consequences would be pretty messy."

Jenna pulled her cell phone from her purse. "See, I'm just an ordinary human, no powers to speak of, but it doesn't take a ton of power to solve this problem." She calmly—okay, semicalmly—pressed 911. Then, before the vampires and raptors below could stop her, she explained to the operator that someone was threatening her, gave the address, screamed a little, and hung up.

She put the phone back into her purse. Everyone below

seemed frozen. "I guess you should get moving. I don't know what the response time is for Philly's finest, but you don't want to be caught here."

Suddenly, the vampires broke and ran. They were nothing but a blur as they scattered. Guess they'd parked their cars somewhere else. Left with no one to fight, Utah and Tor abandoned their raptor forms. From where Jenna was standing, they looked sort of cranky. But not half as cranky as Al.

He glared up at her. "Get down here."

She'd discuss his dictatorial attitude later, but they didn't have time to argue. Jenna ran down the fire escape and over to the car where Utah and Tor were already in the backseat. She climbed in beside Al and they took off.

Safe. But not from Al's fury. His anger filled the car with a dense cloud of disapproval. He said nothing, though, because Utah and Tor filled up the silence with their own complaints.

"You should've stayed out of it." Utah seemed to be aiming his comment at both Al and her. "This was personal pack business."

Since Al didn't seem interested in saying anything, Jenna glanced back at Utah. He'd changed in the short time since Rap had died. No more spiked hair. No more cool piercings. No bright eyes. No smiles. He'd turned dark overnight.

Jenna tried to reach him. "I know how you must feel about your brother, but—"

He turned on her with a snarl. "Wrong. You don't have a clue how I feel, so shut the fuck up."

It wasn't his words that sucked the breath from her lungs, but the expression in his eyes. There was nothing human at home in that gaze. It was cold, flat, and predatory. The eyes of a killer. Jenna knew she was seeing his soul in its basic, stripped-down version, untouched by any kind of humanity. He was terrifying.

Al hit the brake. Without caring that he'd stopped in the middle of the street, he slammed the car into park, shoved open his door, and climbed out. Then he yanked Utah's door open. "Get the hell out of the car."

"Glad to." Utah's eyes almost glowed with all his suppressed rage.

"Ohmigod." Frantically, she stared at Tor. "Stop your brother. He can't go off by himself while he's this way. What if he . . ." *Goes crazy and kills people.*

Tor shrugged. His eyes were just as cold as Utah's, but his anger was contained. And perhaps all the more dangerous for it.

"Never could stop Utah when he had his mind set on something. I'll tag along. Pack stays together." Tor smiled, and his soul lived in that baring of his teeth. "We'll only kill the ones that need killing."

Jenna felt like the top of her head was going to explode. She was surrounded by three men used to expressing every urge in extreme violence, and none of them were thinking straight. She scanned the street. Thank heaven it was so late and the traffic was light. Taking a deep breath, she scrambled from the car and ran around to where Utah and Al faced off.

She tugged at Al's arm. "Stop him."

The gaze he turned on her held the same cold, flat expression as Utah's, but without the murderous rage. "Do you want me to kill him?"

Horrified, she realized he wasn't kidding. "No. God, *no*. Is that how you solve *everything*? Killing?"

His grin was a savage twist of his lips. "It works."

"Look, I don't care what he said to me. That's not Utah the man looking out at us right now. You can't turn him loose on Philly like that."

"I *do* care what he said. Besides, you took killing off the table, so I can't stop him if he wants to go." Al's expression said Utah's departure wouldn't be met with sorrow on his part.

A quick glance at Utah showed he wasn't paying any attention to either of them. He'd turned away and was starting to walk down the street. At least he wasn't wearing his soul on the outside yet.

Tor got out of the car and slammed the door shut with a little too much force. "Damn. I'm tired. I don't feel like doing this shit tonight." But he started to follow his brother.

Without thinking, she punched Al's shoulder. "Do something, damn it. I don't want to wake up to a report of more killings." She watched his eyes light up. "No, not that way. Don't you dare go prehistoric in the middle of Philly. We don't need any soul sightings tonight."

When he turned his hard gaze on her, she instinctively took a step back. *Remember who he is, what he is.* She couldn't go around punching ancient predators and expect to walk away with all her limbs. She'd allowed herself to get too comfortable with him.

Then he smiled, and it was *Al's* smile, human and a little rueful. "Yeah, Fin would shit nails if I let Utah get away."

He turned toward the fast disappearing raptors and shouted after them. "Hey, I thought pack stayed together! You said I was pack now. I'm trying to keep you guys out of trouble with Fin. He's in my head. He knows what's going on. And if he has to come after you, he might just put your souls away for the duration. Give Rap some company. Then how would you get revenge?"

Both raptors stopped, and Jenna held her breath. Tor turned around and headed back to the car. Utah took longer to think about it, but at least he *was* thinking. Finally, he trailed after his brother. They both climbed back into the car without comment. Jenna felt weak with relief as she got in beside Al. He was the last to climb in. He didn't speak to anyone as he continued driving.

"What do you think Fin will do?" Tor sounded a little worried.

Jenna refused to turn around to look at either raptor.

Al shrugged. "Nothing happened. No one died. A slap on the wrist if you're lucky."

Left unsaid was that both raptors could lose their hunting licenses. Like Al. But Jenna thought that Fin couldn't afford to ground more of his men. If things kept going like this, pretty soon all of the Eleven except for Fin would be sitting in different corners of their leader's condo.

Once back at the condo, Al dropped Utah and Tor at the front entrance to face Fin alone. Their car would be ready, so they could drive themselves to their apartment.

Jenna stayed with Al as he parked his car in the underground garage. She was glad he didn't have much to say, because she was busy with her own thoughts. "I think I'll walk in the park for a few minutes before I come up."

"Not alone."

She didn't try to argue with him. He was right. After what she'd seen since arriving, she didn't think she'd ever want to walk alone at night again. "I need my space."

"Sure."

His voice gave nothing away. She crossed the street and wandered along one of the walkways crisscrossing the park. A pretty park. Well lighted and as safe as any park could be after midnight. She liked it.

"You shouldn't have interfered back at the club." He sounded neutral, but she'd bet he was still ticked.

So was she. "And you shouldn't try to order me around."

"You could've gotten yourself killed."

"I had the best plan. Simple and effective."

"You still should have obeyed me and—"

"I don't *obey* anyone." She hoped he realized how close to the edge he was treading.

Whatever he thought, he must have decided to keep it to himself because he walked silently beside her. And when the first few snowflakes drifted down around them, she pushed aside her mad to let a little joy in.

"Snow." She knew he'd hear the excitement in that one word. Snow wasn't a frequent visitor in Houston. "I can't believe it. Look." Jenna lifted her face to the sky as the flakes fell faster and faster. "It's beautiful." Happiness bubbled up, for the moment burying the memories of the night. She dropped onto a park bench to watch.

Al settled beside her, but not before scanning the park for danger.

She refused to let this reminder of the evil still out there dampen her mood. Mesmerized, she stared at the falling snow that was now so thick it gave her only a hazy, impressionistic view of the buildings surrounding the park. It wiped her mind clean of her conflicted feelings for him. Al was with her, and no matter how much his beast terrified her, she still felt safe with him.

Without asking permission, he put his arm across her shoulders and pulled her close against his body. She allowed herself to relax into him, absorbing his heat and a feeling she wasn't quite ready to acknowledge.

"My soul still frightens you."

That sure came out of nowhere. "Shouldn't it?" The falling flakes formed a cocoon around them, muffling sound, isolating them on their own little park bench island. "If it's any comfort, all of the Eleven's souls frighten me."

"Yeah, I guess you'd be stupid not to be afraid." There was no inflection in his voice, nothing to tell her what he felt.

Jenna didn't turn to look at him. A coward? Maybe. But

she didn't want his expression to influence what she would say. "When I first showed up here, all I wanted to do was to get the goods on you guys and drag Kelly home. So it was all about Kelly. Then I found out what you were, what was at stake, and that I had a part in it. So then it became about Kelly and saving humanity. Now I've spent the last few nights watching things happen I'd never thought possible and being scared witless. Along the way, I've started to get to know and sort of like all of you guys. And yes, making love with you was more special than you know. So now it's about Kelly, humanity, and . . . you." She left it up to him to decide whether "you" was singular or plural. "Oh, and saving my own butt is in there somewhere too." She searched for the point to her little speech. "So even though your soul triggers all kinds of survival instincts, I still . . . care about you."

She felt his smile. It sneaked past her guard and stomped through her mental patch of prickly-pear resolves to reach her heart. She'd built a barbwire fence of I–will–nots around that particular organ for the express purpose of keeping out marauding dinosaurs, but it didn't seem to be working.

"Put yourself at the front of the line. It's always about personal survival." The smile was gone.

"Do you really believe that?"

"My soul does. Survival drove everything I did back then, even sex. You know, survival of the species and all that crap."

"What about the human you? What does he believe?" The snow was sticking to the ground, her clothes, her hair, but she gloried in it. *Snow.* People didn't treasure the ordinary, but to a Houstonian this snow was extraordinary and therefore precious. She felt the same way about any peek into his thoughts he might give her, rare and therefore precious.

He exhaled deeply as he stared at the falling flakes. "I'm not sure now. I *was* sure a few days ago."

The silence between thought and words seemed to use up years of her life. What was he trying to say?

"My soul slept for millions of years. So for me, it's only been three months since I hunted in a world without humans, without buildings, without all of this." He swept his hand up to indicate the surrounding city. "Emotions weren't a problem. Didn't have too many. And I was too dumb to appreciate how good I had it."

"You don't like emotions?" He wasn't smiling so maybe he was serious.

He rubbed his hand across his face. "Too much too soon. I *feel* too much." Something in his eyes said she had a thing or two to do with his emotional overload. "I never had to control anything back then. Any emotions I did have were pale imitations of what humans have. I'm not handling them well. And when all the feelings I don't understand stack up in the back of my head, I just . . ." He shrugged.

She took a chance. "Want to explode?"

He nodded. "Lots of repressed rage."

Jenna knew she should stop while she was ahead, but she had to know more. And this definitely wasn't the journalist in her talking. This was personal. "Is the rage just because of all the new emotions?"

For a moment she didn't think he'd answer her, but then he explained. "You already know the Eleven can't be together long without our aggression getting out of control, but there's something more with Fin. He's twice as bad as all the rest. I don't know why. And once I found out he'd erased some of our memories, the anger got even worse." Frustration shone in his eyes. "I don't know. It's just like everything he does makes me mad. No rhyme or reason."

Jenna knew she should keep her thoughts to herself, that what she was going to say might turn his anger toward her, but she spoke anyway. "He's an authority figure. He's the most powerful of the Eleven. That must be tough when you're used to being the biggest and baddest in town." She held her breath for his reaction.

He surprised her. He smiled.

"Ego? I don't think so. Remember, I was used to Fin being in my head, giving orders. Of course, my dinosaur brain wasn't a very complex affair. I had my basic instincts, and that was enough to keep me satisfied."

"Not like now?"

"Not like now."

Something in his gaze made her breathing and heartbeat pick it up a notch, and she didn't have a clue whether it was fear, nerves, or something else altogether.

"Now I think about what I'm feeling. And the emotions batter me from every side. Your feelings are part of your humanity. With me, they're a new experience, and not always a good one."

She nodded, trying to understand.

"For example, I want to have sex with you again. Right now. Right here on this bench."

He left the statement hanging in the frigid air, and Jenna swore she could see the snowflakes melting around the words.

She wanted to say something funny, something to show what he'd said hadn't shaken her all the way to her curling toes. Nothing came to mind, so she just stared at him.

"Back in the day, that wouldn't have been a problem. Thought would become deed with no emotions or any burned brain cells involved."

Words still escaped her, so she just nodded.

"But now things are different, harder."

She finally found her voice. "You can't just bop me over the head with your club and drag me off to your cave."

The slight up tilt of those sexy lips relaxed her a little. "No club. Didn't have opposable thumbs." He shrugged. "Anyway, now I think about what I want and what I'm feeling. Amazingly, there are emotions attached to my sex drive. I'm still trying to untangle them."

As much as she wanted to wallow in this particular topic, she knew she'd better steer the conversation in another direction before she said something she might regret later. But she didn't have to root around for an alternate talking point; without warning, Seir appeared out of the snowy night.

He walked toward them, his long, multi-shades-of-blond hair floating around him on a nonexistent breeze. No snowflakes seemed to touch his leather pants and jacket. His ice-blue eyes seemed to light with real pleasure at finding them.

Al made a disgusted sound as Fin's brother settled his gorgeous body onto the bench next to Jenna. Seir smiled. Al scowled.

"And here I thought I had the night all to myself." His husky voice suggested that being alone with him in the night wouldn't be a bad thing, at least not for Jenna.

Al didn't seem impressed. "You have a reason for being out here?"

"The night calls." Seir's gaze shifted toward where Fin's condo would be if Jenna could see it.

Jenna found something in his voice that he probably wouldn't want her to hear. Surrounded by family, she'd never known loneliness, but that was what she sensed in Seir. It touched her in a surprising way. "He's up there. Why not just go up and say hi?"

His soft laughter held real amusement. "It would take Philly years to rebuild." He met her gaze. "We have a . . . complex family relationship."

"Why'd you decide to talk to us tonight?" Al said.

Seir didn't answer right away. And when he did, Jenna had the feeling what he said came reluctantly.

"I got tired of talking to myself."

That was strange. With his spectacular looks, Seir could

walk into any club in Philly and within minutes have a pile of women's keys sitting next to his drink.

"Keys get old after a while."

She shot him a quick glance. Okay, he could read minds like his brother did.

Seir abandoned the key topic. "So what's happening?"

"Nothing." Al wasn't holding up his end of the conversation.

"We have to spend tomorrow looking for bells." Oops. Jenna didn't need Al's sharp stare to know she'd said too much.

"Bells?" Seir's cold blue eyes sparked with interest.

"Yeah. It's a hobby. Love to search out all kinds of bells when I visit someplace new." Would he buy that?

"Bells." Seir sounded as if she'd just given him the last piece in one of those five-thousand-piece puzzles.

Nope, he wasn't buying it.

Al must've had enough. He glanced at his watch. "It's late and we're heading inside. Say what you came here to say."

"You don't believe I just wanted some company?" For once the mockery was absent from his voice.

"Not a chance."

Jenna wasn't as sure of that as Al seemed.

Seir leaned back against the bench and stared up at the swirling flakes. A sudden frigid breeze whipped around them. Jenna shivered.

"Zero's in town." Seir's slow smile was filled with wicked anticipation.

And at that moment, she could really believe Seir was the demon he claimed. Al stood and pulled Jenna with him. She didn't fight him.

Al met Seir's gaze. "Guess he'll be pissed that you told us."

Seir lifted his brows in mock puzzlement. "Why? He knows I'm telling you." His gaze was still fixed on the falling snow. "Fin can probably feel him. He's that close." Finally he dropped his glance to look at them. "He's mad, but he'll get over it." He smiled. "The question is, will you?"

Without warning, there was an explosion as every light in the square blew out. Jenna figured it must have even knocked out the electricity in the buildings surrounding Rittenhouse Square because she couldn't see even a glimmer of light through the snow.

She felt Al tense beside her. He was ready. As Jenna held her breath, all she could hear was the pounding of her own heart.

"Let's get out of here." Al grabbed her hand and started to run.

Jenna was counting on his sense of direction because she couldn't see a thing. Behind her she heard Seir's laughter.

"You guys are lucky. Zero's feeling playful tonight!" Seir's amusement followed them out of the park.

For whatever reason, Fin's condo was the only one with any lights. And as they took the elevator up, Jenna leaned against the wall. Al didn't offer any comments.

Fin met them at the door. He didn't look upset. "Zero has an immature streak in him. Always has."

Al looked around at the brightly lit room. "How did this building keep all its lights?"

Fin started to walk away from them. "I've protected this building. He can't touch it."

Jenna caught up with him. "Wait. If he wants to destroy you guys, why didn't he kill Al and me?"

Fin paused to look at her. "Zero's like a cat. He likes to play with his prey. Killing can come later. That's his weakness. He's overconfident. He always assumes he'll get a second shot. Besides, Seir was with you." Without giving her a chance to throw another question at him, he left the room.

Jenna stared after him and then turned to look at Al. "Do you understand anything that just happened?"

He shook his head. "I guess our exalted leader didn't think we deserved to know the truth."

She could see his rage building. This was something he'd have to work through himself. He wouldn't appreciate her hanging around watching him try to get back his control.

"Look, I'm beat. I'll see you around noon. I have to find that bell I'm supposed to ring." Without giving him a chance to argue with her, she left the room.

And as she walked away, she heard his muffled curse and the sound of breaking glass. She winced. All of Fin's vases had looked expensive.

Chapter Fourteen

Jenna woke with the same sexual buzz she'd felt going to sleep. It was always there now, but each hour it seemed to get louder and louder. She'd tried to swat it away, because there was something totally selfish about imagining sensual scenarios with Al when the fate of humanity hung in the balance.

She thought about those scenarios as she headed toward the dining room. Even though eight hours of restless dreams separated her from Al, she felt as if they'd never parted last night. Because her dreams had all been about him. But every time she'd reached for him in her sleep, he'd morphed into his beast. And that was still a buzz kill for her. Would she ever be able to accept both sides of his nature?

She almost snorted. Not that she'd ever get to a place in their relationship where it mattered. He was too wrapped up in his rage and devotion to duty to feel anything beyond a healthy lust for her.

And if she concentrated hard enough, she could almost be glad about that.

As she entered the dining room, she realized it wasn't going to be a comfortable meal. Fin sat alone at the table. None of the Eleven were there to act as buffers.

Sighing, she sat down, not too close but not too far away either. Didn't want to give Fin the impression she was afraid of him. But her subconscious whispered that if ever a man deserved to be feared, it was this one.

"Sleep well, Jenna?" Those strange silver eyes said he knew damn well she hadn't.

She shrugged. "Not really. I had a lot on my mind." *I had Al on my mind.*

He looked away from her to concentrate on his meal: bacon, eggs, and toast. She tried not to be too obvious with her sigh of relief.

"You'll clog your arteries with that stuff." God, she loved the smell of bacon. It brought back memories of younger years when Mom would make breakfast for everyone on a Sunday morning. Simpler times. She missed them.

Fin glanced up and grinned. "Then maybe I'm lucky not to have arteries."

She knew her mouth was hanging open. Not an attractive pose. Jenna didn't know which shocked her more, his artery comment or the absolute beauty of that smile. Luckily for all human women, he didn't smile a lot. She thought about that. Actually, he did smile off and on, but his smiles were never real. This one was *real*.

And he was probably just teasing about his arteries. Pushing away thoughts of smiles and arteries, she allowed Greer to place a plate of bacon and eggs in front of her, too. Hey, after the last few nights, living dangerously wasn't a problem.

"Is Al still sleeping?" Did she sound casual enough?

"No. Utah and Tor picked him up about an hour ago. They're following a few leads on our mole. He's probably the one who gave Rap that card about the restaurant. I thought the raptors deserved a chance to hunt down their brother's betrayer."

"And they still think of Al as part of their pack?"

He pushed his plate away and concentrated on his coffee. "Yes. And I agree with them." His gaze drifted to the window. Even though last night's snow had stopped, the sky still looked gray and threatening. "They've always been three, and it's important that they stay that way."

"You really believe in the number stuff." It boggled her mind how someone like Fin could be so into numerology. Numbers were just numbers. *Yeah, and vampires were just myths a few days ago.* Okay, so she'd keep an open mind. Sort of.

"You'd be surprised what I believe in." He turned his gaze back to her. "Enough about me, though. We need to talk about you."

Rats. She felt a lot more comfortable when Fin's attention was elsewhere. "There's nothing to talk about."

"Sure there is." He seemed thoughtful. "I've noticed how you and Al look at each other."

"He doesn't look at me in any particular way." She wouldn't insult either of them by claiming she didn't look at Al.

"He stares at you all the time, Jenna, and it bothers me. Of course, right now the look is mostly lust, but that's beginning to change."

Jenna hated her automatic shiver of excitement and pleasure. She *didn't* want Al interested. But her emotions didn't play mind games. Every one of them knew the truth. She was screwed.

Fin didn't wait for her to voice a denial. "I saw the same pattern with Ty and Kelly. So it's time I explained the rules of the game you're playing."

Game? Now *that* made her mad. Good. Anger pushed aside her defensive feelings. "Maybe you should hold your lecture until you have something solid to talk about. Yes, I'm attracted to Al, but that's normal. He's the kind of guy every woman would notice. That doesn't mean I want to head down the path my sister took."

"You'll get over your fear of his soul." He sounded matter of fact.

She didn't try to deny that fear. "I don't care how good

you are, you can't predict what I'll feel." Did she believe that? She wasn't sure.

He raked his fingers through that mass of silver hair in a classic gesture of male impatience. She smiled. She was getting to him. Jenna took her moments of power wherever she could find them.

"Okay, so humor me. Here's what you need to know about Al, about any of the Eleven."

No. She didn't want to know. She didn't want any knowledge that would add to the confusion building in her mind, her *heart*.

Fin held his hand up to stop anything she was planning to say. A wasted effort, because she couldn't force any words past the wall of denial she was frantically building brick by tortured brick.

"A wise woman would never fall in love with Al." His expression said he wasn't even close to bestowing the title of "wise" on her stupid head. "To take Al as your mate for life, you'd have to endure a ceremony that would test the limits of your love."

Her imagination went wild. Images of primitive rituals involving piercings and pain came immediately to mind. "I think Al is safe. I don't suffer silently."

"This isn't about physical pain."

He stared at her, and she controlled the urge to glance away. The purple was bleeding into those strange silver eyes—beautiful and terrifying.

"Let's hear it." As long as it didn't involve pain, she thought she could stand just about anything. Not that she'd ever want to do the mating-for-life thing.

"To claim Al, you'd have to walk into the heart of his beast and claim a part of his soul. And he'd have to welcome you."

She frowned. "Exactly what does that mean?"

He exhaled deeply before continuing. She understood the insult. Fin was trying to be patient with her puny human understanding. There were times when she felt like planting her puny human fist in his godlike face.

"You would have to walk into Al's Allosaurus form."

"This would all be symbolic, right?"

"No."

"Eww."

He smiled. Good, she was amusing him. She lived to entertain.

"If Al accepted you as his mate, his dinosaur form would become incorporeal, allowing you to pass into it."

"Well, that's a relief." At the same time, the thought was more than a little terrifying. "I guess if he didn't accept me, I'd just go splat against his mighty chest right before he ate me."

"I think you need to take this a little more seriously."

She shook her head. "If I do that, then I'll run screaming from the room."

"I don't believe you." He studied her with hooded eyes. "I think you're storing all this away so you can write the mother of all features. Someday."

"Someday," she agreed. "So what happens after I breach the dino gates?"

"Before you reach the man who stands at the heart of his beast, you'll see all that he was, all that he experienced." His gaze pierced her. "*All.*"

That "all" hinted at more than just a few scenes of an ancient predator running down dinner. She opted not to joke about it. "And why would this be such a scary trip? Not that I'm thinking about taking it."

"The human mind has its limits."

Ominous. "You're not going to explain, are you?"

"No." He shrugged. "If you take my warning, then you don't need to know more. And if you ignore it"—Fin let the dire implications fill his pause—"then you'll experience everything yourself."

"Let's assume I'm totally stupid and decide to take my chances with Al, why does he have to give me a piece of his soul?" She might be keeping the tone light, but coldness was creeping up her spine.

"By sharing his soul with you, Al becomes a little less than he is and you become a little more." He shifted his gaze to the window. "You'll be mated for all time."

"All time? Not until death do us part?" No, he couldn't mean what his words implied.

"You'll be immortal, Jenna. Just like all of us." Fin was big on dramatic pauses. "Just like your sister."

Her breath left her with an explosive "Huh?"

"Al can survive everything except beheading in his human form." He thought about that. "Probably fire could destroy him too. I'm not sure. Barring those unhappy incidents, Al is immortal. And if he shared his soul with you, the same rules would apply."

Kelly was immortal? Kelly had kept this from her family? Once Jenna's initial surge of anger receded, she admitted that no one would have believed her sister anyway.

Jenna was trying to think of something to say that wouldn't sound inane after Fin's bombshell, but it was tough when her brain was a quivering mess. She needn't have bothered, though, because Shen interrupted.

"Lia is here to talk to Jenna."

Shen smiled at her, but Jenna wasn't buying it. What *was* he beneath that warm and friendly grin? No one connected to the Eleven was what they appeared to be. "Lia? The new vampire queen?"

"Thanks, Shen." Fin didn't speak again until Shen had left the room.

Jenna wondered if he suspected his assistant of being the mole. Probably not. Shen wouldn't still be here if he did.

"I have things to do. Talk to Lia. We need her support. When Al gets back, the two of you can look for bells. Since my vision showed you ringing a bell, I have to believe you'll find the right one. I just hope it's soon. Once Eight gets enough recruits, he'll move on to another city. We have to stop him before that happens." Taking a last sip of coffee, he stood.

"Wait. If you're so all-powerful, why can't you help me find the bell?"

"There're things I can see, and things I can't see. I can't see this." He left the room.

Well, that was helpful. Now she had to talk to Lia. What did she have to say to her newly crowned highness? Uh, nothing.

Lia strode into the room radiating badass-bitch vibes. She'd traded in her jeans for leather pants and knee-high boots. She wore a black T-shirt under a short leather jacket. But her big blue eyes were the same—hard and determined. She dropped into the chair across from Jenna. "So teach me to be human."

Jenna blinked. "What?"

Lia rolled her eyes and indulged in an exaggerated sigh. "Dad said I had to enjoy being a human before he'd give permission for me to become vampire. Let the good times commence. I'm twenty-four, but you'd think I was ten."

"Okay, all this is whizzing right past me. Slow down and elaborate."

Lia helped herself to a slice of toast. She carefully slathered it with butter. "Dad says I've spent my whole life around vampires. He wants me to experience what it's like being human before I make the final decision to change. Without his okay, I'm screwed. It's some archaic vampire rule."

"Great. Just freaking great."

Lia grinned, and it transformed her into a beautiful

woman. "Yeah, tell me about it. But it won't take long. You can just fill me in on how humans think and give me a quick rundown on their emotions. Then we can do some girl things together—shop, get our hair and nails done, hit a few clubs, and call it quits. It'll make Dad happy, and I can get on with my real life."

"Wow, you must think humans are pretty shallow." Jenna was insulted on behalf of all humanity. "Tell me a little about your *real* life."

Lia looked puzzled for a moment before offering a rueful laugh. "Sorry. Didn't mean to belittle humans. It's just that I have to get back to leading my people as soon as possible. Since I'm not vampire yet, I have to be better than my mother for everyone to respect me. I can't make any mistakes. And the longer I'm away from them, the more opportunity for someone to start criticizing."

Something about Lia reminded Jenna of someone. Someone close. Now who did she know who felt she had to do things better than other members of her family? Standing outside and looking in gave Jenna a whole new perspective. "Why is it important to be *better* than your mother?" No way would the term "mom" ever fit Katherine. "I bet if you check it out, you'll find your mother wasn't universally loved." Jenna shuddered just thinking about Katherine's interrogation methods.

The other woman bit her lip in concentration. "My mother never accepted me, never thought of me as an equal. I was human, someone to be hidden and ignored. I want to prove I can lead our people and do it better than she did. It's a matter of pride."

Pride. Had Jenna's eternal search for perfection been all about her own pride? Not a particularly attractive character trait.

"She'll never know." Jenna made the statement as gentle as she could.

"But I will." Lia's words were bands of steely resolve.

Jenna thought of her own loving family and felt sad for the other woman. "I have a few hours to kill, so why don't we do a little shopping and talk about being human?" Al wouldn't want her to leave the condo without him, but what he didn't know wouldn't hurt him. They'd stay close to Rittenhouse Square and be back in a few hours. It was daylight, and a quick glance out the window showed that the snow had already melted from the streets. There was still a white blanket on trees and grass, but that wouldn't keep people inside. The sidewalks would be crowded. Not much chance for an attack.

Jenna grabbed her coat and purse before catching the elevator down. As the door opened, Lia and she almost ran into a big, lethal-looking guy wearing all brown. He looked like a grizzly. He blinked and Jenna got the feeling that was equivalent to a shout of surprise from an ordinary person. As she started to go around him, he stepped in front of her.

"I'm Luke, Fin's driver. I don't think he'd want you going out by yourself." He didn't even attempt to smile.

Rats. Busted. Jenna glanced at Lia. She shrugged.

"I'll drive you wherever you want to go." Luke didn't make it sound as if they had a choice.

"Great." At least they'd get out, and Al couldn't complain when he got back. "We were going to stay right around here, but now that you're driving we can spread our wings." She turned to Lia. "You're from Philly—where should we go?"

Jenna didn't pay too much attention to what Lia told Luke or the walk to his car. Her thoughts had drifted back to Al and to their lovemaking. She knew she was smiling. Never ever had she imagined that physical pleasure, and whatever else was mixed into the total experience, could be so intense. As he'd buried himself deep inside her, every sense had gone supernova on her: his hot male scent, the texture of him—smooth warm flesh and that incredible hair trailing across her skin—and the taste of his arousal as she'd slid her tongue over his body.

And what had happened at the very end, at the moment she clenched around him and exploded into a thousand pleasure points? It was as though for just a heartbeat they'd almost been connected by something beyond the physical. What that something was remained a mystery. She shook her head. Or maybe it had all been a brain burp, a total non-happening.

But she hadn't imagined his emotions. He'd broadcast them loud and clear. His hunger for her body was a driving need that took her breath away.

It was Al's other emotions, though, that still drew shadows in her mind. She'd felt his amazing strength wrapped in so much pain that she'd wanted to scream with the agony of it. Then there was his rage, crippling him with its darkness, shrieking its need to destroy, but with no real target except Fin. How did he live with it?

There was no way she should be able to feel so much for a man she'd known such a short time. The reality of it terrified her.

As she gazed idly out the car window, it occurred to her that not once had she thought of his beast. Maybe she was making progress after all.

She was yanked from her thoughts as the car suddenly accelerated, pushing her back against the seat. What the . . .

Lia laughed. "We're getting on the Schuylkill Expressway, affectionately known as the Sure Kill Expressway. It's merge-or-die here, girlfriend."

Jenna never got to ask where they were going because suddenly all the locks clicked and with lightning speed Luke slapped what looked like a gas mask on his face. Lia didn't bother asking questions. She yanked at the door handle. Locked.

Jenna pulled out her cell phone and frantically hit Kelly's number. She couldn't try to wrestle the steering wheel from Luke. They had to be doing seventy miles an hour. But she was way too slow. The gas was already filling up the car as Kelly answered. Jenna tried to form the words she needed to say, but she wasn't sure if any of them reached her sister as they floated around in her head and slowly drifted away.

Her last thought as darkness closed in was that there was never a dinosaur around when you needed him.

Chapter Fifteen

Al shoved the others aside in his eagerness to get out of the elevator. He reached the condo door in a few strides and then pounded on it. To hell with politely pushing buttons. No matter how much his mind ticked off reasons why he should steer clear of Jenna, the rest of him panted to see her again, touch her again, *talk* to her again.

Amazing that talk even made the list, because what he wanted to do to her lush, sexy body didn't need words. But he was finding that the human part of him craved everything about her.

"Damn, I was sure it was that guy who worked at the desk downstairs." Utah sounded bitter enough to tear the man apart just on principle. "Now what?"

"We'll find the bastard." Tor was coldly determined.

Al figured when the raptors finally found the person responsible for Rap's death, it would be raining body parts for days. "We've eliminated a lot of people. There aren't that many left to check out. We're close." He did some more pounding. *Come on, answer the damn door.*

"Not close enough." Utah's complaint was all frustrated predator.

But Al forgot about the raptors as the door swung open and Fin himself stood in the doorway. Something in his gaze silenced all three men.

"We have a situation." Fin sounded grim.

"Where's Jenna?" Al peered past him.

Fin didn't answer. He turned and led them into the living room, where Jude waited with five other vampires and a woman. Al focused all his attention on the strangers. In his world of eat-or-be-eaten, you survived to old age by being suspicious of everyone. He waited impatiently for Fin to introduce them so he could leave and find Jenna.

But it was Jude who did the honors. He nodded at the five men. "Meet the deadliest vampires in existence." He didn't offer any names. "They belonged to an ancient clan that the Fae destroyed centuries ago. I don't know what they did to piss off the Unseelie Court, and I don't care. As long as no dark fairies try interfering with my business, I'm willing to forget about it."

Al studied the five men. Power, thick and suffocating, flowed from them. It wound around him, poking and prodding, searching for weaknesses. Impressive.

"These men were so dangerous that the rest of the vampire world agreed they had to be destroyed. But that would've meant massive losses on our side and a waste of raw talent on theirs. So I agreed to put them under my protection as long as they did the occasional job for me and didn't eat their handler." He glanced around at the unsmiling faces. "That was a joke, folks. Anyway, I've never regretted it."

Al seemed to remember someone mentioning that these guys had helped Ty and Kelly free the werewolf Neva back in Houston. He studied them more closely. They were all at least six feet five with muscular bodies meant for fighting. But where Jude was dangerous in an understated way, these men reeked of death. They were dressed all in black, their faces carved from jagged granite and forged in the fires of some ancient underworld. They almost crackled with suppressed violence and the need to kill. Al sensed no souls, no flicker of humanity in their cold stares. Even his Allosaurus soul would tread lightly around these predators.

Al glanced at Fin. "Are they here to help with Eight?"

If so, Al felt insulted. The Eleven didn't need outside help for this.

Fin continued to ignore his questions, which was starting to make Al mad.

"This is Sara." Fin turned toward the woman. "She's the pack leader of Philadelphia's werewolves. Macario and Neva asked her to help us."

Utah grunted his disbelief. "A woman can't be pack leader."

Sara smiled at him. Not a nice smile. "She can if she kills every dumbass wolf stupid enough to challenge her."

No one would ever ignore Sara in a crowd. She was tall and lithe, with green eyes and a mass of dark hair that tumbled down her back. She stared at Al, the predatory gleam in her eyes promising that if she chose him as her mate, life would never be boring. It wouldn't be safe either. She'd probably eat her mate when she got tired of him. He wasn't interested.

"Why are they here now?" Al got right to the point. And where was Jenna?

Fin didn't ask anyone to sit down. He paced restlessly in front of the bank of windows. "Jenna and Lia went out this afternoon. They didn't tell anyone they were going, and they didn't leave a note. I assume Jenna was taking Lia shopping or something."

Jenna. Something had happened to his *mate*. The word rose on an ancient and violent need to protect what was his. Al's instinct didn't listen to reason, to the logical list of why Jenna could never be his. His instinct *knew*. And from the depths of what he'd once been, something savage and terrible rose. It beckoned his soul from its cave with promises that together they'd tear apart this city and kill, kill, kill.

"Where. Is. Jenna?" He put all his fury and dread into each word, and everyone stepped away from him except for Fin.

"I don't know." Fin turned to face him, his eyes flat and emotionless. "She got Kelly on her cell phone, but she was only able to say Luke's name before someone ended the call."

The mole. Luke was among the ones they hadn't investigated yet. They'd assumed he was loyal. They'd assumed wrong. And now Jenna and Lia would pay.

His rage, the part of him that simmered just below the surface but wanted, no, *needed*, a target, found it in Fin. "You were supposed to make sure she didn't leave without protection. I go out for a few hours, and you just let her walk away alone."

Fin's eyes changed from silver to solid purple in an instant. That was the only warning they got before the bank of tall windows behind him blew out in an explosion of glass.

"What the fuck . . ." One of Jude's vampires said it for all of them.

Fin moved into Al's space. Al concentrated on not backing away from his leader.

"You think I was sitting in my freaking chair staring at the sky all day? Zero's in town. Who do you think is keeping him distracted and off your backs? I don't walk on water, and I don't have eyes in the back of my head! She wanted to leave, so she left. Shen should've picked her up on the security camera, but he didn't. It happened. Deal with it." He punctuated the last sentence with a crack of thunder that probably had the guys down at the weather bureau scratching their heads.

The cold air swirling in through the gaping windows didn't make Al shiver half as much as Fin's show of temper. Al never doubted that Fin could scramble his atoms and scatter them across the universe if he chose. But he couldn't control his own temper. "Why'd you let her get mixed up in this, anyway? Anyone could ring the damn bells. She should've been safe at home in Houston." The fact that he blamed himself as much as he blamed Fin fanned the flames of his anger. His soul peered eagerly through those flames, waiting for a moment of weakness, a moment when his emotions would overwhelm him, and his soul could break free. He clamped down on those emotions. Losing it wouldn't help Jenna.

Fin nodded as if nothing had happened, his silver eyes calm again and untouched by emotion. "You're learning." He gestured at the others. "I called Jude as soon as I heard, and he brought his men here from Houston."

Utah voiced the obvious. "Must've been a mighty fast plane."

One of Jude's five men spoke for the first time. "We can move through time and space. Why would we need a plane?" He didn't try to hide his contempt for those who did need them.

"Did I mention *how* old they are?" Jude smiled. "They were around when the pyramids were built. Not old by your standards, but old enough to accumulate lots of useful skills. If anyone can find Jenna and Lia, they can. I wouldn't trust the search to the Philly vampires."

"If they're so powerful, why are they working for you?" Tor's expression dismissed Jude's power.

Suddenly the room thrummed with something that raised the hairs on Al's arms. Fin didn't seem concerned, but Tor sure was. He now hung suspended about five feet off the floor.

Jude's smile never changed. "Show respect, raptor. Just because I choose not to show you my power doesn't mean I don't have it." Then without warning, he dropped Tor to the floor. "I'll let you know if we find anything." He nodded to his men, and then in a blur of motion they disappeared through the broken windows.

"Jerks. They couldn't use the elevator like the rest of us?" Utah's complaint sounded halfhearted.

Tor looked one part furious and two parts embarrassed, but he didn't say anything.

Sara laughed. "I think I like your vampire. He has a sense of humor." Her laughter died. "My pack is already on the job. If Jenna and Lia are in the city, we'll find them." She sent one last hard stare at Fin. "You have scary power. I feel sorry for the guy you're hunting."

Al watched her leave before turning to Fin. "Any ideas?"

Fin shook his head. "I can't sense Eight. Nine had success kidnapping Kelly and using her to draw Ty into the Astrodome. Eight might be playing the same game." He speared Al with a hard gaze. "Wherever Jenna and Lia are, I don't want you or any of the Eleven going in after them in human form. Eight could control you too easily. Ty and Gig found that out in Houston."

"I don't care what form I have to take, I want to be there." This wasn't negotiable.

"I agree." Fin finally stopped pacing. "Once we locate them, I'm sending in a team."

"All of us?" Tor had found his voice.

"I never put everyone's life on the line at the same time and place."

That made Al mad all over again. "Jenna and Lia are worth it."

"If all of you get killed at once, who'll be left to fight Zero and the rest of his immortals?" He shrugged. "If I send in a team of four and Eight eliminates you, I'll still have options."

"Ever the optimist." Al didn't care that his comment was a verbal sneer.

"A realist." Fin dropped onto one of the recliners. "The women might already be dead. I'm not ready to sacrifice you to a lost cause."

The word "dead" was a kick in the gut. It almost doubled him over. His soul crept a little closer to the cave entrance, and Al knew if Eight had killed Jenna, nothing, not Fin or ten of his evil twins, could keep his soul from rampaging through Philly. From the expression on Fin's face, he knew it too.

"Who'll be on the team?" Al spoke softly, but he knew from Fin's wince that he must be broadcasting his fury at sonic-boom level. He took a deep breath. This uncontrollable rage was outside anything he'd ever felt before—personal and too intense to describe.

"Us." Utah glanced at his brother. "Wherever Eight is, we want to be there too." His hunger for revenge lived in his eyes.

Fin nodded. "I'll send all three of you along with Ty and Lio. Ty wants to go because Jenna is family, and Lio can take care of anyone who tries to escape by water. Kelly will drive us. She accepts that she'll have to stay with the SUV."

"What happens if the entrance to the building is too small for our beasts?" Tor's expression said he'd get inside even if he had to go in as a human.

"Don't even think about it." Fin didn't raise his voice, but he didn't have to. The words were a bright neon warning that even the craziest of the Eleven would hesitate to ignore. "If the problem arises, I'll give you the strength to get your beasts inside."

Tor nodded, satisfied for the moment.

"And you'll be where?" They'd supply the muscle, but Al knew Fin would take care of any finessing necessary.

"I'll be making sure no mortals notice anything strange." Fin's gaze grew pensive. "And I'll keep Zero from interfering." He smiled. "Or not. Who knows? Zero is an unpredictable bastard."

If Al didn't know any better, he'd almost believe there was a note of affection in Fin's voice. Then he forgot about Fin and Zero. "I have to get back out and start looking."

"No."

Al started to snarl his defiance at Fin and then paused. Maybe for once he needed to listen first. Jenna's life was on the line. "Why not?"

"We have an army of vampires and werewolves as well as the rest of the Eleven looking for them. A few more searchers aren't going to make a difference. I want the team together so as soon as we get word where they are, we can move as one. I don't want you scattered all over the city."

Al hated to admit that Fin's plan made sense. But as much as he needed a clear head and a sense of "team" right now, all he could think of was ditching everyone and laying waste to Philly in his search for Jenna. Reluctantly, he backed away from the edge.

Fin glanced his way, a hint that he was monitoring Al's reactions. "I've called Ty and Lio. They should be here in a little while. I don't care what you do now, but don't leave the condo. And don't try to kill each other." He spared a brief smile for all of them. "It would piss me off." He rose and headed for the doorway. "I'll be in my office. I have to fill Shen in so he can find someone who'll come out this late to fix these windows. If I get any updates, I'll give a shout."

Al didn't stay to talk to the guys. With everything going on in his head, he was close to liftoff. If any of the others said the wrong thing, he might tear Fin's expensive condo apart.

He left on Fin's heels. Al had a vague idea of holing up in his room but then changed his mind. Instead, he turned toward the only room in this place of steel and glass where he could feel close to Jenna.

The door to her room didn't present a problem. A healthy shove fueled by his bad attitude popped the lock. Once inside, he left the room in darkness and stretched out on her bed. He closed his eyes.

Her scent filled the black void behind his closed lids with

images of her. All of her emotions spilled over into his mind, flooding him with memories too new to have hardened. They were still fluid, changing with each of his thoughts. Jenna with eyes huge and frightened as she'd seen the shadow of his beast that first night in the park. Jenna in tears over the death of Rap, a man she'd hardly known. Jenna with her head thrown back and eyes dark with passion.

And while he lay there, a new emotion clamped steel jaws around his heart. This one was all his, and for a moment he didn't recognize it because it was outside his experience. *Fear.* It was jagged glass cutting him apart, taking his breath away with a promise that he might never breathe again. It was terror—for her, for him. It was selfish. What if he never saw her again?

As if the fear wasn't enough, its evil twin joined it. Helplessness. He couldn't do a damn thing until someone found Jenna and Lia. How did humans live with feelings like these? Had his prey felt the same fear and helplessness?

For one of the few times since rising from Machu Picchu, he put aside his rage for something more important. At this moment, it was enough to pray that Jenna and Lia were alive, that he'd reach them in time. He wasn't quite sure who to pray to, so he sent the words out to whatever deity might have some influence.

He had no idea how many hours had slid by before Fin called him. When he strode into the media room where the others waited, Al could feel the bloodlust that stained the air around them. But his need to kill was bigger and badder than all of them put together.

Fin had the picture of a building up on the monitor. Al frowned. It looked like a Greek temple set at the top of a hill. Familiar.

Fin didn't waste words. "Jude's vampires found them. They're in the Museum of Art."

Lio grinned. "Hey, now I'll get to run up those steps like Rocky Balboa did. At the top I'll pump my fists in the air and hum a few bars of 'Gonna Fly Now.'"

Al wasn't amused. The idiot was still in suit, jacket, and expensive tie mode. On the other hand, Al was dressed for killing. Jeans, boots, T-shirt, and black duster. His hair hung loose down his back. Tonight he hunted.

Jenna felt that she'd been fighting her way out of a black pit of goo for eternity. Her only point of reference was Al's face. She didn't understand why that was so. Didn't even *try* to understand.

Finally. Light. She held her breath while awareness caught up with sensation. Wait a minute. The light had been there all along. All she'd had to do was crack her eyelids open and let it in. Dumb.

She opened her eyes wider and then blinked. "Bizarre" and "surreal" were the first words that came to mind. As her brain collected the bits and pieces of her most recent memory, she added "terrifying" to the list. She tried to look around without moving her head.

"Magnificent, isn't it?" The male voice sounded normal and even a little friendly. "You're in the Great Stair Hall of the Philadelphia Museum of Art. The soaring ceiling with that grand staircase leading up to the statue of the goddess Diana makes me all emotional. I've tried to honor the architectural wonder of the building in my own little way."

Uh-oh. Jenna didn't need blinking yellow arrows pointing to "the spot." Luke had kidnapped them. And she didn't have to burn many brain cells to figure out who was signing his paycheck. Jenna looked for Lia. There, she was lying a few feet away. Still out. Then Jenna met the gaze of the man standing in the center of the hall. "You're Eight."

He winced. "Fin really doesn't have much imagination.

Call me Stake. I wasn't expecting guests tonight, but I admire Luke's ability to grasp the moment. I'm afraid you've missed all the fun, though. The killing part is always good for a giggle. Feel free, though, to relax and watch me work."

Jenna kept her mouth shut until she'd taken stock of what was happening. Eight was a tall man, about six one or two. Nice looking in a mature, middle-aged way. Touches of silver at his temples gave him a distinguished look. Expensive suit. He'd give Lio a run for his money.

She glanced into Eight's eyes and froze. His human disguise was perfect except for his eyes. Black, with all the evil of the universe alive in them. Those eyes promised that he could watch the whole of humanity die and enjoy every moment of the dying. Jenna sucked in her breath and looked away.

His chuckle was warm and amused. "Scary, aren't they? I'm among friends here, so I don't feel the need to hide them. If you have any questions, ask me now. I don't like to be interrupted while I work."

For the first time, Jenna allowed herself to acknowledge the bodies arranged in front of Eight. No blood, but they were definitely dead.

"All nice and neat. Not like before. Why?" Did Jenna care about his method? No, but she did care about gaining time until help showed up or else she figured a way out of this herself. Whichever came first.

Oh, and she couldn't forget the fear. She needed a few minutes, or maybe years, to get her terror under control. She tried to ease the pounding of her heart, tried to slow breaths that were coming way too fast. Maybe she needed a paper bag to breathe into.

"My vampires did a superb job. I'm impressed. Two punctures and not a drop of blood spilled." Eight oozed pride in his minions. "I was interested in capturing the flow of lines rather than blood patterns this time. I found an abundance of unwilling models, security people and a few cops who came snooping around before I put up my ward."

Eleven bodies. Someone had arranged them to form the number 2012 on the floor of the hall. Light spotlighted the gruesome scene. Shapes moved restlessly in the shadows where the light didn't reach. She assumed these were Eight's nonhuman recruits.

"Eleven. Clever." She hoped her murmur hid the icy claws tearing at her mind.

"You recognized the symbolism. How bright of you." Eight looked sincerely delighted. "I achieve two goals tonight. I tweak Fin's nose at the same time I point Philadelphia down the path of mass hysteria. When I finish here, I'll notify the media. It'll be delicious."

And the weirdness just went on. Eight had a sketchpad and pencils along with an iPod arranged on a small table beside him. There was a chair so that he could draw in comfort. On the floor beside the table was a cage with a seagull inside. *It* was alive.

"You like birds?" She recognized her mindless babble for what it was. Sound, any sound, kept her panic-stricken gibbering at bay.

"I appreciate anything that comes from the sea, Jenna. May I call you Jenna?" He didn't wait for her reply. "The seagull is a bird of the sea. I found it injured and nursed it back to health. I'll release it when the time is right."

She didn't try to hide her surprise. "Amazing. You get all gleeful about killing humans, but you care for a bird."

He shook his head in mock sorrow. "You disappoint me. I thought that anyone who'd met Fin would realize that both black and white easily turn gray. There are many nuances to good and evil."

Before she could ask him to elaborate, he called her attention to something else.

"I chose this spot because of the inspiration." He swept his arms wide. "I took my pick from the best. I'll take them with me when I leave."

For the first time she noticed that paintings hung from the massive columns surrounding the hall. Obviously Eight had gone shopping in the museum's galleries. The works of art all had one thing in common. The sea.

"Look." He touched her shoulder and pointed.

She controlled her shudder.

"The painting on the third column. *Manet and the Sea.* My favorite."

Jenna could only nod, because she'd seen something else as she'd turned to glance at the painting.

A man. No, not a man. Nothing human looked like that. He was the essence of all things beautiful, all things deadly, all things *unearthly*. His was a beauty forged in darkness.

Well over six feet, he was wrapped in a dark cloak, but it was his face that sucked the breath from her lungs. Every stark line of his jaw and cheekbones, every curve of his full lips spoke of sex. His eyes were deep forest green framed by thick dark lashes. Those eyes revealed what he could do to a woman's body, the unspeakable pleasure-pain he could wring from her, sensations that would leave her screaming in ecstasy as she died because surely no woman could survive making love with him. Smoke-dark hair framed that sensual face, and Jenna knew if she stared into his eyes long enough she might just ask him to strangle her with that tangled glory. He had the kind of power to make a woman beg for even that kind of death. She was sure of it.

Oh God, oh God, oh God. Jenna had to look away, but she couldn't. His gaze gripped her, tore her will away, and dragged her a step closer to him. Clenching her fists, she tried to resist. Because on a level far removed from reason, she knew that once she reached him, she'd tear her clothes from her body and offer herself to him. And there wouldn't be a damn thing she could do to stop herself.

"Glorious, isn't he?"

Eight's voice broke the hypnotic hold the man's gaze had on her. She blinked. Only then did she notice that only his eyes moved. The rest of his body seemed as inanimate as the steel sword that hung at his side.

"Who is he, and what have you done to him?" She forced herself not to look back at the man.

"Ah, my most prized possession." Eight seemed to think about that. "Well, perhaps *Manet and the Sea* might be number one now." Then he brightened. "But I'm still thrilled to have him. This is Kione, a Fae prince of the Unseelie Court. He's an arrogant bastard. I'm sure he never thought anyone could capture him." Eight's smile was smug. "He knows better now. Oh, and he's not moving because he's less troublesome that way."

"Unseelie Court?"

"He's a dark fairy, my dear. A wonderfully evil addition to my collection. I acquire and use beautiful things." Eight's gaze turned predatory. "I'll enjoy him." He turned a speculative glance her way. "I might enjoy you as well."

Over my cold and stiff body.

"Don't tempt me. I find death in all its forms utterly fascinating."

Eight's smile was so normal it just didn't fit the horror of his words. He seemed to sense her fear, and his smile widened. "Terror is the greatest aphrodisiac."

Oh, hell.

Lia made whimpering noises as she regained consciousness. Eight turned his attention on her, and Jenna hated herself for feeling so much relief.

"And Luke also delivered the newly crowned queen of the vampires, who just happens to be human. Delightful. I must reward Luke for the amusement he's giving me."

While Eight's focus was elsewhere, Jenna scanned the hall for possible escape routes. None. She wondered if Al cared that she was missing. Of course he did. The connection they'd forged when they'd made love was real, even if its links were created from the heat of sexual need.

And her sister. Kelly would be frantic.

Fin would sure care. He had bells for her to ring. Jenna got no further with her who-will-care list because Eight turned his attention back to her.

"I'd suggest you explain the facts to your friend. I can't be bothered. I have a scene to capture." He started to pick up his iPod.

"I know you don't think we've got a chance to escape, but aren't you afraid the Eleven will track us here?"

Eight looked mildly amused. "How? Fin can't sense me, and I made sure that he couldn't connect with you mentally. No one followed Luke. I have wards in place that'll discourage interest in the museum." He shrugged. "No, you're completely at my mercy." He winked. "And I have no mercy, none at all. I haven't decided what part you'll play in all this, but I'm thinking about it." Once his iPod was in place, he began to sketch.

Lia was on her knees and about to struggle to her feet when Jenna reached her. Quickly, Jenna whispered what had happened. The other woman took everything in stride. And if she was terrified, she didn't show it. Jenna felt a little resentful about that. She wanted someone to share her fear.

"So how do we get out of here?" Lia looked around the hall. "There're too many of them for us to fight."

"Uh, you think?" Jenna counted pairs of gleaming eyes in the darkness. Eight had brought at least thirty followers to his drawing party. She could only imagine what they were. Vampires for sure. She didn't want to think beyond that.

Lia ignored Jenna's sarcasm as she stared at the museum entrance. "The doors are glass, and so are the panels above them."

"Yeah, but there're a few pesky strips of steel in there too. What're you thinking?"

Lia shrugged. "We can't get out, but something might get in."

Al. It was sort of pitiful how all thoughts led back to him. But they couldn't count on a rescue. They had to come up with their own plan. She took a deep breath and dared to look at the Fae prince. "If we could free him, we might have a chance. If nothing else, he'd be a distraction. How powerful *is* a prince of the Unseelie Court?"

Lia's gaze held raw sexual hunger as she stared at the dark fairy. Jeez, was that how she had looked? Jenna felt embarrassed.

"I guarantee there's nothing in here except for the nutjob drawing pictures of dead people that's more powerful than . . ." Lia never took her gaze from the prince. "What's his name?"

"Kione."

"Right. Anyway, we can't free him. Neither of us knows how."

Jenna narrowed her gaze on Eight. "The 'nutjob' is controlling Kione. If we could come up with a big enough distraction, maybe his hold would weaken and Kione could escape."

Lia didn't seem impressed. "Yeah, Eight would be so focused on killing us that the prince could escape. Fat lot of good that would do our dead butts."

Talk about negativity. Jenna didn't say anything more as she made her own plans to escape. She figured she was dead either way. Eight would kill them. No, wait, he'd have one of his recruits kill them. He couldn't do it himself. Jenna would rather die in a fruitless attempt at escape. Proactive to the end, that was her.

She was still working out the details of her escape attempt when the floor beneath her began to shake.

Chapter Sixteen

His beast's need for violence spurred Al on as he powered up the museum's steps. Beside him, Ty's T. rex matched him stride for stride. Behind them, the two raptors eagerly leaped ten steps at a time. Lio, in his human form, along with Sara and some of her wolves, followed in the rear.

Ordinarily Al would have drawn comfort from the feel of pack around him. Not this time. He didn't care if he was one or one of many. A single purpose drove him—Jenna.

The ground shook and groaned beneath them. Humans close by would suspect an earthquake. Nonhumans inside the museum would know better. No one would see them until it was much too late. Fin had made sure of that.

They reached the top of the steps and pounded toward the glass entrance doors. The glass panels above the doors stretched several stories high. Neither doors nor panels would stop him. He didn't slow down as he felt Fin's power-boost kick in.

Al hurtled through glass and steel. Beside him, he heard Ty's roar of challenge. Utah and Tor moved silently, lethal if smaller shadows ghosting into the Great Stair Hall.

Jude, along with his five vampires, had been crouched on the roof of a nearby building when they'd arrived. The vampires and werewolves would trail them inside, eager to be in on the kill.

Fin had cleared the way. He'd quietly gotten rid of the ward Eight had put around the museum and replaced it with his own. Maybe Zero should've warned his fellow immortal against overconfidence. Eight hadn't posted any lookouts. Al was glad he hadn't. Not that it would have made any difference once Fin arrived.

He analyzed the scene through his predator's eyes. The man in the center must be Eight. His power felt like the controlling force in the room. Off to the sides, half hidden behind large pillars, figures scuttled to escape the flying glass. Those would be Eight's people. But where was the only one he really cared about?

There. Jenna stood a few yards behind Eight. Lia crouched on one side of her, and a man who seemed frozen in place stood on her other side. The intensity of Al's relief stopped him in his tracks while the barbs of fear that had wrapped around his heart loosened and fell away.

Only one man stood between him and his woman. He roared his challenge and then charged. Eight's eyes grew wide as he flung a power burst at Al. If Al had been in human form, it would have ripped him apart. He wasn't, and it didn't. Sure, it slowed him down a little, but nothing Eight could do would stop him now.

The immortal wasn't stupid, though. Al watched Eight glance around, assessing the situation. Then the immortal grabbed some things from a table, picked up a cage that held a seagull, and simply disappeared.

Al screamed his disappointment. He hated to lose prey. While Eight had been focused on him, Jenna and Lia had retreated to a far corner, safe from the fighting for the moment. Al's job was to see that they stayed safe.

He put enthusiasm into his slaughter. Every one of the enemy would've killed Jenna if given the chance. They'd never kill anyone again.

Al clamped his jaws around the head of a vampire. The head separated from the body. Too easy.

Three werewolves leaped at him. He shook them off and

then stomped on them. Luckily for the museum cleaning crew, Fin would make sure this mess was taken care of by morning.

During a brief lull in the action he noticed the human bodies that formed 2012. All Eight's work was for nothing. Fin would get rid of those bodies too.

Then rational thought fled as a group of demons attacked him, and his soul's instincts took over. Grotesque in their true forms, they leaped onto him, digging sharp claws into his back and slashing at his flesh with barbed fangs. They beat the air with leathery wings and screamed their fury. He scraped against a pillar and swung his tail, trying to dislodge them. Twisting his neck as far as it would go, he was able to tear one of them off him. He ripped at the creature, the taste of blood and flesh freeing the savagery that always lurked close to the surface in all of the Eleven. Nothing human remained of him at that moment.

"Holy hell." Lia sounded more awed than afraid.

That was okay, because Jenna was terrified enough for both of them. Eyes wide, she watched the carnage. Even if she were capable of moving, she'd probably never make it across a floor slippery with blood and littered with body parts. The head of a creature she couldn't identify lay near her, the dead eyes glazing over even as it stared sightlessly at her. She swallowed hard to keep from throwing up.

Again and again her eyes returned to Al. No, not Al. She could hardly see his shape inside the animal whose giant teeth were tearing apart the creatures that clung to him. "What are they?" She pointed.

"Demons." Lia's tone was matter of fact.

Jenna watched horrified as a demon's wing wiggled and moved, searching for its lost body. A hysterical giggle rose and was firmly shoved back. "Why are they even fighting? They can't kill each other."

"It's their nature. They were born to destroy."

Lia licked her lips. "If I had my sword I could help." Her eyes gleamed with her desire to leap into the middle of the fight. The rest of her might still be human, but her heart was vampire.

Almost as though she were in a trance, Lia edged away from Jenna, her gaze never leaving the battle. And before Jenna could call her back, she slipped into the shadows and was gone.

They were born to destroy. There it was. The one thing that would always separate her from Al. She didn't have the killer instinct, didn't understand what drove any of them, even Lia.

Jenna narrowed her gaze. Lia. Gone. She was alone in a hall filled with bloodlust-driven nightmares from humanity's darkest imaginings.

But she forgot everything as she glanced back at Al. Bloody remains formed a gruesome circle around him, but some of those remains were pulling themselves together. Literally. The demons didn't die, they just regrouped.

Al didn't seem concerned with his almost-defeated enemies. He had a new worry. A pack of six wolves threw themselves at him. Werewolves? Yeah, the glowing eyes were a dead giveaway. They were huge gray animals as big as small horses, and they leaped and slashed at the already bleeding Allosaurus.

Logically, Jenna knew Al wouldn't die. He was pretty much indestructible in his animal form. At least that's what she'd been told. But what if that supposition was wrong? What if he could be worn down and killed? Rage exploded. Whether they could kill him or not, they were *hurting* him.

Frantically, she scanned the area. She needed a weapon. Then she remembered something. Drawing in a deep breath, she ran the short distance to the dark fairy still frozen on the edge of the action.

"Sorry about this, but I need the weapon more than you do right now." Jenna pushed his cloak aside and pulled out the sword that she'd glimpsed earlier. She refused to look into his eyes. That way lay madness, and she needed a clear head right now.

Thank God no one paid any attention to her. She was human and therefore insignificant. The sword was lighter than she'd expected. Creeping closer to where Al still battled the werewolves, she set her sights on the biggest one, the one who seemed the most aggressive.

She didn't stop to think. If she did, she'd never have the guts to do anything. Once she was close enough, she'd have to strike fast, because even though a human didn't pose a danger to anyone here, a human with a bigass sword did. Then she'd have to run like hell to keep from being ripped apart by the other wolves or trampled by Al. She was counting on the momentary confusion among the wolves to give Al the advantage.

Her heart pounded out a terrified rhythm, and the coppery smell of blood made her want to gag, but she controlled her shaking for the precious seconds it took to raise the sword and strike.

As she brought the sword down, she pushed aside thousands of years of civilization to channel her inner cavewoman. The sword sliced into the wolf, there was a flash of light, and the wolf disappeared. She blinked and stared. Not even a drop of blood on the sword.

Whoa! Al and the rest of the wolves froze. She didn't. Keeping a firm grip on the sword, she ran to the nearest shadowy corner. Breathing hard, she glanced behind her, expecting the pack of ravenous wolves to be in hot pursuit. She almost passed out from relief when she saw that Al was taking full advantage of her help. He methodically tore apart the remaining wolves. They'd *stay* dead. At least she thought so.

Luckily, everyone else was too busy trying to kill each other to pay much attention to a flash of light and one less werewolf. She hunkered down to wait out the fight. Jenna didn't allow herself even to think about the possibility of the good guys losing.

She bit her lip as she watched the battle. It was hard to tell how many of Eight's forces were still fighting. Al and the other members of the Eleven had come in with some vampires and werewolves. She couldn't tell the good from the bad.

Jenna clenched her fists, trying to keep her courage from draining out of her fingertips. A screaming fit of hysterics right now might distract Al from his killing frenzy. No, that was *not* a tear sliding down her face.

Eyes held wide to discourage any more tear-leaking, she shifted her attention to something neutral, something that wasn't clawing, screaming, and dying. And met the gaze of Kione.

But before the impact of that stare could knock her onto her butt, he moved his gaze to something else. She followed his stare.

Ohmigod. There were five massive vampires descending on the Unseelie prince. Swords in hands, hard faces tight with fury, they were definitely the bad guys. And they were going to cut him to pieces where he stood, unable to move.

She could stay right here and be relatively safe. After all, she didn't know Kione. And if Eight were to be believed, the prince wasn't exactly a protector of the light. He was evil, and evil should die. Right?

Jenna sighed. She hoped the sword worked on vampires as well as it did on werewolves, because she couldn't let him be cut down without a chance to protect himself. Especially since she'd taken his sword.

But she wasn't going to be stupid about this. She looked around for some backup. No one. Damn.

"Looking for a white knight, princess?" The deep and sensual male voice was familiar and very close.

"Seir. What're you doing here?" Jenna didn't turn around to look at him. "No, I don't have time to listen. Come with me." She might not be sure of Seir's ultimate loyalty, but he was Fin's brother. That had to count for something.

She reached the Fae prince a few strides before the vampires. Stepping in front of him, she hefted her sword with both hands and pointed it straight out in front of her. "We need to talk about whatever you have planned, guys."

Perhaps this hadn't been such a great idea. Close up, these men were beyond scary. No human emotion showed in their black eyes. The rage and hate surrounding them was so thick, Jenna believed she could reach out and touch it. Hot and sticky, it would cling to her, blocking out light and all other sensation until she suffocated from the pure malevolence of it.

"You wield a mighty phallic symbol, human woman. Too bad you have no male attached to it." The vampire in the middle seemed to feel he'd made a great joke. His lips twitched in what must be a hearty grin for him.

"Move out of our way." The vampire next to him had no sense of humor.

"No. I won't let you kill him." God, why didn't Seir say something? She wanted to turn around to make sure he was there, but she didn't dare take her attention from the five in front of her.

The end vampire hissed at her. "Jude brought us here to save you, but if you persist in defying us, we will do what we need do. Put down the sword."

Jude? These five were on her side? If these were the good guys, she didn't want to ever look into the eyes of the bad ones. Oh, wait, she had. She'd looked into Eight's eyes and they'd looked a lot like these five.

"I won't let you kill a helpless man." She took a quick glance on either side of her. No Seir. Oh, hell.

One of the vampires who hadn't spoken yet stepped forward. "Know you whom you defend, stupid female? He is a Fae prince of the Unseelie Court. He and his destroyed our clan. We will have our revenge."

And without warning, she was swept aside as though a giant hand had slapped her silly. She landed on her behind with the sword still clutched in front of her.

"It's never nice to knock a woman on her butt."

Seir winked on. That was the only way Jenna could describe his sudden appearance. He didn't look white-knightish tonight. Worn jeans, scuffed biker boots, long black coat with hood up—he looked sort of like the grim reaper. Only those icy blue eyes and that quick slashing grin were the same as she remembered.

The five vampires moved so quickly they were just a blur. In a heartbeat they had Seir, Kione, and her surrounded.

"What be you?" The vampire who'd spoken wasn't looking at Jenna. His gaze was fixed on Seir, and he seemed seriously concerned with his inability to identify this new threat. But at least for the moment he wasn't thinking about Kione.

Seir shrugged. "Does it matter?"

A puzzled line formed between the vampire's dark eyes. Jenna had the feeling lines didn't often form there.

Since the five were focused on Seir, Jenna chanced a glance at Al. He was a monster magnet. Between tearing, rending, and stomping, he was scanning the hall. Looking for her? Something in the region of her heart did a hopeful flip-flop.

"I'm whatever you want me to be." Seir the enigmatic.

The vampire leaned closer. "I've heard of only one Seir. Are you a demon prince of hell?" The vampire seemed to dare him not to be. "From what legends tell, you command twenty-six legions of demons."

"Sounds good to me."

"Which side do you battle for on this night?" The vampire tensed.

"My own side."

The vampires didn't seem to know what to do with that answer.

Seir turned to Jenna. "What do you want?"

"These guys want to kill Kione. Eight did something to him so he can't move. I want him to have a fighting chance."

Within the dark cave of his hood, Seir's icy eyes gleamed. "Are you sure? Some things are best kept caged."

Jenna didn't have time for this crap. "Free him."

Seir glanced in Kione's direction, and suddenly the Fae prince moved. Before Jenna could even breathe, "What the hell," the dark fairy had stripped her of his sword.

"I will remember, woman." Kione's voice was dark melted chocolate with a cyanide center.

And she knew that every woman on Earth would happily gobble down that center as long as he gazed at her the way Kione was looking at Jenna now. She fell into that stare, wrapped herself in it, and knew she'd do anything he wanted her to do. *Anything.*

Next to her, Seir made a sound deep in his throat, and the Fae prince shifted his gaze.

Kione smiled, and Jenna almost fell to her knees. My God, what kind of power did he have? Something about her reaction to him was more terrifying than slathering werewolves, bloodsucking vampires, and butt-ugly demons combined. Because Kione, dark prince of the Unseelie Court, had the power to control her will.

Seir didn't react to the smile. Instead, he glanced beyond

their happy little group. "Looks like Jenna's man is joining us. He doesn't look happy. He doesn't even look sane."

Jenna, along with everyone else, turned to stare.

Al had finally found her. Covered in blood, and with his beast's gaze fixed firmly on her, he stomped across the body-strewn hall. Each footfall made the floor vibrate.

She had no idea what would have happened because without warning a thunderclap shook the whole building. At the top of the staircase, Diana rocked on her base. Brilliant flashes of light lit the darkness outside. Finally, what sounded like a series of sonic booms circled the building.

The noise was too much. She clapped her hands over her ears and shouted, "What happened?"

Seir glanced at the charging Allosaurus, and an unspoken message seemed to pass between them. "Zero's arrived. He just took down Fin's ward. They'll be going at it outside. If Zero wins, he'll destroy all of Fin's people. He can't kill you directly, but he has plenty of helpers who can. I have to get you out of here."

"But what about Al?" Desperately, she looked at him, holding his gaze. There was no message in his animal's eyes, so she let her gaze slide down to where she could now clearly see his human form within the beast.

"He wants you safe. Trust me." Seir grabbed her hand and dragged her toward the staircase. "He and the rest of the Eleven here are Fin's last stand. You don't want him distracted because he's worried about you, do you?"

"No, I—"

She didn't get to finish her sentence because he simply picked her up and flew up the staircase. He had to be flying, because no one could run that fast. They'd barely reached the top when another sonic boom shook the building. It was all too much for Diana. The huge statue teetered and fell.

Seir leaped out of the way, and then they both watched the statue crash down the stairs. He shook his head. "First the Astrodome and now Diana. Fin is death on famous landmarks."

Jenna finally found her voice. "Won't all the noise bring the police? Oh, and put me down. I feel silly." She wasn't surprised when he ignored her order.

Did she want the police? She didn't know. Zero might just decide that a bloodbath was fine by him and allow his army to kill all the humans they could. On the other hand, if humans showed up and Zero drew back his forces, then Al would be safe. The selfish part of her desperately wanted the latter, but she wasn't sure she was willing to risk the human population to find out which way Zero would go.

"Won't be any cops."

As he raced through exhibits, she wrapped her arms around his neck. With his heavy hood, the act didn't feel personal in any way.

"Zero took down Fin's ward, but you can bet he's put his own up. No one wants the attention of humans right now. Not during the battle." He stopped and set her on her feet.

She gawked. "This is a Japanese teahouse."

"One of the museum's period rooms. Stay here. Don't make any noise. If Al is standing when this is all over, he'll come for you. If not . . ." He shrugged. "Then I'll come for you."

For the first time in what seemed like centuries, Jenna had a moment to think. "Wait. You never told me whose side you're on."

His eyes gleamed from the depths of his hood. "I didn't, did I?" And then he was gone.

Al was drowning in human emotions, and someone needed to throw him a freaking lifejacket. Once he'd spotted Jenna, he'd shed his attackers and headed toward her. His beast's instinct didn't go beyond telling him that he needed to take her away from all those males. He opened his jaws and roared his intention.

He might be running on his soul's instincts, but that was as far as it went right now. His emotions churned out a million different messages. *Human* messages.

Seir had made things pretty simple when he'd jumped into Al's head. Allow him to take Jenna to a safer spot or let her remain here where some blood-crazed idiot could kill her.

Al wanted Jenna safe, but not with someone he didn't trust. Seir was a danger on a lot of different levels. Okay, okay, so the jerk was the kind of man women liked. Al didn't want Jenna liking Seir or anyone . . . except for him. *Mine.* The one word said it all.

By the time Seir had started up the stairs with Jenna, Al had decided to try to follow them. That was when the statue fell. He stared at the spot where it lay. No way would his Allosaurus get up those stairs.

What the hell should he do? He glanced behind him where a few of Eight's remaining werewolves were stalking him. He knew he was supposed to stay here until the battle was over. His beast thought it was just great that there were still living things left to kill.

But his humanity was too close to the surface right now. What he was feeling had nothing to do with his beast— fear for Jenna, fury at the man who'd taken her, and an emotion that felt an awful lot like . . . He had no name for the emotion. It wasn't a part of his soul's life. And it was demanding that he do something.

Al made his decision. He'd follow Seir in human form. He forced the emotions to the forefront, calling on his humanity to push his soul back into its cave.

"*No.*"

Fin had picked a lousy time to play big boss man. But no matter how angry Fin made him, Al had formed the habit of obedience to his leader over several lifetimes.

"Remain as you are, and finish the fight. You have to win this one on your own. I'm . . . busy."

Al climbed out of his own confused thoughts long enough to listen to what was happening outside. Above the noise of the battle in the hall, which was slowly winding down, he could hear bursts of sound like exploding transformers accompanied by a strange humming and buzzing outside. What the hell were Fin and Zero trying to do to each other?

Al glanced around. Most of those still standing were on his side. They didn't need him. Jenna did.

"We can't take a chance. I can't guarantee I'll be able to hold Zero off. If he gets past me, he'll wipe out every one of you. He's that powerful. Jenna will be unprotected, and he'll just get one of his people to kill her. You have to make sure every supporter of Eight is dead or disabled."

In his heart, Al believed Fin. But he didn't *want* to stay here, he didn't want to leave Jenna to Seir's questionable mercy, he didn't want to *obey*. And so he did what he'd always done. He raged against his leader even as he made a tough choice. He'd keep Jenna safe by helping get rid of every last bastard that Eight had recruited. But heaven help Seir if anything happened to her.

Al let that fury-inducing thought launch him back into battle. The hapless werewolves never knew what hit them. With the sounds of terrified howls echoing in his ears, Al almost didn't hear Fin's last words.

"Thank you."

And Al allowed himself a moment to ponder that. Something in his leader's voice made him uneasy. Then he forgot about Fin in his rush to finish off the fight so he could find Jenna.

Chapter Seventeen

If she lived through this, Jenna would have the mother of all tabloid titles—How I Survived by Hiding in a Japanese Teahouse While Vampires, Werewolves, Demons, and My Dinosaur Lover Battled to the Death.

Too bad she couldn't concentrate on the article to go with it. She could blame her lack of focus on one major worry. If Zero won, would either Al or she survive? The fact that she put Al before herself on her worry list said a lot about her feelings.

Maybe if she'd had this kind of crisis when she was twelve, she wouldn't have wasted her life worrying about things that didn't matter. Nothing like a life-or-death situation to straighten out your priorities. This put everything in perspective. It was all about keeping yourself and the person you cared about alive. Period. And it didn't matter how you managed it. She'd do whatever it took to make sure Al came back to her. Jenna wasn't fussy when it came to the man she loved.

Whoa! She backed up to examine the last word in that sentence. Was it true? Did she love Al? Jenna pulled out her mental checklist for love. Shared interests? Uh, did wanting to save humanity count? She'd give that a yes.

Deep emotional commitment? She hadn't thought that one out, but she couldn't imagine a world without him, a world where she didn't want to be with him. And God knew, if she wasn't running for her life after the last few days, then the whole commitment thing must be serious.

Sexual compatibility? Even in the midst of the present danger, the question almost made her smile. That was a big fat yes.

Willing to die for him? Until now, that question would never have popped onto her radar. In her pre-Eleven world, she'd never have imagined being asked to die for someone. But now, listening to the battle rage below, it seemed perfectly reasonable.

And she realized she'd already answered it. When she'd used Kione's sword on the werewolf attacking Al, she'd known her chances of being ripped to pieces were pretty good. It hadn't stopped her.

Suddenly, she froze. She didn't even breathe as she listened. While she'd been exploring the love question, everything had grown quiet. No sounds of battle, no light and sound show from outside the museum.

Who had won? Was Al okay? She wanted to race through the museum's exhibits screaming his name. She didn't. That could get her killed, and she wouldn't be any help to anyone if she was dead.

Seir had said he'd send Al to her. She didn't have a clue where Seir's real loyalties lay, or even if he had any, but she'd give him a reasonable amount of time to come through on his promise before she ventured from her hiding place.

It seemed like hours as the silence dragged on and on and on. A quick glance at her watch showed that ten minutes had passed. The watch lied.

Just when she'd decided that even the threat of death was better than this feeling of her nerves stretching until they were ready to snap like a rubber band, she heard something. A quiet footfall.

She stilled, not even breathing as she tried to reach beyond the teahouse with her senses. Al, Seir, or someone else?

"Jenna."

Her name was only a soft ripple of sound, but she knew the voice. She exhaled in relief so powerful she shook with it. "Here. I'm in here." She managed to make it to the teahouse's entrance, but her hand trembled as she gripped the doorframe.

Al stood in the shadows amidst the incongruous garden that made up this small piece of Japan. He wore his black duster. His hair was a wild tumble over his shoulders and around his face. He was danger, darkness, and all things delicious.

It was too dark to see if he had any injuries, but he was alive. *Alive.* The miracle of that made her want to cry. She didn't. There were other things, better things she could do with her time than crying.

"Wait for me inside." The shadows hid his expression.

At another time she would've gotten in his face about giving her orders, but she was still floating in a state of euphoria, so she let it pass. She retreated into the unlit room.

Unexpectedly, lights came on outside the teahouse. Then Jenna saw Al's silhouette step in front of the shoji screen that made up half of the front wall. With mouth suddenly dry, she watched him yank off his duster and drop it onto the ground. She could guess where this was going.

He ripped off his T-shirt with controlled violence before reaching for his pants. There was something darkly voyeuristic in watching an anonymous shadow getting naked. But that didn't keep her gaze from staying glued to the screen.

He rid himself of his jeans in one fluid motion. No underwear followed. She slid the tip of her tongue across her lower lip. Then he simply stood facing the screen. His form was all flowing lines delineating a strong muscular body. The translucent screen erased all the hard edges.

When he finally stepped from behind the screen and into clear view, it was like a pure adrenaline shot to every sexual cell in her body. And right now it felt like those were the only kinds of cells she had.

His skin gleamed golden in the soft light. When he shifted his weight, hard muscle moved beneath all that smooth skin. Jenna swallowed hard as she glided her gaze over the length of him, from powerful pecs, to ridged stomach, to muscled thighs and strong legs. That was the appetizer.

She moved on to the main course. His sacs hung heavy between his thighs. His cock was long, thick, and showing signs of intense interest.

Jenna watched him approach, a slow deliberate stalking. Raising her eyes to his, she gasped. His soul looked out of those eyes. The Allosaurus wasn't back in its cave. It might have allowed him to regain human form, but it was still in the driver's seat.

Something moved in her—hot, primitive, and oh, so savage. The terrible fear for his life she'd known a few moments ago rolled over to expose a surprising underbelly.

Jenna wanted what his soul was promising. His beast didn't have anything remotely civilized in mind. Well, good. Because she needed to unsheathe her claws and unleash all the violent emotion stored up inside.

He stepped into the teahouse, so close she could feel his excitement, the emotional high still thrumming through him. His scent was heat, hunger, and a primal craving.

Jenna got it. She might not have an ancient predator's soul, but she'd bet the hot need driving her was just as powerful as his. They'd faced death. Now they'd celebrate life.

And even though she realized she'd eventually have to ask for details about what had happened in the Great Stair Hall, she'd live in the moment for however long they had together.

He took the time to inspect the dim interior of the tea-

house, a predator's instinct when confronted with the un-
known. His sheer size made the room seem tiny. He was a
barbarian invading a place meant for serenity. She smiled.
Serenity wasn't at the top of her wish list right now. What
she needed only this sexy predator could give her.

And would you look at that gorgeous ass—compact, muscular, but nicely rounded. Supremely touchable.

"I like this. Everything here is of the earth. It's right."

She frowned. "I guess so." What did that have to do with
anything? Yes, she knew the teahouse was made of natural
materials. So? A green environment was not a top priority
when it came to sensual settings. She'd make love with him
in a plastic cube, and recycling be damned.

Suddenly he was in front of her, invading her space, backing her against the wall.

"My beast tasted blood tonight and liked it. I've experienced a lot of new emotions since I rose in this time, but my
basic urges are still those of my soul—to kill and to mate."

His heavy-lidded gaze touched her with erotic intent.
And if there were tendrils of dark challenge interwoven
with that intent, all the better.

Al reached out and wrapped his fingers in her hair. He
tugged, pulling her closer. "My soul doesn't want to go back
into its cave. It wants to mate with you deep within the
shadows cast by trees from *my* time, on the hard ground
from *my* time, with the storm winds of *my* time cooling the
fever after the coupling."

She ran her fingers over the side of his face, feeling beard
stubble along with the clenching of his jaw. This small sign
of tension upped her anticipation. This wouldn't be like the
last time. She sensed it. "And what does the human part of
you want?"

His smile was a flash of white in the darkness. "I want
to make love with you in this room surrounded by the

reminders of living things. The scent of cedar, pine, and bamboo connect me to my other life. It's enough." This time his smile was all hungry male. "You're *more* than enough."

Tightening his grip on her hair, he tipped her face up to meet his gaze. "Touch me." Then he covered her mouth with his.

She opened to him, and the heat of his lips, his tongue, ignited a fire that blazed across the millions of years separating her from his soul. His beast lived in his eyes, and she almost imagined it turning its massive head to stare at her. Recognition flared in its alien gaze. *Mate.*

Jenna would meet his soul on its own ground. She tangled her tongue with his, explored the heated wonder of his mouth, and knew she'd remember that taste of dominant male until she died, and beyond.

As he deepened the kiss, she pressed her body against his. She'd taken off her coat a while ago, but there were still too many layers of cloth between them. She wanted bare flesh against bare flesh.

Great minds thought alike, because when he finally broke the kiss he immediately slipped her sweater over her head. Her bra followed quickly. She helped him strip away her jeans and panties. This wouldn't be a slow, sensual mating. Their need was too great.

"Touch me." There was an urgency to his repeated words.

While he nibbled a path along her jaw, down her neck, and across the swell of her breast, she reached between them and clasped his cock.

His low guttural moan sounded appreciative.

Jenna clenched her thighs around the image of him driving deep into her body, filling her, *completing* her. These thoughts from someone who'd always claimed she didn't need *any* man to complete her. She'd been wrong.

"*Touch* me." He didn't sound too coherent.

What did he mean? She *was* touching him. But then she lost her train of thought as he touched *her*, and released something that had slumbered for a very long time. It uncurled and indulged in a long sensual stretch, and then it turned its gleaming gaze on all that hard, sexy, male flesh. It unsheathed long, sharp claws and opened jaws filled with pointy white teeth.

It approved. And in Al's soul it found a kindred spirit.

She flung back her head as he traced the curve of her breast with the tip of his tongue. Around and around, closer and closer to her nipple.

Jenna couldn't wait. With a sound that came scarily close to a growl, she grabbed his hair and yanked him closer. "You've been circling to land for too long. Put us down."

He did. Closing his lips over her nipple, he flicked it with his tongue and then nipped.

"Yes." She demonstrated her satisfaction by reaching behind him to rake her nails down his back and across his ass.

He grunted his surprise before laughing softly. "You challenge my beast."

"You betcha."

Something in the air changed, grew thicker, hotter, and she was almost panting to suck in enough air.

He clasped her butt cheeks in his big hands, digging his fingers into her flesh, kneading, massaging, as he scraped his teeth across her stomach. Only his tight grip kept her upright as he pressed her back against the wall.

"Spread your legs."

His hoarse command didn't meet with any resistance on her part. He kissed his way up to her other breast, closing his lips firmly around the nipple and sucking so hard that every nerve ending in her body screamed with the pleasure-pain of it.

Then he slipped his knee between her spread legs and pressed it tightly *there*. She widened her stance so his knee could press harder and harder and harder. And when he began to slide his knee back and forth over her flesh, she cried out with the intense sensation.

Closing her legs around his thigh, she rode him. He moved harder and faster, lifting her off her feet with the fury of his need. Her back bounced off the teahouse wall, and the wall shook.

"This. Building. Is. Too. Delicate." He forced out each word in time to the hard thrusts of his knee.

"But *I'm* not." She couldn't take any more. She was so wet, and the heaviness low in her belly shrieked for the only thing that could bring relief. Jenna climbed him, clawing at his shoulders as she wrapped her legs around his hips.

He wasn't a slow learner. Once again clasping her behind in his hands, he lifted her above his shaft and then paused.

Glancing between her legs, she could see his cock, so hard and ready that a bead of moisture glistened on its head. Still he didn't lower her onto him.

Okay, if he wanted to play hardball—she paused to admire her own phrasing—two could play that game. Taking one hand from his shoulder, she reached between them and scooped his balls into her palm. She rubbed the pad of her thumb over them—so hard, so tight—before dragging the tips of her nails across them again and again until they tightened even more, if that was possible. He gave up with a groan.

He lowered her until she could feel the tip of his head nudging her open. Nudging wasn't needed, because the door was wide open and the welcome mat already spread out.

Jenna slipped lower and lower, feeling that incredible stretching sensation as he filled more and more of her. She clenched around every inch, focused only on the friction of flesh against flesh, and knew neither of their patience could last much longer.

"My beast thinks this is crap." He tugged at her earlobe with his teeth.

"I agree." Her personal beast thought it was double crap.

Without warning, he forced her down on him at the same time he drove into her. The meeting was cataclysmic.

She was thrust back against the wall and the wall shuddered.

With a "dumbass flimsy wall," Al brought her to the floor in one smooth motion.

His long long hair swept over her as he thrust and withdrew over and over in a sexual dance that knew no past, present, or future. It just *was*. "Touch me, touch me, touch me." His harsh demand was a murmured mantra blending with the rhythm of sex.

Jenna cried out as the pressure, that almost-there feeling grew and grew. But it wasn't just a craving for her orgasm. She was reaching for something else, something she'd almost had last time.

She was beyond reason, beyond everything except sensation and an awareness of the shadowed face of her lover above her. Only the explosion of physical pleasure, the ultimate release mattered. And that other thing, whatever it was.

Faster and faster, she met his thrusts with her own, seeking something, something, something . . .

She found it in that ultimate moment of stillness as her body clenched tightly one final time and then exploded with pleasure. Her orgasm dragged a scream from her as she arched her back. Clasping his broad, sweat-sheened shoulder, she dug her nails into his flesh.

He followed her into his own climax, silently, with the same intensity he must have had when he mated those millions of years before. But his big body shook with the force of his release.

As pleasure ripped through her, Jenna couldn't control

herself. She bucked and rolled and thrashed. He met her with grim ferocity.

Something. There was something else, something too important to miss. She was dimly aware of them crashing into the shoji screen. But she didn't care.

Almost there. She reached into the center of her being and found the thing that craved him with more than a physical need. She stoked its flame, felt it join with her orgasm, and then reach out as far as it could stretch.

It touched him. Not his body, but the essence of who and what he was. For one shining moment, Jenna knew her soul had touched his soul. And nothing would ever be the same again.

The incredible spasms slowly faded, rippling away and disappearing into the larger pool of her heart. But the memory of that mind-blowing *touch* still thrummed through her.

He lay beside her, his breathing slowing, his silence filling up the dark room.

"What just happened?" Why was she whispering? Nothing warranting a reverential whisper had happened. Once she had her head back on straight, she'd think of a logical explanation for all of it.

"We ripped a hole in the damn screen." He sounded disgusted. "Who'd make a wall out of paper?"

She smiled. "It wasn't made with us in mind. It was made to contain serene thoughts."

He snorted his opinion of that. She noticed he'd neatly avoided her question. She'd let him get away with it for the moment, because she needed time to sort through her emotions.

Al stared at the damaged screen, refusing to meet her gaze. If she looked into his eyes, she'd see the turmoil there, the confusion and yes, fear.

What had happened between them was a lot scarier than the battle with Eight's recruits. *Their souls had touched.* And even though Jenna didn't know it, he'd taken a tiny part of her soul for his own. He knew it was wrong, a promise of something he couldn't deliver. Love had no place in his world of rage and hate.

To make things worse, he'd begged her to touch him. And he hadn't been talking about his body. Pure stupidity. When had things gotten so out of control? Al rolled away from her and climbed to his feet. He reached down to help her up.

She watched him, her expression shuttered, not asking her question again. But he knew damn well she was thinking about it, wondering why he'd avoided answering her, and deciding on the best way to drag an explanation from him.

He tried on a smile. It didn't work. Al couldn't make light of what had happened. "I've never made love before." Sex, yes. Lots of it. His Allosaurus had done its part to add to the dinosaur gene pool. But that didn't count, would never count after what Jenna and he had shared. "It was . . . great." Unbelievable, incredible, awesome. But superlatives made him uneasy, embarrassed him. He chose not to address the *soul-touching*.

Her smile said she saw right through his male discomfort with expressing emotion. "You'd make a lousy tabloid reporter. We wallow in overwrought feelings like pigs in a mud hole."

Al felt his tension ease a little. She wasn't pressing the issue. Time to change the topic completely. "No matter where the Eleven go, we destroy stuff." He shook his head ruefully. "Houston lost the Astrodome, and Philly will have to do some major repairs on the museum." He glanced at the screen. "I'll make sure I pay for that."

"What happened downstairs after I left?"

He watched worry darken her eyes. She looked like she was ready to take a blow.

"We won." He exhaled deeply. "Sort of. We killed the ones that could be killed. The ones who couldn't got away. Sara lost a few of her wolves. The vampires were too mean to die."

"Fin?"

He met her gaze. "I don't know. As soon as the job was done downstairs, I came looking for you. We'd better go now." He pulled on his clothes.

"What about Seir?" Jenna didn't object when he helped her into her bra and panties. She took care of her sweater and jeans herself. But he'd gotten to do the fun stuff.

"What about him?" He didn't want to talk about the other male. Jealousy didn't have to make sense. Al was seeing competition wherever he looked, a leftover from his life as a possessive, territorial predator. "He told me where you were. That's all I know."

She nodded, clearly distracted.

He paused before entering the hall and scanned the area for danger. Fin's cleanup crew—all nonhumans—were busy getting rid of any signs of the battle. But they could only do so much. The destroyed entrance, the fallen Diana, and the shoji screen would bear witness to the fact that *something* had happened.

"They put the paintings back."

"What?" He looked around for Fin and found him surrounded by Jude, Sara, Ty, Utah, and Tor. Jude's five supervamps were nearby, looking ready to go a few more rounds.

"Eight had taken seascapes from the museum and put them up around the hall."

Al shrugged. "Guess he gets off on looking at the ocean." He started toward Fin.

She nodded, but she was busy searching the room. "Do you know what happened to the Fae prince?"

Why was she so interested in other men? He took a deep breath. *Down boy.* She'd tried to save the guy, so naturally she'd want to know if he got out in one piece. "He disappeared. Guess he figured he didn't have a horse in this race, so there was no need to stay."

She seemed to accept his explanation. They joined the group around Fin, and for the first time he got a close look at his leader. He sucked in his breath. Fin wasn't bleeding, didn't have any obvious wounds, but his face and eyes . . .

Fin's face was all sharp angles, as if the skin had tightened over his bones or he'd been starved for a few weeks. And his eyes . . . They were deep purple, no silver at all, and looked sunken. There were dark circles under them.

"What happened to you?" Jenna's question was a whisper of horror.

Fin's eyes gave her his attention, but it looked as though he was having a tough time focusing. As much as he loved to hate his leader, seeing him like this didn't give Al the satisfaction he'd expected. It also didn't give him much confidence. The power of the Eleven originated with Fin.

"Zero and I fought to a draw." His smile looked exhausted. "Sure feels like I lost." He seemed to make an effort to pull himself together. "We don't do the physical stuff. Why bother? We can't destroy each other. So we battle psychically. The point is to drive the other one insane. An insane leader is no leader at all."

While Fin was talking, Al counted their little group. Then it hit him. "Where's Lio?"

They all turned their gazes toward Fin.

His words seemed drawn from a deep well of weariness. "Lio came into the museum in human form. He thought he could help. He came in the back entrance. Eight spotted him and materialized just long enough to take Lio with him. I'm sure Eight feels tonight was a roaring success."

"How do you know that's what happened to him?" Sara

seemed pretty subdued. But then she'd lost some of her pack.

Fin shrugged. "I touched his mind before Eight cut him off."

Al registered Jenna's small gasp beside him and felt the fury rolling off the two raptors. He asked the question. "Is Lio dead?"

Fin's gaze grew unfocused. "I don't think so. Not yet, anyway. I felt the death of Rap's body. I haven't felt that from Lio."

Left unsaid was that Zero was one up in their immortal chess game. Al curled his hands into fists and felt his beast's need to strike out at something, anything. He'd liked Lio.

Then he felt Jenna wrap her hand around his fist, and he slowly unclenched his fingers. She clasped his hand and held on tight. And no matter that his soul roared for revenge *now*, he turned from it to accept the warmth and calmness Jenna offered him. He was smart enough to realize that something momentous had just happened to him but too dumb to figure it out.

Jude, cold and contained as usual, bypassed all the roiling emotions to cut to the heart of the matter. "Where do we start looking? Oh, and I hope your cleanup crew is almost done because I can feel the ward weakening. In a little while this place will be crawling with humans."

The vampire's expression said that wouldn't be a totally bad thing. Al noted that the battle had left him extra pale. He probably needed to feed.

Fin seemed to ignore Jude's question. His eyes still burned purple. He turned to focus on Jenna. "You will return to the condo now. You will go to your room and not come out until you've figured out where the bell is. Since you're fated to ring it, I assume you're also fated to find it." He turned his attention back to Jude. "When *she* finds the bell, *we'll* find Eight." He closed his eyes for a moment. "And Lio."

Jenna stared at Fin. She looked disbelieving. "Go to my room? Don't come out?" She glanced at Al. "He's kidding, right?" Then she shook her head. "Never mind. Men with god complexes never have a sense of humor."

Al saw the expression in Fin's eyes and stepped in front of Jenna. "Don't touch her."

Fin grew still, as still as any vampire. Was he even breathing? Al wasn't sure. But the power and threat rolling off Fin pushed everyone around him back a step. Jenna tightened her grip on Al's hand. But when he tried to keep her behind him, she fought her way to his side.

"Look, I'm sorry, Fin. I didn't need to say that. This is a hard time for everyone. I'm sorry about Lio. I'm sorry for those dead people lying in the middle of the hall. I'll do the best I can to figure out which bell will send Eight home."

Al sensed a "but" coming.

"But *never* treat me like a child again."

Uh-oh. Al crouched, ready to defend her. Surprisingly, Fin smiled. And slowly the silver seeped back into his eyes until all the purple was gone.

"Fine. No more godlike orders." His voice was calm and sounded faintly amused. "But know this, Jenna Maloy, if you don't find the bell, Eight's next victim could be any one of us." He paused. "Even Al."

Al looked at Jenna just in time to see her face pale. The fear he saw in her eyes rocked him. Fear for *him*? No one had ever cared enough to be afraid for him. He didn't expect it. Sure, Fin and the others would mourn him, but it wouldn't be the same emotion he felt coming from her. He didn't know what to say, what to do, what to *feel*.

Fin watched her. His expression turned thoughtful. Then

he looked at Al. "Perhaps you should review our mating ceremony with her."

Al wanted to shove the words back down Fin's throat. Of all the things Fin could have said, this was the worst.

Chapter Eighteen

Jenna's stomach plunged ten stories and hit bottom hard. Fin had said the one thing guaranteed to squelch her complaints about his high-handedness. "Low blow."

Fin shrugged. "I use the weapons I have."

Al radiated anger on her behalf. "Cold bastard."

The cold bastard didn't even bother to look insulted. "Why don't you take Jenna home so she can get started?"

"I'll drive them." Jude looked bored now that the fighting had ended. He nodded at his five killing machines, and they rose to follow him.

Ty spoke for the first time. "Kelly is waiting in the SUV."

Frantic to see her sister, Jenna didn't look back as she left the museum. She would always feel conflicted when she thought of it—the horror of the killings, the wonder of their lovemaking.

Jude waited impatiently as she hugged Kelly. "I'm sorry you and Ty had to go through this because of me, sis." Jenna didn't try to hide her tears.

Kelly put her hands on both sides of her sister's face and stared at her. "Let me just look at you. You're alive. That's all that matters. Now go home. I'll wait for Ty."

Jenna nodded as tears clogged her throat. She understood a little better now why Kelly had kept so much from the family. She hadn't wanted to see the same fear in their eyes that Jenna had seen in Kelly's just before her sister realized that both of the people she loved had survived.

Everyone was mostly quiet on the drive to the condo. Jenna didn't know what everyone else was thinking, but her thoughts were a tangled mess—sorrow for Lio, fear for Al, her sister, and all of the Eleven, and worry over how she was going to find that damn bell. Jenna purposely refused to think about where any future relationship with Al would lead. She was already on emotional overload.

When they reached the condo, Jude got out to stand with them for a moment. "When you find Eight, call me, and we'll come."

"Appreciated your help tonight, but what's in it for you?" Al didn't do subtle.

Even splattered with blood, Jude managed to look wickedly sexy.

He smiled, showing just a little fang to make his point. "Self-interest." Jude shrugged. "Right now I'm in a good place, and I don't want any upsets in the status quo." His smile widened. "And I haven't gone on a good old-fashioned killing spree in about twenty years. You guys make being a vampire fun again."

Jenna blinked. "There's such a thing as too much honesty."

Al didn't seem to have a problem with Jude's answer.

Now that the fighting was over, reaction set in. Jenna could hardly put one foot in front of the other as she walked to the elevator.

Al made an impatient sound and simply scooped her into his arms. She didn't fight him. Wrapping her arms around his neck, she rested her head against his chest as he carried her to her room. His familiar scent, the beat of his heart, and his aura of strength calmed her, made her feel safe in a world where danger popped out of every shadow. Once inside, he pushed the door shut and set her down on the couch. He sat beside her.

"You're not leaving." She didn't even try to make it a question.

"No chance." He leaned back and closed his eyes. "You should get some sleep. Don't think you'll be doing much quality thinking until you do. The bell can wait for a few hours."

"But can Lio?" She tried not to think about what had happened to him.

Sorrow and anger etched lines in his face. "He's probably dead. He'd be too dangerous for Eight to keep alive." He opened his eyes and stared at the ceiling. "If he's dead, his soul will be lost unless Fin can get to him soon."

Jenna nodded. "Right. Get me some coffee and my laptop."

He retrieved her laptop from its case and set it on the coffee table in front of her. Then he left to get coffee. Alone for a few minutes, she tried to put her thoughts in some kind of order. No luck.

Okay, she'd concentrate on just one thing. Bells. She Googled "bells in Philadelphia." She'd done this before, but there was a chance she'd missed something the first time around.

The Liberty Bell popped up first. She thought about her editor's tip. Aliens were supposedly trying to steal the symbol of independence. But nothing resonated with her.

With no clues, she could only hope her instincts were in working order and that everything would click into place when she finally found *the* Bell.

According to Google, there were plenty of bells in Philly, but none of them shouted, "I'm the one."

She was staring into space trying to think of another search term she could use for bells when Al returned with coffee. He set the carafe and cups on the coffee table.

"Any luck?" He settled down next to her.

The heat and pressure of his thigh against hers provided a potent distraction. "None. What else could I look up besides bells in Philadelphia, famous bells, or bells that'll send immortal dirtbags home?"

He stirred at least a pound of sugar into his coffee while he thought. "Fin didn't give me much info about bells."

"They symbolize a lot of things. We ring them to celebrate. They toll when someone dies. Bells were rung to warn people or just to mark the time." She tapped her finger impatiently. "We don't use them much now."

"Where would you still find bells?"

"Churches . . . I'm not sure. I guess a few old town halls still have bell towers. Maybe some schools. Ships have bells, but I don't know anything about them."

"Fin is a nut about numbers. I bet the number eight fits into this somewhere."

Jenna stared at him. Duh? Could it be so simple? She put in the words "eight bells" and hit enter. Her fingers almost shook with her need for the right answer.

When the page came up, she skimmed the entries. "There. Ship's bells."

Al leaned closer to read with her. "Okay, so traditionally sailors rang eight bells to signal the end of the last watch."

Excitement pushed aside her exhaustion of a few minutes ago. "They also rang eight bells when a sailor died to symbolize the end of his earthly watch."

Suddenly, it all made sense. She turned to Al, triumph making her feel giddy. "Eight had paintings of the sea hung all around the Great Stair Hall. He had a seagull in a cage. He said he appreciated anything that came from the sea. The bell is on a ship." She flung her arms around his neck. "You're a genius."

"I try." Al didn't waste this opportunity. He covered her mouth with his to show her he was a genius in many, many ways.

Jenna was breathing hard by the time she returned to her laptop. "Where would the ship be?"

"Fin made us read tourist books about Philly. Penn's Landing has a few ships."

"Sounds like a good place to start." It didn't take her long to bring up images of the ships docked there. She pointed. "Maybe that one. A tall ship. It's docked farther north than the other ones, off by itself. It's seaworthy, and Eight would want a ship he could actually sail. We'll check that one first and then work south. Let's go."

He put his hand on her arm, and his touch seared a path directly to her memories of the teahouse. Was that the way it would always be? She shook her head. Stupid. There was no always with them. There was only now.

"First we tell Fin, and then we get our team members together." He frowned. "If Zero came out of their battle looking anything like Fin, then they're both pretty weak right now. We depend on Fin to take care of lots of details."

"Like warding areas so you can keep things private?" She remembered the Astrodome. "I guess he's also your weapon of last resort."

Al looked as if he hated to say something good about Fin. "No matter how many times I butt heads with him, I never doubt his power to destroy at will."

Jenna watched Al stand and wander over to the window. She gave him his moment to do some mental messaging. It must be neat to just open your mind's airwaves and hit send. The phone would've been just as quick, but then she didn't live in his world, so her thinking was more prosaic. Just another reminder of how different they were. The thought made her sad.

Al walked back to the couch. "Fin's calling the team together. We'll meet in the media room."

She stood. Al was only a few inches away, but it might as well have been a million miles. He was focused on death and destruction. She was focused on . . . him. Jenna reached out to sweep a few strands of his hair away from his face. "The way things are going, you may never braid your hair again."

"Maybe not." He smiled, that magic lifting of his sexy lips that turned her heart into Silly Putty. "But if keeping it loose means I'll be hunting *you*, then it's worth it."

His smile slowly faded, and an emotion she couldn't identify flashed in his eyes and was gone.

"I need a quick shower and a change of clothes." It would only take her a few minutes and would give her a chance to regain her emotional center.

Heat flared in his gaze. "Can I come too?"

"No." She smiled to soften her rejection. "It wouldn't be a quick shower then."

Her shower was an oasis in a desert storm of roiling emotions. She didn't think about Al. She didn't think about ringing the bell. She didn't think about returning to Houston. Alone. She turned off everything in her head and gave herself over to lots of white noise and hot water.

When Jenna came out of the bathroom trailing the scent of vanilla and heat, Al felt like he was seeing her for the first time. It was finally settling in that she was his mate.

But knowing she was his mate didn't change anything. Al would still have to hunt Zero and the rest of the immortals. And even if she chose to stay with Kelly, once humanity was safe Jenna would head back to Houston and her human family.

And he'd let her go . . .

Because even if he told her he . . . What was the human word? Loved her? A foreign concept. But "mate" didn't quite fit either. His emotions were all wrapped around this human woman with the long dark hair and big blue eyes. He needed a foreign concept to describe his feelings. Anyway, even if he told her that he loved her, she'd probably run screaming into the night when she found out what she'd have to do to claim him.

Al frowned. This reminded him that Fin of the Big Mouth had told him to explain everything to her. Maybe she'd forget.

"Aren't you going to change?" She walked toward him.

She was near enough now for him to touch, to drag down onto the couch. He wanted to rip the clothes from her body, to bury himself deep inside her, and to buy forgetfulness for a short while.

"No, I'll only get bloody again. Let's get moving." Al didn't care if he sounded impatient. He had to get out of here before temptation floated him right back to that couch.

Jenna cast him a confused glance, but she followed him down to the media room. They were the first ones there. Damn. He didn't need to be alone with her now. She dropped onto a recliner and crossed her legs. Their long length in jeans and boots reminded him of what those legs had felt like wrapped around his body as . . . He exhaled sharply. The others had better hurry.

"Looks like we have a few minutes to kill, so why don't you review the mating ceremony with me." She looked away. "I don't know why Fin thought it was so important for me to know about it."

"Yeah, Fin is hard to figure sometimes." And as much as he should be celebrating her casual attitude, a small *human* part of him hurt.

She glanced back at him, and sadness flickered in her gaze. But then she smiled. "Hey, when you guys have finished kicking immortal butts, I can use all the info I've collected to write the article of my life."

Her job. He'd forgotten about that. "You're losing money every day you're here, aren't you?"

She shrugged. "I'll be okay. I won't be staying much

longer. Besides, I have to track down the aliens that are trying to steal the Liberty Bell."

He knew his expression was blank. The only words that
had registered were "I won't be staying much longer."
Knowing she would be going home was tough, but hearing her say it clenched his stomach into a tight knot.

"Never mind." She waved a hand at him. "So get on
with the review."

Now would be a good time for you to get your ass in here, Fin.
Al sent out a desperate mental SOS.

Fin slammed his mental door closed in Al's face.

Al didn't sit down. He couldn't. He paced restlessly in
front of the bank of windows overlooking Rittenhouse
Square. Why did she freaking have to know this? And why
did *he* have to be the one to tell her?

He stopped in midstride. Wait. She'd said "review." Fin
had said "review." That meant. Horror washed over him.
"You already know about the ceremony."

"Sure. Fin told me. But some of the details have slipped
my mind."

Al closed his eyes, exhaled deeply, and then opened
them again. He'd find Fin right now and destroy his ma-
nipulating ass if he wasn't so relieved. He wouldn't have to
explain. "I'm sure Fin told you the important parts."

"I'm not so sure. For example, how do you know when
you've found your mate?"

"We just do." Al hadn't known he could feel like this—
a roller-coaster ride of emotional highs and lows. A lust
that almost brought him to his knees. A need that gripped
his heart and squeezed until he couldn't think straight. Oh,
yeah, he *knew*.

She raised one brow. "You just do? Any feelings involved here?"

"Probably. You'll have to ask Ty."

"Okay, so what we have so far is that you bond emotionally with a female. You both understand that the bonding is for life. I sort of understand about walking into the heart of your beast, seeing your past, taking a piece of your soul, and becoming immortal."

If Al hadn't seen her white-knuckled grip on the arms of the chair, he would have thought she was cool and detached.

"Fin thinks this can be dangerous for the woman." She waited for his input.

"Fin didn't give a lot of specifics when he first told us about the ceremony, but I got a feeling that the trip into our pasts wouldn't be a safe one." He glanced away.

She watched him, wide-eyed. "Guess the woman would have to really love you."

"Yeah."

The silence stretched on until it became painful.

"We touched souls when we made love in the teahouse, didn't we?"

Al nodded. He decided now wasn't a good time to tell her he'd stolen a small part of her soul for his own. She'd never miss it, and he would treasure it always.

Finally, she sighed. "You were something else before your soul became dinosaur, because dinosaurs didn't have those kinds of mating rituals. Any ideas?"

He waited for the pain, the rolling fog that usually accompanied thoughts of Fin and things he didn't understand. This time there was nothing.

"No."

"And Fin won't tell you."

"No."

He'd never know what she would have said next because Fin strode into the room.

Fin didn't look at either of them. He walked over to the large monitor and fiddled with the computer. "I took some photos of the ships at Penn's Landing off the Web."

He still avoided their gazes. If Al didn't know better, he'd think Fin was ashamed. But that was assigning human emotions to a man who had none. Al thought about Rap's death and Fin's reaction. Okay, so once in a while an emotion popped up, but not often.

"The others are on their way up. As soon as everyone's here, we'll start." Fin finally looked at them. His silver eyes gave nothing away.

Utah and Tor rushed in, raptor eyes glittering with eagerness. Q and Gig followed close behind. Shen slipped in at the end. They all sat down, but the nervous energy in the room was ricocheting off the walls.

"I only want to explain this once. Here's the rundown on why you guys were chosen. Al will keep Jenna safe. Q will supply air support if needed. Utah and Tor deserve revenge for their brother—"

Jenna couldn't keep quiet. "Revenge? Not justice?" Hey, she was a splitting-hairs kind of woman.

Fin's smile didn't touch his eyes. "It's always about revenge. Humans try to pretty it up with different words, but we know it's always about getting even."

Whenever she started to think these guys were civilized, they'd do or say something to remind her they were still ancient predators. With them, violence happened. Did that bother her? Not so much anymore.

Fin continued. "Shen will check out the situation before the attack. Ty wanted to go, but I decided that Kelly had worried enough for one night. He doesn't like lying to her, so I told Kelly that Al and Jenna were just going out to search for more bells. Then I ordered Ty to keep his mouth shut. She'll hate me, but lots of people hate me. You get used to it." He shrugged.."

Something in his eyes made Jenna wonder how true that was.

He glanced at Jenna. "But in the end it's up to you. If you

want her to know the truth, you can talk to her before we leave."

Time to make a tough decision. She wanted to see Kelly, to tell her the truth, to tell her she loved her. But then Kelly would insist on coming or try to keep Jenna from leaving. Jenna would allow neither to happen. *God, I'm sorry, sis.* She shook her head. "No, I'm okay."

"What about Gig?" Tor sounded as though he wasn't sure about including Gig.

Jenna wasn't sure either. She hadn't met Gig, and she wasn't sure she wanted to now. About six feet six, he wore torn jeans, scuffed boots, and a ratty old jacket with no shirt underneath. He had a wild mane of dark hair, and his tan contrasted with his eerily pale eyes. He had an insane gleam in those scary eyes.

But she was nothing if not polite. "I never got the chance to meet you." She didn't offer her hand because she was afraid he'd bite it off. "I saw a skeleton of a Giganoto-saurus. Impressive size."

"Everywhere, babe, everywhere." He didn't smile when he said it. "Al needs to keep your hot little ass away from me. You make me hungry."

The rumbling that came from Al's throat couldn't be mistaken for anything but a challenge.

Gig answered him in kind.

Oh, shit. "Starve then. You're a prehistoric punk, and I'll put my 'hot little ass' wherever I want." Why didn't Fin step in? She chanced a quick glance in his direction. He looked amused.

If ever a dinosaur looked surprised, it was Gig. Then he flung back his head and laughed. For the first time, Jenna realized how gorgeous he really was under all that atti-tude.

"Sweetheart, you ever get tired of your puny little Al-losaurus, come play with the big boys."

Al was broadcasting so much fury that Jenna felt her head would explode.

Fin finally intervened. "I chose Gig because he's crazy. And a fifty-foot-long, eight-ton carnivore patrolling the dock area will discourage Eight's recruits from trying to escape."

Jenna rushed in to take the focus off Gig. "What does Shen do?"

Fin shrugged. "He sneaks."

Why couldn't Fin answer a freaking question with a straight answer? He was a reporter's nightmare. She'd opened her mouth to ask for specifics, but Fin didn't give her the chance.

He hit a computer key and the photo of a ship appeared on the screen. "This is the *Serafina*. She's a one-hundred-seventy-seven-foot-long, three-masted barkentine. A tall ship. Don't ask me what that means, because it isn't important. The bell should be in the back next to the steering wheel." He cast his gaze around the group. "And yes, I know the front and back of boats have specific names, but front and back works for me."

"Are we sure this is the right ship?" Q winked at Jenna when she glanced his way.

Thank God, Al was still glaring at Gig.

"I did a little research on the *Serafina*. The ship recently changed hands. I couldn't find any info on the new owner, and the old owner conveniently died right after the sale. Sounds suspicious to me." Fin hit another key. "But just in case, here are our other two possibilities."

Jenna let him drone on, because her gut was telling her that the *Serafina* was Eight's ship. She tuned in again when he moved onto specific plans.

"Gig, you know your job. Al, you'll go on board first with Jenna behind you. The deck's long enough for you, but you won't be able to move freely. Too much stuff to get in your way, and you're not exactly light on your feet. So go as far as you can, and then let Utah and Tor take over. They can leap and move fast. Q will take to the air and eliminate anyone who gets past the raptors."

Fin must've seen Al opening his mouth to object. "You will all follow my orders. And no one except for Jenna will be in human form on that ship. Remember Lio."

There was a somber silence. Fin exhaled wearily. "Try to find out what Eight did with him before you send the bastard away for a few million more years. And remember, your sole goal is to get Jenna to that bell. Eight can't touch her, but his recruits sure can."

"What about you?" For someone with such a crappy attitude, Gig sounded strangely respectful with Fin.

Jenna thought about that. Or maybe Al was the strange one, the only one who harbored so much rage against his leader.

"I'll be nearby, but I won't be much help. I have to recharge the old batteries. Zero and I cancelled each other out. If it's any comfort, he shouldn't be a factor in this either."

"No wards?" Al sounded worried.

"It's late." Fin's eyes hardened. "If you're lucky, everyone will be tucked up in their beds and far away from the *Serafina*. If they're not?" He shrugged. "Gig is an equal opportunity enforcer. Collateral damage *will* happen."

Jenna didn't want to analyze Fin's scary index. She had lots of other things to worry about. Like would Al and she come out the other end in one piece? *Please let everyone survive, and let me do this right.* She didn't give a damn if Kelly had kicked Nine's butt with more panache, she just wanted to get rid of Eight forever.

They all headed for the condo door. Before she could take a step to follow, Al took her hand and pulled her against his side. He leaned close to her ear.

"I will let no one hurt you. If I have to tear that ship apart, you *will* be kept safe. Trust and believe me." He met her gaze. "Because . . ."

Tell me. He had to finish that sentence. She willed him to keep talking. He didn't. He didn't say anything all the way down in the elevator, and his silence continued into the SUV. Rats.

Tension thrummed through her as they parked about a block from Penn's Landing. She turned to Fin. "Maybe you and Zero aren't in great shape, but won't Eight be able to put up wards to keep us off the ship?"

Fin shrugged. "Maybe. But he put up his own wards at the museum, so he won't be operating at full psychic strength for a few hours either. I'm not completely helpless. I can manage his wards if I have to." He glanced at the others. "Okay, we separate here. I don't want everyone converging on the ship as a mob. Once you're close to the *Serafina*, Shen will go onto the ship and take a look around, make sure Eight is there." His silver eyes shone in the darkness. "And keep your eyes open for Lio."

Jenna could feel the anger and sadness from the others. "Will Jude and his men be helping?"

Fin's smile flashed white. "They'll be in the wind, like me." And then he was gone.

The others faded away until it was just Al and her. She stayed behind him as he skulked through the shadows. This would probably be exciting if possible death didn't wait at the end.

Suddenly, he stopped, turned, and put his finger to his lips. Then they waited. It seemed as though they stood like that for an hour before something happened. Something turned out to be a six-foot-long snake. It slithered out of the darkness, and she had to clap a hand over her mouth to keep from screaming.

"It's just Shen." Al's urgent whisper calmed her. Sort of.

Unblinking, she watched as Shen took his human form. He was naked, but she was too shocked to notice the details. "Why didn't Fin warn me? Why didn't *you* warn me?" She punched Al in the arm.

"I didn't think of it. And Fin enjoys being cryptic. He doesn't give straight answers unless it suits him. You must have noticed." He focused on Shen. "Is this the ship?"

Shen's eyes gleamed black in the dark. He shivered in the cold. "Yeah. This is it. Eight's down in the cabin with some of his recruits." He was silent for a moment. "Lio's in the water beside the ship. In his beast's form. He's not moving. Probably still alive. I don't think even Eight could kill Lio unless he was in human form. I guess Eight put some kind of whammy on him."

"Whammy? Great grasp of magical terms, Shen." Al's heart didn't seem to be in his teasing. "I can't see Eight keeping Lio around for long. Come morning, people would tend to notice an eighty-foot-long sea creature that definitely isn't a whale."

"Lio's still alive? We have to help him." Something lightened in Jenna just knowing he wasn't dead.

"We need Fin." Al sounded reluctant to admit that. "I don't know how we'll pull this off without involving humans. Even at this time of night, there're some around. We need to cloak our presence. And whatever Eight did to Lio, none of us can undo."

"But I can." The voice was low, husky, and carried its special brand of sexual compulsion.

"Kione?" She peered into the darkness.

The dark fairy didn't so much step out of the night as coalesce from the blackness around him. He was dark within dark.

Jenna felt Al tense and knew he was ready to free his soul

if needed. Shen didn't look worried. She didn't know what kind of snake Shen was, but she'd bet it wasn't a garden variety.

"How can you help, and why would you bother?" Al the eternally suspicious.

Kione's soft laughter was more of a deadly threat than an expression of amusement. "I can make the humans you worry about stay away from the ship, and I can break whatever spell Eight is using on your comrade. Why would I do this?" He shrugged. "I owe the woman for my freedom."

Jenna found that some of Al's suspicion had rubbed off on her. "It's probably the same spell Eight used on you. If you couldn't break it then, how do you expect to do it now?" Oh, what the hey, may as well annoy him completely by asking her second question. "And if you're a Fae prince of the Unseelie Court, why would you feel obligated to repay a human?"

Kione turned the complete focus of his considerable attention on her. Jenna felt a splash of lust wash over her. It was so strong that she wanted to leap on and devour . . . anyone, please, *anyone*. Al was closest. She cast a starving glance his way. Wait, wasn't this entire sexual obsession thing supposed to center only on Kione? Jenna was confused.

"Whatever you're doing, stop it now." Al put a possessive arm across her shoulders.

"Yeah, I'm feeling it too." Shen grinned. "Forget Eight. I need a woman." He studied the Fae prince thoughtfully. "Or not."

Kione made an impatient sound. His dark cloak still hid his body, and his dark hair still framed that unearthly beautiful face. "I am doing nothing. What you feel is what anyone near me always feels. I do not control it. If I focus on one person only, he or she feels it more strongly, but beyond that . . ." He shrugged. "It is your problem to solve. I can do nothing to 'stop it.'"

He seemed to gather himself together. "Unseelie prince or not, I pay back what I owe others. And I owe both the woman and Eight."

Kione's smile flashed in the darkness, and Jenna almost groaned with her need to toss Al to the ground and crawl all over him.

"The woman's name is Jenna." Al sounded calmer. "I'm Al, and this is Shen."

The fairy nodded. "If I say any of your names aloud, it will only make your response more . . . intense." He turned to Jenna to answer her question. "I could not break Eight's spell on me because he caught me by surprise. Once he immobilized me, I was helpless. But this time I'm free and prepared." The word "prepared" sounded ominous coming from Kione's mouth.

Al looked thoughtful. "Okay, do what you can. Lio is beside the ship. See if you can free him." But he wasn't about to abandon his suspicion completely. "Try to harm us and you'll regret it."

Kione hissed his anger. "Do not threaten me. You cannot destroy me, but I can destroy you. Do not forget that."

It was now Al's turn to smile. "Get over yourself, prince. Maybe you could destroy me in my human form, but if you get past me, something bigger and badder will be waiting to take you on. Fin makes Eight look like a kitten."

Uh-oh. Testosterone overload. Jenna needed to redirect their energies. "Look, Kione, ignore Al. He's under lots of pressure. We all are. We appreciate your help." She ignored Al's scowl. "Now, shouldn't we be getting on with things?"

Al simmered for a few moments before mentally concentrating on filling Fin in on what had happened. "I've given Fin Shen's report and told him about our new *ally.*" He made the word "ally" sound like Jack the Ripper had joined forces with them.

Jenna couldn't help it. She hoped a small part of Al's anger was prompted by jealousy. Yes, she was reverting to cavewoman mentality. Al still seemed to be chatting with Fin. But he finally signed off and focused on them. "We move in now. Fin says he'll do what he can to help."

She barely had time to draw in a deep breath of courage before Al freed his soul. He loomed above her in the darkness, a forty-foot-long, sixteen-foot-high prehistoric monster with four-inch serrated teeth and short arms with clawed, three-fingered hands. It was too dark for her to see the human form within the beast. Jenna took only a moment to appreciate the total weirdness of standing next to an ancient predator while she watched cars whiz across the nearby Benjamin Franklin Bridge.

When she glanced around, Shen was gone. He was probably back in snake form slithering toward the ship.

A million uncertainties flashed through her mind at warp speed. They were near Market Street. No matter how late it was, cars still rolled along. What were the chances that no one would notice a battle between the Earth's greatest predators and an immortal who probably wouldn't hesitate to launch a sound-and-light show?

They had a big open parking lot to cross. The few cars there must belong to Eight's people. But no one could convince her that Eight didn't know they were coming. He could just zap himself out of there as he'd done at the museum.

Fin was an uncertainty. Did he have the strength to take down any ward Eight managed to throw up? Could he cloak his people until they at least got to the ship?

And then there was their very own Unseelie prince. He was the true wild card.

Jenna traded a brief glance—very brief—with the Fae prince. "Time to take this show on the road."

Chapter Nineteen

Jenna followed blindly behind Al, running to keep up with his giant stride. She couldn't see past his huge body, and even though she knew the raptors must be close behind them, she couldn't see or hear them. She resisted the urge to glance back to make sure everyone was still there.

Al didn't bother trying to be sneaky as he strode toward the ramp leading onto the ship. Not that anything as big as his Allosaurus could "sneak" anywhere. The ground vibrated with each step.

And in the eternity it took to cross the parking lot, Jenna thought of many things—how easy it would be for someone to kill her once she emerged from Al's shadow, what she'd regret most if she died, what she'd regret most if *he* died.

It all came down to one truth. She loved him and she should have told him so. Too late now. The truth would only distract him at a bad time. But afterward, she'd tell him. And there *would* be an afterward. She'd make it happen.

Maybe he'd just look at her blankly when she told him. Then she'd smile a lot as she caught the first flight back to Houston. And she'd keep smiling because, well, life went on. Didn't it?

Jenna felt when Al picked up his pace. The ground vibrated faster. Someone somewhere must be cloaking them, because Eight and his cronies should have been on deck by now firing away. Nonhumans weren't dumb. They'd have guns. And where were the lookouts?

Al took the ramp in one stride. Which was a good thing, because it probably would have crumpled under his weight if he'd spent any more time on it.

On each side of the ramp, she spotted the bodies of several werewolves. Guess Eight did have lookouts. Shen's work? He must be one lethal snake.

And then violence exploded. Al was already moving along the deck toward the bell when Eight and the rest of his recruits erupted from below. The immortal didn't target Al or her. He couldn't touch Jenna, and he knew from the museum that it'd be tough to bring down Al.

So as his assorted vampires, werewolves, demons, and unidentified nonhuman entities tried to get to her, Eight took aim at the raptors.

But Utah and Tor were determined moving targets. They leaped past Al and raced in different directions. Eight's power blasts left a fiery trail of destruction but didn't quite catch up with either raptor.

Al moved his massive body forward while fighting to protect Jenna. His tail swept charging werewolves aside at the same time he ripped a vampire into bloody bits.

Jenna was officially freaked. She'd never thought it was possible to be this scared and still be alive. When a demon took flight, beating its leathery wings madly as it gained height and then plunging toward her, she shrieked. Al was involved with other attackers. He wouldn't be able to help her.

Then Jenna heard a strange cry that jerked her attention away from the demon. Before she could even wonder what it was, a huge shape plummeted from the dark sky. With a wingspan of what had to be close to forty feet and a huge head ending in a long, long beak, she didn't have to see the human form within the beast to know that Q had arrived. He skewered the demon and flung it far out into the Delaware River. The demon would take a few minutes to recover, precious minutes that would get her closer to the bell.

Suddenly, something rose from the water beside the boat. Something so horrific that everyone paused to stare. The whole of the creature was too amazing to take in all at once.

Jenna felt as if her heart was about to explode from her chest, her breaths came in panting gulps. *Oh. My. God.*

It was almost half as long as the ship. Huge head. Teeth that had to be eight inches long. It lunged after the demon and clamped those enormous teeth onto him. Then it dragged the demon beneath the now-red-tinged water.

Kione had done his job. Lio was one pissed off Liopleurodon. He'd make sure that any enemies who dropped into the water wouldn't rejoin the fight.

Then the scene on deck became a maelstrom of twisting bodies and bloody death.

At some point Eight climbed the middle mast. He balanced high above them and shouted his defiance. "You will *not* take my ship."

He accompanied his prediction by sending streamers of fire across the surface of the water, forcing Lio farther out into the river. Then he caught one of the raptors with a blast of energy that spiraled him off the ship and all the way across the parking lot. A bunch of demons crowded around the ramp to make sure he didn't get back on the ship.

Uh-oh. Al had stopped moving. He was too big to go any farther without damaging the ship so much that she wouldn't be able to reach the bell.

Jenna was able to crawl around him while he blocked as much of the area as he could and dealt out destruction

Too bad several werewolves were near the bell. Checkmate. What the hell would she do now? Al didn't want her to try for it. She could feel his fear for her pounding against her will. But she didn't have a choice. She had to go on.

Jenna didn't even see the werewolf that flattened her. All she knew was that suddenly she was looking up into a pair of slathering jaws filled with huge teeth.

She heard Al's crazed roar a second before he lunged forward. There was a snapping sound at the same time that the wolf disappeared from sight. Its blood sprayed her face, her hair, and her coat just as she realized what the snapping sound had been.

Looking up, she screamed as the nearest mast crashed to the deck. It missed her, it missed Al, and that's all that mattered. She rolled onto her stomach and crawled toward the bell as Al fought nightmare creatures above her.

Sobbing, she was finally there. Dragging herself to her feet she reached for the rope attached to the bell's clapper.

That's when she saw Utah. He'd leaped past Eight's remaining recruits to reach her. Now as she watched, his soul faded and he stood there in his human form. He looked as shocked as she did.

"I don't know . . ." He raked shaking fingers through his blond hair, returning its spikes to their former glory. "Rap died as a human. What I'm feeling is human emotion." His blue eyes blazed with sorrow and hate. "I can't hold it all in." He thumped his chest with his fist. "I need to witness justice for him as a man."

Drawing his lips away from his teeth, he glared up to where Eight stared down at them. "The prick doesn't have a clue what's about to happen." He lowered his gaze to her. "Do it. Now."

"No. *You* do it." Where the hell had that come from? But even as she said it, she knew it was the right thing to do. She didn't need to be Kickbutt Heroine of the Universe. Even though she'd been in Fin's vision, she wasn't the important part of the equation, the bell was. This moment belonged to Rap's brothers.

Eagerness glittered in Utah's blue eyes. "You sure?"

Eight must have realized that something suspicious was going on because he suddenly loosed a thunderous blast of energy. It hit right behind Jenna and Utah. She glanced back in time to see Al stagger and fall.

"No!" She grabbed Utah. "Ring the damn bell. Eight times." And then she scrambled back to Al.

Confused, Al had returned to human form. He didn't even notice as Tor, still a raptor, leaped over him so he could protect Utah as he rang the bell.

Jenna knelt beside him, leaning over to shield him from Eight. The immortal could kill Al while he was in human form, but he couldn't do a damn thing to her directly.

Eight shouted his triumph from above them, where he still clung to one of the two remaining masts. "You're beaten. You're all beaten. There are more of my workers left than yours. Where's your great and mighty leader Fin? Where're your reinforcements? All I see are two of the Eleven in human form, one stupid human, and one raptor. Oh, and I guess you can count the big dumb monster in the parking lot. He doesn't matter though, because I'm not going back to shore. I'll create a new mast, and then I'm sailing this ship out of here."

Eight glanced around. "I suppose the Fae prince is skulking around somewhere, and I really wanted to keep the Liopleurodon. What a magnificent sea creature. But I suppose one doesn't always get what one wants in life." He started to climb down from his perch.

Awareness returned to Al's eyes. They blazed into hers. What she read there made her weak. Then she heard the bell.

Utah yanked on the rope attached to the clapper, and with each ring he shouted, "This is for Rap."

By the third ring, Eight realized what was happening. But it was too late; he'd begun to shimmer. He screamed his fury. "No! What the fuck are you doing? You can't send me back. I have to sail my ship into the Atlantic. I've waited millions of years to ride the fucking waves."

The shimmer grew brighter and brighter. Eight slid down the rest of the mast and tried to cover his ears with his hands. Rocking back and forth he shouted, "No, no, no!"

The bell rang for the sixth time, and Eight began to break into millions of sparkling bits. Faster and faster he disintegrated until only his mouth remained.

And at the end, he stopped screaming. "Free my seagull," were his last words.

As the bell rang for the eighth time, the millions of sparkling pieces of what had been Eight spiraled into a shining ball of light and disappeared.

The shocked silence lasted only until Eight's recruits realized they were on their own. They charged down the ramp—no one was willing to take a chance with Lio—and were met by Gig, Jude, and his five vampires. The ones who tried to fly away found Q waiting for them.

Jenna didn't watch. She could only stare at Al. Until she felt a presence above her. She looked up.

Kione stared down at them. "I've repaid my debt, woman."

"Thanks. We don't know anything about you. Any little insights you want to leave with us?" What a stupid question, but Jenna was at the dumb-question stage of exhaustion.

Without answering, he flung his cloak wide. Jenna gasped, and Al cursed. Kione wore no shirt, and every inch of exposed skin was covered with angry red welts that seemed to pulse with a life of their own.

"What the hell happened to you?" Al's sympathy was real.

Kione didn't answer his question. He stared into the darkness. "A reminder that power always has its price. Tell that to your leader." And then he was gone.

The proof of Kione's suffering along with every other horrible thing she'd witnessed left Jenna feeling numb. Quiet had settled over the dock. Al rose and helped Jenna to her feet. Then they picked their way past the carnage and destruction. But she stopped Al before they got off the ship.

"The seagull."

Al nodded and disappeared belowdecks. A minute later he returned with the seagull's cage. He put the cage on the deck and opened it. The seagull stepped out, glanced around, and then took flight. They watched it disappear into the darkness.

"He loved the bird. Do you think that counted? I mean, after all the evil he committed?" She pushed a strand of her hair away from her face and tried not to think about the blood coating it.

Now that her life wasn't hanging in the balance, Jenna realized the wind blowing in off the Delaware was damn cold. She pulled up her collar and stuck her hands into her pocket.

Al shrugged. "I guess every little bit counts. The sea was his weakness. If he wasn't so determined to save this ship, if he'd just disappeared when we attacked, he wouldn't be heading home right now." He guided her off the ship.

They'd only taken a few steps when Utah and Tor caught up with them.

"Thank you."

Jenna didn't know whether Utah or Tor had spoken, but it didn't matter. There were no shadows in their eyes now. And for that she was glad. "Wherever he is, I know that Rap is cheering you tonight."

Al wrapped his arm around her waist and guided her

away from the parking lot and what was happening there. When he reached a quiet spot where no one could see them, he stopped.

"I learned something tonight. When I saw that wolf on top of you and knew you might die, I packed a lot of regrets into a few seconds."

Jenna tried not to hold her breath.

He trailed his fingers along her jaw, leaving behind a path of warmth and hope. "I regretted spending so much time being mad at Fin and the whole world that I didn't leave room for other feelings."

"Uh-huh. Feelings." *What feelings?*

"I didn't want to like you. You were part of my punishment, someone who was keeping me from my nightly rampages. The ones when I pretended that every demon, every vampire, every werewolf I destroyed was really Fin."

"You hate him that much? Why?" Jenna wasn't comfortable with that side of Al; but love was nothing if not flexible. She wasn't perfect either, and that was okay.

Something broke free inside her. She would never be the best at anything, but she could be damn good at something. And that something would be loving Al, if he'd let her.

Al shrugged. "I've never understood why. Maybe Fin knows, but he's not the sharing kind. But we're not talking about Fin here."

All movement seemed to stop, even her breathing, as Jenna waited.

"For a while my human emotions were too new for me to recognize them. I understand them now." He leaned forward, touching his lips to hers, murmuring his message. "I love you, Jenna Maloy. What you do with that love is up to you, but it's there for the taking."

"Consider it taken, Al Endeka. I love you, and I want to walk into the heart of your beast."

Al stepped back as though giving her room to breathe, to

run away if she chose. "You'll be immortal. We'll be bonded forever, however long that might be. Think about your family. Either you or Kelly will eventually have to explain things to them. How will they feel?" He took a deep breath. "And claiming a piece of my soul can be a one-way trip to insanity. At least that's what Fin said." He seemed hesitant to let her make the journey.

"It's my choice, and I choose to take the chance. I love you way too much to let a hike through your past stop me. And my family only wants Kelly and me to be happy. When the time comes, they'll accept our choices."

Happiness turned his hazel eyes luminous. "Ty and Kelly went through an ancient ceremony." His expression grew puzzled. "I don't know where the ceremony came from, but it felt right at the time. Something else that Fin didn't explain."

Jenna wrapped her arms around his waist and rested her head against his chest. "We don't need a ceremony that you can't remember. We don't need a lot of people watching." She looked up at him. "Let's do it now."

Al scanned the area. They were out of sight of everyone. He nodded. When she would've spoken, he placed a finger over her lips.

She couldn't help it. Jenna slid her tongue over the tip of his finger and watched his gaze darken.

"Don't distract me."

He clasped his bottom lip with his teeth and then released it, providing a distraction of his own. The damp sheen of it stirred something primal and sexual in her.

His gaze grew serious. "If at any time you can't go on, just turn and walk back out. I want you safe."

"I won't be turning around, and I'll always be safe with you." She was sure of that.

There was nothing more to be said. Al backed up farther and then released his soul.

Jenna decided she'd never be able to see the Allosaurus materialize without experiencing a breathless moment of wonder. She controlled her need to gulp. The massive body looked way too substantial. She'd have to trust that when she reached him she wouldn't just bounce off his body. But then she saw the man waiting within the beast and knew everything would be okay.

Taking a deep breath, she began walking. And when she reached his beast, Jenna took a leap of faith and didn't slow down. She passed through him and into him. Then the world as she knew it disappeared.

His beast's world was a blur of vibrant colors and unspeakable savagery. But it didn't shock her. She knew this world because of him and what she'd read of this time. Still, treading in his pack's footsteps, watching them bring down a hapless plant eater, smelling the scents of blood and hunger, and then seeing them feed, almost made her bolt.

And when the Al of that long-past time turned his massive head to look at her, she froze. Fear trembled through her as she scanned the area for a tree big enough to climb. Then she forced herself to relax, to remember. She was a spectator to his life, not a participant. She wouldn't die here.

As the pattern of his beast's life passed before her in ever-quickening scenes, she wondered why Fin would think it could drive her insane. It would be a weak woman who couldn't survive this. She was feeling pretty smug about the whole thing and anxious for it all to be over so she could touch Al again.

Then everything changed. She was in a different place, in a different time. Jenna instinctively knew this was the time "before," the time that Fin refused to discuss with his men.

This was the stuff of insanity.

Terror hammered at her—unreasoning, unrelenting. The world around her was dark, with the spiraling shapes of alien-looking buildings towering over streets filled with indescribable carnage. Death swept out of swirling, black, death-clouds. It came in the form of giant, wingless machines like none she'd ever seen before. In the distance, she could hear explosions and see fires lighting the darkness.

I'm only a spectator, a spectator, a spectator. This time the mantra didn't work. She could *feel* the evil—oppressive, heavy, moving like a massive rolling blanket of misery and death. And it was coming her way.

It would catch her, smother her within its terrifying folds, and she'd never reach Al. Never, never, never.

Jenna ran. She didn't know where, or why, or how she'd outrace the spreading extinction of all life in this city. Because that's what was coming, and she had to find Al. She sobbed as she ran, felt the tears trailing down her face only to be swept away by the sudden wind that whipped up debris from the chaotic streets.

The smell of death gagged her, but she couldn't stop long enough to throw up. Couldn't stop, couldn't stop.

Her breaths came in tortured gasps, and her legs felt ready to collapse under her, but she kept going. A shadow detached itself from the darkness, and for a moment she thought it was Al. No, not Al, but someone else. Someone she knew. A glint of silver and the shadow was gone. But she couldn't stop to think. Had to keep going. Had to find Al.

She'd never understood the saying about something breathing down your neck. Jenna understood it now. Death had a hot, fetid breath, and he was reaching for her. She strained to get one more burst of speed from pumping lungs and a pounding heart that had no more to give. She closed her eyes and screamed Al's name.

Without warning, strong arms wrapped around her and pulled her against a warm, solid chest. A *familiar* chest. She sobbed into Al's shirt as he ran his hand over her hair and made low, comforting sounds. And when he spoke, she somehow knew the words weren't his.

"You touch my soul, Jenna. You touch what I am, what I once was, and what I will be."

She wasn't surprised when the ritual response formed in her mind. "I accept what you share with me today—your love, your soul. I give my love and my soul in return."

His lips brushed hers as he murmured the last words. "Take what is mine, and let it join us forever."

Their kiss was long and deep, filled with acceptance of past suffering and joy in all their tomorrows. Jenna finally understood the power of what she'd briefly touched in the teahouse. It was love to the power of ten. Okay, maybe eleven. And yes, that was the over-the-top tabloid writer speaking, but who cared?

She could *feel* the part of him she shared. It was the heat of the sun after a long, cold winter. And she knew she'd never tire of rolling around in it. Naked. With him. Also naked.

Which gave her ideas. "Let's go home. Now."

His smile was a sexy twist of his lips, and his eyes blazed his erotic intent. "Sounds good to me."

Al sat on the park bench in Rittenhouse Square. It was almost dawn. After making love with so much intensity that he knew his shouts must've wakened everyone in the condo, he'd gathered Jenna to him and fallen asleep.

He woke a little later with a sense of someone calling him. Jenna was deep in exhausted sleep, and feeling her warmth curled against him, he almost ignored the summons. But he wanted to know.

Pulling on his clothes, he'd left the condo. Now he sat enjoying a feeling he'd never experienced before. He was totally happy. No rage against his new life, against Fin. The joy came with a sense of freedom, and he just let it soak in.

Al was almost ready to believe he'd dreamed the call when Fin emerged from the darkness and sat down next to him.

"Two down, seven to go. Plus Zero."

"Why'd you call me?" Al wanted to get back to Jenna.

"Oh, and Kione sent a message. Power always has its price."

Fin simply nodded. He didn't look Al's way. "I gave Ty a wedding gift, and now I have one for you."

For him? Al was intrigued in spite of himself. He waited.

"You've always wondered why you hate me so much." Fin held up his hand. "I know, I know. You'd say it isn't really hate. But it is." His silver hair gleamed and sparkled.

"Whatever." Al wondered about that hair. The silver seemed to glow even when there wasn't a light source.

Fin finally turned his head to meet Al's gaze. "I'm going to give you a slice of your memory to explain why."

Al barely had time to register what Fin had said before he was flung into a different place, a familiar place. Buildings he knew rose on either side of the street where he lay. The dark sky was filled with roiling clouds and death.

He was dying. He knew it, accepted it. They'd fought for days, but now his friends and family lay dead around him. No more reason to fight, to live. He closed his eyes.

And when he opened them, someone was leaning over him. Rage surged through him, giving him temporary strength. He tried to rise, to strike at the face, but he couldn't. He fell back, unable to move.

"I need your soul." The voice was not one he knew, but it represented something hated.

"Never."

"Life beyond this time, this place. Forever. That is what I offer you tonight. And since I don't feel that you're emotionally able to make a wise choice right now, I'll make it for you."

There was a touch of amusement in the voice that made him hate its owner even more.

The face came closer, and only two things registered before everything went black.

Long silver hair.

And the word "enemy."

Epilogue

"You know, I think Zero fits. The beginning, the end. It's whatever you want it to be. Fin was complimenting you." Seir grinned. He liked his reasoning.

The man standing at the edge of the roof staring down at traffic made a rude noise. "That's crap and you know it. Fin wanted me to know he thought I was nothing, worthless." He reached down to stroke Balan.

The black jaguar turned his head to study Seir from golden eyes. *"You hid your identity from me when last we met. That is not the act of a friend."*

"I'm no one's friend." And then he pushed the jaguar from his mind.

Seir didn't walk over to join them. Heights bothered him. A weakness he wasn't proud of. "Fin's not stupid. He knows what you are."

The man turned away from the edge, his long, dark-red hair swinging in a glittering arc behind him. He walked over to where Seir stood. "He's grown stronger. I couldn't . . . What's the vernacular in this time period?"

"Whip his ass?"

"I suppose that will do. He fought me to a draw."

"Guess you need to practice harder."

"Maybe I should begin practicing by heaving *your* ass off this roof." His smile was a slash of wicked enjoyment at the thought.

Seir contemplated the idea with a lot less enthusiasm. "Where're you going next?"

"Wherever Fin goes next. That's your job. Find out." He studied Seir from eyes that refused to stay one color. Right now they were bad-tempered red.

"Maybe I feel like I've earned some vacation time." Seir never tired of agitating.

"Maybe you need to make up your mind whose side you're on." With that parting shot, he jerked open the door leading from the roof and disappeared.

Seir met Balan's amused stare. "And you shut up, cat."

☐ YES!

Sign me up for the Love Spell Book Club and send my
FREE BOOKS! If I choose to stay in the club, I will pay
only $8.50* each month, a savings of $6.48!

NAME: _____

ADDRESS: _____

TELEPHONE: _____

EMAIL: _____

☐ I want to pay by credit card.

☐ **VISA**   ☐ **MasterCard**   ☐ **DISCOVER**

ACCOUNT #: _____

EXPIRATION DATE: _____

SIGNATURE: _____

Mail this page along with $2.00 shipping and handling to:
Love Spell Book Club
PO Box 6640
Wayne, PA 19087
Or fax (must include credit card information) to:
610-995-9274
You can also sign up online at **www.dorchesterpub.com**.

*Plus $2.00 for shipping. Offer open to residents of the U.S. and Canada only.
Canadian residents please call 1-800-481-9191 for pricing information.
If under 18, a parent or guardian must sign. Terms, prices and conditions subject to
change. Subscription subject to acceptance. Dorchester Publishing reserves the right
to reject any order or cancel any subscription.